DESTINY RAISED HER QUIVERING JIB-BOOM LIKE A LANCE . . .

She seemed to hang motionless on the edge of another trough before she plunged forward and down. From the corner of his eye Bolitho saw something fall from overhead. It hit the deck and exploded with a loud bang.

Rearing and plunging, her sails booming and thundering in wild confusion, *Destiny* began to swing away from the oncoming vessel.

Bolitho felt the young midshipman by his side.

"What'll we do, sir?"

Bolitho used something like physical strength to control his stampeding thoughts. Nobody else was here to lead, to advise. He was in charge . . .

ALEXANDER KENT
STAND INTO DANGER

A JOVE BOOK

This Jove book contains the complete
text of the original hardcover edition.
It has been completely reset in a typeface
designed for easy reading, and was printed
from new film.

STAND INTO DANGER

A Jove Book / published by arrangement with
G. P. Putnam's Sons

PRINTING HISTORY
G. P. Putnam's edition / February 1981
Jove edition / April 1983

ISBN: 0-515-06888-8

Jove books are published by Jove Publications,
Inc., 200 Madison Avenue, New York, N.Y. 10016.
The words ''A JOVE BOOK'' and the ''J'' with sunburst
are trademarks belonging to Jove Publications, Inc.

PRINTED IN THE UNITED STATES OF AMERICA

To Winifred,
with my love

Contents

Far away where sky met sea
A majestic figure grew,
Pushed along by Royal decree
Her aggressive pennants flew.

Blazing red, dark plumes of grey,
Destruction overall,
As shot and grape found its way
Into a human wall.

From *A Mariner's Tale*
by DANIEL BYRNE

STAND INTO DANGER

I

Welcome Aboard

Richard Bolitho thrust some coins into the hand of the man who had carried his sea-chest to the jetty and shivered in the damp air. It was halfway through the forenoon, and yet much of the land and the sprawling houses of Plymouth were hidden in drifting mist. No wind at all to speak of, so that the mist made everything look eerie and dismal.

Bolitho squared his shoulders and stared across the swirling water of the Hamoaze. As he did so he felt the unfamiliar touch of his lieutenant's uniform which, like everything in his sea-chest, was new: the white lapels of his coat, the cocked hat set squarely across his black hair. Even his breeches and shoes had come from the same shop in Falmouth, in his own county just across the river, from the tailor whose family had been making clothing for sea officers since anyone could remember.

It should be his proudest moment. All he had worked and hoped for. That first, seemingly impossible step from midshipman's berth to wardroom, to become a King's officer.

He tugged his hat more firmly across his forehead as if to make himself believe it. It *was* his proudest moment.

'Be you joinin' th' *Destiny,* zur?'

Bolitho saw that the man who had carried the chest was still beside him. In the dull light he looked poor and ragged, but there was no mistaking what he had once been: a seaman.

Bolitho said, 'Yes, she's lying out there somewhere.'

1

The man followed his glance across the water, his eyes faraway.

'Fine frigate, zur. Only three years old, she be.' He nodded sadly. 'She's bin fittin' out for months. Some say for a long voyage.'

Bolitho thought of this man and all the hundreds like him who roamed the shorelines and harbours looking for work, yearning for the sea which they had once cursed and damned with the best of them.

But this was February 1774, and to all accounts England had been at peace for years. Wars still erupted around the world, of course, but always in the name of trade or self-preservation. Only the old enemies remained the same, content to bide their time, to seek out the weakness which might one day be exploited.

Ships and men, once worth their weight in gold, were cast aside. The vessels to rot, the seamen, like this ragged figure with all the fingers missing from one hand and a scar on his cheek as deep as a knife, left without the means to live.

Bolitho asked, 'What were you in?'

Astonishingly, the man seemed to expand and straighten his back as he answered, 'Th' *Torbay*, zur. Cap'n Keppel.' Just as quickly he slumped down again. 'Any chance of a berth in your ship, zur?'

Bolitho shook his head. 'I'm new. I don't know the state aboard *Destiny* as yet.'

The man sighed. 'I'll call 'e a boat then, zur.'

He put his good hand in his mouth and gave a piercing whistle. There was an answering clatter of oars in the mist, and very slowly a waterman's boat nudged towards the jetty.

Bolitho called, '*Destiny*, if you please!'

Then he turned to give some more coins to his ragged companion, but he had vanished into the mist. Like a ghost. Gone perhaps to join all the others.

Bolitho clambered into the boat and drew his new cloak around him, his sword gripped between his legs. The waiting was done. It was no longer the day after tomorrow and then tomorrow. It was now.

The boat dipped and gurgled in a cross-current, the oarsman watching Bolitho with little enthusiasm. Another young luff going to make some poor jack's life hell, he thought. He wondered if the young officer with the grave features and black hair tied to the nape of his neck was so new he would not know the proper waterman's fare. But then again, this one had a West Country touch in his voice, and even if he was a 'foreigner' from across the border in Cornwall, he would not be fooled.

Bolitho went over all that he had discovered about his new ship. Three years old, the ragged man had said. He would know. All Plymouth probably pondered over the care which was being taken to equip and man a frigate in these hard times.

Twenty-eight guns, fast and agile, *Destiny* was what most young officers dreamed of. In time of war, free of the fleet's apron strings, swifter than any larger vessel, and more heavily armed than anything smaller, a frigate was a force to be reckoned with. Better hopes of promotion, too, and if you were lucky enough ever to reach the lofty peak of command, so too would a frigate offer the chance of action and prize-money.

Bolitho thought of his last ship, the seventy-four-gun *Gorgon*. Huge, slow-moving, a teeming world of people, miles of rigging, vast spans of canvas, and the spars to carry it. It was also a schoolroom, where the young midshipmen learned how to control and sustain their unwieldy charge, and they learned the hard way.

Bolitho looked up as the waterman said, 'Should be seeing her about now, sir.'

Bolitho peered ahead, glad of the interruption to his thoughts. As his mother had said when he had left her in the big grey house at Falmouth, '*Put it behind you, Dick. You cannot bring him back. So take care of yourself now. The sea is no place for the unwary.*'

The mist darkened and edged aside as the anchored ship loomed into view. The boat was approaching her starboard bow and past the long tapering jib-boom. Like Bolitho's new uniform on the wet jetty, the *Destiny* seemed to shine through the drifting murk.

From her lithe black and buff hull to her three mastheads she was a thoroughbred. All her shrouds and standing rigging were freshly blacked down, her yards crossed, and each sail neatly furled to match its neighbour.

Bolitho raised his eyes to the figurehead as it reached out as if to greet him. It was the most beautiful one he had ever seen. A bare-breasted girl with her out-thrust arm pointing to the next horizon. In her hand she held the victor's crown of laurels. Only the laurels and her unwavering blue stare had been inserted to break her white purity.

The waterman said between pulls, 'They *say* that the wood-carver used his young bride to copy for that, sir.' He showed his teeth in what might have been a grin. 'I reckon he had to fight a few away from *her*!'

Bolitho watched the frigate slipping past the boat, the occasional activity on her nearest gangway and high above the deck.

She was a beautiful ship. *He was lucky.*

'Boat ahoy!'

The waterman bawled in reply, 'Aye, aye!'

Bolitho saw some movement at the entry port, but not enough to excite much attention. The waterman's answer to the challenge had said it all. An officer was joining the ship, but nobody senior enough to bother about, let alone her captain.

Bolitho stood up as two seamen leapt into the boat to help make fast and to collect his chest. Bolitho glanced at them quickly. He was not fully eighteen years old, but he had been at sea since he was twelve and had learned to assess and measure the skills of sailormen.

They looked tough and hardy, but the hull of a ship could hide a lot. The sweepings of jails and assize courts, being sent to sea to serve the King rather than face deportation or a hangman's halter.

The seamen stood aside in the pitching boat as Bolitho handed the oarsman some money.

The man pushed it into his jerkin and grinned. '*Thankee*, sir. Good luck!'

Bolitho climbed up the frigate's tumblehome and stepped through the entry port. He was astonished at the difference even though he had been expecting it. After a ship of the line, the *Destiny* seemed crowded to a point of confusion. From the twenty twelve-pounders on her gun deck to the smaller weapons further aft every inch of space seemed to have a purpose and to be in use. Neatly flaked lines, halliards and braces, tiered boats and racks of pikes at the foot of each mast, while in and around every item were men he must soon know by name.

A lieutenant stepped through the side party and asked, 'Mr Bolitho?'

Bolitho replaced his hàt. 'Aye, sir. Come aboard to join.'

The lieutenant nodded curtly. 'Follow me. I'll have your gear taken aft.' He said something to a seaman and then shouted, 'Mr Timbrell!' Put some more hands in the foretop. It was like bedlam up there when I last inspected it!'

Bolitho just remembered in time to duck his head as they walked aft beneath the quarterdeck. Again the ship appeared to be crowding in on him. More guns, firmly tethered behind each sealed port, the aromas of tar and cordage, fresh paint and crowded humanity, the smells of a living vessel.

He tried to assess the lieutenant who was leading him aft to the wardroom. Slim and round-faced, with that harassed look of a man left in charge.

'Here we are.'

The lieutenant opened a screen door and Bolitho stepped into his new home. Even with the black muzzled twelve pounders along one side, a reminder, if one was needed, that there was no place in a ship-of-war which was safe when the iron began to fly, it looked surprisingly comfortable. A long table, with high-backed chairs instead of benches like those endured by lowly midshipmen. There were racks for drinking glasses, others for swords and pistols, and on the deck there was a covering of painted canvas.

The lieutenant turned and studied Bolitho thoughtfully. 'I'm Stephen Rhodes, Second Lieutenant.' He smiled, the change making him more youthful than Bolitho had realized. 'As this is your first ship as lieutenant, I'll try to make the way as easy as I can. Call me Stephen, if you wish, but sir in front of the hands.' Rhodes threw back his head and yelled, 'Poad!'

A scrawny little man in a blue jacket bustled through a screen door.

'Some wine, Poad. This is the new third lieutenant.'

Poad bobbed. 'Pleasure, sir, I'm sure.'

As he hurried away Rhodes remarked, 'Good servant, but

light-fingered, so don't leave anything too valuable lying about.' He became serious again. 'The first lieutenant is in Plymouth, doing something or other. His name is Charles Palliser, and might seem a bit stiff at first meeting. He's been in *Destiny* with the captain from her first commissioning.' He changed tack suddenly. 'You were lucky to get this appointment.' It sounded like an accusation. 'You're so young. I'm twenty-three, and was only promoted to second lieutenant when my predecessor was killed.'

'*Killed?*'

Rhodes grimaced. 'Hell, it was nothing heroic. He was thrown off a horse and broke his neck. Good fellow in many ways, but there it is.'

Bolitho watched the wardroom servant putting goblets and a bottle within Rhodes' reach.

He said, 'I *was* surprised to get this appointment myself.'

Rhodes eyed him searchingly. 'You don't sound too sure? Don't you *want* to join us? God, man, there are a hundred who would jump at the chance!'

Bolitho looked away. A bad beginning.

'It's not that. My best friend was killed a month back.' It was out in the open. 'I just can't believe it.'

Rhodes' eyes softened and he pushed a glass towards him. 'Drink this, Richard. I didn't understand. Sometimes I wonder why we do this work when others live easily ashore.'

Bolitho smiled at him. Except for his mother's benefit he had not smiled much lately.

'What are our orders, er, Stephen?'

Rhodes relaxed. 'Nobody really knows except the lord and master. A long haul to the south'rd is all I *do* know. The Caribbean, maybe further still.' He shivered and glared at the nearest gunport. 'God I'll be glad to see the back of this wet misery here!' He took a quick swallow. 'We've a good company for the most part, but with the usual seasoning of gallows-birds. The sailing master, Mr Gulliver, is newly promoted from master's mate, but he's a fine navigator, even if he is a bit awkward amongst his betters. By tonight we shall have a full complement of midshipmen, two of whom are twelve and thirteen respectively.' He grinned. 'But don't be slack with 'em, Richard, just because you were one yourself a dog-watch ago. Your head will be on the block, not theirs!'

Rhodes tugged a watch from his breeches. 'First lieutenant will be coming off shortly. I had better chase up the hands. He likes a smart display when he steps aboard.'

He pointed to a small screened cabin. 'That one is yours, Richard. Tell Poad what you need and he will get the other servants to deal with it.' Impulsively he thrust out his hand. 'Good to have you with us. Welcome aboard.'

Bolitho sat in the empty wardroom listening to the clatter of blocks and rigging, the unending slap of feet above his head. Hoarse voices, the occasional trill of a boatswain's call as a piece of gear was piped up from a boat alongside, to be stored and checked into its own special place in the hull.

Soon Bolitho would know their faces, their strengths and weaknesses. And in this low-beamed wardroom he would share his hopes and daily life with his fellows. The two other lieutenants, the marine officer, the newly appointed sailing master, the surgeon and the purser. The select few in a company which was listed as being 200 souls.

He had wanted to ask the second lieutenant about *the lord and master,* as he had described him. Bolitho was very young for his rank, but not so much that he did not know it would have been wrong. To share a confidence and to give a personal opinion of *Destiny*'s captain would be a little short of madness from Rhodes' point of view when he had only just met the new arrival.

Bolitho opened the door of his tiny cabin. About the length of the swinging cot and enough room to sit down. A place for privacy, or as near to it as one could get in a small, bustling man-of-war. After the midshipman's berth on the orlop deck it was a palace.

His advancement had been very swift, as Rhodes had remarked. But for all that, if the unknown lieutenant had not been killed by a fall from his horse the vacancy for third lieutenant would not have been posted.

Bolitho unlocked the top half of his sea-chest and then hung a mirror on one of the massive timbers beside his cot. He looked at himself, seeing the small lines of strain around his mouth and grey eyes. He was leaner, too, honed down to a youthful toughness which only shipboard food and hard work could produce.

Poad peered at him. 'I could pay a waterman to go into town and purchase some extra victuals for you, sir.'

Bolitho smiled. Poad was like a stall-holder at a Cornish fair.

'I have some coming aboard directly, thank you.' He saw the disappointment and added, 'But if you see that it's stowed properly I'll be *obliged*.'

Poad nodded quickly and scuttled away. He had made his play. Bolitho's reaction had been the right one. There would be payment somewhere along the way if Poad looked after the new lieutenant's personal stores.

A door crashed open and a tall lieutenant strode into the wardroom, hurling his hat on one of the guns and yelling for Poad in one breath.

He examined Bolitho very slowly, his eyes taking in everything from his hair to his new buckled shoes.

He said, 'I'm Palliser, the senior.'

He had a crisp way of speaking. He glanced away as Poad ran through the door with a jug of wine.

Bolitho watched the first lieutenant curiously. He was very tall, so that he had to stoop between the deckhead beams. In his late twenties, but with the experience of a man far older. He and Bolitho wore the same uniform, but they were so far apart they could have been standing on either side of an abyss.

'So *you're* Bolitho.' The eyes swivelled back towards him above the rim of the goblet. 'You have a fair report, in *words,* that is. Well, this is a frigate, Mr Bolitho, not some overmanned third-rate. I need every officer and man working until this ship, *my* ship, is ready to weigh.' Another fierce swallow. 'So report on deck, if you please. Take the launch and get yourself ashore. You must know the lie of the land around here, eh?' He gave a fleeting smile. 'Lead a recruiting party to the west bank and examine those villages. Little, gunner's mate, will assist. He understands the game. There are some posters you can put up at the inns as you go. We need about twenty sound hands, no rubbish. We are up to full complement, but at the end of a long passage that's another matter. We shall lose a few, have no doubt of it. Anyway, the captain wants it done.'

Bolitho had been thinking of unpacking, of meeting his companions, of having a meal after the long coach journey from Falmouth.

To settle things quite firmly, Palliser said offhandedly, 'This is Tuesday, be back aboard noon on Friday. Don't lose any of your party, and *don't* let them pull the wool over your eyes!'

He banged out of the wardroom, calling for somebody else.

Rhodes appeared in the open door and smiled sympathetically. 'Hard luck, Richard. But his manner is rougher than his thoughts. He has picked a good shore-party for you. I've known some first lieutenants who would give a new junior a collection of moonstruck felons for company, just to give him hell when he returned.' He winked. 'Mr Palliser intends to have a command of his own soon. Bear that in mind at all times as I do, it helps considerably!'

Bolitho smiled. 'I'd better go at once, in that case.' He hesitated. 'And thank you for making me welcome.'

Rhodes sank down in a chair and thought about the noon meal. He heard the clatter of oars alongside and the shout of the launch's coxswain. What he had seen of Bolitho he liked. Young certainly, but with the restless quality of one who would do well in a tight corner or in a screaming hurricane.

It was strange how you never considered the worries and problems of your betters when you were a midshipman. A lieutenant, junior or not, was a kind of superior being. One who berated and was quick to find fault with the youthful beginners. Now he knew better. Even Palliser was frightened of the captain. Probably the lord and master was terrified of upsetting his admiral, or someone higher still?

Rhodes smiled. But for a few more precious moments there was peace.

Little, the gunner's mate, stood back, his broad hands on where his hips should have been, and watched as one of his men tacked up another recruiting poster.

Bolitho pulled out his watch and looked across the village green as a church clock chimed midday.

Little said gruffly, 'Mebbee time for a wet, sir?'

Bolitho sighed. Another day, after a sleepless night in a

tiny, none too clean inn where he worried that his small recruiting party might desert, in spite of what Rhodes had said about their selection. But Little had made sure that part had gone well. He was totally at odds with his name; squat, overweight, even gross, so that his belly sagged heavily over his cutlass belt like a sack. How he managed it on purser's rations was a marvel. But he was a good hand, seasoned and experienced, and would stand no nonsense.

Bolitho said, 'One more stop, Little. Then . . .,' he gave a rueful smile, 'I'll buy you all a drink.'

They brightened up immediately. Six seamen, a marine corporal and two drummer boys who looked like toy soldiers freshly out of a box. They did not care about the miserable results of their trek from one village to the next. Usually the sight of Bolitho's party aroused little interest, except amongst the childen and a few snapping dogs. Old habits died hard so near the sea. Many still recalled the dreaded press-gangs when men could be torn from their families and put in a King's ship to suffer the harsh conditions of a war which few understood even now. And a goodly number had never come back at all.

Bolitho had managed to obtain four volunteers so far. Four, and Palliser was expecting twenty. He had sent them back with an escort to the boat in case they should have a change of heart. Two of them were seamen, but the others were labourers from a farm who had lost their jobs, 'unfairly', they both said. Bolitho suspected they were willing to volunteer for a more pressing reason, but it was no time to ask questions.

They tramped across the deserted green, the muddy grass splashing up from Bolitho's shoes and on to his new stockings.

Little had already quickened his pace, and Bolitho wondered if he had done the right thing to offer them all a drink.

He shrugged inwardly. So far nothing had gone right. Matters could hardly get much worse.

Little hissed, 'There be some men, sir!' He rubbed his big hands together and said to the corporal, 'Now, Dipper, get your little lads to strike up a tune, eh?'

The two minute marines waited for their corporal to relay the order, then while one beat a lively tap on his drum the other drew a fife from his cross-belt and broke into what sounded like a jig.

The corporal's name was Dyer. Bolitho asked, 'Why do you call him Dipper?'

Little grinned, baring several broken teeth, the true mark of a fighter.

'Bless you, sir, 'cause he were a pickpocket afore he saw the light and joined the bullocks!'

The little group of men by the inn seemed to melt away as the seamen and marines drew near.

Two figures remained, and a more incongruous pair it was hard to imagine.

One was small and darting, with a sharp voice which carried easily above the fife and drum. The other was big and powerful, stripped to the waist, his arms and fists hanging at his sides like weapons waiting to be used.

The small man, a barker, enraged earlier by the sudden departure of his audience, saw the sailors and beckoned excitedly.

'Well, well, well, wot 'ave we 'ere then? Sons of the sea, the British Jack Tar!' He doffed his hat to Bolitho. 'An' a real gentleman in command, no doubt of that!'

Bolitho said wearily, 'Fall the men out, Little. I'll have the landlord send some ale and cheese.'

The barker was shouting, 'Which one of you brave lads will stand up to this fighter of mine?' His eyes darted amongst them. 'A *guinea* for the man who can stand two minutes against 'im!' The coin flashed between his fingers. 'You don't 'ave to win, my brave boys, just stand and fight for *two minutes*!'

He had their full attention now, and Bolitho heard the corporal murmur to Little, 'Wot about it, Josh? An 'ole bleedin' guinea!'

Bolitho paused by the inn door and glanced at the prize-fighter for the first time. He looked as strong as ten, and yet there was something despairing and pathetic about him. He was not looking at any of the seamen but apparently staring into space. His nose had been broken, and his face showed the punishment of many fights. Country fairs, for the farming gentry, for anyone who would wager on seeing men fight for a bloody victory. Bolitho was not certain which one he despised more, the man who lived off the fighter or the one who laid bets on his pain.

He said shortly, 'I shall be inside, Little.' All at once the thought of a glass of ale or cider beckoned him like a wilful spirit.

Little was already thinking of other things. 'Aye, sir.'

It was a friendly little inn, and the landlord hurried to greet Bolitho, his head almost brushing the ceiling. A fire burned brightly in its box, and there was a smell of freshly baked bread and smoked hams.

'You sit down there, Lieutenant. I'll see to your men presently.' He saw Bolitho's expression. 'Begging your pardon sir, but you're wasting your time hereabouts. The war took too many away to follow the drum, an' those what came back went elsewhere to the big towns like Truro an' Exeter to get work.' He shook his head. 'Me now, if I was twenty years younger I might have signed on.' He grinned. 'Then again . . .'

Some while later, Richard Bolitho sat in a high-backed chair beside the fire, the mud drying on his stockings, his coat unbuttoned to allow for the excellent pie the landlord's wife had brought him. A big, elderly dog lay by his feet, pulsating gently as it enjoyed the heat and dreamed of some past exploit.

The landlord whispered to his wife, 'Did you *see* him? A King's officer, no less. Lord, he looks more like a boy!'

Bolitho stirred from his drowsiness and yawned. Then his arms froze in mid air as he heard loud shouts of anger interposed with laughter. He jumped to his feet, groping for his sword and hat and trying to button his coat at the same time.

He almost ran to the door, and when he stumbled into the keen air he saw the seamen and marines falling against each other, convulsed with laughter, while the little barker screamed, 'You *cheated*! You *must* 'ave cheated!'

Little spun the gold guinea and caught it deftly in his palm. 'Not me, matey. Fair an' square, that's Josh Little!'

Bolitho snapped, 'What's going on?'

Corporal Dyer said between gasps of laughter, ''E put the big prize-fighter on 'is back, sir! Never seen the like!'

Bolitho glared at Little. 'I'll speak to you later! Now fall the men in, we've miles to go to the next village!'

He swung round and stared with astonishment as the barker turned on the fighter. The latter was standing as before, as if he had never moved, let alone been knocked down.

The barker picked up a length of chain and screamed, '*This* is for yer bloody stupidity!' The chain slashed across the man's naked back. '*This* is for losin' my money!' *Crack*.

Little glanced at Bolitho uneasily. ' 'Ere, sir, I'll give the bugger 'is money, I'll not see that poor devil beaten like a cur!'

Bolitho swallowed hard. The big fighter could have killed his tormentor with one blow. Perhaps he had been on the way down for so long he no longer felt pain or anything else.

But it was more than enough for Bolitho. His bad beginning aboard *Destiny*, his failure to find the required volunteers were all he could take. This degrading sight tipped the balance completely.

'You there! Belay that!' Bolitho strode forward, watched with both awe and amusement by his men. 'Put down that chain at once!'

The barker quailed and then quickly regained his earlier confidence. He had nothing to fear from a young lieutenant. Especially in a district where he was often paid for his services.

'I've me rights!'

Little snarled, 'Let me 'andle the bugger, sir! I'll give 'im bloody rights!'

It was all getting out of hand. Some villagers had appeared, too, and Bolitho had a mental picture of his men having a pitched battle with half the countryside before they could get to the launch.

He turned his back on the defiant barker and faced up to the fighter. Near to he was even bigger, but in spite of his size and strength Bolitho saw only his eyes, each of which was partly hidden by lids battered shapeless over the years.

'You know who I am?'

The man nodded slowly, his gaze fixed on Bolitho's mouth as if he was reading every word.

Gently Bolitho asked, 'Will you volunteer for the King's service? Join the frigate *Destiny* at Plymouth,' he hesitated, seeing the painful understanding in the man's eyes, 'with me?'

Then just as slowly as before he nodded, and without a glance at the gaping barker he picked up his shirt and a small bag.

Bolitho turned to the barker, his anger matched only by his feeling of petty triumph. Once clear of the village he would release the fighter anyway.

The barker yelled, 'You can't do that!'

Little stepped forward threatingly. 'Stow the noise, matey, an' show respect for a King's officer, or . . .' He left the rest in little doubt.

Bolitho licked his lips. 'Fall in, men. Corporal, take charge there!'

He saw the big fighter watching the seamen and called, 'Your name, what is it?'

'Stockdale, sir.' Even the name was dragged out. His chords must have been mangled in so many fights that even his voice was broken.

Bolitho smiled at him. 'Stockdale. I shall not forget you. You will be free to leave us whenever you wish.' He glanced meaningly at Little. 'Before we reach the boat.'

Stockdale looked calmly at the little barker who was sitting on a bench, the chain still dangling from his hand.

Then he wheezed very carefully, 'No, sir. I'll not leave you. Not now. Not never.'

Bolitho watched him join up with the others. The man's obvious sincerity was strangely moving.

Little said quietly, 'You've no need to worry. This'll be all round the ship in no time.' He leaned forward so that Bolitho could smell the ale and cheese. 'I'm in your division, sir, an' I'll beat the block off any bugger who tries to make trouble!'

A shaft of watery sunlight played across the church clock, and as the recruiting party marched stoically towards the next village Bolitho was glad of what he had just done.

Then it began to rain, and he heard Little say, 'Not much further, Dipper, then back to the ship for a wet!'

Bolitho looked at Stockdale's broad shoulders. Another volunteer. That made five in all. He lowered his head against the rain. Fifteen to go.

The next village was even worse, especially as there was no inn, and the local farmer only allowed them to sleep for the night in an unused barn, and that was with obvious reluctance. He claimed his house was full of visitors, and anyway. . . . That word 'anyway' spoke volumes.

The barn leaked in a dozen places and stank like a sewer, and the sailors, like most of their kind, used to the enforced cleanliness of living in close quarters, were loud voiced in their discontent.

Bolitho could not blame them, and when Corporal Dyer came to tell him that the volunteer Stockdale had vanished, he replied, 'I'm not surprised, Corporal, but keep an eye on the rest of the party.'

He thought about the missing Stockdale for a long time, and wondered at his own sense of loss. Perhaps Stockdale's simple words had touched him more deeply than he had realized, that he had represented a change of luck, like a talisman.

Little exclaimed, 'God Almighty! *Look at this!*'

Stockdale, dripping with rain, stepped into the lantern light and placed a sack at Bolitho's feet. The men crowded round as the treasures were revealed in the yellow glow. Some chickens, fresh bread and crocks of butter, half a meat pie and, more to the point, two big jars of cider.

Little gasped, 'You two men, start plucking the chickens, you, Thomas, watch out for unwanted visitors.' He faced Stockdale and thrust out the guinea. ''Ere, matey, you take it. You've bloody earned it!'

Stockdale barely heard. As he bent over his sack he wheezed, 'No. 'T'were '*is* money. You keep it.'

To Bolitho he said, 'This is for you, sir.'

He held out a bottle which looked like brandy. It made sense. The farmer was probably mixed up with the smuggling 'trade' hereabouts.

Stockdale watched Bolitho's face searchingly, then he added, 'I'll make you comfortable, you see.'

Bolitho saw him moving about amongst the busy seamen as if he had been doing it all his life.

Little said quietly, 'Reckon you can stop frettin' now, sir. Old Stockdale will be worth fifteen men all on his bloody own, by my reckonin'!'

Bolitho drank some of the brandy, the grease from a chicken leg running unheeded across the cuff of his new shirt.

He had learned a lot today, not least about himself.

His head lolled, and he did not feel Stockdale remove the cup from his fingers.

And there was always tomorrow.

2

Leave the Past Behind

Bolitho pulled himself up the *Destiny*'s side and raised his hat to the quarterdeck. Gone was the mist and dull cloud, and the houses of Plymouth beyond the Hamoaze seemed to be preening themselves in hard sunshine.

He felt stiff and tired from tramping from village to village, dirty from sleeping in barn and inn alike, and the sight of his six recruits being mustered and then led forward by the master-at-arms did little to raise his spirits. The sixth volunteer had come up to the recruiting party less than an hour before they had reached the long-boat. A neat, unseamanlike figure aged about thirty, who said he was an apothecary's assistant but needed to gain experience on a long voyage so that he might better himself.

It was as unlikely a story as that of the two farm labourers, but Bolitho was too weary to care.

'Ah, I see you are back, Mr Bolitho!'

The first lieutenant was standing at the quarterdeck rail, his tall figure framed against the washed-out sky. His arms were folded and he had obviously been watching the new arrivals from the moment the returning launch had been challenged.

In a crisp voice he added, 'Lay aft, if you please.'

Bolitho climbed to the larboard gangway and made his way to the quarterdeck. His companion of three days, the gunner's mate Little, was already bustling down a ladder, going to take a 'wet' with his mates, no doubt. He was lost amongst his own

17

world below decks, leaving Bolitho once more a stranger, little different from the moment he had first stepped aboard.

He confronted the first lieutenant and touched his hat. Palliser looked composed and extremely neat, which made Bolitho feel even more like a vagrant.

Bolitho said, 'Six hands, sir. The big man was a fighter, and should be a welcome addition. The last one worked for an apothecary in Plymouth.'

His words seemed to be falling like stones. Palliser had not moved and the quarterdeck was unnaturally quiet.

Bolitho ended, 'It was the best I could do, sir.'

Palliser pulled out his watch. 'Good. Well, the captain has come aboard in your absence. He asked to see you the moment you returned.'

Bolitho stared at him. He had been expecting the heavens to fall. Six men instead of twenty, and one of those would never make a sailor.

Palliser snapped down the guard of his watch and regarded Bolitho coolly. 'Has the long sojourn ashore rendered you hard of hearing? The captain wishes to see you. That does not mean now; aboard this ship it means the moment that the captain *thought* of it!'

Bolitho looked ruefully at his muddy shoes and stockings. 'I—I'm sorry, sir, I thought you said . . .'

Palliser was already looking elsewhere, his eyes busy on some men working on the forecastle.

'I told you to obtain twenty men. Had I ordered you to bring six, how many would you have found? Two? None at all?' Surprisingly he smiled. 'Six will do very well. Now be off to the captain. Pork pie today, so be sharp about your business or there'll be none left.' He turned on his heel, yelling, 'Mr Slade, what *are* those idlers doing, damn your eyes!'

Bolitho ran dazedly down the companion ladder and made his way aft. Faces loomed past him in the shadows between the decks, voices fell silent as they watched him pass. *The new lieutenant. Going to see the captain. What is he like? Too easy or too hard?*

A marine stood with his musket by his side, swaying slightly as the ship tugged at her anchor. His eyes glittered in the lantern which spiralled from the deckhead, as it did night and day when the captain was in his quarters.

Bolitho made an effort to straighten his neckcloth and push the rebellious hair from his forehead.

The marine gave him exactly five seconds and then rapped smartly on the deck with his musket.

'Third lieutenant, *sir*!'

The screen door opened and a wispy-haired man in a black coat, probably the captain's clerk, gave Bolitho an impatient, beckoning gesture. Rather like a schoolmaster with a way-ward pupil.

Bolitho tucked his hat more firmly beneath his arm and entered the cabin. After the rest of the ship it was spacious, with a second screen separating the stern cabin from the dining space, and what Bolitho took to be the sleeping quarters.

The slanting stern windows which crossed the complete rear of the cabin shone in the sunlight, giving an impression of warmth, while the overhead beams and the various pieces of furniture rippled cheerfully in the sea's reflections.

Captain Henry Vere Dumaresq had been leaning against the sill, apparently peering down at the water, but he turned with unusual lightness as Bolitho entered through the dining space.

Bolitho tried to appear calm and at ease, but it was impossible. The captain was like nobody he had ever seen. His body was broad and thickset, and his head stood straight on his shoulders as if he had no neck at all. It was like the rest of the man, powerful and giving an impression of immense strength. Little had said that Dumaresq was only twenty-eight years old, but he looked ageless, as if he had never changed and never would.

He walked to meet Bolitho, putting each foot down with forceful precision. Bolitho saw his legs, made more promi-nent by his expensive white stockings. The calves looked as thick as a man's thigh.

'You appear somewhat knocked about, Mr. Bolitho.'

Dumaresq had a throaty, resonant voice, one which would carry easily in a full gale, yet Bolitho suspected it might also convey quiet sympathy.

He said awkwardly, 'Aye, sir, I—I mean, I was ashore with the recruiting party.'

Dumaresq pointed to a chair. 'Sit.' He raised his voice very slightly. 'Some claret!'

It had the desired effect, and almost immediately his servant was busily pouring wine into two beautifully cut glasses. Then just as discreetly he withdrew.

Dumaresq sat down opposite Bolitho, barely a yard away. His power and presence were unnerving. Bolitho recalled his last captain. In the big seventy-four he had always been remote, aloof from the happenings of wardroom and gunroom alike. Only at moments of crisis or ceremony had he made his presence felt, and then, as before, always at a distance.

Dumaresq said, 'My father had the honour of serving with yours some years back. How is he?'

Bolitho thought of his mother and sister in the house at Falmouth. Waiting for Captain James Bolitho to return home. His mother would be counting the days, perhaps dreading how he might have changed.

He had lost an arm in India, and when his ship had been paid off he had been told he was to be placed on the retired list indefinitely.

Bolitho said, 'He is due home, sir. But with an arm gone and no chance to remain in the King's service, I'm not certain what will become of him.' He broke off, startled that he had spoken his thoughts aloud.

But Dumaresq gestured to the glass. 'Drink, Mr Bolitho, and speak as you will. It is more important that I should know you than you should care for my views.' It seemed to amuse him. 'It comes to all of us. We must consider ourselves fortunate indeed to have *her*!' His big head swivelled round as he looked at the cabin. He was speaking of the ship, his ship, as if he loved her more than anything.

Bolitho said, 'She is a fine vessel, sir. I am honoured to join her.'

'Yes.'

Dumaresq leaned over to refill the glasses. Again he moved with catlike ease, but used his strength, like his voice, sparingly.

He said, 'I learned of your recent grief.' He raised one hand. 'No, not from anyone in this ship. I have my own means, and I like to know my officers just as I know my command. We shall be sailing shortly on what may prove a rewarding voyage, then again it may be fruitless. Either way it will not be easy. We must put old memories behind us, reserve not forget them. This is a small ship and each man in her has a part to play.

'You have served under some distinguished captains and you obviously learned well from your service. But in a frigate there are few passengers, and a lieutenant is not one of them. You will make mistakes, and I will allow for that, but misuse your authority and I will fall upon you like a wall of rock. You must avoid making favourites, for they will end up using you if you are not careful.'

He chuckled as he studied Bolitho's grave features.

'There is more to being a lieutenant than growing up. The people will look to you when they are in trouble, and you will have to act as you think best. Those other days ended when you quit the midshipman's berth. In a small ship there is no room for friction. You have to become a *part* of her, d'you see?'

Bolitho found himself sitting on the edge of his chair. This strange man gripped his attention like a vice. His eyes, set wide apart, equally compelling, insistent.

Bolitho nodded. 'Yes, sir. I do.'

Dumaresq looked up as two bells chimed out from forward.

'Go and have your meal. I've no doubt you're hungry. Mr Palliser's crafty schemes for recruiting new hands usually bring an appetite if nothing more.'

As Bolitho rose to his feet Dumaresq added quietly, 'This voyage will be important to a lot of people. Our midshipmen are mostly from influential parents who are eager to see they get a chance to distinguish themselves when most of the fleet is rotting or laid up in-ordinary. Our professional warrant officers are excellent, and there is a strong backbone of prime seamen. The rest will learn. One last thing, Mr Bolitho, and I trust I will not have to repeat it. In *Destiny*, loyalty is paramount. To me, to this ship, and to His Britannic Majesty, *in that order*!'

Bolitho found himself outside the screen door, his senses still reeling from the brief interview.

Poad was hovering nearby, bobbing excitedly. 'All done, sir? I've 'ad yer gear stowed where it'll be safe, just like you ordered.' He led the way to the wardroom. 'I managed to 'old up the meal 'til you was ready, sir.'

Bolitho stepped into the wardroom and, unlike the last time, the place was noisy with chatter and seemingly full of people.

Palliser stood up and said abruptly, 'Our new member, gentlemen!'

Bolitho saw Rhodes grinning at him and was glad of his friendly face.

He shook hands and murmured what he hoped was the right thing. The sailing master, Julius Gulliver, was exactly as Rhodes had described him, ill at ease, almost furtive. John Colpoys, the lieutenant who commanded the ship's marine contingent, made a splash of scarlet as he shook Bolitho's hand and drawled, 'Charmed, m'dear fellah.'

The surgeon was round and jolly-looking, like an untidy owl, with a rich aroma of brandy and tobacco. There was Samuel Codd, the purser, unusually cheerful for one of his trade, Bolitho thought, and certainly no subject for a portrait. He had very large upper teeth and a tiny receding chin, so that it looked as if half of his face was successfully devouring the other.

Colpoys said, 'I hope you can play cards.'

Rhodes smiled. 'Give him a chance.' To Bolitho he said, 'He'll have the shirt off your back if you let him.'

Bolitho sat down at the table next to the surgeon. The latter placed some gold-rimmed glasses on his nose. They looked completely lost above his red cheeks.

He said, 'Pork pie. A sure sign we are soon to leave here. After that'—he glanced at the purser—'we will be back to meat from Samuel's stores, most of it condemned some twenty years ago, I daresay.'

Glasses clinked, and the air became heady with steam and the smell of food.

Bolitho looked along the table. So this was what wardroom officers were like when out of sight of their subordinates.

Rhodes whispered, 'What did you make of him?'

'The captain?' Bolitho thought about it, trying to keep his memories in their proper order. 'I was impressed. He is so, so . . .'

Rhodes beckoned Poad to bring the wine jug. 'Ugly?'

Bolitho smiled. 'Different. A bit frightening.'

Palliser's voice cut through the conversation. 'You will inspect the ship when you have eaten, Richard. Truck to keel, fo'c'sle to taffrail. What you cannot understand, ask me. Meet as many of the junior warrant officers as you can, and memorize your own divisional list.' He dropped one eyelid to the marine but not quickly enough for Bolitho to miss it. 'I am certain he will wish to see that his men measure up to those he so skilfully brought us today.'

Bolitho looked down as a plate was thrust before him. There was little of the actual plate left visible around the pile of food.

Palliser had called him by his first name, had even made a casual joke about the volunteers. So these were the real men behind the stiff attitudes and the chain of command on the upper deck.

He raised his eyes and glanced along the table. Given a chance he would be happy amongst them, he thought.

Rhodes said between mouthfuls, 'I've heard we're sailing on Monday's tide. A fellow from the port admiral's office was aboard yesterday. He is usually right.'

Bolitho tried to remember what the captain had said. *Loyalty.* Shelve all else until there was time for it, when it could do no damage. Dumaresq had almost echoed his mother's last words to him. The sea is no place for the unwary.

Feet clattered overhead, and Bolitho heard more heavy nets of stores being swayed inboard to the twitter of a call.

Away from the land again, from the hurt, the sense of loss. Yes, it would be good to go.

True to Lieutenant Rhodes' information, His Britannic Majesty's Ship *Destiny* of twenty-eight guns made ready to weigh anchor on the following Monday morning. The past few days had gone so swiftly for Bolitho he thought life might be quieter at sea than it had been in harbour. Palliser had kept him working watch-on, watch-off with hardly a break. The first lieutenant took nothing at face value and made a point of questioning Bolitho on his daily work, his opinions and suggestions for changing some of the men around on the watch and quarter bills. If he was swift with his sarcasm, Palliser was equally quick to put his subordinate's ideas to good use.

Bolitho often thought of Rhodes' words about the first lieutenant. *After a command of his own.* He would certainly do his best for the ship and her captain, and be doubly quick to stamp on any incompetence which might eventually be laid at his door.

And Bolitho had worked hard to know the men he would deal with directly. Unlike the great ships of the line, a frigate's survival depended on her agility and not the thickness of her timbers. Likewise, her company was divided into divisions where they could work with the best results for the ship's benefit.

The foremast, with all its spread of canvas, course and topsails, topgallants and royals, with the additional foresails, jib and flying jib provided the means to turn with haste, through the wind's eye if need be, or to luff and cut across an enemy's vulnerable stern. At the opposite end of the ship the helmsmen and sailing master would use each mast, each scrap of canvas to lay the vessel on the course required with the least need for manoeuvre.

Bolitho was in charge of the mainmast. The tallest in the ship, it too was graded like the men who would soon be swarming aloft when ordered, no matter how they felt or what the weather threw against them.

The nimble topmen were the cream of the company, while on the deck itself, working at braces and halliards and manning the capstan bars, were the landmen, the newly recruited, or old sailors who could no longer be expected to fight salt-hardened canvas a hundred feet and more above the hull.

Rhodes had the fore, while a master's mate took charge of the mizzen-mast, supposedly the easiest one in any ship with its limited sail plan and where bodily strength was the first requirement. The afterguard, marines and a handful of seamen were sufficient to attend the mizzen.

Bolitho made a point of meeting the boatswain, a formidable-looking man named Timbrell. Tall, weather-beaten and scarred like an ancient warrior, he was the king of the vessel's seamen. Once clear of the land, Timbrell would work under the first lieutenant to rectify storm damage, repair spars and rigging, maintain the paintwork, ensure all the seams were free of leaks, and generally keep an eye on the professionals who would carry out those needs. The carpenter and his crew, the cooper and the sailmaker, the ropemaker and all the rest.

A seaman to his fingertips, he was a good friend to a new officer, but could be a bad enemy if provoked.

This particular Monday morning had begun early, before daybreak. With the cook providing a hasty meal, as if he too was conscious of the need to get under way.

Lists were checked yet again, names to match voices, faces to put into jobs where they belonged. To a landsman it would have looked like chaos, with lines snaking across the decks, men working aloft astride the great yards as they loosened the sails, hardened overnight by an unexpected frost.

Bolitho had seen the captain come on deck several times. Speaking with Palliser or discussing something with Gulliver, the master. If he was anxious he did not show it, but strode around the quarterdeck with his sure-footed tread like a man thinking of something else beyond the ship.

The officers and warrant officers had changed into their faded sea-going uniforms, so that only Bolitho and most of the young midshipmen looked alien in their new coats and shining buttons.

Bolitho had received two letters from his mother, both together from the Falmouth Mail. He could picture her as he had last seen her. So frail, and so lovely. The lady who had never grown up, some local people said. The Scottish girl who had captivated Captain James Bolitho from their first meeting. She was really too frail to carry the weight of the house and the estate. With his elder brother Hugh at sea somewhere, back aboard his frigate after a short period in command of the revenue cutter *Avenger* at Falmouth, and their father not yet home, the burden would seem doubly hard. His grown-up sister Felicity had already left home to marry an army officer, while the youngest in the family, Nancy, should have been thinking of a coming marriage of her own.

Bolitho crossed to the gangway where the hands were stowing the hammocks brought up from below. Poor Nancy, she would be missing Bolitho's dead friend more than any-one, and with nothing to keep her mind free of her loss.

Someone stood beside him and he turned to see the surgeon peering at the shore. The time he had found to speak with the rotund surgeon had been well spent. Another strange member of their company. Ship's surgeons, in Bolitho's experience, had been of the poorest quality, butchers for the most part, and their bloody work with knife and saw was as feared by sailors as any enemy broadside.

But Henry Bulkley was a world apart. He had been in a comfortable living in London, at a prestigious address where his clients had been wealthy but demanding.

Bulkley had explained to Bolitho during the quiet of a dog-watch, 'I got to hate the tyranny of the sick, the selfishness of the people who are only content if they are ill. I came to sea to escape. Now I *repair* and do not have to waste my time on those too rich to know their own bodies. I am as much a specialist as Mr Vallance, our gunner, or the caprenter, and I share their work in my own way. Or poor Codd, the purser, who frets over each mile logged and sets it against his stores of cheese and salt beef, candles and slop clothing.'

He had smiled contentedly. 'And I enjoy the pleasure of seeing other lands. I have sailed with Captain Dumaresq for three years. He, of course, is never sick. He would not *permit* it to happen!'

Bolitho said, 'It is a strange feeling to leave like this. To an unknown destination, a landfall which only the captain and two or three others may know. No war, yet we sail ready to fight.'

He saw the big man called Stockdale mustering in line with the other seamen around the trunk of the mainmast.

The surgeon followed his glance and observed, 'I heard something of what happened ashore. You have made a firm convert in that one. My God, he looks like an oak. I say that Little must have tripped him to win his money.' He shot a glance at Bolitho's profile. 'Unless he wanted to come with you? To escape from something, like most of us, eh?'

Bolitho smiled. Bulkley did not know the half of it. Stockdale had been allotted to the mizzen-mast for sail drill, and the quarterdeck six-pounders when the ship cleared for action. It was all in writing and signed with Palliser's slashing signature.

But somehow Stockdale had managed to alter things. Here he was in Bolitho's division, and would be stationed on the starboard battery of twelve-pounders which were in Bolitho's charge.

A quarter-boat pulled strongly from the shoreline, all the others having been hoisted inboard on their tier before the first cock had even considered crowing.

The last link with the land. Dumaresq's final letters and despatches for the courier. Eventually they would end up on somebody's desk at the Admiralty. A note would be passed to the First Sea Lord, a mark might be made on one of the great charts there. A small ship leaving under sealed orders. It was nothing new, only the times had changed.

Palliser strode to the quarterdeck rail, his speaking trumpet beneath his arm, his head darting around like a bird of prey seeking the next victim.

Bolitho looked up at the mainmast truck and was just able to discern the long red masthead pendant as it snapped out towards the quarter. A north-westerly wind. Dumaresq would need at least that to work clear of the anchorage. Never easy at the best of times, and after three months without sea-going activity, it would only require some forgetful seaman or petty officer to relay the wrong order and a proud exit might become a shambles in minutes.

Palliser called, 'All officers lay aft, if you please.' He sounded irritable, and was obviously conscious of the importance of the moment.

Bolitho joined Rhodes and Colpoys on the quarterdeck, while the master and the surgeon hovered slightly in the background like intruders.

Palliser said, 'We shall weigh in half an hour. Take up your stations, and watch every man. Tell the boatswain's mates to start anyone shirking his work, and take the name of each malingerer for punishment.' He glanced at Bolitho curiously. 'I have put that Stockdale man with you. I am uncertain as to why, but he seemed to feel it was his place. You must have some special gift, Mr Bolitho, though for the life of me I cannot see it!'

They touched their hats and walked away to their various stations.

Palliser's voice followed them, hollow and insistent through the speaking trumpet.

'Mr Timbrell! Ten more hands on the capstan! Where is that damn shantyman?'

The trumpet swivelled round like a coachman's blunder-buss. 'Hell's teeth, Mr Rhodes, I want the anchor hove short this morning, *not next week!*'

Clink, clink, clink, the pawls on the capstan moved reluctantly as the men threw themselves on the bars. Whippings and lashings had been cast off from the various coils of halliards and other running rigging, and while the officers and midshipmen were placed at intervals along the decks, like blue and white islets amongst a moving tide of seamen, the ship seemed to come alive, as if she too was aware of the time.

Bolitho darted a glance at the land. No more sun, and a light drizzle had begun to patter across the water, touching the ship and making the waiting men shiver and stamp their bare feet.

Little was whispering fiercely to two of the new seamen, his big hands stabbing out like spades as he made some point or other. He saw Bolitho and sighed.

'Gawd, sir, they're like blocks o' wood!'

Bolitho watched his two midshipmen and wondered how he should break the barrier which had sprung up as he had appeared on deck. He had spoken only briefly to them the previous day. *Destiny* was the first ship to both of them, as she was to all but two of the 'young gentlemen'. Peter Merrett was so small he seemed unable to find a place amidst the straining ropes and panting, thrusting seamen. He was twelve years old, the son of a prominent Exeter lawyer, who in turn was the brother of an admiral. A formidable combination. Much later on, if he lived, little Merrett might use such influence to his own advantage, and at the cost of others. But now, shivering and not a little frightened, he looked the picture of misery. The other one was Ian Jury, a fourteen-year-old youth from Weymouth. Jury's father had been a distinguished sea officer but had died in a shipwreck when Ian had still been a child. To the dead captain's relatives the Navy must have seemed the obvious place for Jury. It would also save them a great deal of trouble.

Bolitho nodded to them.

Jury was tall for his age, a pleasant-faced youth with fair hair and a barely controlled excitement.

Jury was the first to speak. 'Do we know where we are bound, sir?'

Bolitho studied him gravely. Under four years between them. Jury was not really like his dead friend, but the hair was similar.

He cursed himself for his brooding and replied, 'We shall know soon enough.' His voice came out more sharply than he had intended and he said, 'It is a well-kept secret as far as I am concerned.'

Jury watched him, his eyes curious. Bolitho knew what he was thinking, all the things he wanted to ask, to know, to discover in his new, demanding world. As he had once been himself.

Bolitho said, 'I shall want you to go aloft to the maintop, Mr Jury, and watch over the hands as they work. You, Mr Merrett, will remain with me to pass messages forrard or aft as need be.'

He smiled as their eyes explored the towering criss-cross of shrouds and rigging, the great main-yard and those above it reaching out on either beam like huge long-bows.

The two senior midshipmen, Henderson and Cowdroy, were aft by the mizzen, while the remaining pair were assisting Rhodes by the foremast.

Stockdale happened to be nearby and wheezed, 'Good mornin' for it, sir.'

Bolitho smiled at his battered features. 'No regrets, Stockdale?'

The big man shook his head. 'Nah. I needs a change. This will do me.'

Little grinned from across a twelve-pounder. 'Reckon you could take the main-brace all on yer own!'

Some of the seamen were chattering or pointing out land-marks on the shore as the light began to strengthen.

From the quarterdeck came the instant reprimand. 'Mr Bolitho, sir, keep those hands in order! It is more like a cattle-fair than a man-o'-war!'

Bolitho grimaced. 'Aye, aye sir!'

He added for Little's benefit, 'Take the name of anyone who . . .'

He got no chance to finish as Captain Dumaresq's cocked

hat appeared through the after companion and then with
apparent indifference his bulky figure moved to one side of
the quarterdeck.

Bolitho whispered fiercely to the midshipmen, 'Now listen,
you two. Speed is important, but not more so than getting
things done correctly. Don't badger the men unnecessarily,
most of them have been at sea for years anyway. Watch and
learn, be ready to assist if one of the new hands gets in a
tangle.'

They both nodded grimly as if they had just heard words
of great wisdom.

'Standing by forrard, sir!'

That was Timbrell, the boatswain. He seemed to be everywhere. Pausing to put a new man's fingers properly around a
brace or away from a block so that when his companions
threw their weight on it he would not lose half of his hand.
He was equally ready to bring his rattan cane down with a
crack on somebody's shoulders if he thought he was acting
stupidly. It brought a yelp of pain, and unsympathetic grins
from the others.

Bolitho heard the captain say something, and seconds later
the red ensign ran smartly up to the peak and blew out in the
wind like painted metal.

Timbrell again. 'Anchor's hove short, sir!' He was leaning
over the beak-hard, peering intently at the current as it swirled
beneath the bowsprit.

'Stand by on the capstan!'

Bolitho darted another glance aft. The place of command.
Gulliver with his helmsmen, three today at the big double
wheel. Taking no chances. Colpoys with his marines at the
mizzen braces, the midshipman of the watch, and the signals
midshipman, Henderson, still staring up at the wildly flapping
ensign to make sure the halliards had not fouled. With the
ship about to leave port, it would be more than his life was
worth.

At the quarterdeck rail, Palliser with a master's mate, and
slightly apart from them all, the captain, stout legs well
braced, hands beneath his coat-tails, as he stared the full
length of his command. To his astonishment, Bolitho saw that
Dumaresq was wearing a scarlet waistcoat beneath his coat.

'*Loose heads' ls!*'

The men up forward stirred into life, an unwary landman almost getting trampled underfoot as the great areas of canvas flapped and writhed in their sudden freedom.

Palliser glanced at the captain. There was the merest nod. Then the first lieutenant lifted his speaking trumpet and yelled, 'Hands aloft there! *Loose tops' ls!*'

The ratlines above either gangway were filled with seamen as they rushed up like monkeys towards the yards, while other fleet-footed topmen dashed on higher still, ready to play their part when the ship was under way.

Bolitho smiled to hide his anxiety as Jury sped after the clawing, hurrying seamen.

By his side Merrett said hoarsely, 'I feel sick, sir.'

Slade, the senior master's mate, paused and snarled, 'Then contain it! Spew up 'ere, my lad, an' I'll stretch you across a gun an' give you six strokes to sharpen your wits!' He hurried on, snapping orders, pushing men to their proper stations, the small midshipman already forgotten.

Merrett sniffed. 'Well, I *do* feel sick!'

Bolitho said, 'Stand over there.'

He peered towards the speaking trumpet and then aloft at his men strung out along the yards, the great billowing mass of the main-topsail already catching pockets of wind and trying to wrench itself free.

'Man the braces! Stand by . . .'

'*Anchor's aweigh, sir!*'

Like a released animal the *Destiny* paid off into the wind, her sails thundering out from her yards, banging and puffing in a frenzy until with the men straining at the braces to haul the yards round and the helm hard over she came under command.

Bolitho swallowed bile as a man slipped on the mainyard but was hauled to safety by one of his mates.

Round and further still, so that the land seemed to be whirling past the bows and the graceful figurehead in a wild dance.

'More hands to the weather forebrace! Take that man's name! Mr Slade! See to the anchor and lively now!'

Palliser's voice was never still. As the anchor rose dripping

to the cathead and was swiftly made fast to prevent it batter-
ing at the ship's hull, more men were rushed elsewhere by his
demanding trumpet.

'Get the fore and main-courses set!'

The biggest sails boomed out from their yards and hardened like iron in the driving wind. Bolitho paused to straighten
his hat and draw breath. The land where he had searched for
volunteers was safely on the opposite beam now, and with her
masts lining up to the wind and rudder *Destiny* was already
pointing towards the narrows, beyond which the open sea
waited like a field of grey.

Men fought with snaking lines, while overhead blocks
screamed as braces and halliards took on the strain of muscle
against the wind and a growing pyramid of canvas.

Dumaresq had not apparently moved. He was watching the
land sliding abeam, his chin tightly jammed into his neckcloth.

Bolitho dashed some rain or spray from his eyes, feeling
his own excitement, suddenly grateful he had not lost it.
Through the narrows and into the Sound, where Drake had
waited to match the Armada, where a hundred admirals had
pondered and considered their immediate futures. And where
after that?

'Leadsman in the chains, Mr Slade!'

Bolitho knew he was in a frigate now. No careful, portly
manoeuvre here. Dumaresq knew there would be many eyes
watching from the land even at this early hour. He would cut
past the headland as close as he dared, with just a fathom
between the keel and disaster. He had the wind, he had the
ship to do it.

Behind him he heard Merrett retching helplessly and hoped
Palliser would not see him.

Stockdale was bending a line round his palm and elbow in
a manner born. On his thick arm it looked like a thread. He
and the captain made a good pair.

Stockdale said huskily, 'Free, that's what I am.'

Bolitho made to reply but realized the battered fighter was
speaking for his own benefit.

Palliser's tone stung like a lash. 'Mr Bolitho! I shall tell
you *first*, as I need the t'gan'sls set as soon as we are through
the narrows! It may give you time to complete your dream
and attend to your duties, sir!'

Bolitho touched his hat and beckoned to his petty officers. Palliser was all right in the wardroom. On deck he was a tyrant.

He saw Merrett bending over a gun and vomiting into the scuppers.

'Damn your eyes, Mr Merrett! Clean up that mess before you dismiss! And control yourself!'

He turned away, confused and embarrassed. Palliser was not the only one, it seemed.

3

Sudden Death

The week which followed *Destiny*'s departure from Plymouth was the busiest and the most demanding in Richard Bolitho's young life.

Once free of the land's protection, Dumaresq endeavoured to set as much canvas as his ship could safely carry in a rising wind. The world was confined to a nightmare of stinging, ice-cold spray, violent swooping thrusts as the frigate smashed her way through troughs and rearing crests alike. It seemed as if it would never end, with no time to find dry clothing, and what food the cook had been able to prepare and have carried through the pitching hull had to be gulped down in minutes.

Once as Rhodes relieved Bolitho on watch he shouted above the din of cracking canvas and the sea surging inboard along the lee side, 'It's the lord and master's way, Dick! Push the ship to the limit, find the strength of every man aboard!' He ducked as a phantom of freezing spray doused them both. 'Officers, too, for that matter!'

Tempers became frayed, and once or twice small incidents of insubordination flared openly, only to be quenched by some heavy-fisted petty officer or the threat of formal punishment at the gratings.

The captain was often on deck, moving without effort between compass and chartroom, discussing progress with Gulliver, the master, or the first lieutenant.

And at night it was always worse. Bolitho never seemed to get his head buried in a musty pillow for his watch below before the hoarse cry was carried between deck like a call to arms.

'All hands! All hands aloft an' reef tops'ls!'

And it was then that Bolitho really noticed the difference. In a ship of the line he had been forced to claw his way aloft with the rest of them, fighting his loathing of heights and conscious only of the need not to show that fear to others. But when it was done, it was done. Now, as a lieutenant, it was all happening just as Dumaresq had prophesied.

In the middle of one fierce gale, as *Destiny* had tacked and battered her way through the Bay of Biscay, the call had come to take in yet another reef. There had been no moon or stars, just a rearing wall of broken water, white against the outer darkness, to show just how small their ship really was.

Men, dazed by constant work and half blinded by salt spray, had staggered to their stations, and then reluctantly had begun to drag themselves up the vibrating ratlines, then out along the topsail yards. The *Destiny* had been leaning so steeply to leeward that her main-yard had seemed to be brushing the broken crests alongside.

Forster, the captain of the maintop, and Bolitho's key petty officer, had yelled, 'This man says 'e won't go aloft, sir! No matter what!'

Bolitho had seized a stay to prevent himself from being flung on his face. 'Go yourself, Forster! Without you up there God knows what might happen!' He had peered up at the remainder of his men while all the time the wind had moaned and shrieked, like a demented being enjoying their torment.

Jury had been up there, his body pressed against the shrouds by the force of the wind. On the foremast they had been having the same trouble, with men and cordage, sails and spars all pounded together while the ship had done her best to hurl them into the sea below.

Bolitho had then remembered what Forster had told him. The man in question had been staring at him, a thin, defiant figure in a torn checkered shirt and seaman's trousers.

'What's the matter with you?' Bolitho had had to yell above the din.

'I can't go, sir.' The man had shaken his head violently. *'Can't!'*

Little had come lurching past, cursing and blaspheming as

he helped to haul some new cordage to the mainmast in readiness for use.

He had bellowed, 'I'll drag 'im aloft, sir!'

Bolitho had shouted to the seaman, 'Go below and help relieve the pumps!'

Two days later the same man had been reported missing. A search of the ship by Poynter, the master-at-arms, and the ship's corporal, had revealed nothing.

Little had tried to explain as best as he knew how. 'It were like this, sir. You should 'ave *made* 'im go aloft, even if 'e fell and broke 'is back. Or you could 'ave taken 'im aft for punishment. 'E'd 'ave got three dozen lashes, but 'e'd 'ave been a *man!*'

Bolitho had reluctantly understood. He had taken away the seaman's pride. His messmates would have sympathized with a man seized up at the gratings and flogged. Their contempt had been more than that lonely, defiant seaman had been able to stand.

On the sixth day the storm passed on and left them breathless and dazed by its intensity. Sails were reset, and the business of clearing up and repairing put aside any thought of rest.

Now, everyone aboard knew where the ship was first headed. To the Portuguese island of Madeira, although what for was a mystery still. Except for Rhodes, who had confided that it was merely to lay in a great store of wine for the surgeon's personal use.

Dumaresq had obviously read the report of the seaman's death in the log, but had said nothing of it to Bolitho. At sea, more men died by accident then ever from ball or cutlass.

But Bolitho blamed himself. The others, Little and Forster, years ahead of him in age and experience, had turned to him because he was their lieutenant.

Forster had remarked indifferently, 'Well, 'e weren't much bloody good anyway, sir.'

All Little had offered had been, 'Could 'ave been worse, sir.'

It was amazing to see the difference the weather made. The ship came alive again, and men moved about their work without glancing fearfully across their shoulders or clinging to the shrouds with both arms whenever they went aloft to splice or reeve new blocks.

On the morning of the seventh day, while the smell of cooking started the wagers going as to what the dish would eventually be, the masthead lookout yelled, 'Deck there! Land on the lee bow!'

Bolitho had the watch, and beckoned Merrett to bring him a telescope. The midshipman looked like a little old man after the storm and a week of back-breaking work. But he was still alive, and was never late on watch.

'Let me see.' Bolitho levelled the glass through the black shrouds and past the figurehead's curved shoulder.

Dumaresq's voice made him start. 'Madeira, Mr Bolitho. An attractive island.'

Bolitho touched his hat. For so heavy a man the captain could move without making a sound.

'I—I'm sorry, sir.'

Dumaresq smiled and took the telescope from Bolitho's hands. As he trained it on the distant island he added, 'When I was a lieutenant I always made sure that somebody in my watch was ready to warn me of my captain's approach.'

He glanced at Bolitho, the wide, compelling eyes seeking something. 'But not you, I suspect. Not yet anyway.'

He tossed the glass to Merrett and added, 'Walk with me. Exercise is good for the soul.'

So up and down along the weather side of the quarterdeck the *Destiny*'s captain and her most junior lieutenant took their stroll, their feet by-passing ring-bolts and gun-tackles without conscious effort.

Dumaresq spoke briefly of his home in Norfolk, but only as a place. He did not sketch in the people there, his friends, or whether he was married or not.

Bolitho tried to put himself in Dumaresq's place. Able to walk and speak of other, unimportant things while his ship leaned to a steady wind, her sails set one above the other in ordered array. Her officers, her seamen and marines, the means to sail and fight under any given condition, were all his concern. At this moment they were heading for an island, and afterwards they would sail much further. The responsibility seemed endless. As Bolitho's father had once wryly remarked, 'Only one law remains unchanged for any captain. If he is successful others will reap the credit. If he fails he will take the blame.'

Dumaresq asked suddenly, 'Are you settled in now?'

'I think so, sir.'

'Good. If you are still mulling over that seaman's death, I must ask you to desist. Life is God's greatest gift. To risk it is one thing, to throw it away is to cheat. He had no *right*. Best forgotten.'

He turned away as Palliser appeared on deck, the master-at-arms bringing up the rear.

Palliser touched his hat to the captain, but his eyes were on Bolitho.

'Two hands for punishment, sir.' He held out his book. 'You know them both.'

Dumaresq tilted forward on his toes, so that it appeared as if his heavy body would lose its balance.

'See to it at two bells, Mr Palliser. Get it over and done with. No sense in putting the people off their food.' He strode away, nodding to the master's mate of the watch like a squire to his gamekeeper.

Palliser closed his book with a snap. 'My compliments to Mr Timbrell, and ask him to have a grating rigged.' He crossed to Bolitho's side. 'Well, now?'

Bolitho said, 'The captain told me of his home in Norfolk, sir.'

Palliser seemed vaguely disappointed. 'I see.'

'Why does the captain wear a red waistcoat, sir?'

Palliser watched the master-at-arms returning with the boat-swain. 'Really, I am surprised your confidences did not extend that far.'

Bolitho hid a smile as Palliser strode away. He did not know either. After three years together that was something.

Bolitho stood beside Rhodes at the taffrail and watched the colourful activity of Funchal Harbour and its busy waterfront. *Destiny* lay at her anchor, with only the quarter-boat and the captain's gig in the water alongside. It did not look as if anyone would be allowed ashore, Bolitho thought.

Local boats with quaint curling stems and stern-posts milled around the frigate, their occupants holding up fruit and bright shawls, big jars of wine and many other items to tempt the sailors who thronged the gangways or waved from the shrouds and tops.

Destiny had anchored in mid-afternoon, and all hands had stayed on deck to watch the final approach, drinking in the beauty of what Dumaresq had rightly described as an attractive island. The hills beyond the white buildings were filled with beautiful flowers and shrubs, a sight indeed after the wild passage through the Bay. That, and the two floggings which had been carried out even as the ship had changed tack for their final approach, were forgotten.

Rhodes smiled and pointed at one boat. It contained three dark-haired girls who lay back on their cushions and stared boldly up at the young officers. It was obvious what they hoped to sell.

Captain Dumaresq had gone ashore almost as soon as the smoke of the gun salute to the Portuguese governor had dispersed. He had told Palliser he was going to meet the governor and pay his respects, but Rhodes said later, 'He's too excited for a mere social visit, Dick. I smell intrigue in the air.'

The gig had returned with instructions that Lockyer, the captain's clerk, was to go ashore with some papers from the cabin strong-box. He was down there now fussing about with his bag of documents while the side-party arranged for a boatswain's chair to sway him out and down into the gig.

Palliser joined them and said disdainfully, 'Look at the old fool. Never goes ashore, but when he does they have to rig a chair in case he falls and drowns!'

Rhodes grinned as the clerk was finally lowered into the boat. 'Must be the oldest man aboard.'

Bolitho thought about it. That was something else he had discovered. It was a young company, with very few senior hands like those he had known in the big seventy-four. The sailing master of a man-of-war was usually getting on in years by the time he was appointed, but Gulliver was under thirty.

Most of the hands lounging at the nettings or employed about the decks looked in good health. It was mostly due to the surgeon, Rhodes had said. That was the value of a medical man who cared, and who had the knowledge to fight the dreaded scurvy and other diseases which could cripple a whole ship.

Bulkley was one of the few privileged ones. He had gone
ashore with orders from the captain to purchase all the fresh
fruit and juices he thought necessary, while Codd, the purser,
had similar instructions on the matter of vegetables.

Bolitho removed his hat and let the sun warm his face. It
would be good to explore that town. Sit in a shady tavern like
those Bulkley and some of the others had described.

The gig had reached the jetty now and some of *Destiny*'s
marines were making a passage through a watching crowd for
old Lockyer to get through.

Palliser said, 'I see that your shadow is nearby.'

Bolitho turned his head and saw Stockdale kneeling beside
a twelve-pounder on the gun-deck. He was listening to Vallance,
the ship's gunner, and then making gestures with his hand
beneath the carriage. Bolitho saw Vallance nod and then clap
Stockdale on the shoulder.

That was unusual. He already knew that Vallance was not
the easiest warrant officer to get along with. He was jealous
about everything in his domain, from magazine to gun crews,
from maintenance to the wear and tear of tackle.

He came aft and touched his hat to Palliser.

'That new man Stockdale, sir. He's solved a problem with
a gun I've been bothered with for months. It was a replace-
ment, y'see. I've not been happy about it.' He gave a rare
smile. 'Stockdale thinks we could get the carriage reset by . . .'

Palliser spread his hands. 'You amaze me, Mr Vallance.
But do what you must.' He glanced at Bolitho. 'Your man
may not say much, but he is certainly finding his place.'

Bolitho saw Stockdale looking up at him from the gun-
deck. He nodded and saw the man smile, his battered face
screwed up in the sunlight.

Jury, who was the midshipman of the watch, called, 'Gig's
shoved off, sir!'

'That was quick!' Rhodes snatched a telescope. 'If it's the
captain coming back already, I'd better . . .' He gasped and
added quickly, 'Sir, they're bringing Lockyer with them!'

Palliser took a second glass and levelled it on the green-
painted gig. Then he said quietly, 'The clerk's dead. Sergeant
Barmouth is holding him.'

Bolitho took the telescope from Rhodes. For the moment
he could see nothing unusual. The smart gig was pulling

strongly towards the ship, the white oars rising and falling in perfect unison, the crew in their red checkered shirts and tarred hats a credit to their coxswain.

Then as the gig swung silently to avoid a drifting log, Bolitho saw the marine sergeant, Barmouth, holding the wispy-haired clerk so that he would not fall into the sternsheets.

There was a terrible wound across his throat, which in the sunlight was the same colour as the marine's tunic.

Rhodes murmured, 'And the surgeon's ashore with most of his assistants. God, there'll be hell to pay for this!'

Palliser snapped his fingers. 'That man you brought aboard with the other new hands, the apothecary's assistant? Where is he, Mr Bolitho?'

Rhodes said quickly, 'I'll fetch him, sir. He was doing some jobs in the sick-bay, just to test him out, the surgeon said.'

Palliser looked at Jury. 'Tell the boatswain's mate to rig another tackle.' He rubbed his chin. 'This was no accident.'

The local boats parted to allow the gig to glide to the main chains.

There was something like a great sigh as the small, untidy boat was hauled up the side and swung carefully above the gangway. Some blood ran down on to the deck, and Bolitho saw the man who had joined his recruiting party hurrying with Rhodes, to take charge of the corpse.

The apothecary's assistant's name was Spillane. A neat, self-contained man, not the sort who would leave security to seek adventure or even experience, Bolitho would have thought. But he seemed competent, and as he watched him telling the seamen what to do, Bolitho was glad he was aboard.

Sergeant Barmouth was saying, 'Yessir, I'd just made sure that the clerk was safely through the crowd, an' was about to take my stand on the jetty again, when I 'eard a cry, then everyone started yellin' an' carryin' on, you know, sir, like they does in these parts.'

Palliser nodded abruptly. 'Quite so, Sergeant. What then?'

'I found 'im in an alley, sir. 'Is throat was slit.'

He paled as he saw his own officer striding angrily across the quarterdeck. He would have to repeat everything for Colpoys' sake. The marine lieutenant, like most of his corps, disliked interference by the sea officers, no matter how pressing the reason.

Palliser said distantly, 'And his bag was missing.'

'Yessir.'

Palliser made up his mind. 'Mr Bolitho, take the quarter-boat, a midshipman and six extra hands. I'll give you an address where you will find the captain. Tell him what has happened. No dramatics, just the facts as you know them.'

Bolitho touched his hat, excited, even though he was still shocked by the suddenness of Lockyer's brutal death. So Palliser did know more of what the captain was doing than he proclaimed. When he looked at the scrap of paper which Palliser thrust into his hand he knew it was not the governor's residence, or any other official place for that matter.

'Take Mr Jury, and select six men yourself. I want them smartly turned out.'

Bolitho beckoned to Jury and heard Palliser say to Rhodes, 'I might have sent you, but Mr Bolitho and Jury have newer uniforms and may bring less discredit on my ship!'

In next to no time they were being pulled across the water towards the shore. Bolitho had been at sea for a week, but it seemed longer, so great was the change in his surroundings.

Jury said, 'Thank you for taking me, sir.'

Bolitho thought of Palliser's parting shot. He could not resist a sarcastic jibe. And yet he had been the one to think of Spillane, the one to see what Stockdale was doing with the gun. A man of many faces, Bolitho thought.

He replied, 'Don't let the men wander about.'

He broke off as he saw Stockdale, half hidden by the boat's oarsmen. Somehow he had found time to change into his checked shirt and white trousers and equip himself with a cutlass.

Stockdale pretended not to see his surprise.

Bolitho shook his head. 'Forget what I said. I do not think you will have any trouble after all.'

What had the big man said? *I'll not leave you. Not now. Not never.*

The boat's coxswain watched narrowly and then thrust the tiller bar hard over.

'Toss yer oars!'

The boat came to a halt by some stone stairs and the bowman hooked on to a rusty chain.

Bolitho adjusted his sword-belt and looked up at the watching townspeople. They appeared very friendly. Yet a man had just been murdered a few yards away.

He said, 'Fall in on the jetty.'

He climbed up the stairs and touched his hat to Colpoys' pickets. The marines looked extremely cheerful, and despite their rigid attitudes in front of a ship's officer, they smelled strongly of drink, and one of them had a flower protruding from his collar.

Bolitho took his bearings and strode towards the nearest street with as much confidence as he could muster. The sailors tramped behind him, exchanging winks and grins with women on balconies and in windows above the street.

Jury asked, 'Who would want to kill poor Lockyer, sir?'

'Who indeed?'

Bolitho hesitated and then turned down a narrow alley where the roofs nodded towards each other as if to blot out the sky. There was a heady scent of flowers, and he heard someone playing a stringed instrument in one of the houses.

Bolitho checked his piece of paper and looked at an iron gate which opened on to a courtyard with a fountain in its centre. They had arrived.

He saw Jury staring round at the strangeness of everything, and remembered himself in similar circumstances.

He said quietly, 'You come with me.' He raised his voice, 'Stockdale, take charge out here. Nobody is to leave until I give the word, understood?'

Stockdale nodded grimly. He would probably batter any would-be troublemaker senseless.

A servant led them to a cool room above the courtyard where Dumaresq was drinking wine with an elderly man who had a pointed white beard and skin like finely tooled leather.

Dumaresq did not stand. 'Yes, Mr Bolitho?' If he was startled by their unheralded arrival he hid it very well. 'Trouble?'

Bolitho glanced at the old man but Dumaresq said curtly, 'You are with friends here.'

Bolitho explained what had happened from the moment the clerk had left the ship with his bag.

Dumaresq said, 'Sergeant Barmouth is nobody's fool. If the bag had been there he would have found it.'

He turned and said something to the courtly gentleman with the beard, and the latter showed a brief flash of alarm before regaining his original composure.

Bolitho pricked up his ears. Dumaresq's host might live in Madeira, but the captain was speaking in Spanish, unless he was much mistaken.

Dumaresq said, 'Return to the ship, Mr Bolitho. My compliments to the first lieutenant and ask him to recall the surgeon and any other shore party immediately. I intend to weigh before nightfall.'

Bolitho closed his mind to the obvious difficulties, to say nothing of the risk of leaving harbour in the dark. He sensed the sudden urgency, the apprehension which Lockyer's murder had brought amongst them.

He nodded to the elderly man and then said to Dumaresq, 'A lovely house, sir.'

The old man smiled and bowed his head.

Bolitho strode down the stairs with Jury in his shadow, sharing every moment without knowing what was happening.

Bolitho wondered if the captain had noticed. That his host had understood exactly what he had said about his fine house. So if Dumaresq had spoken to him in Spanish it was so that neither he nor Jury should understand.

He decided it was one part of the mystery he would hold to himself.

That night, as promised, Dumaresq took his ship to sea. In light airs, and with all but her topsails and jib brailed up, *Destiny* steered slowly between other anchored vessels, guided by the ship's cutter with a lantern close to the water like a firefly to show her the way.

By dawn, Madeira was just a purple hump on the horizon far astern, and Bolitho was not certain if the mystery still remained there in the alley where Lockyer had drawn his last breath.

4

Spanish Gold

Lieutenant Charles Palliser closed the two outer screen doors of Dumaresq's cabin and said, 'All present, sir.'

In their various attitudes the *Destiny*'s lieutenants and senior warrant officers sat and watched Dumaresq expectantly. It was late afternoon, two days out of Madeira. The ship had a feeling of leisurely routine about her, as with a light north-easterly wind laying her on a starboard tack she cruised steadily into the Atlantic.

Dumaresq glanced up at the skylight as a shadow moved past it. Most likely the master's mate of the watch.

'Shut that, too.'

Bolitho glanced at his companions, wondering if they were sharing his growing sense of curiosity.

This meeting had been inevitable, but Dumaresq had taken great pains to ensure it would come well after his ship had cleared the land.

Dumaresq waited for Palliser to sit down. Then he looked at each man in turn. From the marine officer, past the surgeon, the master and the purser, finally to his three lieutenants.

He said, 'You all know about the death of my clerk. A reliable man, even if given to certain eccentricities. He will be hard to replace. However, his murder by some persons unknown means more than the loss of a companion. I have been under sealed orders, but the time is come to reveal some of the task we shall soon be facing. When two people know something it is no longer a secret. An even greater enemy in a small ship is rumour, and what it can do to idle minds.'

Bolitho flinched as the wide, compelling eyes paused on him momentarily before passing to some other part of the cabin.

Dumaresq said, 'Thirty years ago, before most of this ship's company had drawn breath, one Commodore Anson took an expedition south around Cape Horn and into the Great South Sea. His purpose was to harry Spanish settlements for, as you should know, we were then at war with the Dons.' He nodded grimly. 'Again.'

Bolitho thought of the courtly Spaniard in the house behind the harbour at Funchal, the secrecy, the missing bag for which a man had died.

Dumaresq continued, 'One thing is certain. Commodore Anson may have been courageous, but his ideas of health and caring for his people were limited.' He looked at the rotund surgeon and allowed his features to soften. 'Unlike us, maybe he had no proper doctors to advise him.'

There were several chuckles, and Bolitho guessed the remark had been made to put them more at their ease.

Dumaresq said, 'Be that as it may, within three years Anson had lost all of his squadron but his own *Centurion*, and had left thirteen hundred of his people buried at sea with his various escapades. Most of them died from disease, scurvy and bad food. It is likely that if Anson had returned home without further incident he would have faced a court martial and worse.'

Rhodes shifted in his chair, his eyes shining as he whispered, 'I *thought* as much, Dick.'

Dumaresq's glance silenced whatever it was Rhodes had been about to impart.

The captain brushed some invisible dust from his red waistcoat and said, 'Anson fell in with a Spanish treasure ship homeward bound with bullion in her holds valued at more than a million guineas.'

Bolitho vaguely remembered reading of the incident. Anson had seized the ship after a swift fight, had even broken off the action in order that the Spaniards could douse a fire which had broken out in their rigging. He had been that eager and desperate to take the treasure ship, *Nuestra Senora de*

Covadonga, intact. Prize courts and the powers of Admiralty
had long looked on such captures as of greater value than the
lives lost to obtain them.

Dumaresq cocked his head, his calm attitude momentarily
lost. Bolitho heard the hail from the masthead to report a sail
far off to the north. They had already sighted it twice during
the day, for it seemed unlikely there would be more than one
vessel using this same lonely route.

The captain shrugged. 'We shall see.' He did not elaborate
but continued, 'It was not known until recently that there was
another treasure ship on passage to Spain. She was the *Asturias,*
a larger vessel than Anson's prize, and therefore more heavily
laden.' He darted a glance at the surgeon. 'I can see *you* have
heard of her?'

Bulkley sat back and interlaced his fingers across his ample
stomach. 'Indeed I have, sir. She was attacked by an English
privateer under the command of a young Dorset man, Captain
Piers Garrick. His letter of marque saved him many times
from the gallows as a common pirate, but today he is Sir
Piers Garrick, well respected, and the past holder of several
government posts in the Caribbean.'

Dumaresq smiled grimly. 'True, but I suggest you confine
your suspicions to the limits of the wardroom! The *Asturias*
was never found, and the privateer was so damanged by the
engagement that she too had to be abandoned.'

He looked round, irritated as the sentry called through the
door, 'Midshipman of the watch, *sir!*'

Bolitho could picture the anxiety on the quarterdeck. Should
they disturb the meeting below their feet and risk Dumaresq's
displeasure? Or should they just note the strange sail in the
log and hope for the best?

Dumaresq said, 'Enter.' He did not seem to raise his voice
and yet it carried to the outer cabin without effort.

It was Midshipman Cowdroy, a sixteen-year-old youth who
Dumaresq had already punished for using unnecessary sever-
ity on members of his watch.

He said, 'Mr Slade's respects, sir, and that sail has been
reported to the north'rd again.' He swallowed hard and seemed
to shrink under the captain's stare.

Dumaresq said eventually, 'I see. We shall take no action.'

As the door closed he added, 'Although I fear that stranger is not astern of us by coincidence.'

A bell chimed from the forecastle and Dumaresq said, 'Recent information has been found and sworn to that most of the treasure is intact. A million and a half in bullion.'

They stared at him as if he had uttered some terrible obscenity.

Then Rhodes exclaimed, 'And we are to discover it, sir?'

Dumaresq smiled at him. 'You make it sound very simple, Mr Rhodes, perhaps we shall find it so. But such a vast amount of treasure will, and has already, aroused interest. The Dons will want it back as their rightful property. A prize court will argue that as the ship had already been seized by Garrick's privateer before she managed to escape and hide, the bullion is the property of His Brittanic Majesty.' He lowered his voice, 'And there are some who would seize it to further a cause which would do us nothing but harm. So, gentlemen, now you know. Our outward purpose is to complete the King's business. But if the news of this treasure is allowed to run riot elsewhere, I will want to know who is responsible.'

Palliser rose to his feet, his head bowed uncomfortably between the deckhead beams. The rest followed suit.

Dumaresq turned his back and stared at the glittering water which stretched to the horizon astern.

'First we go to Rio de Janeiro. Then I shall know more.'

Bolitho caught his breath. The South Americas, and Rio was all of 5000 miles from his home at Falmouth. It would be the furthest he had yet sailed.

As they made to leave Dumaresq said, 'Mr Palliser and Mr Gulliver, remain, if you please.'

Palliser called, 'Mr Bolitho, take over my watch until I relieve you.'

They left the cabin, each immersed in his own thoughts. The far-off destination would mean little to the ordinary sailor. The sea was always there, wherever he was, and the ship went with him. Sails had to be trimmed and reset at all hours, no matter what, and a seaman's life was hard whether the final landfall was in England or the Arctic. But let the rumour of treasure run through the ship and things might be very different.

As he climbed to the quarterdeck Bolitho saw the men assembling for the first-watch looking at him curiously, then turning away as he met their eyes, as if they already knew.

Mr Slade touched his hat. 'The watch is aft, sir.'

He was a hard master's mate and unpopular with many of the people, especially those who did not rise to his impressive standards of seamanship.

Bolitho waited for the helmsmen to be relieved, the usual handing over from one watch to the next. A glance aloft at the set of the yards and sails, examine the compass and the chalked notes on the slate made by the midshipman on duty.

Gulliver came on deck, banging his palms together as he did when he was worried.

Slade asked, 'Trouble, sir?'

Gulliver eyed him warily. He had been in Slade's position too recently to take any comment as casual. Seeking favours perhaps? Or a way of suggesting that he was out of his depth with the wardroom officers aft?

He snapped, 'At the next turn of the glass we will alter course.' He peered at the tilting compass, 'Sou'-west by west. The captain intends to see the t'gan'sls, though with these light winds under our coat-tails I doubt if we can coax another knot out of her.'

Slade squinted up at the masthead lookout. 'So the strange sail means something.'

Palliser's voice preceded him up the companion ladder. 'It *means,* Mr Slade, that if that sail is still there tomorrow morning she is indeed following us.'

Bolitho saw the worry in Gulliver's eyes and guessed what Dumaresq must have said to him and Palliser.

'Surely there is nothing we can do about that, sir? We are not at war.'

Palliser regarded him calmly. 'There is quite a lot we can do about it.' He nodded to emphasize the point. 'So be ready.'

As Bolitho made to leave the quarterdeck in his care Palliser called after him., 'And I shall be timing those laggards of yours when all hands are piped to make more sail.'

Bolitho touched his hat. 'I am honoured, sir.'

Rhodes was waiting for him on the gun-deck. 'Well done, Dick. He'll respect you if you stand up to him.'

They walked aft to the wardroom and Rhodes said, 'The lord and master is going to take that other vessel, you know that, don't you, Dick?'

Bolitho threw his hat on to one of the guns and sat down at the wardroom table.

'I suppose so.' His mind drifted back again, to the coves and cliffs of Cornwall. 'Last year, Stephen, I was doing temporary duty aboard a revenue cutter.'

Rhodes was about to make a joke of it but saw the sudden pain in Bolitho's eyes.

Bolitho said, 'There was a man then, a big and respected landowner. He died trying to flee the country. It was proved he had been smuggling arms for an uprising in America. Maybe the captain thinks this is similar, and all this time that gold has been waiting for the right use.' He grimaced, surprised at his own gravity. 'But let's talk about Rio. I am looking forward to that.'

Colpoys strolled into the wardroom and arranged himself carefully in a chair.

To Rhodes he said, 'The first lieutenant says you are to select a midshipman to assist with the clerical duties in the cabin.' He crossed his legs and remarked, 'Didn't know the young fellas could write!'

Their laughter died as the surgeon, unusually grim-faced, entered, and after a quick glance around to make certain they were undisturbed, said, 'The gunner's just told me something interesting. He was asked by one of his mates if they would need to move some of the twelve-pounder shot forward to make room for the bullion.' He let his words sink in. 'How long has it been? Fifteen minutes? Ten? It must be the shortest secret of any day!'

Bolitho listened to the regular creak and clatter of rigging and spars, the movement of the watch on deck overhead.

So be ready, Palliser had said. It had suddenly adopted another meaning altogether.

The morning after Dumaresq's disclosures about the treasure ship found the strange sail still lying far astern.

Bolitho had the morning-watch, and had sensed the growing tension as the light hardened across the horizon and faces around him took on shape and personality.

Then came the cry, 'Deck there! Sail to th' nor'-east!'

Dumaresq must have been ready for it, expecting it. He came on deck within minutes, and after a cursory glance at the compass and the flapping sails, observed, 'Wind's dropping off.' He looked at Bolitho. 'This is a damnable business.' He recovered himself instantly. 'I shall have breakfast now. Send Mr Slade aloft when he comes on watch. He has an eye for most craft. Tell him to study that stranger, though God knows she is cunning enough to keep her distance and still not lose us.'

Bolitho watched him until he had disappeared below and then looked along *Destiny*'s full length. It was the ship's busiest time, with seamen at work with holy-stones on the deck planking, others cleaning guns and checking running and standing rigging under Mr Timbrell's critical eye. The marines were going through one of their many, seemingly complicated drills with muskets and fixed bayonets, while Colpoys kept at a distance, leaving the work to his sergeant.

Beckett, the carpenter, was already directing some of his crew to begin repairs on the larboard gangway which had been damaged when a purchase had collapsed under the weight of some incoming stores. The upper deck with its double line of twelve-pounders was like a busy street and a market-place all in one. A place for hard work and gossip, for avoiding authority or seeking favour.

Later, with the decks cleaned up, the hands were piped to sail drill with Palliser at his place on the quarterdeck to watch their frantic efforts to knock seconds off the time it took to reef or make more sail.

And all the while as they lived through the daily routine of a man-of-war, that other sail never left them. Like a tiny moth on the horizon it was always there. When *Destiny* shortened sail and the way fell from beneath her beakhead, the stranger too would follow suit. Spread more canvas and the lookout would immediately report a responding action by the stranger.

Dumaresq came on deck as Gulliver was just completing his supervision of the midshipman's efforts as they took the noon sights to fix the ship's position.

Bolitho was close enough to hear him ask, 'Well, Mr Gulliver, how will the weather favour us tonight?' He sounded impatient, even angry that Gulliver should be doing his normal duties.

The sailing master glanced at the sky and the red masthead pendant. 'Wind's backed a piece, sir. But the strength is the same. Be no stars tonight, too much cloud in the offing.'

Dumaresq bit his lip. 'Good. So be it.' He swung round and called, 'Pass the word for Mr Palliser.' He saw Bolitho and said, 'You have the dog-watches today. Make certain you gather plenty of lanterns near the mizzen. I want our 'friend' to see our lights later on. They will give him confidence.'

Bolitho watched the change in the man, the power running through him like a rising wave, a need to crush this impudent follower.

Palliser came striding aft, his eyes questioning again as he saw Dumaresq speaking with his junior lieutenant.

'Ah, Mr Palliser, I have work for you.'

Dumaresq smiled, but Bolitho could see from the way a nerve was jumping at the corner of his jaw, the stiffness in his back and broad shoulders, that his mind was less relaxed.

Dumaresq made a sweeping gesture. 'I shall require the launch ready for lowering at dusk, earlier if the light is poor. A good man in charge, if you please, and extra hands to get her mast stepped and sails set as soon as they are cast off.' He watched Palliser's inscrutable face and added lightly, 'I want them to carry several of the large lanterns, too. We shall douse ours and darken ship completely as soon as the launch is clear. Then I intend to beat hard to wind'rd, come about and *wait*.'

Bolitho turned to look at Palliser. To tackle another vessel in the dark was not to be taken flippantly.

Dumaresq added, 'I shall flog any man aboard who shows so much as a glow-worm!'

Palliser touched his hat. 'I'll attend to it, sir. Mr Slade can take charge of the boat. He's so keen on promotion it'll do him good.'

Bolitho was astounded to see Dumaresq and the first lieutenant laughing together like a pair of schoolboys, as if this was an everyday occurrence.

Dumaresq looked at the sky and then turned to stare astern. Only from the masthead could you see the other vessel, but it was as if he was able to reach beyond the horizon itself. He was calm again, in control of his feelings.

He said, 'Something to tell you father about, Mr Bolitho. It would appeal to him.'

A seaman tramped past carrying a great coil of rope across his shoulder like a bundle of dead snakes. It was Stockdale. As the captain vanished below he wheezed, 'We goin' to fight that one, sir?'

Bolitho shrugged. 'I—I think so.'

Stockdale nodded heavily. 'I'll grind an edge on my blade, then.' That was all it apparently meant to him.

Left alone to his thoughts, Bolitho crossed to the rail and looked down at the men already working to free the launch from the other boats on the tier. Did Slade, he wondered, yet realize what might become of him? If the wind rose after they had dropped the launch, Slade could be driven miles off course. It would be harder than finding a pin in a haystack.

Jury came on deck, and after some hesitation joined him by the rail.

Bolitho stared at him. 'I thought you were sent aft to do poor Lockyer's work?'

Jury met his gaze. 'I asked the first lieutenant if he would send Mr Midshipman Ingrave instead.' Some of his composure collapsed under Bolitho's gaze. 'I'd prefer to stay in your watch, sir.'

Bolitho clapped him on the shoulder. 'On your head be it.' But he felt pleased all the same.

The boatswain's mates hurried from hatchway to hatchway, their silver calls trilling in between their hoarse cries for the watch below to assist in swaying out the launch.

Jury listened to the shrill whistles and said, 'The Spithead nightingales are in full cry this evening, sir.'

Bolitho hid a smile. Jury spoke like an old sailor, a real sea-dog.

He faced him gravely, 'You'd better go and see what is being done about the lanterns. Otherwise Mr Palliser will have the both of us in full cry, I'm thinking.'

As dusk came down to conceal their preparations the masthead lookout reported that the other sail was still in sight.

Palliser touched his hat as the captain came on deck. 'All ready, sir.'

'Very well.' Dumaresq's eyes shone in the reflected glare
from the array of lanterns. 'Shorten sail and stand by to lower
the boat.' He looked up as the main-topsail filled and boomed
sullenly from its yard. 'After that, every stitch she can carry.
If that ferrett back there is a friend, and merely seeking our
protection on the high seas, we shall know it. If not, Mr
Palliser, he shall know *that,* I promise you!'

An anonymous voice whispered, 'Cap'n's comin' up, sir!'
Palliser turned and waited for Dumaresq to join him by the
quarterdeck rail.
Gulliver's shadow moved through the gloom. 'South by
east, sir. Full and bye.'
Dumaresq gave a grunt. 'You were right about the clouds,
Mr Gulliver, though the wind's fresher than I expected.'
Bolitho stood with Rhodes and three midshipmen at the lee
side of the quarterdeck ready to execute any sudden order.
More to the point, they were able to share the drama and the
tension. Dumaresq's comment had sounded as if he blamed
the master for the wind.
He looked up and shivered. *Destiny,* after thrashing and
beating her way to windward for what had seemed like an
eternity, had come about as Dumaresq had planned. With a
stiff wind sweeping over the laboard quarter she was plunging
across a procession of breaking white-horses, the spray rising
above the weather rigging and sweeping on to the crouching
seamen like tropical rain.
Destiny had been stripped down to her topsails and jib with
her big forecourse holding two reefs in readiness for a swift
change of tack.
Rhodes murmured, 'That other vessel is out there somewhere, Dick.'
Bolitho nodded and tried not to think of the launch as it had
vanished into a deepening darkness, the lanterns making a
lively show on the water.
It was an eerie feeling, with the ship so quiet around him.
Nobody spoke, and the heavily greased gear was without its
usual din and clatter. Just the sweeping sea alongside, the
occasional rush of water through the lee scuppers as *Destiny*
dropped her bows into a deep trough.
Bolitho wanted to forget what was happening around him

and to concentrate on what he had to do. Palliser had selected the best seamen in the ship for a boarding party if it came to that. But the sudden upsurge of wind might have changed Dumaresq's ideas, he thought.

He heard Jury moving restlessly by the nettings, and Rhodes' midshipman, Mr Cowdroy, who had been in the ship for two years. He was a haughty, bad-tempered youth of sixteen who would be impossible as a lieutenant. Rhodes had had cause to report him to the captain more than once, and the last time he had been ignominiously caned across a six-pounder by the boatswain. It did not seem to have changed him. Little Merrett made up the trio, trying to keep out of sight, as usual.

Rhodes said softly, 'Soon now, Dick.' He loosened the hanger in his belt. 'Might be a slaver, who knows?'

Yeames, master's mate of the watch, said cheerfully, 'Not likely, sir. You'd *smell* a blackbirder by now!'

Palliser snapped, 'Be silent there!'

Bolitho watched the sea curling above the dipping side in a frothing white bank. Beyond it there was nothing but an occasional jagged crest. As black as a boot, as Colpoys had remarked. His marksmen were already aloft in the tops, trying to keep their muskets dry and watching for the first sight of the stranger.

If the captain and Gulliver had timed it correctly, the stranger should appear on *Destiny's* starboard bow. The frigate would hold the wind-gage and the other vessel would have no chance of slipping away. The men at the starboard battery were ready, the gun captains on their knees as they prepared to run out as soon as the word came from aft.

To a civilian sitting by his hearth in England it might all seem like a kind of madness. But to Captain Dumaresq it was something else entirely, and it mattered. The other vessel, whatever she was, was interfering with the King's affairs. That made it personal, not to be taken lightly.

Bolitho gave another shiver as he recalled his first meeting with the captain. *To me, to this ship, and to His Brittanic Majesty, in that order*!

Destiny raised her quivering jib-boom like a lance and seemed to hang motionless on the edge of another trough before she plunged forward and down, her bows smashing through solid water and flinging spray high above the forecastle.

From one corner of his eye Bolitho saw something fall from overhead. It hit the deck and exploded with a loud bang.

Rhodes ducked as a ball whined dangerously past his face and gasped, 'A damned bullock has dropped his musket!'

Startled voices and harsh accusations erupted from the gun-deck, and Lieutenant Colpoys ran to the quarterdeck ladder in his haste to deal with the culprit.

It all happened in a swift sequence of events. The sudden explosion as *Destiny* ploughed her way towards the next array of crests, the attention of officers and seamen distracted for just a few moments.

Palliser said angrily, 'Stop that noise, damn your eyes!'

Bolitho turned and then froze as out of the darkness, running with the wind, came the other vessel. Not safely down-wind to starboard, but right here, rising above the larboard side like a phantom.

'Put up your helm!' Dumaresq's powerful voice stopped some of the startled men in their tracks. 'Man the braces there, stand by on the quarterdeck!'

Rearing and plunging, her sails booming and thundering in wild confusion, *Destiny* began to swing away from the on-coming vessel. Gun crews who minutes earlier had been nursing their weapons in readiness for a fight were caught totally unawares, and even now were tumbling across to help the men on the opposite side where the twelve-pounders still pointed at their sealed ports.

More spray burst over the quarterdeck as another sea surged jubilantly across the nettings and drenched the men nearby. Order was being restored, and Bolitho saw seamen straining back on the braces until they seemed to be touching the deck itself.

He shouted, 'Stand to, men!' He was groping for his hanger even as he realized that Rhodes and his midshipman had already gone running to the bows. 'She'll be into us directly!'

A shot echoed above the din of sea and wind, but whether fired by accident or by whom, Bolitho did not know or care.

He felt Jury by his side.

'What'll we do, sir?'

He sounded frightened. As well he might, Bolitho thought.

Merrett was clinging to the nettings as if nothing would ever shift him.

Bolitho used something like physical strength to control his stampeding thoughts. He was in charge. Nobody else was here to lead, to advise. Everyone on the upper deck was too occupied with his own role.

He managed to shout, 'Stay with me.' He pointed at a running figure. 'You, clear the starboard battery and prepare to repel boarders!'

As men floundered cursing and shouting in all directions, Bolitho heard Dumaresq's voice. He was on the opposite side of the deck, yet seemed to be speaking into Bolitho's ear.

'*Board*, Mr Bolitho!' He swung round as Palliser sent more men to shorten sail in a last attempt to delay the impact of collision. 'She must not escape!'

Bolitho stared at him, his eyes wild. 'Aye, sir!'

He was about to draw his hanger when with a thundering crash the other vessel drove hard alongside. But for Dumaresq's quick action she would have rammed into the *Destiny*'s broadside like a giant axe.

Yells changed to screams as a tumbling mass of cordage and broken spars crashed on and between the two hulls. Men were knocked from their feet as the sea lifted the vessels together yet again, bringing down another tangle of rigging and blocks. Some men had fallen, too, and Bolitho had to drag Jury by the arm as he shouted, 'Follow me!' He waved his hanger, keeping his eyes away from the sea which appeared to be boiling between the two snared hulls. One slip and it would all be over.

He saw Little brandishing a boarding axe, and of course Stockdale holding his cutlass like a dirk against his massive frame.

Bolitho gritted his teeth and leapt for the other vessel's shrouds, his legs kicking in space as he struck out seeking a foothold. His hangar had gone from his hand and swung dangerously from his wrist as he gasped and struggled to hold on. More men were on either side of him, and he retched as someone fell between the two vessels, the man's scream cut off abruptly like a great door being slammed shut.

As he dropped to the unfamiliar deck he heard other voices and saw vague shapes rushing across the fallen wreckage, some with blades in their fists, while from aft came the sharp crack of a pistol.

He groped for his hanger and shouted, 'Drop your weapons in the King's name!'

The roar of voices which greeted his puny demand was almost worse than the danger. Perhaps he had been expecting Frenchmen or Spaniards, but the voices which yelled derision at his upraised hanger were as English as his own.

A spar plunged straight down into the deck, momentarily separating the two opposing groups and smashing one of the figures to pulp. With a final quiver the two vessels wrenched themselves apart, and even as a sword-blade darted from the shadows toward him, Bolitho realized that *Destiny* had left him to fend for himself.

5

Blade to Blade

Calling to each other by name, and matching curses with their
unknown adversaries, the *Destiny*'s small boarding party struggled to hold together. All the while the deck was flung about
by the sea, the motion made worse by fallen spars and great
creepers of rigging which trailed over the bulwarks and pulled
the hull into each trough like a sea-anchor.

Bolitho slashed out at someone opposite him, his blade
jarring against steel as he parried away another thrust. Bolitho
was a good swordsman, but a hanger was a poor match for a
straight blade. Around him men were yelling and gasping,
bodies interlocked while they fought with cutlass and dirk,
boarding axe and anything which they could lay hands on.

Little bellowed, 'Aft, lads! Come on!' He charged along
the littered deck, hacking down a crouching shadow with his
axe as he ran, and followed by half of the party.

Near Bolitho a man slipped and fell, and then rolled over,
protecting his face from the one who stood astride him with a
raised cutlass. Bolitho heard the swish of steel, the sickening
thud of the blade driving into bone. But when he turned he
saw Stockdale wrenching his own blade free before tossing
the dead man unceremoniously over the side.

It was a wild, jumbled nightmare. Nothing seemed real,
and Bolitho could feel the numbness thrusting through his
limbs as he fought off another attacker who had slithered
down the shrouds like an agile ape.

He ducked, and felt the man slice above his head, the

breath rasping out of him from the force of his swing. Bolitho punched him in the stomach with the knuckle-bow of his hanger, and as he reeled away hacked him hard across the neck, the pain lancing up his arm as if he had been the one to be cut down.

Despite the horror and the danger, Bolitho's mind continued to respond, but like that of an onlooker, somebody uninvolved with the bloody hand-to-hand fighting around him. The vessel was a brigantine, her yards in disarray as she continued to fall downwind. There was a smell of newness about her, a freshly built craft. Her crew must have been dumbfounded when *Destiny*'s canvas had loomed across their bows, and that shock was the only thing which had so far saved the depleted boarding party.

A man bounded forward, regardless of the slashing figures and sobbing wounded who were being trampled underfoot.

Through his reeling mind one more thought came to Bolitho. This gaunt figure in a blue coat and brass buttons must be the vessel's master.

The brigantine was temporarily out of control, but within hours that could be put right. And *Destiny* was nowhere to be seen. Perhaps her damage was much worse than they had thought. You never really considered it might happen to your own ship. Always to another.

Bolitho saw the dull glint of steel and guessed dawn was not far away. Surprisingly, he thought of his mother, glad that she would not see his body when he fell.

The gaunt man yelled, 'Drop your sword, rot you!'

Bolitho tried to shout back at him, to rally his men, to give himself a last spur of defiance.

Then the blades crossed, and Bolitho felt the strength of the man through the steel as if it was an extention of his own arm.

Clash, clash, clash, Bolitho parried and cut at the other man, who took every advantage to press and follow each attack.

There was a clang, and Bolitho felt the hanger torn from his fingers, the lanyard around his wrist severed by the force of the blow.

He heard a frantic voice yell, 'Here, sir!' It was Jury, as he hurled a sword across the writhing bodies hilt-first.

Bolitho's desperation came to his aid. Somehow he caught it, twisting it in his grip as he felt its balance and length. Tiny pictures flashed through his mind. His father teaching him and his brother Hugh in the walled kitchen-garden at Falmouth. Then later, matching careful movements against each other.

He sobbed as the other man's sword cut through his sleeve just below his armpit. Another inch and . . . He felt the fury sweeping everything else aside, an insanity which seemed to give him back his strength, even his hope.

Bolitho locked blades again, feeling his opponent's hatred, smelling his strength and his sweat.

He heard Stockdale calling in his strange, husky voice and knew he was being pressed too hard to reach his side. Others had stopped fighting, their wind broken as they stared with glazed eyes at the two swordsmen in their midst.

From another world, or so it seemed, came the crash of a single cannon. A ball hissed over the deck and slammed through a flapping sail like an iron fist. *Destiny* was nearby, and her captain had taken the risk of killing some of his own men to make his presence felt and understood.

Some of the brigantine's men threw down their weapons instantly. Others were less fortunate and were felled by the inflamed boarders even as they tried to grasp what was happening.

Bolitho's adversary shouted wildly, 'Too late for you, *sir*!'

He thrust Bolitho back with his fist, measured the distance and lunged.

Bolitho heard Jury cry out, saw Little running towards him, his teeth bared like a wild animal.

After all the agony and the hate, it was too easy and without any sort of dignity. He held his balance and did not even have to guide his feet and arms as he stepped aside, using the other man's charge to flick his blade in one ringing encounter and then drive his own beneath the lost guard and into his chest.

Little dragged the man away and raised his bloodied axe as he tried to struggle free.

Bolitho shouted, 'Belay that! Let him be!'

He looked round, feeling dazed and sick, as some of his men gave a wild cheer.

Little let the man fall to the deck and wiped his face with

the back of his wrist, as if he too was slowly but reluctantly letting go of the madness. Until the next time.

Bolitho saw Jury sitting with his back against a broken spar, his hand clasped across his stomach. He knelt down and tried to drag Jury's fingers away. Not him, he thought. Not so soon.

A seaman Bolitho recognized as one of his best maintopmen bent down and jerked the midshipman's hands apart.

Bolitho swallowed hard and tore the shirt open, remembering Jury's fear and his trust at the moment of boarding. Bolitho was young, but he had done this sort of thing before.

He peered at the wound and felt like praying. A blade must have been stopped by the large gilt plate on Jury's cross-belt, he could see the scored metal even in the poor light. It had taken the real force, and the attacker had only managed to scar the youth's stomach.

The seaman grinned and fashioned a wad from Jury's torn shirt. 'He'll be all right, sir. Just a nick.'

Bolitho got shakily to his feet, one hand resting on the man's shoulder for support.

'Thank you, Murray. That was well said.'

The man looked up at him as if trying to understand something.

'I saw him throw that sword to you, sir. It was then that some other bugger made his play.' He wiped his cutlass absently on a piece of sailcloth. 'It was the last bloody thing he *did* do on this earth!'

Bolitho walked aft towards the abandoned wheel. Voices from the past seemed to be following him, reminding him of this particular moment.

They will be looking to you now. The fight and fury has gone out of them.

He turned and shouted, 'Take the prisoners below and put them under guard.'

He sought out a familiar face from others who had followed him blindly without really knowing what they were doing.

'You, Southmead, man the wheel. The rest go with Little and cut free the wreckage alongside.'

He glanced quickly at Jury. His eyes were open and he was trying not to cry out from the pain.

Bolitho forced a smile, his lips frozen and unreal. 'We have a prize. Thank you for what you did. It took real courage.'

Jury tried to reply but fainted away again.

Through the wind and spray Bolitho heard the booming challenge of Captain Dumaresq's voice through a speaking trumpet.

Bolitho called to Stockdale, 'Answer for me. I am spent!'

As the two vessels drew closer, their fine lines marred by broken spars and dangling rigging, Stockdale cupped his big hands and yelled, 'The ship is ours, sir!'

There was a ragged cheer from the frigate. It seemed obvious to Bolitho that Dumaresq had not expected to find a single one of them left alive.

Palliser's crisp tones replaced the captain's resonant voice. 'Lay to if you are able! We must recover Mr Slade and his boat!'

Bolitho imagined he could hear someone laughing.

He raised his hand as the frigate tacked slowly and awkwardly away, men already working on her yards to haul up fresh canvas and reeve new blocks.

Then he looked at the brigantine's deck, at the wounded men who were moaning quietly or trying to drag themselves away like sick animals will do.

There were some who would never move.

As the light continued to strengthen, Bolitho examined the sword which Jury had flung to save him. In the dull light the sword was like black paint, on the hilt and up to his own wrist.

Little came aft again. The new third lieutenant was young. In a moment he would fling the sword over the side, his guts soured by what they had done together. That would be a pity. Later he would want it to give to his father or his sweetheart.

Little said, ' 'Ere, sir, I'll take that an' give it a shamper for you.' He saw Bolitho's hesitation and added affably, 'It's bin a real mate to you. Always look after yer mates, that's what Josh Little says, sir.'

Bolitho handed it to him. 'I expect you're right.'

He straightened his back, even though every muscle and fibre seemed to be cutting him like hot bands.

'Lively, men! There's much to do.' He recalled the captain's words. 'It won't do it by itself!'

From beneath the foremast and its attendant pile of fallen debris Stockdale watched him and then gave a satisfied nod. One more fight had ended.

Bolitho waited wearily by Dumaresq's table in *Destiny*'s cabin, his aching limbs at odds with the frigate's motion. Dull daylight had revealed the brigantine's name to be *Heloise*, outward bound from Bridport in Dorset to the Caribbean, by way of Madeira to take on a cargo of wine.

Dumaresq finished leafing through the brigantine's log-book and then glanced at Bolitho.

'Do sit, Mr. Bolitho. Before you fall down.'

He rose and walked to the quarter windows, pressing his face against the thick glass to seek out the brigantine which was lying in *Destiny*'s lee. Palliser and a fresh boarding party had gone across earlier, the first lieutenant's experience in much demand as they sought to repair the damage and get the vessel under way again.

Dumaresq said, 'You performed well. Extremely so. For one so young and as yet inexperienced in leading men, you achieved more than I'd dared to hope.' He clasped his powerful hands behind his coat-tails as if to contain his anger. 'But seven of our people are dead, others badly injured.' He reached up and banged the skylight with his knuckles. '*Mr Rhodes!* Be so good as to find out what the damned surgeon is about!'

Bolitho forgot his tiredness, his previous resentment at being ordered from his prize to make way for the first lieutenant. It was fascinating to watch the slow rise of Dumaresq's anger. Like a smouldering fuse at it edges towards the first cask of powder. It must have made poor Rhodes jump to hear his captain's voice rising from the deck at his feet.

Dumaresq turned to Bolitho. 'Good men killed. Piracy and murder, no less!'

He had made no mention of the miscalculation which all but wrecked or dismasted both ships.

He was saying, 'I knew they were up to something. It was evident at Funchal that too many ears and eyes were abroad.' He ticked off the points on his strong fingers. 'My clerk, just to get the contents of his satchel. Then the brigantine, which must have quit England about the same time as we left Plymouth, *happens* to be in harbour. Her master must have known I could not beat to wind'rd and make a chase of it. So long as he kept his distance he was safe.'

Bolitho understood. If *Destiny* had clawed round to approach the other vessel in daylight, the *Heloise* would have had the advantage of the wind and the distance. The frigate could outpace her in any fair chase, but under cover of darkness the brigantine would easily slip away if expertly handled. Bolitho thought of the gaunt man he had cut down in the fight to hold the deck. He could almost pity him. Almost. Dumaresq had ordered him to be brought across so that Bulkley, the surgeon, could save his life, if that were possible.

Dumaresq added, 'By God, it proves something, if more proof were needed. We are on the right scent.'

The marine sentry called, 'Surgeon, sir!'

Dumaresq glanced at the perspiring surgeon. 'And about bloody time, man!'

Bulkley shrugged, either indifferent to Dumaresq's explosive temper or so used to it that it meant nothing to him.

'The man is alive, sir. A bad wound but a clean one.' He glanced curiously at Bolitho. 'He's a strong fellow, too. I'm surprised and gratified to see you in one portion!'

Demaresq snapped, 'Never mind all that. How dare that ruffian interfere with a King's ship. He'll get no mercy from me, be certain of it!'

He calmed slowly. It was like watching the sea receding, Bolitho thought.

'I must find out what I can from him. Mr Palliser is searching the *Heloise*'s hull, but in view of what Mr Bolitho took pains to discover, I think it unlikely we will gain much. According to the log she was launched last year and completed just a month back. Though she's hardly big enough for useful commerce, I'd have thought.'

Bolitho wanted to leave, to try and wash the stain of combat from his hands and mind.

The surgeon remarked, 'Mr Jury is well enough. A nasty cut, but he is a healthy boy. There'll be no after effects.'

Dumaresq gave a smile. 'I spoke with him when he was

brought up from the cutter. A touch of hero-worship there, I think, Mr Bolitho?'

'He saved my life, sir. He's no cause to praise me for that.'

Dumaresq nodded. 'Hmmm. We shall see.'

He changed tack. 'We shall be sailing in company before nightfall. Keep all hands busy, that's the thing. Mr Palliser will need to rig a jury topgallant mast on that damned pirate, but it must be done.' He glanced at Bolitho. 'Pass the word to the quarterdeck. Change masthead lookouts every hour. We'll use this enforced respite to keep our eyes open for other would-be followers. As it stands, we have a fine little prize, and nobody yet knows anything about it. It might assist in some way.'

Bolitho stood up, his legs heavy again. So there was to be no rest.

Dumaresq said, 'Turn up the hands at noon to witness burial, Mr Bolitho. We'll send the poor fellows on their last journey while we lie to.' He scattered the sentiment by adding, 'No sense in wasting time once we are under way.'

Bulkley followed Bolitho past the sentry and towards the ladder which led below to the main-deck.

The surgeon gave a sigh. 'He has the bit between his teeth now.'

Bolitho looked at him to try and understand his feelings. But it was too dark between decks, with only the ship's sounds and smells rising around them for company.

'Is it the bullion?'

Bulkley lifted his head to listen to the muffled shouts from a boat coming alongside, booming against the hull in the deep swell.

'You are still too young to understand, Richard.' He laid a plump hand on Bolitho's sleeve. 'And that was no sort of criticism, believe me. But I have met men such as our captain, and I know him better than many. He is a fine officer in most respects, if a trifle headstrong. But he *yearns* for action like a drunkard craves the bottle. He commands this fine frigate, but he feels deep down that it is too late or too early for him. With England at peace, the chances of distinction and advancement are few. It suits me very well, but . . .,' he shook his head. 'I have said enough, but I know you will respect my confidence.'

He ambled to the ladder, leaving an aroma of brandy and tobacco to join the other smells already present.

Bolitho walked forward into the daylight and then ran quickly up a ladder to the quarterdeck. He knew that if he did not keep moving he would fall asleep on his feet.

Destiny's gun-deck was littered with broken rigging, amidst which the boatswain and the ropemarker stood and discussed what might still be save. Above the decks the seamen were busy splicing and hammering, and the torn sails were already brought down to be patched and stowed away for emergencies. A ship-of-war was self-sufficient. Nothing could be wasted. Some of that canvas would soon be gliding into the sea-bed, weighted down with round shot to carry the dead to the place where there was only darkness and peace.

Rhodes crossed to his side. 'Good to have you back, Dick.' He dropped his voice as they both turned to look across at the drifting brigantine. 'The lord and master was like an enraged lion after you'd broken free from the side. I shall tread very warily for the next week.'

Bolitho studied the other vessel. It was more like a dream than ever now. It was hard to believe he had managed to rally his men and take the *Heloise* after all which had happened. Men had died. He had probably killed at least one of them himself. But it had no meaning. No substance.

He walked to the rail and saw several of the faces on the deck below turn up towards him. What did they think, he wondered? Rhodes seemed genuinely pleased for him, but there would be envy, others might feel he had been too lucky, too successful for one so junior.

Spillane, the surgeon's new helper, appeared on the lee gangway and threw a parcel over the side.

Bolitho felt sick. What was it? An arm or a leg? It could have been his.

He heard Slade, the master's mate, yelling abuse at some unfortunate seaman. The *Destiny's* recovery of the launch and the thankful shouts of the exhausted crew when she had eventually discovered them had apparently done nothing to make Slade any gentler.

In due course the dead men were buried, while the living stood with bared heads as the captain read a few words from his prayer book.

Then, after a hasty meal and a welcome tot of brandy, the hands turned to again, and the air was filled with the noise of saws and hammers, with strong smells of paint, and tar for the seams, to mark their progress.

Dumaresq came on deck at the end of the afternoon-watch and for several minutes looked at his ship and then at the clearing sky which told him more than any instrument.

He said to Bolitho, who was once more officer of the watch, 'Look at our people working. Ashore they are branded as hawbucks and no-good drunkards. But give 'em a piece of rope or a span of timber an' you'll see what they can do.'

He spoke with such feeling that Bolitho ventured to ask, 'Do you think another war is coming, sir?'

For an instant he thought he had gone too far. Dumaresq turned quickly on his thick legs, his eyes hard as he said, 'You have been speaking with that damned sawbones, eh?'

Then he gave deep chuckle. 'There is no need to answer. You have not yet learned deceit.' He moved to the opposite side for his usual stroll, then added, 'War? I am depending on it!'

Before darkness closed in to hide one ship from another, Palliser sent word to say he was ready to proceed and would repair the less important damage in the days on passage for Rio.

Slade had gone across to the *Heloise* to take charge of the prize crew, and Palliser returned in the quarter-boat even as nightfall joined the sky to the horizon like a curtain.

Bolitho marvelled at the way Palliser kept going. He showed no sign of tiredness, and did not spare himself as he bustled about the ship using a lantern to examine every repair and shouting for the culprit if he discovered something which he considered to be shoddy workmanship.

Thankfully Bolitho climbed into his cot, his coat on the deck where it had fallen. Around him *Destiny* shivered and groaned as she rode a quarter sea without effort, as if she too was grateful for a rest.

It was the same throughout the hull. Bulkley sat in his sick-bay drawing on a long clay pipe and sharing some of his brandy with Codd, the purser.

Outside, barely visible on the orlop deck, the remaining sick and wounded slept or whimpered quietly in the darkness.

In the cabin Dumaresq was at his table writing busily in his personal diary, without a coat, and with his shirt open to the waist. Occasionally he glanced at the screen door as if to pierce it and see the length of his command, his world. And sometimes he looked up at the deckhead as Gulliver's footsteps told him that the master was still brooding over the collision, fearful the blame might be laid at his door.

Throughout the main-deck, where there was barely room to stand upright, the bulk of the ship's company swung in their hammocks to *Destiny*'s regular plunging motion. Like lines of neat pods, waiting to give birth in an instant if the wind so ordered or the drums beat to quarters.

Some men, unable to sleep or working their watch on deck, still thought of the short, bitter fight, of moments when they had known fear. Of familiar faces which had been wiped away, or of the prize money the handsome brigantine might bring them.

Tossing in his cot in the sick-bay, Midshipman Jury went over the attack yet again. Of his desperate need to help Bolitho as the lieutenant's hanger had been hurled away, of the sudden agony across his stomach like a hot iron. He thought of his dead father whom he could scarcely remember and hoped he would have been proud of what he had done.

And *Destiny* carried them all. From the grim-faced Palliser who sat opposite Colpoys in the deserted wardroom, the cards mocking him from the table, to the servant, Poad, snoring in his hammock, they were all at her mercy as her figurehead reached out for the horizon which never drew any nearer.

Two weeks after seizing the brigantine, *Destiny* crossed the Equator on her way south. Even the master seemed pleased with their progress and the distance covered. A convenient wind and milder, warmer air did much to raise the men's spirits and keep them free of illness.

Crossing the line was a new experience for over a third of the ship's company. Boisterous horse-play and skylarking which accompanied the ceremony by a four days' allowance of wine and spirits for everybody.

With Little, the gunner's mate, making a formidable Neptune in a painted crown and a beard of spunyarn, accompanied by his bashful queen in the shape of one of the ship's boys, all the newcomers to his kingdom were soundly ducked and abused.

Afterwards, Dumaresq joined his officers in the wardroom and stated his satisfaction with the ship's performance and swift passage. They had left the *Heloise* far astern, with some of her damage still being repaired. Dumaresq was obviously in no mood to delay his own landfall, and had ordered Slade to meet him off Rio with all the haste he could manage.

On most days *Destiny* pushed her way along under all plain sail, and would have made a fine sight had there been any other vessel to share their ocean. Working high above the decks, or employed in regular sail and gun drill, the new hands began to fit into the routine, and Bolitho saw the pallid skins of those who had come from the debtors' jails or worse taking on a deeper hue as the sun grew stronger with each passing day.

Another of the men who had been wounded in the fight had died, bringing the total to eight. Watched night and day by one of Colpoys' marines, the *Heloise's* master continued to regain his strength, and Bolitho imagined Dumaresq was set on keeping him alive if only to see him hang for piracy.

Midshipman Jury had been allowed to return to duty, but was confined to working on deck or standing his watch aft. Strangely enough, their brief moment of shared danger and courage seemed to hold him and Bolitho apart, and, although they met several times every day, Bolitho could sense a certain discomfort between them.

Maybe the captain had been right. Perhaps Jury's hero-worship, as he had termed it, had created an embarrassment rather than a bond.

Little Merrett, on the other hand, seemed to have gained more confidence than anyone would have thought possible. It was as if he had expected to be killed, and that now he was convinced nothing worse could ever happen to him. He ran up the shrouds with the other midshipmen, and during the dog-watches his shrill voice was often heard in some contest or argument with his companions.

One evening, as the ship ghosted along under her courses and topsails and Bolitho took over the first watch for Lieutenant Rhodes, he saw Jury watching the other midshipmen skylarking in the fighting tops, probably wishing he was up there with them.

Bolitho waited for the helmsman to call, 'Steady as she goes, sir! Sou'-sou'-west!' Then he crossed to the midshipman's side and asked, 'How is the wound?'

Jury looked at him and smiled. 'It no longer hurts, sir. I am lucky.' His fingers strayed to his cross-belt and touched the scar on the gilt plate. 'Were they really pirates?'

Bolitho shrugged. 'I believe they were intent on following us, spies perhaps, but in the eyes of the law they will be seen as pirates.'

He had thought a great deal about it since that terrible night. He suspected Dumaresq and Palliser knew a lot more than they were telling, that the captured brigantine was deeply involved with *Destiny*'s secret mission and her brief stay at Funchal.

He said, 'But if we maintain this pace we shall be in Rio in a week's time. Then I daresay we shall learn the truth.'

Gulliver appeared on the quarterdeck and peered up at the hardening canvas for a long minute without speaking. Then he said, 'Wind's getting up. I think we should shorten sail.' He hesitated, watching Bolitho's face. 'Will you tell the captain, or shall I?'

Bolitho looked at the topsails as they filled and tightened to the wind. In the dying sunlight they looked like great pink shells. But Gulliver was right, and he should have seen it for himself.

'I'll tell him.'

Gulliver strode to the compass, as if unable to contain his restlessness. 'Too good to last. I knew it.'

Bolitho beckoned to Midshipman Cowdroy who was temporarily sharing his watches until Jury was fully recovered.

'My respects to the captain. Tell him the wind is freshening from the nor'-east.'

Cowdroy touched his hat and hurried to the companion. Bolitho bit back his dislike. An arrogant, intolerant bully. He wondered how Rhodes put up with him.

Jury asked quietly, 'Are we in for a storm, sir?'

'Unlikely, I think, but it's best to be prepared.' He saw something glitter in Jury's hand and said, 'That is a fine looking watch.'

Jury held it out to him, his face filled with pleasure. 'It belonged to my father.'

Bolitho opened the guard carefully and saw inside a tiny but perfect portrait of a sea officer. Jury was already very like him.

It was a beautiful watch, made by one of the finest craftsmen in London.

He handed it back and said, 'Take good care of it. It must be very valuable.'

Jury slipped it into his breeches pocket. 'It is worth a great deal to me. It is all I own of my father.'

Something in his tone affected Bolitho deeply. It made him feel clumsy, angry with himself for not seeing beyond Jury's eagerness to please him. He had no one else in the world who cared.

He said, 'Well, my lad, if you keep your wits about you on this voyage it will stand you in good stead later on.' He smiled. 'A few years ago who had even heard of James Cook, I wonder? Now he is the country's hero and when he returns from his latest voyage, I've no doubt he'll be promoted yet again.'

Dumaresq's voice made him spin round. 'Do not excite the boy, Mr Bolitho. He will want my command in no time!'

Bolitho waited for Dumaresq's decision. You never knew where you were with him.

'We shall shorten sail presently, Mr Bolitho.' He rocked back on his heels and examined each sail in turn. 'We'll run while we can.'

As he disappeared through the companion, the master's mate of the watch called, 'The cutter is workin' free on the boat tier, sir.'

'Very well.' Bolitho sought out Midshipman Cowdroy again. 'Take some hands and secure the cutter, if you please.' He sensed the midshipman's resentment and knew the reason for it. He would be glad to be rid of him from his watch.

Jury was guessed what was happening. 'I'll go, sir. It's what I should be doing.'

Cowdroy turned on him and snapped, 'You are unwell, *Mr* Jury. Do not strain yourself on our behalf!' He swung away, shouting for a boatswain's mate.

Later, as true to Gulliver's prediction the wind continued to rise and the sea's face changed to an angry array of white crests, Bolitho forgot about the rift he had created between the two midshipmen.

First one reef was taken in, then another, but as the ship staggered and dipped into a worsening sea, Dumaresq ordered all hands aloft to take in all but the main-topsail, so that *Destiny* could lie to and ride out the gale.

Then, to prove it could be gentle as well as perverse, the wind fell away, and when daylight returned the ship was soon drying and steaming in the warm sunshine.

Bolitho was exercising the starboard battery of twelve-pounders when Jury reported that he had been allowed to return to full duty and was no longer to bunk in the sick-bay.

Bolitho had a feeling that something was wrong, but was determined not to become involved.

He said, 'The captain intends that ours will be the smartest gun salute they have ever seen or heard in Rio.' He saw several of the bare-backed seamen grinning and rubbing their palms together. 'So we'll have a race. The first division against the second, with some wine for the winners.' He had already asked the purser's permission to grant an extra issue of wine.

Codd had thrust out his great upper teeth like the prow of a galley and had cheerfully agreed. 'If you pay, Mr Bolitho, *if you pay!*'

Little called, 'All ready, sir.'

Bolitho turned to Jury. 'You can time them. The division to run out first, twice out of three tries, will take the prize.'

He knew the men were getting impatient, fingering the tackles and handspikes with as much zeal as if they were preparing to fight.

Jury tried to meet Bolitho's eyes. 'I have no watch, sir.'

Bolitho stared at him, aware that the captain and Palliser were at the quarterdeck rail to see his men competing with each other.

'You've lost it? Your father's watch?' He could recall Jury's pride and his sadness as he had shown it to him the previous evening. 'Tell me.'

Jury shook his head, his face wretched. 'It's gone, sir. That's all I know.'

Bolitho rested his hands on Jury's shoulder. 'Easy now. I'll try to think of something.' Impetuously he tugged out his own watch, which had been given to him by his mother. 'Use mine.'

Stockdale, who was crouching at one of the guns, had heard all of it, and had been watching the faces of the other men nearby. He had never owned a watch in his life, nor was he likely to, but somehow he knew this one was important. In a crowded world like the ship a thief was dangerous. Sailors were too poor to let such a crime go unpunished. It would be best if he was caught before something worse happened. For his own sake as much as anybody's.

Bolitho waved his arm. *'Run out!'*

The second division of guns won easily. It was only to be expected, the losers said, as it contained both Little and Stockdale, the two strongest men in the ship.

But as they shared out their mugs of wine and relaxed beneath the shade of the main-course, Bolitho knew that for Jury at least the moment was spoiled.

He said to Little, 'Secure the guns.' He walked aft, some of his men nodding at him as he passed.

Dumaresq waited for him to reach the quarterdeck. 'That was smartly done!'

Palliser smiled bleakly. 'If we must bribe our people with wine before they can handle the great guns, we shall soon be a dry ship!'

Bolitho blurted out, 'Mr Midshipman Jury's watch has been stolen.'

Dumaresq eyed him calmly, 'And so? What must I do, Mr Bolitho?'

Bolitho flushed. 'I'm sorry, sir. I—I thought . . .'

Dumaresq shaded his eyes to watch a trio of small birds as they dashed abeam, seemingly inches above the water. 'I can almost smell the land.' He turned abruptly to Bolitho again. 'It was reported to you. Deal with it.'

Bolitho touched his hat as the captain and first lieutenant began to pace up and down the weather side of the deck.

He still had a lot to learn.

6

A Matter of Discipline

With all her canvas, except topsails and jib, clewed up, *Destiny* glided slowly across the blue water of Rio's outer roadstead. It was oppressively hot with barely enough breeze to raise much more than a ripple beneath her beakhead, but Bolitho could sense the expectancy and excitement around him as they made their way towards the protected anchorage.

Even the most experienced seaman aboard did not deny the impressive majesty of the landfall. They had watched it grow out of the morning mist, and it was now spread out on either beam as if to enfold them. Rio's great mountain was like nothing Bolitho had seen, dwarfing all else like a giant boulder. And beyond, interspersed with patches of lush green forest, were other ridges, steep and pointed likes waves which had been turned to stone. Pale beaches, necklaces of surf, and nestling between hills and ocean the city itself. White houses, squat towers and nodding palms, it was a far cry from the English Channel.

To larboard Bolitho saw the first walled battery, the Portuguese flag flapping only occasionally above it in the hard sunlight. Rio was well defended, with enough batteries to dampen the keenest of attackers.

Dumaresq was studying the town and the anchored vessels through his glass.

He said, 'Let her fall off a point!'

'West-nor'-west, sir!'

Palliser looked at his captain. 'Guard-boat approaching.'

Dumaresq smiled briefly. 'Wonders what the hell we are doing here, no doubt.'

Bolitho plucked his shirt away from his skin and envied the half naked seamen while the officers were made to swelter in their heavy dress-coats.

Mr Vallance, the gunner, was already checking his chosen crews to make sure nothing went wrong with his salute to the flag.

Bolitho wondered how many unseen eyes were watching the slow approach of the English frigate. A man-of-war, what did she want? Was she here for peaceful purposes, or with news of another broken treaty in Europe?

'Begin the salute!'

Gun by gun the salute crashed out, the heavy air pressing the thick smoke on the water and blotting out the land.

The Portuguese guard-boat had turned in her own length, propelled by great sweeps, so that she looked like a giant water-beetle.

Somebody commented, 'The bugger's leadin' us in.'

The last gun recoiled and the crews threw themselves on the tackles to sponge the smoking muzzles and secure each weapon as a final gesture of peaceful intentions.

A figure waved a flag from the guard-boat, and as the long sweeps rose dripping and still on either beam, Dumaresq remarked dryly, 'Not too close in, Mr Palliser. They're taking no chances with us!'

Palliser raised his trumpet to his mouth. 'Lee braces there! Hands wear ship!'

Like parts of an intricate pattern the seamen and their petty officers ran to their stations.

'Tops'l sheets!' Palliser's voice roused the sea-birds from the water upon which they had only just alighted after the din of the salute. 'Tops'l clew-lines!'

Dumaresq said, 'So be it, Mr Palliser. Anchor.'

'Helm a'lee!'

Destiny turned slowly into the wind, the way going off her as she responded to the helm.

'Let go!'

There was a splash from forward as the big anchor plummeted down, while strung out on the topsail yards the seamen deftly furled the sails as if each mast was controlled by one invisible hand.

'Away gig's crew! Away quarter-boat!'

Bare feet stampeded across the hot decks while *Destiny* took the strain of her cable and then swung to the pull of the ocean.

Dumaresq thrust his hands behind his back. 'Signal the guard-board alongside, if you please. I shall have to go ashore and pay my respects to the Viceroy. It is best to get such ponderous matters over and done with.'

He nodded to Gulliver and his mates by the wheel. 'Well done.'

Gulliver searched the captain's face as if expecting a trap. Finding none, he replied thankfully, 'My first visit here as master, sir.'

Their eyes met. Had the collision been any worse it would have been the last time for both of them.

Bolitho was kept busy with his own men and had little time to watch the Portuguese officers come aboard. They looked resplendent in their proud uniforms and showed no discomfort in the blistering heat. The town was almost hidden in mist and haze, which gave it an added air of enchantment. Pale buildings, and craft with colourful sails and a rig not unlike Arab traders which Bolitho had seen off the coast of Africa.

'Dismiss the watch below, Mr Bolitho.' Palliser's brisk voice caught him off guard. 'Then stand by with the marine escort to accompany the captain ashore.'

Bolitho ducked thankfully beneath the quarterdeck and made his way aft. In contrast with the upper deck it seemed almost cool.

In the gloom he all but collided with the surgeon as he clambered up from the main-deck. He seemed unusually agitated and said, 'I must see the captain. I fear the brigantine's master is dying.'

Bolitho went through the wardroom to his tiny cabin to collect his sword and his best hat for the journey ashore.

They had discovered little about the *Heloise*'s master, other than he was a Dorset man named Jacob Triscott. As Bulkley had remarked previously, it was not much incentive to stay alive when only the hangman's rope awaited him. Bolitho found that the news troubled him deeply. To kill a man in self-defence, and in the line of duty, was to be expected. But now the man who had tried to cut him down was dying, and the delay seemed unfair and without dignity.

Rhodes stamped into the wardroom behind him. 'I'm parched. With all these visitors aboard, I'll be worn out in no time.'

As Bolitho came out of his cabin Rhodes exclaimed, 'What is it?'

'The brigantine's master is dying.'

'I know.' He shrugged. 'Him or you. It's the only way to see it.' He added, 'Forget about it. The lord and master will be the one to get annoyed. He was banking on getting information from the wretch before he expired. One way or another.'

He followed Bolitho through the screen door and together they looked forward, to the waiting glare of the upper deck.

Rhodes asked, 'Any luck with young Jury's watch?'

Bolitho smiled grimly. 'The captain told me to deal with it.'

'He would.'

'I expect he's forgotten about it by now, but I must do something. Jury has had enough trouble already.'

Johns, the captain's personal coxswain, dressed in his best blue jacket with gilt buttons, strode past. He saw Bolitho and said, 'Gig's in the water, sir. You'd best be there, too.'

Rhodes clapped Bolitho on the shoulder. 'The lord and master would not take kindly to being kept waiting!'

As Bolitho was about to follow the coxswain, Rhodes said quietly, 'Look, Dick, if you'd like me to do something about that damned watch while you're ashore . . .'

Bolitho shook his head. 'No, but thank you. The thief is most likely from my division. To search every man and turn his possessions out on deck would destroy whatever trust and loyalty I've managed to build up so far. I'll think of something.'

Rhodes said, 'I just hope young Jury has not merely mislaid the timepiece; a loss is one thing, a theft another.'

They fell silent as they approached the starboard gangway where the side-party had fallen in to pay its respects to the captain.

But Dumaresq was standing with his thick legs apart, his head jutting forward as he shouted to the surgeon, 'No, sir, *he shall not die*! Not until I have the information!'

Bulkley spread his hands helplessly. 'But the man is *going*, sir. There is nothing more I can do.'

Dumaresq looked at the waiting gig and at the quarterboat nearby with Colpoys' marine escort already crammed aboard. He was expected at the Viceroy's residence, and to delay might provoke bad feelings which he would certainly wish to avoid if he needed Portuguese co-operation.

He swung on Palliser. 'Dammit, *you* deal with it. Tell that rogue Triscott that if he will reveal the details of his mission and his original destination I shall send a letter to his parish in Dorset. It will ensure that he is remembered as an honest man. Impress upon him what that will mean to his family and his friends.' He glared at Palliser's doubtful features. 'God damn it, Mr Palliser, think of something, will you?'

Palliser asked mildly, 'And if he spits in my face?'

'I'll hang him here and now, and see how his family like *that*!'

Bulkley stepped forward. 'Be easy, sir, the man is dying, he cannot hurt anyone.'

'Go back to him and do as I say. That is an order.' He turned to Palliser. 'Tell Mr Timbrell to rig a halter to the main-yard. I'll run that bugger up to it, dying or not, if he refuses to help!'

Palliser followed him to the entry port. 'It will be a signed declaration, sir.' He nodded slowly. 'I'll get a witness and have his words written down for you.'

Dumaresq smiled tightly. 'Good man. See to it.' He saw Bolitho and snapped, 'Into the gig with you. Now let us see this Viceroy, eh?'

Once clear of the side Dumaresq turned to study his ship, his eyes almost closed against the reflected glare.

'A fine surgeon is Bulkley, but a bit of an old woman at times. Anyone would think we are here for our health, instead of seeking a hidden fortune.'

Bolitho tried to relax, his buttocks burning on the sun-heated thwart as he attempted to sit as squarely as his captain.

The brief confidence led him to ask, 'Will there really be any treasure, sir?' He was careful to keep his voice low so that the stroke oarsman should not hear him.

Dumaresq tightened his fingers around his sword hilt and stared at the land.

'It is somewhere, that I do know. In what form it now is remains to be seen, but that is why we are here. Why we were in Madeira when I went to the house of a very old friend. But something immense is happening. Because of it my clerk was killed. Because of it the *Heloise* played the dangerous game of trying to follow us. And now poor Bulkley wants me to read a prayer for a rogue who may hold a vital clue. A man who nearly killed my young and *sentimental* third lieutenant.' He turned and regarded Bolitho curiously. 'Are you still in irons over Jury's watch?'

Bolitho swallowed. The captain had not forgotten after all.

'I am going to deal with the matter, sir. Just as soon as I can.'

'Hmmm. Don't make a drudgery of it. You are one of my officers. If a crime is committed the culprit must be punished. Severely. These poor fellows have barely a coin between them. I'll not see them abused by some common thief, though God knows many of them began life like that!'

Dumaresq did not raise his voice nor look at his coxswain, but said, 'See what you can do, Johns.'

It was all he said, but Bolitho sensed a powerful bond between the captain and his coxswain.

Dumaresq stared toward the landing-stairs. There were more uniforms and some horses. A carriage, too, probably to carry the visitors to the residency.

Dumaresq pouted and said, 'You can accompany me. Good experience for you.' He chuckled. 'When the treasure ship *Asturias* broke off the engagement all those thirty years ago, it was later rumoured she entered Rio. It was also suggested that the Portuguese authorities had a hand in what happened to the bullion.' He smiled broadly. 'So some of the people on that jetty are probably more worried than I at this moment.'

The bowman raised his boat-hook as with oars tossed the gig moved against the landing-stairs with barely a quiver.

Dumaresq's smile was gone. 'Now let us get on with it. I want to get back as soon as possible and see how Mr Palliser's persuasion is progressing.'

At the top of the stairs a file of Colpoys' marines, their faces the colour of their coats in the blazing sunshine, snapped to attention. Opposite them, in white tunics with brilliant yellow trappings, was a guard of Portuguese soldiers.

Dumaresq shook hands and bowed to several of the waiting dignitaries as greetings were formally exchanged and translated. A crowd of onlookers stood watching nearby, and Bolitho was struck by the number of black faces amongst them. Slaves or servants from the big estates and plantations. Brought thousands of miles to this place where, with luck, they might be bought by a kind master. If unlucky, they would not last very long.

Then Dumaresq climbed into the carriage with three of the Portuguese while others mounted their horses.

Colpoys sheathed his sword and glared up at the Viceroy's residence on a lush hillside and complained, 'We shall have to march, dammit! I am a marine, not a bloody foot-soldier!'

By the time they reached the fine-looking building Bolitho was soaking with sweat. While the marines were led to the rear of the house by a servant, Bolitho and Colpoys were ushered into a high-ceilinged room with one side open to the sea and a garden of vivid blossoms and shady palms.

More servants, soft-footed and careful to keep their eyes averted from the two officers, brought chairs and wine, and above their heads a great fan began to sway back and forth.

Colpoys stretched out his legs and swallowed the wine with relish.

'Sweet as a hymn in chapel!'

Bolitho smiled. The Portuguese officials, the military and traders lived well here. They would need something to sustain them against the heat and the risk of fever and death in a dozen forms. But the wealth of the growing empire was said to be too vast to be assessed. Silver, precious stones, strange metals and miles of prospering sugar plantations, no wonder they needed an army of slaves to satisfy the demands from far-off Lisbon.

Colpoys put down his glass and got to his feet. In the time it had taken them to march up from the jetty to the residence, Dumaresq had apparently completed his business.

From his expression as he appeared through an arched doorway, Bolitho guessed he was far from satisfied.

Dumaresq said, 'We shall return to the ship.'

The farewells were completed at the residence this time, and Bolitho began to realize that the Viceroy was not in Rio, but would return as soon as he was told of *Destiny*'s visit.

Dumaresq explained as much as he strode into the sunlight, touching his hat to the saluting guards as he went.

He growled in his resonant voice, 'That means he *insists* I wait for his return. I was not born yesterday, Bolitho. These people are our oldest allies, but some of them are not above a little piracy. Well, Viceroy or not, when *Heloise* catches up with us I shall weigh when I'm good and ready!'

To Colpoys he said, 'March your men back.' As the scarlet coats moved away in a cloud of dust, Dumaresq climbed into the carriage. 'You come with me. When we reach the jetty I want you to take a message for me.' He pulled a small envelope from his coat. 'I had it ready. I always expect the worst. The coachman will carry you there, and I have no doubt the news of your visit will be all over the town within an hour.' He smiled grimly. 'But the Viceroy is not the only man with cunning.'

As they clattered past Colpoys and his sweating marines, Dumaresq said, 'Take a man with you.' He glanced at Bolitho's expectant face. 'A body-guard, if you like. I saw that prize-fighting fellow in the quarter-boat. Stockdale, that's his name? Take him.'

Bolitho marvelled. How *could* Dumaresq contain so many things at once? Out there a man was dying, and Palliser's own life would not be worth much if he failed to obtain some information. There was someone in Rio who must be connected with the missing bullion, but not the one for whom he was carrying Dumaresq's letter. There was a ship, her people and the captured *Heloise,* and thousands of miles still lay ahead before they knew success or failure. For a post-captain of twenty-eight, Dumaresq certainly carried a great burden on his shoulders. It made Jury's missing watch seem almost trivial.

A tall, black-haired half-caste with a basket of fruit on her head paused to watch the carriage as it rolled past. Her bare shoulders were the colour of honey, and she gave a bold smile as she saw them watching her.

Dumaresq said, 'A fine looking girl. And a prouder pair of catheads I never did see. It would be worth the risk of a painful payment later on just to relish her!'

Bolitho did not know what to say. He was used to the

coarse comments of sailors, but from Dumaresq it seemed vulgar and demeaning.

Dumaresq waited for the carriage to stop. 'Be as fast as you can. I intend to take on fresh water tomorrow and there's a lot to be done before that.' He strode to the stairs and vanished into his gig.

Later, with Stockdale sitting opposite him and filling half the carriage, Bolitho directed his coachman to the address on the envelope.

Dumaresq had thought of everything. Bolitho or any other stranger might have been stopped and questioned here. But the sight of the carriage with the Viceroy's insignia on either door was enough to gain access anywhere.

The house where the carriage eventually pulled to a halt was a low building surrounded by a thick wall. Bolitho imagined it was one of Rio's oldest houses, with the additional luxury of a large garden and a well-tended driveway to the entrance.

A Negro servant greeted Bolitho without a flicker of surprise and led him into a great circular entrance hall with some marble vases which contained flowers like those he had seen in the garden and several statues which stood in separate alcoves like amorous sentries.

Bolitho hesitated in the centre of the hall, uncertain of what to do next. Another servant passed, eyes fixed on some distant object as he ignored the letter in Bolitho's hand.

Stockdale rumbled, 'I'll go an' stir their stumps for 'em, sir!'

A door opened noiselessly, and Bolitho saw a slightly built man in white breeches and a deeply frilled shirt watching him.

He asked, 'Are you from the ship?'

Bolitho stared. He was English, 'Er, yes, sir. I am Lieutenant Richard Bolitho of His Britannic . . .'

The man came to meet him, his hand outstretched. 'I *know* the name of the ship, Lieutenant. All Rio knows it by now.'

He led the way to a book-lined room and offered him a chair. As the door was closed by an unseen servant, Bolitho saw Stockdale standing massively where he had left him. Ready to protect him, to tear the house down brick by brick, he suspected.

'My name is Jonathan Egmont.' He smiled gently. 'That will mean nothing to you. You must be very young for your rank.'

Bolitho rested his hands on the arms of the chair. Heavy, well carved. Like the house, it had been here for a long time.

Another door opened and a servant waited for the man named Egmont to notice him.

'Some wine, Lieutenant?'

Bolitho's mouth was like a kiln. He said, 'I would welcome a glass, sir.'

'Rest easy then, while I read what your captain has to tell me.'

Bolitho glanced around the room as Egmont walked to a desk and slit opened Dumaresq's letter with a gold stiletto. Shelf upon shelf of books, while on the floor were several rich-looking carpets. It was difficult to see very much because his eyes were still half blinded by the sun's glare, and anyway the windows were so heavily shaded that it was almost too dark to study his host. An intelligent face, he thought. A man about sixty, although he had heard that in such a climate men could age rapidly. It was hard to guess what he was doing here, or how Dumaresq had discovered him.

Egmont laid the letter carefully on the desk and looked across at Bolitho.

'Your captain has said nothing of this to you?' He saw Bolitho's expression and shook his head. 'No, of course he would not, and it was wrong of me to ask.'

Bolitho said, 'He wished me to bring the letter without delay. That is all I know.'

'I see.' For a few moments he looked unsure, even apprehensive. Then he said, 'I shall do what I can. It will take time, of course, but with the Viceroy away from his residence I have no doubt your captain will wish to remain for a while.'

Bolitho opened his mouth and then shut it as the door swung inwards and a woman entered the room carrying a tray.

He got to his feet, very conscious of his crumpled shirt, of his hair plastered to his forehead by the sweat of the journey. Set against what he was certain was the most beautiful creature he had ever seen, he felt like a vagrant.

She was dressed all in white, the waist of her gown nipped

in with a thin golden belt. Her hair was jet black like his own, and although held in check by a ribbon at the nape of her neck, was arranged to fall on her shoulders, the skin of which looked like silk.

She glanced at him and then studied him from top to toe, her head slightly on one side.

Egmont was also on his feet and said stiffly, 'This is my wife, Lieutenant.'

Bolitho bowed. 'I am honoured, ma'am.' He did not know what to say. She made him feel clumsy and unable to form his words, and all without saying anything to him.

She placed the tray on a table and raised her hand towards him.

'You are welcome here, Lieutenant. You may kiss my hand.'

Bolitho took it, feeling her softness, her perfume which made his head spin.

Her shoulders were bare, and despite the darkened room he saw that she had violet-coloured eyes. She was beautiful and more. Even her voice as she had offered her hand to him was exciting. How could she be his wife? She must be many years younger. Spanish or Portuguese, certainly not English. Bolitho would not have cared if she had just stepped from the moon.

He stammered, 'Richard Bolitho, ma'am.'

She stood back and put her fingers to her mouth. Then she laughed. 'Bo-li-tho! I think it will be easier for me to call you Lieutenant.' She swung her gown across the floor, her eyes moving to her husband. 'Later, I think I may call you Richard.'

Egmont said, 'I will write a letter for you to take with you, Lieutenant.' He seemed to be looking past, even through her. As if she was not there. 'I will do what I can.'

She turned to Bolitho again. 'Please call on us while you are in Rio. Our house if yours.' She gave a slow curtsy, her eyes on his face, until she said softly, 'I have *enjoyed* our meeting.'

Then she was gone, and Bolitho sat down in the chair as if his legs had broken under him.

Egmont said, 'I shall be a few moments. Enjoy the wine while I put pen to paper.'

Eventually it was done, and as he sealed the envelope with scarlet wax Egmont remarked distantly, 'Memory has a long reach. I have been here for many years and have rarely strayed but for the needs of my business. Then one day there comes a King's ship, commanded by the son of a man once dear to me, and now everything is changed.' He stopped abruptly and then said, 'But you will be in a hurry to return to your duties.' He held out the letter. 'I bid you good day.'

Stockdale eyed him curiously as he left the book-lined room. 'All done, sir?'

Bolitho paused as another door opened and he saw her standing there, her gown making her look like another perfect statue against the dark room beyond. She did not speak, or even smile, but just looked at him, directly, as if, Bolitho thought, she was already committing herself to something. Then her hand moved and stayed momentarily at her breast, and Bolitho felt his heart pounding as if trying to join hers in her hand.

The door closed, and he could almost believe he had imagined it or that the wine had been too strong.

He glanced at Stockdale and saw the look on his battered face and knew it was no lie.

'We had better get back to the ship, Stockdale.'

Stockdale followed him towards the sunlight. Not a bit too soon, he thought.

It was dusk by the time the boat from the landing-stairs made fast to the main chains. Bolitho climbed up to and through the entry port thinking of the beautiful woman in the white gown.

Rhodes was waiting with the side-party and whispered quickly, 'The first lieutenant is looking for you, Dick.'

'Lay aft, Mr Bolitho!' Palliser's brusque tones silenced Rhodes before he could say more.

Bolitho climbed to the quarterdeck and touched his hat. 'Sir?'

Palliser snapped, 'I have been *waiting* for you!'

'Yes, sir. But the captain ordered me on an errand.'

'And a fine time it has taken you!'

Bolitho controlled his sudden anger with an effort. Whatever he did or tried to do, Palliser was never satisfied.

He said quietly, 'Well, sir, I am here now.'

Palliser peered at him as if to seek out some kind of insolence.

Then he said, 'During your absence ashore, the master-at-arms, who was acting upon my orders, searched some of the people's messes.' He waited for Bolitho to react. 'I do not know what kind of discipline you are trying to instil into your division, but let me assure you it will take a lot more than a bribe of spirits and wine to achieve it! Mr Jury's watch was found in the possession of one of your maintopmen, Murray, so what say you?'

Bolitho stared at him incredulously. Murray had saved Jury's life. But for his swift action on the *Heloise*'s deck that night, the midshipman would be dead. And if Jury had not thrown the sword to replace Bolitho's lost hangar, he too would be a corpse. It had been their bond, of which none of them had spoken.

He protested, 'Murray is a good hand, sir. I cannot see him as a thief.'

'I'm certain of *that*. But you have a lot to learn, Mr Bolitho. Men like Murray would not dream of thieving from a messmate, but an officer, even a lowly midshipman, is fair game.' He controlled his voice with an obvious effort. 'But that isn't the worst part. Mr Jury had the impertinence, the monstrous audacity, to tell me he had given the watch to Murray as a gift! Can you, *even you*, Mr Bolitho, believe it?'

'I can believe he said it to save Murray, sir. He was wrong, but I can well understand.'

'Just as I thought.' He leaned forward. 'I will see that Mr Jury is put ashore for passage to England the moment we are in company with some higher authority, and what do you think of that?'

Bolitho said hotly, 'I think you are acting unfairly!'

He could feel his anger giving way to despair. Palliser had tried to provoke him, but this time it had got suddenly out of hand.

He said, 'If you are trying to discredit me through Mr Jury, then you are succeeding. But even to contemplate it, knowing he has no family, and that he will give his very soul to the Navy, is damnable! And if I were you, *sir*, I'd be sick with shame!'

Palliser stared at him as if he had been struck. *'You what!'*

A small figure bobbed from the shadows. It was Macmillan, the captain's servant.

He said, 'Beg pardon, gentlemen, but the cap'n would like you in 'is cabin at once.'

He shrank back as if expecting to be knocked senseless.

Dumaresq was standing in the centre of the day-cabin, legs apart, hands on hips, as he glared at his two lieutenants.

'I'll not have you brawling on my quarterdeck like a pair of louts! What in hell's name has got into you?'

Palliser looked shocked, even pale, as he said, 'If you had heard what Mr Bolitho said, sir . . .'

'Heard? *Heard?*' Domaresq jabbed one fist towards the skylight. 'I'd have thought the whole ship *heard* well enough!'

He looked at Bolitho. 'How dare you show insubordination to the first lieutenant. You will obey him without question. Discipline is paramount if we are not to become a shambles. I expect, no, I *demand* that the ship is at all times ready to act as I dictate. To bicker over some petty matter within earshot of anyone present is a madness, and I'll not tolerate it!' He examined Bolitho's face and added in a calmer tone, 'It must not happen again.'

Palliser tried again. 'I was telling him, sir . . .' He fell silent as the compelling eyes turned on him like lamps.

'You are my first lieutenant, and I shall uphold what you do under my command. But I will not have you using your temper on those too junior to hit back. You are an experienced and skilled officer, whereas Mr Bolitho is new to the wardroom. As for Mr Jury, he knows nothing of the sea but that which he has learned since we left Plymouth; would you say that is a fair assessment?'

Palliser swallowed hard, his head bowed beneath the beams as if he was in prayer.

'Yes, sir.'

'Good. That is something we agree upon.'

Dumaresq walked to the stern windows and stared at the reflected lights on the water.

'Mr Palliser, you will pursue the matter of the theft. I do not wish a useful hand like Murray punished if he is innocent. On the other side of the coin, I'll not see him evade it if he is guilty. The whole ship knows what has happened. If he walks free from this because of our inability to discover the truth, there will be no controlling the real trouble-makers and sea-lawyers amongst us.' He held out his hand to Bolitho. 'You have a letter for me, I expect.' As he took it he added slowly, 'Deal with Mr Jury. It is up to you to treat him fairly but severely. It will be as much a test for you as it is for him.' He nodded. 'Dismiss.'

As Bolitho closed the door behind him he heard Dumaresq say, 'That was a fine statement you took from Triscott. It makes up for the earlier set-back.'

Palliser mumbled something and Dumaresq replied, 'One more piece and the puzzle may be solved more quickly than I thought.'

Bolitho moved away, conscious of the sentry's eyes as they followed him into the shadows. He entered the wardroom and sat down carefully, like a man who has just fallen from a horse.

Poad said, 'Somethin' to drink, sir?'

Bolitho nodded, although he had barely heard. He saw Bulkley seated against one of the ship's great timbers and asked, 'Is the *Heloise*'s master dead?'

Bulkley looked up wearily and waited for his eyes to focus.

'Aye. He passed away within minutes of putting his name to the statement.' The surgeon's voice was very slurred. 'I hope it was worth it.'

Colpoys came from his cabin and threw one elegant, white-clad leg over a stool.

'I am growing sick of this place. Anchored right out here. Nothing to do . . .' He looked from Bolitho to Bulkley and said wryly, 'I was wrong it seems. Here we have gaiety a-plenty!'

Bulkley sighed. 'I heard most of it. Triscott was making the one voyage as master. It seems he was ordered to join us at Funchal and determine what we were about.' He accidentally knocked over a goblet of brandy but did not appear to notice as the spirit ran over his legs. 'Having seen us on our way, he was supposed to head for the Caribbean and hand over the vessel to her new owner, the one who had paid for her to be built.' He coughed and dabbed his chin with a red handkerchief. ' 'Stead o' that, he got too nosey and tried to follow us.' He peered vaguely aft as if to seek Dumaresq through the bulkhead. 'Imagine that? The mouse hunting the tiger! Well, now he's paid for it in full.'

Colpoys asked impatiently, 'Well then, who is this mysterious buyer of brigantines?'

Bulkley turned towards the marine, as if it hurt him to move. 'I thought you were cleverer than that. Sir Piers Garrick, o' course! One-time privateer in the King's name and a damned pirate in his own!'

Rhodes entered the wardroom and said, 'I heard that. I suppose we should have known, as the lord and master was so careful to mention him. All those years ago. He must be over sixty now. And d'you really believe he still knows what happened to the *Asturia*'s bullion?'

Colpoys said wearily, 'The sawbones has dozed off, Stephen.'

Poad, who had been hovering close by, said, 'Fresh pork tonight, gentlemen. Sent off shore with the compliments of a Mr Egmont.' He waited for just the right moment. 'The boatman said it was to mark Mr Bolitho's visit to 'is 'ouse.'

Bolitho flushed as they all stared at him.

Colpoys shook his head sadly. 'My God, we've only just arrived here and I see a woman's hand in all this.'

Rhodes took him aside as Gulliver joined Colpoys and the purser at the table.

'Was he hard on you, Dick?'

'I lost my temper.' Bolitho smiled ruefully. 'I think we all did.'

'Good. Stand up to him. Don't forget what I said.' He made sure nobody else was listening. 'I've told Jury to wait for you in the chartroom. You'll be uninterrupted there for a while. Get it over with. I've been through all this myself.' He sniffed and exclaimed, 'I can smell that pork, Dick. You *must* have influence.'

Bolitho made his way forward to the small chartroom which was just beside the main companion. He saw Jury standing by the empty table, probably seeing his career wiped away like Gulliver's calculations.

Bolitho said, 'I was told what you did. Murray's case will be investigated, the captain has given his word. You will not be put ashore when we join the nearest squadron. You are staying in *Destiny*.' He heard Jury's quick intake of breath and said, 'So it's up to you now.'

'I—I don't know what to say, sir.'

Bolitho could feel his determination crumbling. He had once been like Jury, and knew what it was like to face apparent disaster.

He made himself say, 'You did wrong. You told a lie to protect a man who may well be guilty.' He silenced Jury's attempted protest. 'It was not your place to act for one in a way you might not have acted for another. I was equally at fault. If I was to be asked if I would have cared as much if Murray had been one of the bad apples in the barrel, or had you been like one of the other midshipmen, I should have had to admit to being biased.'

Jury said tightly, 'I am sorry for the trouble I have caused. Especially to you.'

Bolitho faced him for the first time, seeing the pain in his eyes.

'I know. We have both learned something from all this.' He hardened his tone. 'If not, we are neither of us fit to wear the King's coat. Carry on to your berth, if you please.'

He heard Jury leave the chartroom and waited for several minutes to recover his composure.

He had acted correctly, even if he had been late. In future Jury would be on his guard and less willing to depend on others. Hero-worship, the captain had termed it.

Bolitho sighed and walked to the wardroom. Rhodes looked up at him as he opened the door, his eyes questioning.

Bolitho shrugged. 'It was not easy.'

'It never is.' Rhodes grinned and twitched his nose again. 'It will be a delayed dinner because of the pork's late arrival in our midst, but I feel the waiting will put a worthwhile edge to the appetite!'

Bolitho took a goblet of wine from Poad and sat in a chair. It was better to be like Rhodes, he thought. Live for today, with no care for the next horizon and what it might bring. That way, you never got hurt. He thought of Jury's dismayed features and knew otherwise.

7

Divided Loyalties

Two more days passed with no sign that the Portuguese
Viceroy had returned, or, if he had, that he intended to
receive Dumaresq.

Sweltering under a blazing sun, the seamen went about
their work with little enthusiasm. Tempers flared, and on
several occasions men were taken aft to be awarded punishment.

And as the bell chimed each passing watch, Dumaresq,
whenever he appeared on the quarterdeck, seemed to be
growing more intolerant and angry. A seaman was given
extra work merely for staring at him, and Midshipman Ingrave,
who had been acting as his clerk, was sent back to his normal
shipboard duties with 'Too stupid to hold a pen!' still ringing
in his unhappy ears.

Even Bolitho, who had little experience of the politics used
in foreign ports, was aware of *Destiny*'s enforced isolation. A
few hopeful craft hovered near the ship with local wares for
barter, but were openly discouraged by the vigilant guard-
boat. And there had certainly been no message sent by the
man called Egmont.

Samuel Codd, the purser, had gone aft to complain about
his inability to preserve his supply of fresh fruit, and half of
the ship must have heard Dumaresq's fury break over him
like a tidal wave.

'What do you take me for, you miser? D'you think I have
nothing to do but buy and sell like a common tinker? Take a
boat and get ashore yourself, and *this* time tell the merchant

the stores are for *me*!' His powerful voice had pursued Codd from the cabin. 'And don't return empty handed!'

In the wardroom the atmosphere was little changed. The usual grumbles and exaggerated yarns about what had happened during the daily routine. Only when Palliser appeared did the climate become formal, even strained.

Bolitho had seen Murray and had confronted him with the accusation of theft. Murray had firmly denied any part of it, and had pleaded with Bolitho to speak on his behalf. Bolitho was deeply impressed by the man's sincerity. Murray was more resentful at the prospect of an unjust flogging than fearful. But that would come unless something could be proved.

Poynter, the master-at-arms, was adamant. He had discovered the watch in Murray's ditty-box during a quick search of several messes. Anybody could have put it there, but what was the point? It was obvious that something would be done to discover the missing watch. A careful thief would have hidden it in one of a hundred secret places. It did not make any sense.

On the evening of the second day the brigantine *Heloise* was sighted heading for the land, her sails shining in the dying sunlight as she completed a leisurely tack for the final approach.

Dumaresq watched her with his telescope and was heard to mutter, 'Taking his damn time. He'll have to do better if he wants promotion!'

Rhodes said, 'Have you noticed, Dick? The freshwater lighters have not been sent out to us as promised? Our stocks must be running low. No wonder the lord and master grows pink with anger.'

Bolitho recalled what Dumaresq had told him. That *Destiny* was to take on water the day after anchoring. He had forgotten, with so much else to occupy his thoughts.

'Mr Rhodes!' Dumaresq strode to the quarterdeck rail. 'Signal *Heloise* to anchor in the outer roadstead. Mr Slade'll not likely attempt an entrance in the dark, but just to be sure, send a boat with my instructions to moor clear of the headland.'

The trill of calls brought the boat's crew running aft. There were several groans when they saw how far the brigantine was standing from the land. A long, hard pull in two directions.

Rhodes sought out the midshipman of the watch. 'Mr Lovelace, go with the boat.' He kept his face straight as he looked at Bolitho. 'Damned midshipmen, eh, Dick? Must keep 'em busy!'

'Mr Bolitho!' Dumaresq was watching him. 'Come here, if you please.'

Bolitho hurried aft until they were both at the taffrail, well out of earshot of everyone.

'I have to tell you that Mr Palliser is unable to discover any other culprit.' He watched Bolitho closely. 'That troubles you, I see.'

'Yes, sir. I have no proof either, but I am convinced Murray is innocent.'

'I'll wait until we are at sea. Then punishment will be carried out. It does no good to flog men before the eyes of foreigners.'

Bolitho waited, knowing there was more to come.

Dumaresq shaded his eyes to stare up at the masthead pendant. 'A fair breeze.' Then he said, 'I shall need another clerk. There is more writing and copying in a man-of-war than powder and shot.' His tone hardened. 'Or fresh water, for that matter!'

Bolitho stiffened as Palliser came aft and then paused as if at an invisible line.

Dumaresq said, 'We are done. What is it, Mr Palliser?'

'Boat approaching, sir.' He did not look at Bolitho. 'It is the same one which brought the pork for cabin and wardroom.'

Dumaresq's brows lifted. 'Really? That interests me.' He turned on his heel, then said, 'I shall be in my quarters. And on the matter of my clerk, I have decided to put the surgeon's new helper, Spillane, to the task. He seems educated and well-disposed to his betters, and I'll not *spoil* the good surgeon by overloading him with aid. He has enough loblolly boys to run his sick-bay.'

Palliser touched his hat. 'So be it, sir.'

Bolitho walked to the larboard gangway to watch the approaching boat. Without a glass he could see no one aboard he recognized. He felt like mocking himself for his stupidity. What had he expected? That the man, Jonathan Egmont, would be coming out to see the captain? Or that his lovely wife would take the fatiguing and uncomfortable journey just to wave to him? He was being ridiculous, childish. Perhaps he had been at sea too long, or his last visit to Falmouth which had brought so much unhappiness had left him open to fantasy and impossible dreams?

The boat came to the main chains, and after a great deal of sign language between the oarsmen and a boatswain's mate an envelope was passed up to Rhodes and then carried aft to the cabin.

The boat waited, idling a few yards from the frigate's hull, the olive-skinned oarsmen watching the busy sailors and marines and probably assessing the strength of *Destiny*'s broadside.

Eventually Rhodes returned to the entry port and handed another envelope down to the boat's coxswain. He saw Bolitho watching and crossed to join him by the hammock nettings.

'I know you will be sorry to hear this, Dick.' He could not prevent his mouth from quivering. 'But we are invited ashore to dine tonight. I believe you know the house already?'

'Who will be going?' Bolitho tried to control his sudden anxiety.

Rhodes grinned. 'The lord and master, *all* of his lieutenants, and, out of courtesy, the surgeon.'

Bolitho exclaimed, 'I cannot believe it! Surely the captain would never leave his ship without at least one lieutenant aboard?' He looked round as Dumaresq appeared on deck. 'Would he?'

Dumaresq shouted, 'Fetch Macmillan and my new clerk, Spillane!' He sounded different, almost jubilant. 'I shall require my gig in half an hour!'

Rhodes hurried away as Dumaresq added loudly, 'I want you and Mr Bolitho and our gallant redcoat ready and presentable at that time!' He smiled. 'The surgeon, too.' He strode away as his servant scurried in his wake like a terrier.

Bolitho looked at his hands. They appeared steady enough, and yet, like his heart, they seemed to be out of control.

In the wardroom there was complete confusion as Poad and his assistants tried to produce clean shirts, pressed uniform coats and generally attempted to transform their charges from sea officers into gentlemen.

Colpoys had his own orderly and was cursing like a trooper as the man struggled with his gleaming boots while he examined himself in a hand-mirror.

Bulkley, as owl-like and crumpled as ever, muttered, 'He's only taking me because of the wrong he did in my sick-bay!'

Palliser snapped, 'For God's sake! He probably doesn't trust you alone in the ship!'

Gulliver was obviously delighted to be left aboard in temporary command. After the long passage from Funchal he had seemingly gathered more confidence, and anyway he hated 'the ways of the quality', as he had once confided to Codd.

Bolitho was the first at the entry port. He saw Jury taking over the watch on the quarterdeck, their eyes met and then moved on. It would all be different once the ship was at sea again. Working together would drive away the differences, except that there was still Murray's fate to be considered.

Dumaresq came on deck and inspected his officers. 'Good. Quite good.'

He looked down at his gig alongside, at the oarsmen in their best checked shirts and tarred hats, with his coxswain ready and waiting.

'Well done, Johns.'

Bolitho thought of the other time he had gone ashore here with Dumaresq. How he had casually asked Johns to look into the matter of Jury's missing watch. Johns, as captain's coxswain, was held in great respect by the petty officers and senior hands. A word in the right place, and a hint to the master-at-arms, who never needed much encouragement when it came to harrying the people, and a swift search had done the rest.

'Into the boat.'

In strict order of seniority, and watched from the gangway by several of the off-duty seamen, *Destiny*'s officers descended into the gig.

Last of all, resplendent in his gold-laced coat with the white lapels, Dumaresq took his place in the stern-sheets.

As the boat moved carefully away from the frigate's hull, Rhodes said, 'May I say, sir, how grateful we are to be invited?'

Dumaresq's teeth showed very white in the gloom. 'I asked all my officers to join me, Mr Rhodes, because we are of one company.' His grin broadened. 'Also, it suits my purpose for the folk ashore to know we are *all* present.'

Rhodes answered lamely, 'I see, sir.' Clearly he did not.

In spite of his earlier misgivings and worries, Bolitho settled down and watched the lights on the land. He was going to enjoy himself. In a foreign, exotic country which he would remember and describe in detail when he returned to Falmouth.

No other thought would interfere with this evening.

Then he recalled the way she had looked at him when he had left the house, and felt his resolve giving way. It was absurd, he told himself, but with that glance she had made him feel like a man.

Bolitho stared along the loaded table and wondered how he would manage to do justice to so many glistening dishes. He was already wishing he had heeded Palliser's curt advice as they had climbed ashore from the gig. 'They'll try to make you drunk, so take care!' And that had been nearly two hours ago. It did not seem possible.

The room was large with a curved ceiling and hung around with colourful tapestries, the whole made even more impressive by hundreds of candles, glittering chandeliers at regular intervals overhead, while along the table's length were some candelabra which must be solid gold, Bolitho thought.

The *Destiny*'s officers had been carefully seated, and made patches of blue and white, separated by the richer clothing of the other guests. They were all Portuguese, most of whom spoke little English and shouted at one another to demand an instant translation or a means of making a point clear to the visitors. The commandant of the shore batteries, a great hogshead of a man, was matched only by Dumaresq in voice and appetite. Occasionally he would lean towards one of the ladies and bellow with laughter, or thump the table with his fist to emphasize his remarks.

A parade of servants came and went, ushering an endless procession of dishes, which ranged from succulent fish to steaming platters of beef. And all the time the wine continued to flow. Wine from their homeland or from Spain, sharp-tasting German hocks and mellow bottles from France. Egmont was certainly generous, and Bolitho had the impression that he was drinking little as he watched over his guests with an attentive smile on his lips.

It was almost too painful to look at Egmont's wife at the

opposite end of the table. She had nodded to Bolitho when he
had arrived, but little else. And now, squashed between a
Portuguese ship-chandler and a wrinkled lady who never
seemed to stop eating, even to draw breath, Bolitho felt
ignored and lost.

But just to look at her was breathtaking. Again she was
dressed in white, against which her skin seemed golden by
contrast. The gown was cut very low across her breasts, and
around her neck she wore a double-headed Aztec bird with
trailing tail feathers, which Rhodes had knowledgeably identi-
fied as rubies.

As she turned her head to speak with her guests the ruby
tails danced between her breasts, and Bolitho swallowed another glass of claret without realizing what he had done.

Colpoys was already half drunk and was describing in
some length to his lady companion how he had once been
caught in a woman's chamber by her husband.

Palliser on the other hand seemed unchanged, eating steadily but sparingly, and careful to keep his glass always half
filled. Rhodes was less sure of himself now, his voice thicker,
his gestures more vague than when the meal had begun. The
surgeon held his food and drink very well, but was sweating
badly as he tried to listen to the halting English of a Portuguese official and answer a question from the man's wife at
the same time.

Dumaresq was incredible. He turned nothing away and yet
seemed completely at ease, his resonant voice reaching along
the table to keep a lagging conversation alive or to arouse one
of his worse for wear officers.

Bolitho's elbow slipped from the table and he almost fell
forward amongst the decimated dishes. The shock helped to
steady him, to realize just how badly the drink had taken
effect. Never again. Never, *never* again.

He heard Egmont announce, 'I think, gentlemen, if the
ladies are about to withdraw, we should transfer to a cooler
room.'

Somehow Bolitho managed to get to his feet in time to
assist the wrinkled lady from her chair. She was still chewing
as she followed the others through a door to leave the men at
their ease.

A servant opened another door and waited for Egmont to

lead his guests into a room which looked out over the sea. Thankfully, Bolitho walked on to the terrace and leaned on a stone balustrade. After the heat of the candles and the power of the wine the air was like water from a mountain stream.

He looked at the moon and then across the anchorage where the lights from *Destiny*'s open gun-ports glittered on the water as if the ship was burning.

The surgeon joined him by the balustrade and said heavily, '*That* was a meal of substance, my boy!' He belched. 'Enough to feed a village for a month. Just imagine it. All that way from France or Spain, no expense spared. When you consider some people are lucky to get a loaf of bread, it makes you wonder.'

Bolitho looked at him. He had thought about it, although not from the point of injustice. How could a man like Egmont, a stranger in this foreign land, make so much wealth? Enough to obtain anything he wanted, even a beautiful wife who must be half his age. The double-headed bird about her throat was gold, a fortune in its own right. Was that part of the *Asturias*'s treasure? Egmont had known Dumaresq's father, but had obviously never met his son before. They had barely spoken, when you thought about it, and when they had it seemed to be through one of the others, light and trivial.

Bulkley leaned forward and adjusted his spectacles. 'There's a work-hungry master, eh? Can't wait for the morning tide.'

Bolitho turned and looked at the anchorage. His practised eye soon discovered the moving vessel, in spite of the queasiness in his stomach.

A vessel under way, her sails making a flitting shadow against the riding lights of other anchored craft as she headed out into the roadstead.

Bulkley said vaguely, 'Local man, must be. Any stranger'd go aground here.'

Palliser called from the open doorway. 'Come in and join us.'

Bulkley chuckled. 'Always a generous fellow when it's someone else's cellar!'

But Bolitho remained where he was. There was enough noise coming from the room anyway, laughter and the clink of glasses, and Colpoys' voice rising higher and higher above the rest. Bolitho knew his absence would not be noticed.

He walked along the moonlit terrace, letting the sea air cool his face.

As he passed another room he heard Dumaresq's voice, very close and very insistent.

'I did not come all this way to be fobbed off with excuses, Egmont. You were in it up to the neck right from the beginning. My father said as much before he died.' The contempt in his voice was like a whip. 'My father's "gallant" first lieutenant who held off when he was sorely needed!'

Bolitho knew he should draw back, but he could not move. The tone of Dumaresq's voice seemed to chill his spine. It was something which had been pent-up for years and now could not be restrained.

Egmont protested lightly, 'I did *not* know. You must believe me. I was fond of your father. I served him well, and always admired him.'

Dumaresq's voice was muffled. He must have turned away with impatience, as Bolitho had seen him do often enough aboard ship.

'Well, my father, whom you so much *admired,* died a pauper. But then, what could you expect for a discarded sea-captain with one arm and one leg, eh? But he kept your secret, Egmont, he at least understood the meaning of loyalty! This could be the end of everything for you.'

'Are you threatening me, sir? In my own house? The Viceroy respects me, and will soon have something to say if I choose to complain!'

'Really?' Dumaresq sounded dangerously calm. 'Piers Garrick was a pirate, of gentle birth maybe, but a bloody pirate for all his manners. If the truth had leaked out about the *Asturias,* even his *letter of marque* would not have saved his neck. The treasure ship put up a good fight, and Garrick's privateer was severely damanged. Then the Don struck his colours, probably did not realize that Garrick's hull was so badly shot through. That was the worst thing he ever did in his life.'

Bolitho waited, holding his breath, fearful that the sudden silence meant they had somehow discovered his presence.

Then Dumaresq added quietly, 'Garrick scuttled his own command and took control of the *Asturias.* He probably butchered most of the Spaniards, or left them to rot somewhere where they could not be found. It was all made so simple for him. He sailed the treasure ship into this port on some excuse or other. England and Spain were at war, *Asturias* would be allowed to remain here for a short while, outwardly to effect repairs, but really to prove she was afloat after Garrick's alleged encounter with her.'

Egmont said shakily, 'That is surmise.'

'Is it? Let me continue, and then you shall decide if you intend to call for the Viceroy's aid.'

His voice was so scathing that Bolitho could almost feel pity for Egmont.

Dumaresq continued, 'A certain English ship was sent to investigate the loss of Garrick's vessel and the escape of the treasure which should rightfully have been a King's prize. That ship was commanded by my father. You, as his senior, were sent to take a statement from Garrick, who must have realized that without your connivance he was for the gallows. But his name was cleared, and while he gathered up his gold from where he had hidden it after destroying the *Asturias*, you resigned from the Navy, and quite mysteriously rose to the surface right here in Rio where it all begin. But this time you were a rich man, a *very* rich man. My father, on the other hand, continued to serve. Then in '62, when he was with Rear-Admiral Rodney at Martinique, driving the French from their Caribbean islands, he was cruelly wounded, broken for life. There is a moral in that, surely?'

'What do you want me to do?'

He sounded dazed, stunned by the completeness of Dumaresq's victory.

'I shall require a sworn testimony to confirm what I have just said. I intend to enlist the Viceroy's aid if need be, and a warrant will then be sent from England. The rest you can well imagine for yourself. With your statement and the power invested in me by His Majesty and their lordships, I intend to arrest *Sir* Piers Garrick and take him to England for trial. I want that bullion, or what is left of it, but most of all I want *him*!'

'But why do you treat me like this? I had no part in what happened to your father at Martinique. I was not then in the Navy, you know that yourself!'

'Piers Garrick was supplying weapons and military stores

to the French garrisons at Martinique and Guadeloupe. But
for him my father might have been spared, and but for *you*,
Garrick would not have had the chance to betray his country a
second time!'

'I—I must have time to think, to . . .'

'It has all run out, Egmont. All thirty years of it. I require
to know Garrick's whereabouts and what he is doing. Anything you can tell me about the bullion, *anything*. If I am
satisfied, I will sail from here and you shall not see me again.
If not . . .' He left the rest unsaid.

Egmont said, 'Can I trust you?'

'My father trusted *you*.' Dumaresq gave a short laugh.
'Choose.'

Bolitho pressed his shoulders against the wall and stared up
at the stars, Dumaresq's energy was not merely inspired by
duty and an eagerness for action. Hate had kept him sifting
vague information, hate had made him hunt down the key
which would unlock the mystery surrounding Garrick's rise to
power. No wonder the Admiralty had selected Dumaresq for
the task. The added spur of revenge would put him leagues
ahead of any other captain.

A door banged open and Bolitho heard Rhodes singing and
then protesting as he was dragged bodily back into the room.

He walked slowly along the terrace, his mind reeling from
what he had heard. The enormity of the secret was unsettling.
How could he go about his duties without giving away what
he had discovered? Dumaresq would see through him in
seconds.

He was suddenly completely sober, the dullness gone from
his mind like a sea mist.

What would become of her if Dumaresq carried out his
threat?

He swung angrily on his heel and made his way towards
the open doors. When he entered he realized that some of the
guests had already gone, and the commandant of the batteries
was bowing almost to the floor as he swept his hat across his
corpulent belly.

Egmont was there with his wife, his face pale but otherwise
impassive.

Dumaresq too seemed as before, nodding to the departing
Portuguese, kissing the gloved hand of the chandler's lady.

It was like seeing two different people from the ones he had overheard just a few rooms away.

Dumaresq said, 'I think my officers are unanimous in their delight at your table, Mr Egmont.'

His glance settled on Bolitho for a second. No more, but Bolitho sensed the question as if it had been shouted aloud.

'I hope we can repay your kindness. But duty is duty, as you will know from experience.'

Bolitho glanced round, but nobody had noticed the sudden tension between Egmont and the captain.

Egmont turned away and said, 'We will say good-night, gentlemen.'

His wife came forward, her eyes in shadow as she held out her hand to Dumaresq.

'It is good-morning now, no?'

He smiled and kissed her hand. 'You are a delight to see at any hour, ma'am.'

His gaze lingered on her bared bosom, and Bolitho flushed as he recalled what Dumaresq had said about the girl who had watched their carriage.

She smiled at the captain, her eyes clear now in the candle-light. 'Then I think you have seen enough for one day, sir!'

Dumaresq laughed and took his hat from a servant while the others made their farewells.

Rhodes was carried bodily from the house and laid in a waiting carriage, a blissful smile on his face.

Palliser muttered, 'Damned disgrace!'

Colpoys, whose pride was the only thing which prevented his collapsing like Rhodes, exclaimed thickly, 'A fine night, ma'am.' He bowed and almost fell over.

Egmont said tersely, 'I think you had better go inside, Aurora, it grows damp and chill.'

Bolitho stared at her. *Aurora*. What an exquisite name. He retrieved his hat and made to follow the others.

'Well now, Lieutenant, have you nothing to say to me?'

She looked at him as she had the first time, her head slightly on one side. He saw it in her eyes, the dare, the challenge.

'I am sorry, ma'am.'

She held out her hand. 'You must not apologize so often. I wish we had had more time to speak. But there were so many.' She tossed her head and the ruby tails flashed on her bosom. 'I hope you were not too bored?'

Bolitho realized that she had removed her long white glove before she offered her hand.

He held her fingers and said, 'I was not bored. I was in despair. There is a difference.'

She withdrew her hand, and Bolitho thought he had ruined everything by his clumsiness.

But she was looking at her husband who was listening to Bulkley's parting words. Then she said softly, 'We cannot have you in despair, Lieutenant, now can we?' She looked at him steadily, her eyes very bright. 'It would never do.'

Bolitho bowed and murmured, 'May I see you?'

Egmont called, 'Come along, the others are leaving.' He shook Bolitho's hand. 'Do not delay your captain. It does not pay.'

Bolitho walked out to one of the waiting carriages and climbed inside. She knew and understood. And now, after what he had overheard, she would need a friend. He stared blindly into the darkness, remembering her voice, the warm touch of her fingers.

'Aurora.' He started, realizing he had spoken her name aloud.

But he need not have bothered, his companions were already fast asleep.

She was twisting in his arms, laughing and provoking him as he tried to hold her, to feel the touch of her bare shoulder against his lips.

Bolitho awoke gasping in his cot, his head throbbing wildly as he blinked at the lantern above his face.

It was Yeames, master's mate, his eyes curious as he watched the lieutenant's confusion, his reluctance to let go of a dream.

Bolitho asked, 'What time is it?'

Yeames grinned unsympathetically. 'Dawn, sir. The 'ands is just turnin' to to 'olystone and scrub down.' He added as an afterthought. 'The cap'n wants you.'

Bolitho rolled out of his cot and kept his feet well apart on the deck for fear of falling. The brief respite of Egmont's cool terrace had gone, and his head felt as if it contained a busy anvil, while his throat tasted vile.

Dawn, Yeames had said. He had not been in his cot for more than two hours.

In the next cabin he heard Rhodes groaning as if in agony, and then yelping in protest as an unknown seaman dropped something heavy on the quarterdeck overhead.

Yeames prompted, 'Better 'urry, sir.'

Bolitho tugged on his breeches and groped for his shirt which had been tossed in one corner of the tiny space. 'Trouble?'

Yeames shrugged. 'Depends wot you mean by trouble, sir.'

To him Bolitho was still a stranger and an unknown quantity. To share what he knew, merely because Bolitho was worried, would be stupid.

Bolitho found his hat, and tugging on his coat he hurried through the wardroom and blundered aft towards the cabin.

The sentry called, 'Third lieutenant, *sir*!' and Macmillan, the captain's servant, opened the screen door as if he had been waiting behind it.

Bolitho stepped through into the after cabin and saw Dumaresq by the stern windows. His hair was awry, and he looked as if he had not found time to undress after his return from Egmont's house. In a corner by the quarter windows, Spillane, the newly appointed clerk, was scratching away with his pen, trying to show no concern at being called at such an early hour. The other two present were Gulliver, the master, and Midshipman Jury.

Dumaresq glared at Bolitho. 'You should have come immediately! I do not expect my officers to dress as if they are going to a ball when I need them!'

Bolitho glanced down at his crumpled shirt and twisted stockings. Also, with his hat clamped beneath one arm, his hair was falling over his face, just as it had been on the pillow. Hardly suitable for a ball.

Dumaresq said, 'During my absence ashore, your seaman Murray escaped. He was not in his cell, but being taken to the sick-bay because he had complained about a severe pain in his stomach.' He turned his wrath on the master. 'God damn it, Mr Gulliver, it was obvious what he was doing!'

Gulliver licked his lips. 'I was in charge of the ship, sir. It was my responsibility. I saw no cause for Murray to suffer, an' the man not yet found guilty as charged.'

Midshipman Jury said, 'The message was brought aft to me, sir. It was my fault.'

Dumaresq replied tersely, 'Speak when you are addressed. It was not your fault, because midshipmen do not *have* responsibility. Neither do they possess the wit or the brains to be in a position to say what this or that man shall do!' His eyes trained round on Gulliver again. 'Tell Mr Bolitho the rest.'

Gulliver said harshly, 'The ship's corporal was escorting him when Murray pushed him down. He was outboard and swimming for the shore before the alarm was raised.' He looked downcast and humiliated at having to repeat his explanation for a junior lieutenant's benefit.

Dumaresq said, 'So there it is. Your trust in that man was wasted. He escaped a flogging, but when he is taken he will hang.' He glanced at Spillane. 'Note it in the log. Run.'

Bolitho looked at Jury's dismay. There were only three ways for a man to quit the Navy, and they were noted as R, D, or DD. *Run* implied desertion, D stood for discharged. Murray's next entry would be the last. *Discharged—Dead*.

And all because of a watch. And yet, in spite of the disappointment over his trust in Murray, Bolitho was strangely relieved at what had happened. The punishment for a man he had known and liked, who had saved Jury's life, was no longer a threat. And its aftermath of suspicion and bitterness had been averted.

Dumaresq said slowly, 'So be it. Mr Bolitho, you will remain. The others may carry on.'

Macmillan closed the door behind Jury and Gulliver. The master's shoulders were stiff with resentment.

Dumaresq asked, 'Hard, you are thinking? But it may prevent weakness later on.'

He calmed as only he could, the rage falling away without apparent effort.

'I am glad you carried yourself well last night, Mr Bolitho. I hope you kept your eyes and ears open?'

The sentry's musket thumped on the deck again. 'First lieutenant, *sir*!'

Bolitho watched as Palliser entered the cabin, his routine list of work for the day beneath his arm. He looked gaunter than usual as he said, 'The water lighters may come out to us today, sir, so I shall tell Mr Timbrell to be prepared. Two men are to see you for promotion, and there is the question of punishment for the ship's corporal for negligence and allowing Murray to desert.'

His eyes moved to Bolitho and he gave a curt nod.

Bolitho wondered if it was mere chance that Palliser always seemed to be nearby whenever he was with the captain.

'Very well, Mr Palliser, though I'll believe those water lighters when I see them.' He looked at Bolitho. 'Go and put your appearance to rights and take yourself ashore. Mr Egmont has a letter for me, I believe.' He gave a wry smile. 'Do not dally too long, although I know there are many distractions in Rio.'

Bolitho felt his face going hot. 'Aye, sir. I'll leave directly.'

He hurried from the cabin and heard Dumaresq say, 'Young devil!' But there was no malice in his voice.

Twenty minutes later Bolitho was sitting in the jolly-boat being pulled ashore. He saw that Stockdale was acting as the boat's coxswain, but did not question him on this. Stockdale seemed to make friends easily, although his fearsome appearance might also have something to do with his apparent freedom of movement.

Stockdale called hoarsely, 'Easy all!'

The oars rose dripping in the rowlocks, and Bolitho realized that the jolly-boat was losing way in order not to be run down by another vessel. She was a brig, a sturdy, well-used vessel with patched canvas and many a scrape on her hull to mark encounters with sea and weather.

She had already spread her topsails, and there were men sliding down backstays to the deck to set the forecourse before she cleared the rest of the anchored vessels nearby.

She moved slowly between *Destiny*'s jolly-boat and some incoming fishermen, her shadow falling across the watching oarsmen as they rested on their looms and waited to proceed.

Bolitho read her name across the counter, *Rosario*. One of hundreds of such craft which daily risked storm and other dangers to trade and to extend the outposts of a growing empire.

Stockdale growled, 'Give way all!'

Bolitho was about to turn his attention to the shore when he saw a movement at the stern windows above the name *Rosario*. For an instant he imagined he was mistaken. But he was not. The same black hair and oval face. She was too far off for him to see the violet of her eyes, but he saw her looking towards him before the brig changed tack and the sunlight made the windows into a fiery mirror.

He was heavy-hearted when he reached the house with the age-old wall around it. Egmont's steward told him coolly that his master had departed, his wife, too. He did not know their destination.

Bolitho returned to the ship and reported to Dumaresq, expecting a further eruption of fury at this latest set-back.

Palliser was with him as Bolitho blurted out what he had discovered, although he did not mention he had seen Egmont's wife in the *Rosario*.

He did not need to. Dumaresq said, 'The only vessel to leave here was the brig. He must be aboard. Once a damned traitor always a traitor. Well, he'll not escape this time, by God no!'

Palliser said gravely, 'So this was the reason for the delay, sir. No fresh water, no audience with the Viceroy. They had us over a gate.' He sounded suddenly bitter. 'We can't move, and they know it!'

Surprisingly, Dumaresq gave a great grin. Then he shouted, 'Macmillan, I want a shave and a bath! Spillane, prepare to write some orders for Mr Palliser.' He walked to the stern windows and leaned on the sill, his massive head lowered towards the rudder. 'Select some prime seamen, Mr Palliser, and transfer to the *Heloise*. Do not rouse the guard-boat's attention with too much fuss, so take no marines. Weigh and chase that damned brig, and don't lose her.'

Bolitho watched the change in the man. It explained why Dumaresq had stopped Slade from entering the protected anchorage. He had anticipated something like this and had a trick to play, as always.

Palliser's mind was already busy. 'And you, sir?'

Dumaresq watched his servant as he prepared a bowl and razor by his favourite chair.

'Water or no water, Mr Palliser, I shall weigh tonight and come after you.'

Palliser eyed him doubtfully. 'The battery might open fire, sir.'

'In daylight maybe. But there is a lot of so-called honour at stake here. I intend to test it.' He turned away, dismissing them, but added, 'Take the third lieutenant. I shall require Rhodes, even if his head is still falling apart from his drinking, to assume your duties here.'

At any other time Bolitho would have welcomed the offer gladly. But he had seen the look in Palliser's eyes, and remembered the face at the brig's cabin windows. She would despise him after this. Like the dream, it was over.

8

The Chase

Lieutenant Charles Palliser strode to the *Heloise*'s compass box and then consulted the masthead pendant.

To confirm his fears, Slade, the acting-master, said dourly, 'The wind's backed a piece, but it's also falling away.'

Bolitho watched Palliser's reactions and compared him with Dumaresq. The captain was in Rio aboard *Destiny*, outwardly dealing with the ship's affairs, even to the extent of seeing two seamen who had been put up for promotion. Fresh water, the prospect of a summons from the Portuguese Viceroy, it would mean nothing to most of the frigate's company. But Bolitho knew what was really uppermost in Dumaresq's thoughts: Egmont's refusal to yield and his sudden departure in the brig *Rosario*. Without Egmont, Dumaresq would have little choice but to seek higher naval authority for instructions, and in that time the scent would go cold.

Slade had said that the brig had been steering north-north-east as she had cleared the roadstead. Egmont was heading along the coast, probably all the way to the Caribbean. In a small trading vessel like that it would be extremely uncomfortable for his lovely wife.

Palliser crossed to his side. On the brigantine's confined deck he looked like a giant, but unusually content, Bolitho thought. Palliser was free of his captain's word, could act as he pleased. Always provided he did not lose the *Rosario*. And with the wind dropping fast, that was a possibility.

He said, 'They'll not be expecting a chase. That is all we have on our side.'

He glanced up, irritated, as the forecourse boomed and flapped, empty of wind and allowing the heat to seek out the men on deck.

'*Damn!*' Then he said, 'Mr Slade says the brig will stay inshore. Unless the wind shifts, I accept that. We shall continue as we are. Change the lookouts as you think fit, and have the weapons which are still aboard this vessel inspected.' He clasped his hands behind him. 'Don't work the people too hard.' He saw the surprise on Bolitho's face and gave a thin smile. 'They will have to take to the oars shortly. I intend to warp *Heloise* with the boats. They'll need all their muscle for that!'

Bolitho touched his hat and walked forward. He should have guessed. But he had to confess admiration for Palliser's preparations. He thought of everything.

He saw Jury and Midshipman Ingrave waiting for him by the foremast. Jury looked tense but Ingrave, who was a year older, could barely conceal his delight at being freed from his task of acting-clerk for the captain.

Beyond them were other familiar faces amongst the hastily selected hands. Josh Little, gunner's mate, his stomach hanging over his cutlass-belt. Ellis Pearse, boatswain's mate, a bushy-browed man who had shown the same satisfaction as Bolitho that Murray had deserted. Pearse would have been the man to flog him, and he had always liked Murray. And of course, there was Stockdale, his thick arms folded over his chest as he surveyed the brigantine's deck, remembering perhaps that fierce, desperate struggle when Bolitho had fought hand to hand with the vessel's master.

Dutchy Vorbink, foretopman, who had left the East India Company and exchanged their ordered and well-paid life for that of a man-of-war. He spoke little English, unless he wanted to, so nobody had discovered his true reason for volunteering.

There were faces which had now become people to Bolitho. Some coarse and brutalized, others who would brawl with the best of them but were equally quick to put right a wrong for a less outspoken messmate.

Bolitho said, 'Mr Spillane, examine the arms chest and

make a list of weapons. Little, you had better go through the
magazine.' He looked around at the few swivel guns, two of
which had been sent across from *Destiny*. 'Hardly enough to
start a war.'

It brought a few grins and chuckles, and Stockdale muttered, 'There's still some prisoners battened below, sir.'

Bolitho looked at Little. He had forgotten about the *Heloise*'s
original company. Those not killed or wounded had been
detained here. Safe enough, but in the event of trouble they
would have to be watched.

Little showed his uneven teeth. 'All taken care of, sir. I got
Olsson on guard. They'd be too scared to challenge 'im!'

Bolitho agreed. Olsson was a Swede and was said to be
half mad. It shone from his eyes which were like washed-out
blue glass. A good seaman who could reef and steer and turn
his hand to anything, but when they had boarded this same
brigantine Bolitho had chilled to Olsson's crazy screams as he
had cleaved his way through his opponents.

He forced a grin. 'I'd think twice myself.'

Pearse groaned as the sails shivered and then flapped dully
against rigging and spars.

'There goes the bloody wind.'

Bolitho crossed to the bulwark and leaned out over the blue
water. He saw the wind's ripple on the surface moving away
far ahead of the bows like a great shoal of fish. The brigantine
lifted and sighed in the swell, blocks and sails clattering in
protest as the power went with the wind.

'Man your boats!' Palliser was watching from beside the
helmsmen.

Bare feet padded over the hot deck seams as the first
crews went away in the quarter-boat, as well as *Destiny*'s
cutter which they had kept in tow beneath the counter.

It took far too long to lay out the towing warps and pass
them to the boats. Then with each boat angled away on either
bow the painful, dreary business began.

They could not hope to make any speed, but it would
prevent the vessel from drifting completely out of command,
and when the wind came they would be ready.

Bolitho stood above the larboard anchor and watched the
towlines tautening and then sagging beneath the glittering
water as the oarsmen threw their weight into play.

Little shook his head. 'Mr Jury's no'and for this sir. 'E'll need to use 'is starter on that lot.'

Bolitho could see the difference between the two towing boats. Jury's was yawning badly, and a couple of the oars were barely cutting beneath the surface. The other boat, with Midshipman Ingrave in charge, was making better progress, and Bolitho knew why. Ingrave was not a bully, but he was well aware of his superiors watching from the brigantine, and was using a rope's end on some of his men to make them work harder at the oars.

Bolitho walked aft and said to Palliser, 'I'll change the crews in an hour, sir.'

'Good.' Palliser was watching the sails and then the compass. 'She's got steerage-way at least. Few thanks to the larboard boat.'

Bolitho said nothing. He knew only too well what it was like as a midshipman to be suddenly thrown into an unpopular job. But Palliser did not press the point, which was something. Bolitho thought of his own sudden acceptance of his new role. He had not asked Palliser about changing the boats' crews, he had told him, and the first lieutenant had accepted without question. Palliser was as wily as Dumaresq. In their very different ways they were able to draw out exactly what they required from their subordinates.

He glanced at Slade, who was shading his eyes to peer at the sky. A man who wanted promotion above all else. Dumaresq used that too, to extract the best from the intolerant master's mate, which in turn would aid him when his chance of advancement finally came. Even Palliser had his mind set on his own command, and this temporary duty in charge of *Heloise* would stand very well on this record.

All through the day the relentless boat-pulling went on, while not even a faint breeze came to revive the sails. They hung from the yards, limp and useless, like the men who tumbled aboard from the boats as soon as they were relieved. Too exhausted to do much more than gulp down a double ration of wine which Slade had broached from the hold, they fell about like dead men.

In the cabin aft, tiny as it was, but adequate when compared with the rest of the space between decks, the relieved midshipmen and their lieutenants tried to find escape from the heat and the dangerous need to drink and keep on drinking.

With Palliser asleep and Slade on watch, Bolitho sat at the small table, his head lolling as he tried to keep his mind awake. Opposite him, his lips cracked from the sun's glare, Jury rested his head on his hands and looked into space.

Ingrave was away with the boats again, but even his keenness was flagging badly.

Bolitho asked, 'How do you feel?'

Jury smiled painfully, 'Dreadful, sir.' He tried to straighten his back and plucked his sodden shirt away from his skin.

Bolitho pushed a bottle towards him. 'Drink this.' He saw the youth hesitate and insisted, 'I'll stand your trick in the boats if you like. It's better than sitting here and waiting.'

Jury poured a cup of wine and said, 'No, sir, but thank you. I'll go when I'm called.'

Bolitho smiled. He had toyed with the idea of telling Stockdale to go with the midshipman. One sight of him would put a stopper on any slackness or insubordination. But Jury was right. To make it easy for him when he most needed confidence and experience would only lay a snare for later on.

'I—I was thinking, sir.' He looked across guardedly. 'About Murray. D'you think he'll be all right?'

Bolitho thought about it. Even that was an effort. 'Maybe. Provided he stays away from the sea. I've known men who have quit the Navy to return and find security under a different name in the service they had originally reviled. But that can be dangerous. The Navy is a family. There is always a familiar face and a memory to match it.'

He thought of Dumaresq and Egmont. Each linked by Dumaresq's dead father, just as he was now involved with whatever they might attempt.

Jury said, 'I often think about him. Of what happened on deck.' He glanced up at the low beams as if expecting to hear the ring of steel, the desperate shuffling of men circling each other for a kill. Then he looked at Bolitho and added, 'I'm sorry. I was told to put it from my mind.'

A call shrilled and a voice yelled, 'Away boats' crews! Lively there!'

Jury stood up, his fair hair brushing the deckhead.

Bolitho said quietly, 'I was told much the same when I joined the *Destiny*. Like you, I still have the same difficulty.'

He remained at the table, listening to the thump of boats alongside, the clatter of oars as the crews changed around yet again.

The door opened, and bent double like a crippled sailor, Palliser groped his way to a chair and thankfully sat down. He too listened to the boats thrashing away from the hull, the sluggish response from the tiller-head as the brigantine submitted to the tow.

Then he said flatly, 'I'm going to lose that devil. After getting this far, it's all been cut from under me.'

Bolitho could feel the disappointment like a physical thing, and the fact Palliser had made no effort to hide his despair was strangely sad.

He pushed the bottle and cup across the table. 'Why not take a glass, sir.'

Palliser looked up from his thoughts, his eyes flashing. Then he smiled wearily and took the cup.

'Why not, Richard?' He slopped the wine carelessly over the rim. 'Why not indeed?'

While the sun moved towards the opposite horizon, the two lieutenants sat in silence, occasionally taking a sip of the wine which by now was as warm as milk.

Then Bolitho dragged out his watch and said, 'One more hour with the boats and then we shall secure for the night, sir?'

Palliser had been in deep thought and took several seconds to reply.

He said, 'Yes. There's nothing else we *can* do.'

Bolitho was stunned by the change in him, but knew if he tried to cheer him up the truce would be shattered.

Feet shuffled through the main-deck and Little's great face squinted in at them.

'Beg pardon, sir, but Mr Slade sends 'is respects and says 'e can 'ear gunfire to the north'rd!'

An empty bottle rolled across the deck at the lieutenants' feet and clinked against the side as the cabin suddenly tilted.

Palliser stared at the bottle. He was still seated, but his head was touching a beam without difficulty.

He exclaimed, '*The wind!* The damned, wonderful wind!' He clawed his way to the door. 'Not a moment too soon!'

Bolitho felt the hull give a shiver, as if it was awakening from a deep sleep. Then with a bound he hurried after the lanky Palliser, sobbing with pain as his skull came in contact with a ring-bolt.

On deck the men were staring around with disbelief as the big forecourse filled and boomed noisily from its yard.

Palliser yelled, 'Recall the boats! Stand by to come about!' He was peering at the compass and then up at the masthead pendant, just visible against the early stars.

Slade said, 'Wind's shifted, sir, veered a little, sou'-west.'

Palliser rubbed his chin. 'Gunfire, you say?'

Slade nodded. 'No doubt. Small pieces is my guess.'

'Good. As soon as the boats are secured, get under way again and lay her on the larboard tack. Steer nor'-west by north.'

He stood aside as the men ran through the deepening shadows to their stations.

Bolitho tested their new relationship. 'Will you not wait for *Destiny,* sir?'

Palliser held up his hand and they both heard the muted sounds of gunfire.

Then he said tersely, 'No, Mr Bolitho, I will not. Even if my captain succeeds in leaving harbour, and is able to discover more favourable winds than ourselves, he'll not thank me for allowing the evidence he so sorely needs to be destroyed.'

Pearse yelled, 'Boats secured aft, sir!'

'Man the braces! Stand by to come about!'

The wind hissed over the water and thrust against the canvas with new strength, pushing the brigantine over as a white froth gathered around her stem.

Palliser said sharply, 'Darken ship, Pearse! I want nothing to betray our presence!'

Slade said, 'It might be over an' done with before dawn, sir.'

But the new Palliser snapped, 'Nonsense! That vessel is being attacked, probably by pirates. They'll not risk a collision in darkness.' He turned to seek out Bolitho and added, 'Not like us, eh?'

Little shook his head and breathed out noisily. Bolitho could smell the drink on his breath, as strong as an open cellar door.

'Gawd, Mr Bolitho, 'e's really 'appy at last.'

Bolitho thought suddenly of the face he had seen aboard the ship now under attack.

'Please God we shall be in time.'

Little, not understanding, walked away to join his friend Pearse for another 'wet.'

So the new third lieutenant was as eager as the captain for prize money, he thought, and that could not be such a bad thing for the rest of them.

Palliser prowled across the poop like a restless animal.

'Shorten sail, Mr Bolitho. Take in the t'gan'sls and stays'l. Roundly now!'

Men groped their way to halliards and belaying-pins while others ran swiftly up the ratlines and out along the topgallant yard.

Bolitho always marvelled at the little time it took trained seamen to get used to a strange vessel, even in the dark.

It would soon be dawn, and he could feel the previous day's weariness and hours without sleep clawing at his resistance. Palliser had kept his small company on the move throughout the night. Changing tack, altering course, retrimming sails, as he plotted and estimated the whereabouts of the other vessels. Several times there had been short exchanges of gunfire, but Palliser had said it was more to deter a possible chase than with any hope of close action. One thing had been proved by the occasional cannon fire. There were at least three vessels out there beyond the *Heloise*'s taut jib. Like wolves around a wounded beast, waiting for it to falter or make one fatal mistake.

Little called hoarsely, 'All guns loaded, sir!'

Palliser replied, 'Very well.' In a lower tone to Bolitho he added, '*All* guns. A few swivels and about enough canister to disturb a field of crows!'

Midshipman Ingrave said, 'Permission to run up the colours, sir?'

Palliser nodded. 'Yes. This is a King's ship for the present, and we're not likely to meet another.'

Bolitho recalled some of the muttering he had heard during the night. A few of the hands were troubled at the prospect of engaging pirates or anyone else with so puny an armament.

Bolitho darted a quick glance to starboard. Was there a faint lightening on the horizon? There was a good lookout aloft, and he was their best hope of taking the other vessel by surprise. It was unlikely that pirates intent on capturing and plundering a trader would be bothered about keeping a watch elsewhere.

He heard Slade whispering with Palliser. He was another one who was unhappy about the coming confrontation.

Palliser said fiercely, 'Keep an eye on your course and be ready to change tack if we outrun the enemy. Leave the rest to me, see?'

Bolitho felt his limbs shiver. *The enemy.* Palliser had no doubts anyway.

Stockdale came from the shadows, his great frame angled against the deck as the wind held them over.

'Them buggers are usin' chain-shot, sir. Once or twice I 'eard it when I was aloft.'

Bolitho bit his lip. So they intended to cripple the *Rosario*'s rigging and then pound her into submission with less risk to themselves. They would get a shock when they saw *Heloise* bearing down on them. For a short while anyway.

He said, 'Maybe *Destiny*'s already chasing after us.'

'Mebbee.'

Bolitho turned away as Jury came to join him. Stockdale did not believe that, any more than he did.

Jury asked, 'Will it take much longer, sir?'

'Dawn comes up swiftly. You'll see their topsails or upper yards at any minute now. If one of them fires again, we should be able to plot his bearing.'

Jury watched him in the gloom. 'It does not trouble you, sir?'

Bolitho shrugged. 'Not now. Later perhaps. We are committed, or soon will be.' He turned and put his hand on the midshipman's shoulder. 'Just remember something. Mr Palliser has picked some very experienced hands for this work. But his officers are somewhat youthful.' He saw Jury nod. 'So keep your head and be where you can be seen. Leave the miracles to Mr Palliser.'

Jury smiled and then winced as his cracked lips reminded him of the previous day's boatwork.

He said, 'I'll stay with you.'

Stockdale chuckled. 'Beggin' yer pardon, young gentleman, but don't you be gettin' in my way.' He swung a cutlass across the bulwark like a scythe. 'Wouldn't want you to lose yer 'ead, so to speak!'

Palliser called, 'Stand by to take in the forecourse! Keep it quiet!'

The boatswain's mate pointed abeam. 'Dawn, sir!'

Palliser rasped, 'God dammit, Pearse, we're neither blind nor bloody deaf!'

Pearse grinned at Palliser's back. 'Palliser, you're a real pig!' But he was careful that nobody should hear him.

'Deck there! Sail on the starboard bow! And 'nother to larboard!'

Palliser clapped his hands together. 'We did it! Damn their eyes, we're into them!'

At that moment a gun fired, making an orange flash on the dark water.

Slade said anxiously, 'There's a third to wind'rd!'

Bolitho gripped his hanger and pressed its scabbard against his thigh to calm himself.

Three vessels, the centre one was doubtless the *Rosario*, with her two attackers standing off to form one great triangle. He heard a slithering sound and then a splintering crash, and vaguely through the darkness ahead he saw a jagged patch of spray as some spars and rigging hit the water.

Stockdale nodded. 'Chain-shot right enough, th' buggers.'

'Stand by on deck! Watch your slow-matches!'

There was no need for stealth now. Bolitho heard a shrill whistle from the nearest vessel and the crack of a pistol. It had either exploded in error or had been used as a signal to warn their consort.

With their muskets and powder-horns ready to use, cut-lasses and boarding pikes within easy reach, the *Destiny*'s seamen peered into the darkness.

'Take in the forecourse!'

Men ran to obey, and as the great sail was brailed up to its yard the growing light revealed the crouching figures and trained swivels like the rising of a curtain.

There was a series of bangs, and Bolitho heard the chain-shot screeching overhead like tormented spirits in hell.

Little said between his teeth, 'Too 'igh, thank the livin' Jesus!'

The deadly chain-shot threw up broken spray far to starboard, but in direct line with the brigantine's two masts.

'Lee helm!' Palliser was gripping a backstay as he studied the enemy's blurred outline. 'As close to the wind as you can!'

'Man the braces!'

The brigantine crept round, until her remaining sails were rippling in protest.

'Nor'-west by west, sir! Full an' bye!'

The other vessel fired and a ball slammed down within twenty feet of the *Heloise*'s bow and hurled spray high over the beak-head.

Then firing began in earnest, the balls wide and haphazard as the gun crews tried to guess what the newcomer was trying to do.

Another ball ripped through the driver and left a jagged hole in the canvas large enough for a man's head.

Palliser exploded, 'That bloody fool brig fired at *us*.'

Little grinned. 'Thanks we're pirates, too!'

'I'll give him pirates!'

Palliser pointed at the vessel which was rising out of the darkness to larboard and shortening as she changed tack to run down on the brigantine's impudent approach.

'Schooner! Take her first!'

Little cupped his hands. 'On the uproll, lads!'

Men were still dragging one of the swivels across to mount it on the opposite side and yelled at Little to give them more time.

But Little knew his trade well.

'Easy, lads!' It was like hearing a man quietening a beast. *'Fire!'*

Like glow-worms the matches plunged down and the swivels barked viciously at the oncoming vessel. A murderous hail of closely packed canister swept across her forecastle, and Bolitho thought he heard screams as it found a target.

'Stand by to come about!' Palliser's voice carried easily even without his speaking trumpet. 'Lee braces!'

Palliser walked jerkily down the sloping deck to join Slade by the helm. 'We'll go for another one. Put up your helm.'

Heeling hard over, the brigantine ran to leeward, her canvas banging lustily until the seamen had hauled the yards round again. The second vessel seemed to pivot across the jib-boom until she lay to larboard, her stern end on to the changing *Heloise*.

Palliser yelled, 'Rake her poop, Little!' He swung on Slade and his gasping helmsmen. 'Steady as she goes, you fool!'

Bolitho found time to pity Slade's concern. The *Heloise* was rushing down on the other vessel's stern as if she was about to smash bodily through her quarter like an axe.

'*Fire!*'

Flashes lit up the decks of both vessels as their guns spat out darting orange tongues, accompanied by the crash of iron hitting home. *Heloise*'s canister must have wiped the other vessel's poop clean. Helmsmen, gun crews, there was not enough room to escape as the "daisy cutters" jagged charges swept amongst them. She began to fall downwind, to be raked yet again by Little's other swivels.

'Set the forecourse!' Palliser's voice was everywhere.

Bolitho could see him clearly now, his lean body moving about the poop and framed against the brightening sea like an avenger.

'*Fire!*'

More balls shrieked overhead, and Bolitho guessed that their first target had regained his courage and was closing to the aid of his companion.

He saw the *Rosario* for the first time, and his heart sank at the spectacle. Her foremast had gone completely, and only half of her main appeared to be standing. Wreckage and severed rigging trailed everywhere, and as the sun lifted above the horizon Bolitho saw the thin scarlet threads which ran down from each scupper. It was as if the ship herself and not her defenders was bleeding to death.

'*Hands wear ship!*'

Bolitho jabbed a seaman's shoulder and yelled, 'Join the others!' He felt the man jump before he ran to throw his weight on the braces. He had imagined it to be hot iron and not his hand.

There was a tremendous crash, and Bolitho almost fell to
his knees as two hits were scored on the *Heloise*'s hull.

Bolitho saw Ingrave staring at the nearest vessel, wide-eyed
and unable to move.

He shouted, 'Get below and attend to the damage!' He
strode to the midshipman and gripped his sleeve and shook him
like a doll. '*At once,* Mr Ingrave! Sound the well!'

Ingrave stared at him vacantly, and then with unexpected
determination ran to the companion.

Stockdale unceremoniously dragged Bolitho's arm and held
him aside as a massive block fell from aloft, broken cordage
whipping behind it. It struck the bulwark and bounced over
the side.

Palliser shouted, '*Stand to!*' He had drawn his sword.
'Ready to larboard!'

Against the schooner's cannon, small though they were,
the swivels sounded insignificant. Bolitho saw the canister
blast through the schooner's fore-sail and hurl two men into
bloody bundles before more balls smashed through *Heloise*'s
lower hull. He heard the havoc tearing between decks, the
crack of splinters and collapsing timbers, and knew they had
been badly hit.

Someone had managed to get the pumps going, but he saw
two men fall bleeding badly, and another who had been
working on the topsail yard trying to lower himself to safety
with one leg hanging by a muscle.

Palliser shouted, 'Come aft!'

As Bolitho hurried to join him he said, 'We're doing no
good. Get below yourself and report the damage.' He blinked
as more shots thudded into the reeling hull, and somewhere a
man shrieked in agony. 'Feel her? She's going!'

Bolitho stared at him. It was true. The *Heloise*'s agility had
given way to an ungainly response to both helm and wind. It
did not seem possible. So quickly, and their roles had changed.
There was no aid at hand, and their enemies would not let
them die easily.

Palliser snapped, 'I'm going to steer for the brig. With our
men and her guns there's still a chance.' He looked steadily at
Bolitho. 'Now be a good fellow and get below.'

Bolitho hurried to the companion, his quick glance taking
in the splintered deck planking and stark bloodstains. They

had fought here before. Surely that was enough? Perhaps fate
had always intended they should end thus?

He called to Jury, 'Come with me.' He peered down into
the darkness, dreading the thought of being trapped below if
the ship went down. He spoke carefully to hide his anxiety.
'We will examine the damage together. Then if I fall . . .'
He saw Jury gasp. So he had not yet accepted the idea of
death. '. . . you will relay the details to Mr Palliser.'

Once down the companion ladder he lit a lantern and led
the way forward, careful to avoid some of the jagged splinters
which had been smashed through from the deck above. The
sounds were muffled but filled with menace as the ship
shook and bucked to the bombardment.

The two attacking vessels were working round on either
beam, heedless of the danger of hitting each other in their
eagerness to destroy the little ship with the scarlet ensign at
her peak.

Bolitho dragged open a lower hatch and said, 'I can hear
water.'

Jury whispered, 'Oh, dear God, we're foundering!'

Bolitho laid down and dipped his lantern through the hatch.
It was a scene of complete chaos. Shattered casks and rem-
nants of canvas floated amongst splintered wood, and as he
watched he imagined he saw the water rising still further.

He said, 'Go to the first lieutenant and tell him there's no
hope.' He restrained Jury, feeling his sudden surge of fear as
more balls cracked into the hull. '*Walk*. Remember what I
said. They'll be looking to you.' He tried to smile, to show
that nothing mattered. 'All right?'

Jury backed away, his eyes moving from the open hatch to
Bolitho.

'What will *you* do?'

Bolitho turned his head sharply as a new sound echoed
through the listing hull like a giant's hammer. One of the
anchors had broken free and was smashing into the bows with
every roll. It could only speed their end.

'I'll go to Olsson. We must release the prisoners.'

And then Bolitho was alone. He swallowed deeply and
tried to keep his limbs from shaking. Then very slowly he
groped his way aft again, the regular boom of the anchor
against the hull following him like an execution drum.

There was another thud against the hull, but it was followed instantly by a loud crack. One of the masts, or part of it, was coming down. He tensed, waiting for the final crash as it hit the deck or plunged over the side.

The next instant he was spread-eagled in the darkness, the lantern gone from his hand, although he did not feel anything, nor did he recall the moment of impact.

All he knew was that he was pinned beneath a mass of wreckage and unable to move.

He pressed his ear to a ventilation grating and heard the surge of water as it battered through the bilges and lower hold. He was on the edge of terror, and knew that in seconds he could be screaming and kicking in a hopeless attempt to free himself.

Thoughts crowded through his mind. His mother as she had watched him leave. The sea below the headland at Falmouth where he and his brother had first ventured out in a fisherman's boat, and his father's wrath when he had discovered what they had done.

His eyes smarted, but when he tried to move his fingers to his face the fallen debris held him as cruelly as any trap.

The anchor had stopped its incessant boom against the hull, which meant it was probably under water with the forepart of the vessel.

Bolitho closed his eyes and waited, praying that his nerve would not break before the end.

9

Palliser's Ruse

Bolitho felt a growing pressure against his spine as some of the fallen timber shifted to the brigantine's motion. He heard a scraping sound somewhere overhead, the clang of metal as one of the guns broke free and tumbled across the deck. The angle was more acute, and he could hear the sea piling against the hull, but much higher than before as the vessel continued to settle deeper and deeper.

There was still some shooting, but it seemed as if the victors were standing off to wait for the sea to complete their work for them.

Slowly, but with mounting desperation, Bolitho tried to wriggle free from the debris across his body. He could hear himself groaning and pleading, gasping meaningless words as he struggled to rid himself of the trap.

It was useless. He only succeeded in dislodging some more broken woodwork, a piece of which ploughed past his head like a spear.

With something like panic he heard sounds of a boat being manned, some hoarse cries and more musket shots.

He clenched his fists and pressed his face against the deck planking to prevent himself from screaming. The vessel was going fast and Palliser had ordered her to be abandoned.

Bolitho tried to think clearly, to accept that his companions were doing what they must. It was no time for sentiment or some useless gesture. He was already as dead as the others who had been shot down in the heat of the fighting.

He heard voices and someone calling his name. Needles of light probed through the tangled wreckage, and as the deck gave another lurch Bolitho shouted, *'Go back! Save yourselves!'*

He was shocked and stunned by his words and the strength of his voice. More than anything he had wanted to live until he had realized someone had cared enough to risk death for his sake.

Stockdale's throaty voice said, ' 'Ere, work that spar clear!'

Somebody else said doubtfully, 'Too late, by the looks of it, mate. We'd best get aft.'

Stockdale rasped, 'Take 'old like I told you! Now, together, lads! *'Eave!'*

Bolitho cried out as the pain pushed harder into his spine. Feet moved down from the other side of the pile and he saw Jury on his knees peering through a gap to look for him.

'Not long, sir.' He was shaking with fear but trying to smile at the same time. 'Hold on!'

As suddenly as it had smashed him down the weight of broken planking and one complete spar were levered and hoisted clear.

A man seized Bolitho's ankles and dragged him roughly up the sloping deck, while Stockdale appeared to be holding back a wall of wreckage all on his own.

Jury gasped, 'Quickly!' He would have fallen but for a seaman's ready grip, and then they were all staggering and lurching like drunks running from a press-gang.

On deck at last, Bolitho forgot the pain and the lurking moments of bare terror.

In the strengthening light he saw that the *Heloise* was already a total wreck, her fore-topmast gone completely and her main nothing more than a jagged stump. Her canvas, broken spars and an entangled mesh of fallen rigging completed the scene of devastation.

To drive it home, Bolitho saw that both boats were manned and standing clear, and the nearer of the two was already higher than the *Heloise*'s lee side.

Palliser stood in the cutter directing some of his men to use their muskets on one of the schooners. The dying brigantine acted as a barrier, the only thing which still stood between the enemy and their chance to run down on the boats and finish the one-sided fight.

Stockdale grunted, 'Over th' side, lads!'

His mind reeling, Bolitho saw that two of the men who had come back for him were Olsson, the mad Swede, and one of the farm-workers who had volunteered to his Plymouth recruiting party.

Jury kicked off his shoes and secured them inside his shirt. He looked at the water as it came swirling over the bulwark and exclaimed huskily, 'It's a long swim!'

Bolitho flinched as a musket ball smacked into the deck and raised a splinter as high as a goose quill within feet of where they were standing.

'Now or never!' He saw the sea thundering through the companion and turning one of the corpses in a wild dance as it forced the bows deeper and deeper below the surface.

With Stockdale panting and floundering between them, Bolitho and Jury sprang into the water. It seemed to take an age to reach the nearest boat, and even then they had to join the others who were hanging to the gunwales and trying not to hamper the oarsmen as they headed for the dismasted *Rosario*.

Most of the men around Bolitho were strangers, and he realized they must be the released prisoners. Olsson had looked so wild it was a wonder he had not left them to drown with their ship.

Then all at once the brig's side towered above them. She was a small vessel, but viewed from the water as he fought for breath and clung to a thrown line, Bolitho thought she looked as big as a frigate.

Eventually they were pushed, dragged and man-handled up and over the side where they were confronted by the brig's own company, who stared at them as if they had come from the sea itself.

Palliser left nobody in doubt as to who was in command.

'Little, take the prisoners below and put them in irons. Pearse, discover the chance of a jury-rig, anything to give us steerage-way!' He strode past some dazed and bleeding men and snapped, 'Have these guns loaded, d'you hear? God dammit, you're like a pack of old women!'

A man of some authority pushed through his sailors and said, 'I am the master, John Mason. I know why you're here, but I give thanks to God for it, sir, though I fear we are no match for them pirates.'

Palliser eyed him coldly. 'We shall see about that. But for now, do as I direct. How you and your people behave today may decide what happens to you.'

The man gaped at him. 'I don't understand, sir?'

'Do you have a passenger, one Jonathan Egmont?'

Bolitho leaned on the bulwark sucking in great gulps of air, the sea-water streaming from his limbs to mingle with the blood around the nearest gun.

'Aye, sir, but . . .'

'Alive?'

'Was when I last saw him. I put my passengers below when the attack began.'

Palliser gave a grim smile. 'That is fortunate. For both of us, I think.' He saw Bolitho and added sharply, 'Make sure Egmont is secure. Tell him nothing.' He was about to turn his attention to one of the schooners but instead watched the *Heloise*'s final moment, as with a last burst of spray from her hatches she plunged to the bottom. He said, 'I am glad you were able to stay with us. I ordered the vessel to be abandoned.' His eyes rested momentarily on Jury and Stockdale. 'However . . .'

Bolitho staggered to an open hatch, his bruised mind still grappling with the *Rosario*'s lay-out as she pitched about in the swell.

The brig had taken a terrible beating. Upended guns, corpses and pieces of men lay strewn with the other debris, ignored in the frantic efforts to keep their attackers from boarding.

A seaman with one hand wrapped in a crude bandage, the other gripping a pistol, called, 'Down 'ere, sir!'

Bolitho clambered down a ladder, his stomach rebelling against the stench of pain and suffering. Three men lay unconscious or dying, another was crawling back to his station as best he could in makeshift dressings and a sling.

Egmont stood at a table, wiping his hands on a rag, while a seaman trimmed a lantern for him.

He saw Bolitho and gave a tired shrug. 'An unexpected meeting, Lieutenant.'

Bolitho asked, 'Have you been attending the wounded?'

'You know the Navy, Lieutenant. For me it is a long, long

time ago since I served your captain's father, but it is something you never lose.'

Bolitho heard the urgent clank of pumps, the sounds of blocks and tackles being hauled noisily across the upper deck. The *Destiny*'s seamen were working again, and he was needed up there to help Palliser, to keep them at it, driving them by force if necessary.

They had been in a savage fight and some had died, as he had nearly done. Now they were needed again. Let them falter and they would drop. Allow them time to mourn the loss of a friend and they would lose the stuff of fighting.

But he asked, 'Your wife, is she safe?'

Egmont gestured towards a bulkhead door. 'In there.'

Bolitho thrust his shoulder against it, the fear of being trapped below decks still scraping at his mind.

By lantern-light in a sealed, airless cabin he saw three women. Aurora Egmont, her maid and a buxom woman he guessed to be the master's wife.

He said, 'Thank God you're safe.'

She moved towards him, her feet invisible in the cabin's gloom so that she appeared to be floating.

She reached up and felt his wet hair and his face, her eyes large as she said quietly, 'I thought you were still in Rio.' Her hands touched his chest and his arms as they hung at his sides. 'My poor lieutenant, what have they done to you?'

Bolitho could feel his head swimming. Even here, amidst the stench of bilge and death, he was conscious of her perfume, the cool touch of her fingers on his face. He wanted to hold her, to press her against his body like the dream. To share his anxiety for her, to reveal his longing.

'Please!' He tried to step away. 'I am filthy. I just wanted to be sure you were safe. Unhurt.'

She pushed his protest aside and put her hands on his shoulders. 'My brave lieutenant!' She turned her head and called sharply to her maid, 'Stop weeping, you silly girl! Where is your pride?'

In those few seconds Bolitho felt her breast press against his wet shirt, as if there was nothing between their bodies.

He murmured, *'I must go.'*

She was staring at him as if to memorize everything about him. 'Will you fight again? Do you have to?'

Bolitho felt the strength returning to his body. He could even smile as he said, 'I have someone to fight *for*, Aurora.'

She exclaimed, 'You remembered!'

Then she pulled his head down and kissed him firmly on the mouth. Like him, she was shaking, her earlier anger with her maid a pretence like his own.

She whispered, 'Be careful, Richard. My young, *so*-young lieutenant.'

With Palliser's voice ringing in the distance, Bolitho walked back to the ladder and ran to the upper deck.

Palliser was examining the two big schooners with a telescope, and without lowering it he asked dryly, 'May I assume that all is well below?'

Bolitho made to touch his hat, but remembered it had gone a long time ago.

'Aye, sir. Egmont is helping the wounded.'

'Is he indeed?' Palliser closed his glass with a snap. 'Now listen. Those devils will try to divide our defences. One will stand off while the other attempts to board.' He was thinking aloud. 'We may have survived one fight, but they will see *Heloise*'s loss as their victory. They'll give no quarter now.'

Bolitho nodded. 'We might hope to hold them off if we had every gun fully manned, sir.'

Palliser shook his head. 'No. We are adrift and cannot prevent one or both of them from raking our stern.' He glanced at some of the brig's seamen as they staggered past with a trailing serpent of rigging. 'These people are done for, no stomach left. It's up to us.' He nodded firmly, his mind made up. 'We shall allow one of the buggers to grapple. Divide them and see how they like *that*.'

Bolitho looked at the fallen masts and sprawled bodies, amongst which *Destiny*'s seamen moved like scavengers on a battle-field. Then he touched his mouth with his fingers, as if he expected to feel a difference there where she had kissed him with such fervent passion.

He said, 'I'll tell the others, sir.'

Palliser eyed him bleakly. 'Yes. Just *tell* them. Explanations may come later. If they do, we shall know we have won. If not, they won't matter.'

*   *   *

Palliser lowered his telescope and said bitterly, 'They are better manned than I thought.'

Bolitho shaded his eyes to watch the two schooners, their big fore and aft sails like wings against the bright sky as they tacked slowly to windward of the helpless brig.

The larger of the two vessels, her canvas pock-marked by their canister-shot during the dawn engagement, was a topsail schooner. She touched off a memory and Bolitho said, 'I think she was the one I saw leaving harbour when we were at Egmont's house. I recognize her rig.'

'Most probably. Not many of them in these waters.'

Palliser was studying the schooners' methodical approach. One standing well up to windward, the other maneuvring towards the *Rosario*'s larboard bow where she would be best shielded from her remaining guns. They were sturdy six-pounders, and under Little's skilled supervision could still make a mark on anything which ventured too close.

Palliser handed Bolitho the glass. 'See for yourself.' He walked over to speak with the brig's master and Slade by the compass box.

Bolitho held his breath and steadied the glass on the nearest schooner. She was weather-worn and ill-used, and he could see the many men who were staring across at the defiant, mastless brig. Some were waving their weapons, their jeers and threats lost only in distance.

He thought of the girl in the cabin, what they would do to her, and gripped his hanger so tightly that it hurt his palm.

He heard the brig's master say, 'I can't argue with a King's officer to be sure, but I'll not answer for what may happen!'

And Slade said urgently, 'We'll never hold 'em, sir, and it's not right to put it to the test!'

Palliser's voice was flat and uncompromising. 'What do you suggest? Wait for a miracle perhaps? Pray that *Destiny* will rise from the deep and save all our wretched souls?' He did not conceal his sarcasm or his contempt. 'God damn your eyes, Slade, I'd have expected better from you!'

He turned and saw Bolitho watching the tense little group. 'In about fifteen minutes that cut-throat will try to grapple us. If we drive him off he will stand clear and the both of them will rake us for a while. Then they will try again. And again.'

He waved his arm slowly towards the torn decks and weary, red-eyed seamen. 'Do you see these people holding out?'

Bolitho shook his head. 'No, sir.'

Palliser turned away. 'Good.'

But Bolitho had seen the expression on his face. Relief perhaps, or surprise that someone was agreeing with him in spite of the terrible odds.

Then Palliser said, 'I am going below. I must speak with the prisoners we took from *Heloise.*'

Little said quietly to his friend the boatswain's mate, 'Them stupid clods won't know wot side they be on, eh, Ellis?' They both guffawed as if it was some huge joke.

Jury asked, 'What will we do next?'

Ingrave suggested shakily, 'Parley, sir?'

Bolitho watched the approaching schooner, the expert way her mainsail was being reset to give her a perfect heading for the last half cable.

'We shall meet them as they attempt to board.'

He saw his words moving along the littered deck, the way the seamen gripped their cutlasses and axes and flexed their muscles as if they were already in combat. The brig's men were only hired hands, not professional and disciplined like *Destiny's* people. But the latter were tired, and there were too few of them when set against the threatening mob aboard the schooner. He could hear them now, yelling and jeering, their combined shouts like an animal roar.

If there had been only one vessel they might have managed. Perhaps it would have been better to die with the *Heloise* rather than prolong the agony.

Palliser returned and said, 'Little, stand by the forrard guns. When I so order, fire at will, but make quite certain the shots do no real damage.' He ignored Little's disbelief. 'Next, load the remainder with a double charge of grape and canister. At the moment of coming alongside I want those bastards raked.' He let his words drive home. 'If you lose every man in doing it, I need those guns to fire!'

Little knuckled his forehead, his heavy features grim with understanding at last. The brig's bulwark offered little protection, and with the other vessel grinding alongside to grapple them together, the gun crews could be cut down like reed.

Palliser unclipped his scabbard and tossed it aside. He

sliced his sword through the air and watched the bright sun-light run along the blade like gold.

'It will be warm work today.'

Bolitho swallowed, his mouth horribly dry. He too drew his hanger and removed the leather scabbard as he had seen Palliser do. To lose a fight was bad enough, to die because you had tripped over your scabbard was unthinkable.

Muskets banged across the narrowing strip of water be-tween the two hulls, and several men ducked as the balls struck the timbers or whined menacingly overhead.

Palliser sliced down an imaginary foe with his sword and then said sharply, *'Fire!'*

The leading guns hurled themselves inboard on their tack-les, the smoke billowing back through the ports as their crews did their best to follow Little's orders.

A hole appeared in the schooner's big fore-sail, but the other shots went wide, throwing up spindly waterspouts nearer to the other vessel than the one which was bearing down on them.

There were wild cheers and more shots, and Bolitho bit his lip as a seaman was hurled back from the bulwark, his jaw smashed away by a musket ball.

Palliser called, 'Stand by to repel boarders!'

All at once the long schooner was right there opposite them, and Bolitho could even see his own shadow on her side with those of his companions.

Musket shots whipped past him and he heard another man cry out, the sound of the ball smashing into his flesh making Ingrave cover his face as if to save himself from a similar fate.

The sails were falling away, and as the tide of men surged across the schooner's deck, grapnels soared above them to clatter and then grip the *Rosario*'s hull like iron teeth.

But someone aboard the schooner must have anticipated a last trick from men who could fight like this. Several shots swept through the crouching gun crews and two men fell kicking and screaming, their blood marking their agony until they lay still.

Bolitho glanced quickly at Jury. He was holding his dirk in one hand, a pistol in the other.

Between his teeth Bolitho said, 'Keep with me. Don't lose

your footing. Do what you told me to do.' He saw the wildness in Jury's eyes and added, *'Hold on!'*

There was a great lurch as with a shuddering crash the schooner came hard downwind and continued to drive alongside until the grapnel lines took the strain and held her fast.

'Now!' Palliser pointed with his sword. *'Fire!'*

A gun belched flame and smoke and the full charge exploded in the exact centre of the massed boarders. Blood and limbs flew about in grisly array, and the momentary terror changed to a wild roar of fury as the attackers formed up again and hurled themselves over the side and on to the brig's hull.

Steel scraped on steel, and while a few men tried to fire and reload their muskets, others thrust wildly with pikes, flinging shrieking boarders between the two hulls to be ground there like bloody fenders.

Palliser yelled, *'Another!'*

But Little and his men were cut off on the forecastle, a wedge of slashing, yelling figures already on the deck between them and the remaining unfired cannon. Its crew lay sprawled nearby, either dead or dying Bolitho did not know. But without that final burst of grape and canister they were already beaten.

A seaman crawled towards the gun, a slow-match gripped in one fist, but he fell face down as an attacker vaulted over the bulwark and hacked him across the neck with a boarding axe. But the force of the blow threw him off balance and he slipped helplessly in his victim's blood. Dutchy Vorbink shouldered Jury aside and charged forward, his jaws wide in a soundless oath as he struck the scrambling figure on the head with his cutlass. The blade glanced from his skull, and Bolitho saw an ear lying on the deck even as Vorbink finished the job with a carefully measured thrust.

When he looked again, Bolitho saw Stockdale by the abandoned gun, his shoulder bleeding from a deep cut, but apparently oblivious to it as he swept up the slow-match and jabbed it to the gun.

The explosion was so violent that Bolitho imagined it must have split the barrel. A whole section of the schooner's bulwark had vanished, and amidst the charred woodwork and cut rigging the men who had been waiting their chance to leap across were entwined in a writhing heap.

Palliser yelled, *'At 'em, lads!'* He cut down a running figure and fired his pistol into the press of boarders as the thin line of defenders surged to meet it.

Bolitho was carried forward with the rest, his hanger rasping against a cutlass, the breath burning in his lungs as he parried the blade clear and slashed a wild-eyed man across his chest. A pistol exploded almost in his ear, and he heard Jury cry out to someone to watch his back as two kicking, yelling boarders cut their way through the exhausted seamen.

A pike slid past Bolitho's hip and pinioned a man who had been trying to follow his comrades through the breach. He was still screaming and dragging at the pike with his bloodied fingers as Stockdale loomed out of the throng and killed him with his cutlass.

Midshipman Ingrave was down, holding his head with both hands as the fight-maddened figures lurched over him in a tide of hatred.

Above it all Bolitho heard Palliser's voice. 'To me, my lads!' It was followed by a burst of cheering and wild cries, and with amazement he saw a tightly packed crowd of men surge through the companionway and forward hatch to join Palliser amidships, their bared blades already clashing with the surprised boarders.

'Drive 'em back!' Palliser pushed through his men, and this seemed to inflame them to greater efforts.

Bolitho saw a shadow waver towards him and struck out with all his strength. The man coughed as the hanger's blade took him right across the stomach and fell to his knees, his fingers knitted across the terrible wound as the cheering sailors blundered over him.

It could not be happening, but it was. Certain defeat had changed to a renewed attack, and the enemy were already falling back in a broken rout as the wave of men charged into them.

Bolitho understood that they must be the prisoners, the *Heloise*'s original crew, which Palliser had released and had put to his own use. But it was all confused in his mind as he cut and thrust with the rest, his shoulder knotted in pain, his sword-arm like solid lead. Palliser must have offered them something, as Dumaresq had done for their master, in exchange for their aid. Several had already fallen, but their sudden arrival had put back the heart into the *Destiny*'s men.

He realized too that some of the pirates had gone over the side, and when he lowered his guard for the first time he saw that the lines had been severed and the schooner was already drifting clear.

Bolitho let his arm fall to his side and stared at the other vessel spreading her sails and using the wind to stand away from the mastless, blood-stained but victorious brig.

Men were cheering and slapping each other on the back. Others ran to help their wounded companions, or called the names of friends who would never be able to answer.

One of the pirates who had been feigning death ran for the bulwark when he finally realized his own vessel was breaking off the battle. It was Olsson's moment. With great care he drew a knife from his belt and threw it. It was like a streak of light, and Bolitho saw the running man spin round, his eyes wide with astonishment as the haft quivered between his shoulders.

Little jerked out the knife and tossed it to the pale-eyed Swede. 'Catch!' Then he picked up the corpse and pitched it over the bulwark.

Palliser walked the length of the deck, his sword over his shoulder where it made a red stain on his coat.

Bolitho met his gaze and said huskily, 'We did it, sir. I never thought it would work.'

Palliser watched the released prisoners handing back their weapons and staring at each other as if stunned by what they had done.

'Nor I, as a matter of fact.'

Bolitho turned and saw Jury tying a bandage round Ingrave's head. They had survived.

He asked, 'D'you think they'll attack again?'

Palliser smiled. 'We have no masts. But they have, with the masthead lookouts who can see far further than we. I have no doubt we owe our victory to more than a momentary and unorthodox ruse.'

Palliser, as always, was right. Within the hour *Destiny*'s familiar pyramid of sails was etched against the horizon in bright sunshine. They were no longer alone.

10

No Childish Desire

The *Destiny*'s stern cabin seemed unnaturally large and remote after the embattled brig.

In spite of what he had endured, Bolitho felt wide awake, and wondered what had given him this renewal of energy.

All day the frigate had been hove to with the mastless *Rosario* wallowing in her lee. While the rest of Palliser's party and the wounded had been ferried across to *Destiny*, other boats had been busy carrying men and material to help the brig's company set up a jury-rig and complete minimum repairs to take them into port.

Dumaresq sat at his table, a litter of papers and charts scattered before him, all of which Palliser had brought from the *Rosario*. He was without his coat, and, sitting in his shirt, his neckcloth loosely tied, he looked anything but a frigate captain.

He said, 'You did well, Mr Palliser.' He looked up, his widely spaced eyes turning on Bolitho. 'You also.'

Bolitho thought of that other time when he and Palliser had been demolished by Dumaresq's scathing attack.

Dumaresq pushed the papers aside and leaned back in the chair. 'Too many dead men. *Heloise* gone, too.' He brushed the thought aside. 'But you did the *right* thing, Mr Palliser, and it was bravely done.' He gave a grin. 'I will send *Heloise*'s people with the *Rosario*. From what we have discovered, it would seem that their part in all this was of no importance. They were hired or bribed aboard the brigantine,

137

and by the time they realized they were not going on some short coastal passage they were well out to sea. Their master, Triscott, and his mates, took care to ensure they remained in ignorance. So we'll release them into *Rosario*'s care.' He wagged a finger at his first lieutenant. '*After* you have selected and sworn in any good hands you can use to replace those lost. A spell in the King's service will make a lively change for them.'

Palliser reached out and took a glass of wine as Dumaresq's servant hovered discreetly beside his chair.

'What of Egmont, sir?'

Dumaresq sighed. 'I have ordered that he and his wife be brought across before nightfall. Lieutenant Colpoys has them in his charge. But I wanted Egmont to remain to the last moment so that he could see what his greed and treachery has cost the brig's company as well as my own.' He looked at Bolitho. 'Our plump surgeon has already told me about the vessel you both saw leaving Rio with such stealth. Egmont was safe while he lay hidden, but whoever gave the order for the *Rosario* to be waylaid and seized *wanted him dead*. According to the brig's charts, her final destination was St Christopher's. Egmont was prepared to pay the master anything to take him there, even to avoid his other ports of call in order that he should reach St Christopher's without delay.' He gave a slow smile. 'So that is where Sir Piers Garrick will be.' He nodded as if to emphasize his confidence. 'The hunt is almost over. With Egmont's sworn evidence, and he has no choice left now, we shall run that damn pirate to earth once and for all.' He saw Bolitho's open curiosity and added, 'The Caribbean has seen the making of much wealth. Pirates, honest traders, slavers and soldiers of fortune, they are all there. And where better for *old enemies* to simmer undisturbed?'

He became business-like again. 'Complete this coming and going without too much delay, Mr Palliser. I have advised *Rosario* to return to Rio. Her master will be able to relate his tale to the Viceroy, whereas I was unable to tell mine. He will know that a guise of neutrality must not be so one-sided in future.' As Palliser and Bolitho stood up he said, 'I am afraid we are short of fresh water because of my hasty departure. Mr Codd was able to get all the yams, greens and meat he could desire, but water will have to be found elsewhere.'

Outside the cabin Palliser said, 'You are temporarily relieved of your duties. Even extreme youth has a limit. Go to your quarters and rest while you can.' He saw Bolitho's uncertainty. 'Well?'

'I—I was wondering. What will become of Egmont?' He tried to keep his voice unconcerned. 'And his wife?'

'Egmont was a fool. By remaining quiet he aided Garrick. Garrick was trying to help the French at Martinique against us, and that makes Egmont's silence all the more serious. However, if he has any sense he will tell the captain all he knows. But for us he'd be dead. He'll be thinking of that just now.'

He turned to leave, his movements showing little of the strain he had been under. He was still wearing his old seagoing coat which now had the additional distinction of a blood-stain on one shoulder where he had rested his sword.

Bolitho said, 'I should like to put Stockdale's name forward for advancement, sir.'

Palliser came back and lowered his head to peer at Bolitho beneath a deck-beam.

'Would you indeed?'

Bolitho sighed. It sounded rather like the old Palliser again.

But Palliser said, 'I've already done that. Really, Mr Bolitho, you'll have to think more quickly than that.'

Bolitho smiled, despite the ache in his limbs and the confusion in his thoughts which the girl named Aurora had roused with a kiss.

He entered the wardroom, his body swaying to the frigate's heavier motion.

Poad greeted him like a warrior.

'Sit you down, sir! I'll fetch something to eat and drink.' He stood back and beamed at him. 'Right glad we are to see you again, sir, an' that's the truth!'

Bolitho lay back in a chair and allowed the drowsiness to flow over him. Above and around him the ship was alive with bustling feet and the clatter of tackle.

A job had to be done, and the seamen and marines were used to obeying orders and holding their private thoughts to themselves. Across the darkening water the brig was also busy with working sailors. Tomorrow the *Rosario* would make her way towards safety, where her story would be retold a thousand times. And they would speak of the quiet Englishman with the beautiful young wife who had lived amongst them for years, keeping to themselves and outwardly content with their self-imposed exile. And of the frigate with her grotesque captain which had come to Rio and had slunk away in the night like an assassin.

Bolitho stared up at the deck head, listening to the ship's noises and the sounds of the ocean against her hull. He was privileged. He was right in the midst of it, of the conspiracy and the treachery, and very soon now *she* would be here, too.

When Poad returned with a plate of fresh meat and a jug of madeira he found the lieutenant fast asleep. His legs were out-thrust, the breeches and stockings torn and stained with what appeared to be blood. His hair was plastered across his forehead and there was a bruise on his hand, the one which had been gripping his hanger at the start of the day.

Asleep, the third lieutenant looked even younger, Poad thought. Young, and for these rare moments of peace, defenceless.

Bolitho walked slowly up and down the quarterdeck, avoiding flaked lines and the mizzen bitts without conscious effort. It was sunset and a full day since they had parted company with the battered *Rosario* to leave her far astern. She had looked forlorn and as mis-shapen as any cripple with her crude jury-rig and such a sparse display of sails it would take her several days to reach port.

Bolitho glanced aft at the poop skylight and saw the glow of lanterns reflecting on the driver-boom above it. He tried to picture the dining cabin with her there and the captain sharing his table with his two guests. How would she feel now? How much had she known from the beginning, he wondered?

Bolitho had seen her only briefly when she had been brought across from the brig with her husband and a small mountain of luggage. She had seen him watching from the gangway and had made to raise one gloved hand, but the gesture had changed to less than a shrug. A mark of submission, even despair.

He looked up at the braced yards, the topsails growing darker against the pale fleecy clouds which had been with them for most of the day. They were steering north-north-east and standing well out from the land to avoid prying eyes or another would-be follower.

The watch on deck were doing their usual rounds to inspect the trim of the yards and the tautness of running and standing rigging alike. From below he heard the plaintive scrape of the shantyman's fiddle, the occasional murmur of voices as the hands waited for their evening meal.

Bolitho paused in his restless pacing and grasped the nettings to steady himself against the ship's measured roll and plunge. The sea was already much darker to larboard, the swell in half shadow as it cruised slowly towards their quarter to lift *Destiny*'s stern and then roll beneath her keel in endless procession.

He looked along the upper deck at the regularly spaced guns lashed firmly behind the sealed ports, through the black shrouds and other rigging to the figurehead's pale shoulder. He shivered, imagining it to be Aurora reaching out like that, but for him and not the horizon.

Somewhere a man laughed, and he heard Midshipman Lovelace reprimanding one of the watch who was probably old enough to be his father. It sounded even funnier in his high-pitched voice, Bolitho thought. Lovelace had been awarded extra duties by Palliser for skylarking during the dog-watches when he should have been pondering on his navigational problems.

Bolitho recalled his own early efforts to study, to keep awake and learn the hard-won lessons laid down by his sailing master. It all seemed so long ago. The darkness of the smelly orlop and the midshipman's berth, trying to read the figures and calculations by the flickering light of a glim set in an old oyster shell.

And yet it was no time at all. He studied the vibrating canvas and marvelled at the short period it had taken to make so great a step. Once he had stood almost frozen with fear at the prospect of being left alone in charge of a watch. Now he felt confident enough, but knew if the time came he would and must call the captain. But no one else. He could not turn any more to seek out his lieutenant or some stalwart master's mate for aid or advice. Those days were gone, unless or until he committed some terrible error which would strip him of all he had gained.

Bolitho found himself examining his feelings more closely. He had been afraid when he had believed he was going to go down, trapped below decks in the *Heloise*. Perhaps the closest to terror he had ever been. And yet he had seen action before, plenty of times, even as a twelve-year-old midshipman in his first ship he had gritted his teeth against the thunder of the old *Manxman*'s massive broadside.

In his cot, with the flimsy screen door of his cabin shut to the rest of the world, he had thought about it, wondered how his companions saw and judged him.

They never seemed to worry beyond the moment. Colpoys, bored and disdainful, Palliser, unbreakable and ever-watchful over the ship's affairs. Rhodes appeared carefree enough, so perhaps his own ordeal in the *Heloise* and then aboard the brig had made a deeper impression than he had thought.

He had killed or wounded several men, and had watched others hack down their enemies with apparent relish. But surely you could never get used to it? The smell of a man's breath against your own, the feel of his body heat as he tried to break your guard. His triumph when he thought you were falling, his horror as you drove your blade into muscle and bone.

One of the two helmsmen said, 'Steady as she goes, sir. Nor'-nor'-east.'

He turned in time to see the captain's thickset shadow emerging from the companionway.

Dumaresq was a heavy man but had the stealth of a cat.

'All quiet, Mr Bolitho?'

'Aye, sir.' He could smell the brandy and guessed the captain had just finished his dinner.

'A long haul yet.' Dumaresq tilted on his heels to study the sails and the first faint stars. He changed the subject and asked, 'Are you recovered from your little battle?'

Bolitho felt stripped naked. It was as if Dumaresq had been reading into his very thoughts.

'I think so, sir.'

Dumaresq persisted. 'Frightened, were you?'

'Part of the time.' He nodded, remembering the weight

across his back, the roar of water through the deck below where he had been trapped.

'A good sign.' Dumaresq nodded. 'Never become too hard. Like cheap steel, you'll snap if you do.'

Bolitho asked carefully, 'Will we be carrying the passengers all the way, sir?'

'To St Christopher's at least. There I intend to enlist the governor's aid and have word sent to our senior officer there or at Antigua.'

'The treasure, sir. Is there still a chance of recovering it?'

'Some of it. But I suspect we may recognize it in a very different form from that originally intended. There is a smell of rebellion in the air. It has been growing and smouldering since the end of the war. Sooner or later our old enemies will strike at us again.' He turned and stared at Bolitho as if trying to make up his mind. 'I read something of your brother's recent success when I was at Plymouth. Against another of Garrick's breed, I believe? He caught and destroyed a man who was fleeing to America, a man once respected but who proved to be as rotten as any common felon.'

Bolitho replied quietly, 'Aye, sir. I was there with him.'

'Indeed?' Dumaresq chuckled. 'There was no mention of *that* in the Gazette. Your brother wanted all the glory for himself perhaps?'

He turned away before Bolitho could ask of the connection, if there was one, between the dash down the Channel just a few months back and the mysterious Sir Piers Garrick.

But Dumaresq said, 'I am going to play cards with Mr Egmont. The surgeon has agreed to partner him, whereas I shall have our gallant marine for mine.' He gave a rich chuckle. 'We might empty one of Egmont's money-boxes before we drop anchor off Basseterre!'

Bolitho sighed and walked slowly to the quarterdeck rail. Half an hour and the watch would change. A few words with Rhodes, then down to the wardroom.

He heart Yeames, master's mate of the watch, murmur with unusual politeness, 'Why, good *evenin'*, ladies.'

Bolitho swung round, his heart pounding in immediate response as he saw her moving carefully along the side of the quarterdeck, her arm entwined with that of her maid.

He saw her hesitate and was of two minds what to do next.
'Let me assist you.'

Bolitho crossed the deck and took her proffered hand.
Through the glove he felt the warmth of her fingers, the
smallness of her wrist.

'Come to the weather side, ma'am. There is less spray and
a far better view.'

She did not resist as he led her up the sloping deck to the
opposite side. Then he pulled out his handkerchief and bound
it quickly round the hammock nettings.

He explained as calmly as he could that it was to protect
her glove from tar or any other shipboard substance.

She held herself close to the nettings and stared abeam
across the dark water. Bolitho could smell her fragrant perfume, just as he was very aware of her nearness.

Then she said, 'A long way to St Christopher's Island, is it
not?' She had turned to look at him but her eyes were in
shadow.

'It will take us over two weeks, according to Mr Gulliver,
ma'am. It is a good three thousand miles.'

He saw her teeth white in the gloom, but did not know if
she was showing dismay or impatience.

'A *good* three thousand miles, Lieutenant?' Then she nodded. 'I understand.'

Through the open skylight Bolitho heard Dumaresq's deep
laugh and Colpoys saying something in reply. Dealing his
cards, no doubt.

She had heard too and said quickly to her maid, 'You may
leave us. You have worked hard today.'

She watched the girl reaching for the companionway and
added, 'She has lived all her life on hard dry land. This ship
must be strange to her.'

Bolitho asked, 'What will you do? Will you be safe after
all that has happened?'

She tilted her head as Dumaresq laughed again. 'That will
depend on *him*.' She looked past Bolitho, her eyes shining
like the spray alongside as she asked, 'Does it matter so much
to you?'

Bolitho said, 'You know it does. I care terribly.'

'You do?' She reached out and gripped his arm with her

free hand. 'You are a kind boy.' She felt him stiffen and added gently, 'I apologize. You are a man to have done what you did back there when I thought I was going to be killed.'

Bolitho smiled. 'I am the one to apologize. I want you to like me so much that I act like a fool.'

She twisted round and moved closer to look at him. 'You mean it. I can tell that, if nothing else.'

'If only you could have remained in Rio.' Bolitho was searching his mind for some solution which might help. 'Your husband should not have risked your life.'

She shook her head, the movement of her hair striking at Bolitho's heart like a dagger.

'He has been good to me. Without him I would have been lost long ago. I was a stranger in Rio. I am of Spanish blood. When my parents died I was to have been bought as a wife by a Portuguese trader.'

She gave a shudder. 'I was only thirteen. He was like a greasy pig!'

Bolitho felt betrayed. 'Was it not love which made you marry your husband?'

'Love?' She tossed her head. 'I do not find men very attractive, you know. So I was content with his arrangements for me. Like his many fine possessions, I think he sees me as a decoration.' She opened the shawl which she had carried on deck. 'Like this bird, yes?'

Bolitho saw the same two-headed bird with the ruby tail feathers she had worn at her house in Rio.

He said fervently, 'I love you!'

She tried to laugh but nothing came. She said, 'I suspect you know even less about loving than I do.' She reached up and touched his face. 'But you meant what you said. I am sorry if I hurt you.'

Bolitho grasped her hand and pressed it firmly against his cheek. She had not laughed or piled scorn on him for his clumsy advances.

He said, 'You will be left in peace soon.'

She sighed. 'And then you will come like a knight on your charger to save me, yes? I used to dream of such things when I was a child. Now I think as a woman.'

She pulled his hand down and pressed it against her skin,

so that the warmth of the jewelled bird on his fingers was like a part of her.

'Do you feel that?' She was watching him intently.

He could feel the urgent beat of her heart rising to match his own as he touched the smooth skin and the firm curve of her breast.

'That is no childish desire.' She made to move away but when he held her she said, 'What is the use? We are not alone to act as we please. If my husband thinks I am betraying him, he will refuse to help your captain.' She put her hand on his lips. 'Hear me! Dear Richard, do you not see what that would mean? My husband thrown into some English prison to await trial and death. I, as his wife, might be taken also, or left destitute to await another Portuguese trader, or worse.' She waited for him to release her and then murmured, 'But do not think I would not or could not love you.'

Voices echoed along the deck and Bolitho heard a boat-swain's mate calling out names as the watch trooped aft to relieve his own men.

In those few seconds Bolitho found himself hating the boatswain's mate with all his soul.

He exclaimed, 'I must see you again.'

She was already making her way to the opposite side, her slim outline like a ghost against the dark water beyond.

'Three thousand miles you said, Lieutenant? It is such a long way. Each day will be torture.' She hesitated and glanced back at him. 'For both of us.'

Rhodes clattered up through the companionway and stood aside to let her pass. He nodded to Bolitho and remarked, 'A beauty indeed.' He seemed to sense Bolitho's mood, that he was prepared to be hostile if he mentioned her again.

He added, 'That was clumsy of me. Stupid, too.'

Bolitho pulled him to one side, oblivious of the watch mustering beyond the quarterdeck rail.

'I am in hell, Stephen! I can tell no one else. It is driving me mad.'

Rhodes was deeply moved by Bolitho's sincerity and by the fact he was sharing his secret with him.

He said, 'We shall think of something.' It sounded so unconvincing in the face of his friend's despair that he said, 'A lot can happen before we sight St. Christopher's.'

The master's mate touched his hat. 'The watch is aft, sir.'

Bolitho walked to the companionway and paused with one foot on the ladder. Her perfume was still hanging there, or if not it must be clinging to his coat.

Aloud he exclaimed, 'What can I do?'

But the only answer came from the sea and the rumble of the rudder beneath Dumaresq's cabin.

The first week of the *Destiny*'s passage passed swiftly enough, with several blustery squalls to keep the hands busy and to hold back the scorching heat.

Up and around Cabo Branco then north-west for the Spanish Main and the Indies. There were longer periods of low breezes, and some of no wind at all when the boats were put down and the gruelling work of warping the ship by muscle and sweat was enforced.

Fresh water ran lower as a direct consequence, and with neither rain nor the prospect of an early landfall it was rationed. After a week it was cut further still to a pint a day per man.

During his daily watches under the blazing sun, Bolitho saw very little of Egmont's wife. He told himself it was for her good as well as his own. There were troubles enough to contend with. Outbreaks of insubordination which ended in fists and kicks or the use of a petty officer's starter. But Dumaresq refrained from having any of his men flogged, and Bolitho wondered if it was because he was eager to keep the peace or holding his hand for his passengers' benefit.

Bulkley was showing signs of anxiety, too. Three men had gone down with scurvy. In spite of his care and the regular issue of fruit juce, the surgeon was unable to prevent it.

Once, while he had been lingering in the shadow of the big driver, Bolitho had heard Dumaresq's voice through the cabin skylight, dismissing Bulkley's pleas, even blaming him for not taking better precautions for his sick seamen.

Bulkley must have been examining the chart, because he had protested, 'Why not Barbados, Captain? We could anchor off Bridgetown and arrange for fresh water to be brought to us. What we have left is crawling with vermin, and I'll not answer for the people's health if you insist on driving them like this!'

'God damn your eyes, sir! I'll tell you who you shall answer to, believe me! I'll not go to Barbados and shout to the whole world what we are doing. You attend to your duties and I shall do the same!'

And there it had ended.

Seventeen days after parting from the *Rosario* the wind found them again, and with even her studding-sails set *Destiny* gathered way like the thoroughbred she was.

But perhaps it was already too late to prevent some kind of explosion. It was like a chain reaction. Slade, the master's mate, still brooding over Palliser's contempt, and knowing it would likely hinder, even prevent any chance of promotion, poured abuse on Midshipman Merrett for failing to calculate the ship's noon position correctly. Merrett had overcome his early timidity, but he was only twelve years old. To be berated so harshly in front of several hands and the two helmsmen were more than enough for him. He burst into tears.

Rhodes was officer of the watch and could have intervened. Instead he remained by the weather side, his hat tilted against the sun, his ears deaf to Merrett's outburst.

Bolitho was below the mainmast watching some of his topmen reeving a new block at the topgallant yard and heard most of it.

Stockdale was with him, and muttered, 'It's like an overloaded waggon, sir. Somethin's got to give.'

Merrett dropped his hat and was rubbing his eyes with his knuckles when a seaman picked up the hat and handed it to him, his eyes angry as he glanced at the master's mate.

Slade yelled, 'How dare you interfere between your betters?'

The seaman, one of the after-guard, retorted hotly, 'Dammit, Mr Slade, 'e's doin' 'is best! It's bad enough for the bloody rest of us, let alone fer 'im!'

Slade seemed to go purple.

He screamed, 'Master-at-arms! Secure that man!' He turned on the quarterdeck at large. 'I'll see his backbone at the gratings!'

Poynter and the ship's corporal arrived and seized the defiant seaman.

The latter showed no sign of relenting. 'Like Murray, eh?

A good 'and an' a loyal shipmate, and they was goin' to flog 'im, too!'

Bolitho heard a growl of agreement from the men around him.

Rhodes came out of his torpor and called, 'Pipe down there! What's going on?'

Slade said, 'This man defied me, and swore at me, so he did!' He was becoming dangerously calm and glaring at the seaman as if he would strike him dead.

Rhodes said uncertainly, 'In that case . . .'

'In *that* case, Mr Rhodes, have the man put in irons. I'll have no defiance in my ship.'

Dumaresq had appeared as if by magic.

Slade swallowed and said, 'This man was interfering, sir.'

'I heard you.' Dumaresq thrust his hands behind his back. 'As did the whole ship, I would imagine.' He glanced at Merrett and snapped, 'Stop snivelling, boy!'

The midshipman stopped, like a clock, and looked about him with embarrassment.

Dumaresq eyed the seaman and added, 'That was a costly gesture, Adams. A dozen lashes.'

Bolitho knew that Dumaresq could do nothing but uphold his subordinates, right or wrong, and a dozen lashes was minimal, just a headache, the old hands would term it.

But an hour later, as the lash rose and then cracked with terrible force across the man's naked back, Bolitho realized just how frail was their hold over the ship's company with land so far away.

The gratings were unrigged, the man named Adams was carried below grunting with pain to be revived with a wash-down of salt water and a liberal dose of rum. The spots of blood were swabbed away, and to all intents everything was as before.

Bolitho had relieved Rhodes in charge of the watch, and heard Dumaresq say to the master's mate, 'Discipline is upheld. For all our sakes.' He fixed Slade with his compelling stare. 'For your own safety, I would suggest you stay out of my way!'

Bolitho turned aside so that Slade should not see him watching. But he had seen Slade's face. Like that of a man who had been expecting a reprieve only to feel his arms being pinioned by the hangman.

All that night Bolitho thought about the girl named Aurora. It was impossible to get near her. She had been given half of the stern cabin, while Egmont made the best of a cot in the dining space. Dumaresq slept in the chartroom nearby, and there was always the servant and the marine sentry to prevent any casual caller from entering.

As he lay in his cot, his naked body sweating in the unmoving air, Bolitho pictured himself entering her cabin and holding her in his arms. He groaned at the torment, and tried to ignore the thirst which had left his mouth like a kiln. The water was foul and in short supply, and to keep drinking wine as a substitute was inviting disaster.

He heard uncertain footsteps in the wardroom and then a gentle tap on his screen door.

Bolitho rolled out of the cot, groping for his shirt as he asked, 'Who is it?'

It was Spillane, the captain's new clerk. Despite the hour he was neat and tidy, and his shirt looked as if it had just been washed, although how he had managed it was a mystery.

Spillane said politely, 'I have a message for you, sir.' He was looking at Bolitho's tousled hair and casual nakedness as he continued, 'From the lady.'

Bolitho darted a quick glance around the wardroom. Only the regular creaks and groans of the ship's timbers and the occasional murmur of canvas from above broke the silence.

He found he was whispering. 'Where is it, then?'

Spillane replied, 'By word of mouth, sir. She'd not put pen to paper.'

Bolitho stared. Now Spillane was a conspirator whether he wanted to be or not.

'Go on.'

Spillane lowered his voice further still. 'You take over the morning-watch at four o'clock, sir.' His precise, landsman's expression made him seem even more out of place here.

'Aye.'

'The lady will endeavour to come on deck. For a breath of air, if someone is bold enough to question her.'

'Is that all?'

'It is, sir.' Spillane was watching him closely in the faint light from a shuttered lantern. 'Did you expect more?'

Bolitho glanced at him guardedly. Was that last remark a show of familiarity, a testing insolence because of their shared conspiracy? Maybe Spillane was nervous, eager to get it over with.

He said, 'No. Thank you for telling me.'

Bolitho stood for a long moment, his body swaying to the motion, as he went over everything Spillane had said.

Later, he was still in the wardroom, sitting in a chair, the same shirt dangling from his fingers as he stared into the shadows.

A boatswain's mate found him and whispered, 'I see you don't need a call, sir. The watch is musterin' now. Fair breeze up top, but another blazin' day is my guess.'

He stood back as Bolitho pulled on his breeches and fumbled around for a clean shirt. The lieutenant was obviously half asleep still, he decided. It was a cruel waste to don any clean garment for the morning-watch. It would be a wet rag by six bells.

Bolitho followed the man on deck and relieved Midshipman Henderson with the briefest possible delay. Henderson was next in line for lieutenant's examination and Palliser had allowed him to stand the middle-watch on his own.

The midshipman almost fled from the deck, and Bolitho could well imagine his thoughts as he tumbled into his hammock on the orlop. His first watch alone. Reliving it. What had nearly gone wrong, when he had nearly decided to rouse Palliser or the master. The feeling of triumph as Bolitho had appeared, knowing the watch was ended without mishap.

Bolitho's men settled down in the shadows, and after checking the compass and the set of the topsails he walked towards the companionway.

Midshipman Jury crossed to the weather side and wondered when he would get his chance to stand a watch unaided. He turned and saw Bolitho moving aft by the mizzen-mast, and then blinked as another pale figure glided to meet him.

He heard the helmsmen whispering together and noticed that the boatswain's mate of the watch had moved discreetly to the weather gangway.

'Watch your helm there!' Jury saw the seamen stiffen at the great double-wheel. Beyond them the two pale figures seemed to have merged into one.

Jury walked to the quarterdeck rail and gripped it with both hands.

To all intents he *was* standing his first watch unaided, he thought happily.

11

A Close Thing

Under topsails, forecourse and jib only, the *Destiny* headed slowly towards the green humpbacked island. So gentle was the breeze that her progress was a snail's pace, an impression which grew as she approached the small ridge of land.

The masthead had sighted it the previous day, just before dusk, and throughout the night-watches until the break of dawn there had been a buzz of speculation from wardroom to messdeck.

Now, in the harsh forenoon sunlight it lay across their bows and shimmered in a low haze, as if it might vanish at any second like a mirage.

It was higher towards its centre, where thick clusters of palms and other foliage were bunched together, to leave the slopes and the tiny, crescent-shaped beaches totally devoid of cover.

'Deep six!'

The hollow chant from a leadsman in the chains reminded Bolitho of the shallows nearby, the hint of a reef lying to starboard. A few sea-birds dotted the water, and others cruised watchfully around the topgallant mastheads.

Bolitho heard Dumaresq conferring with Palliser and the master. The island was marked on the chart but apparently unclaimed. The known survey was poor, and Dumaresq was probably regretting his impulse to touch land in search for water.

But the ship was down to her last barricoes of water, and

the contents were so vile that Bulkley and the purser had joined forces in another plea to the captain for him to seek a new supply. Enough at least to take them to their destination.

'By th' mark seven!'

Gulliver tried to relax his stance as the keel glided into deeper water. The ship was still standing two cables clear of the nearest beach. If the wind rose or changed direction, *Destiny* might be in trouble, with no depth at all to beat free of the land and out-thrust reef.

Every man but the cook and the sick ones in Bulkley's care was on deck or clinging to the shrouds and ratlines, strangely silent as they peered towards the little island. It was one of hundreds in the Caribbean, but the hint of fresh, drinkable water made it appear special and priceless.

'By th' mark five!'

Dumaresq grimaced at Palliser. 'Hands wear ship. Stand by to anchor, if you please.'

With her sails barely flapping in the intense heat, the frigate turned wearily on the blue water until the order to let go was yelled along the deck. The anchor splashed down, pushing great circles away from the bows and churning up pale sand from the bottom.

Once anchored the heat seemed to force into the ship still more, and as Bolitho made his way to the quarterdeck he saw Egmont and his wife standing right aft by the taffrail, sheltering beneath a canvas awning which George Durham, the sailmaker, had rigged for them.

Dumaresq was studying the island slowly and methodically with the signal midshipman's big telescope.

He remarked, 'No smoke, or signs of life. Can't see any marks on the beach either, so there aren't any boats on this side.' He handed the glass to Palliser. 'That ridge looks promising, eh?'

Gulliver said, cautiously, 'Could be water there, right enough, sir.'

Dumaresq ignored him and turned instead to his two passengers. 'Might be able to stretch your legs ashore before we weigh.' He chuckled.

He had addressed both of them, but Bolitho somehow knew that his words had been aimed at the woman.

He thought of that one moment when she had come on

deck to see him. It had been unreal but precious. Dangerous, and all the more exciting because of it.

They had spoken very little. All through the following day Bolitho had thought about it, relived it, hung on to each moment for fear of losing something.

He had held her close to his body while the ship had ploughed into the first misty light of dawn, feeling her heart beat against his, wanting to touch her and afraid he would spoil it with his boldness. She had freed herself from his arms and had kissed him lightly on the mouth before merging with the remaining shadows to leave him alone.

And now, just to hear Dumaresq's casual familiarity towards her, his mention of stretching her legs, was like a barb, a spur of jealousy which he had never known before.

Dumaresq broke his thoughts. 'You will take a landing-party, Mr Bolitho. Determine if there is a stream or any useful rock pools. I will await your signal.'

He walked aft, and Bolitho heard him speaking again with Egmont and Aurora.

Bolitho flinched. He saw Jury watching him and imagined for an instant he had again spoken her name aloud.

Palliser snapped, 'Get a move on. If there is no water, we'd best know about it quickly.'

Colpoys was standing languidly by the mizzen. 'I will send some of my fellows as pickets, if you wish.'

Palliser exclaimed, 'Hell's teeth, we're not expecting a pitched battle!'

The cutter was hoisted outboard and lowered alongside. Stockdale, now promoted to gun-captain, was already detailing some hands for the shore-party, while the boat's coxswain supervised the loading of extra tackle for the water-barricoes should they require them.

Bolitho waited until the boat was manned and then reported to Palliser. He saw the girl watching him, the way one hand was resting on her necklace, remembering perhaps, or reminding him that his had once lain there.

Palliser said, 'Take a pistol. Fire if you find anything.' His eyes narrowed against the fierce glare. 'Once the casks are filled they'll discover something else to grumble about!'

The cutter pulled away from the side, and Bolitho felt the

sun burn across his neck as they left the *Destiny*'s protective shadow.

'Give way all!'

Bolitho trailed his arm over the side, feeling the sensual touch of cool water, and imagined her with him, swimming and then running hand in hand up the pale beach to discover each other for the first time.

When he looked over the gunwale he saw the bottom quite clearly, dotted with white stones or shells, and isolated humps of coral, deceptively harmless in the shimmering reflections.

Stockdale said to the coxswain, 'Looks like nobody's ever been 'ere, Jim.'

The man eased the tiller-bar and nodded, the movement bringing a trickle of sweat from under his tarred hat.

'Easy all! Bowman, boat yer oar!'

Bolitho watched the cutter's shadow rising to meet them as the bowman vaulted over the side to guide the stem into the sand while the others hauled their blades inboard and hung panting over the looms like old men.

And then there was total stillness. Just a far-off murmur of surf on a reef, the occasional gurgle of water around the grounded cutter. No bird lifted from the crowded hump of palms, not even an insect.

Bolitho climbed over the gunwale and waded to the beach. He was wearing an open shirt and breeches, but his body felt as if he was dressed in thick furs. The thought of tearing off his crumpled clothing and running naked into the sea mingled with his earlier fantasy, and he wondered if she was watching from the ship, using a telescope to see him.

Bolitho realized with a start that the others were waiting.

He said to the coxswain, 'Remain with the boat. The crew, too. They may have to do several journeys yet.' To Stockdale he said, 'We'll take the others up the slope. It's the shortest way and probably the coolest.'

He ran his eye over the small landing-party. Two of them were from the *Heloise*'s original company, now sworn-in members of His Majesty's Navy. They still appeared dazed at their swift change of circumstances, but they were good enough seamen to avoid the harsher side of the boatswain's tongue.

Apart from Stockdale, there was none of his own division in the group, and he guessed there had been little enthusiasm for volunteering to tramp round an uninhabited island. Later, if they discovered water, it would be very different.

Stockdale said, 'Follow me!'

Bolitho walked up the slope, his feet sinking in the loose sand, the pistol in his belt burning his skin like a piece of hot iron. It felt strange to walk here, he thought. A tiny, unknown place. There might be human bones nearby. Shipwrecked mariners, or men cast adrift and marooned by pirates to die horribly without hope of rescue.

How inviting the palms looked. They were moving gently, and he could hear them rustling as he drew nearer. Once he stopped to look back at the ship. She seemed far away, balanced perfectly on her own reflection. But in distance she had lost her rakish lines, and her masts and loosely furled sails seemed to be swaying and bending in the haze, as if the whole ship was melting.

The small party of seamen tramped gratefully into a patch of shade, their ragged trousers catching in some large fronds which displayed teethlike barbs around the edges. There were different smells here, too, of rotting undergrowth, and from vividly coloured blossoms.

Bolitho looked up at the sky and saw a frigate-bird circling high overhead, its scimitar-shaped wings motionless as it ghosted on the hot current. So they were not completely alone.

A man called excitedly, 'Look yonder, sir! *Water!*'

They pressed forward, all tiredness momentarily forgotten.

Bolitho looked at the pool with disbelief. It was shivering slightly, so he guessed there was some sort of underground source close by. He could see the surrounding palms reflected on its surface and the images of his men as they peered down at the water.

Bolitho said, 'I'll have a taste.'

He clambered along the sandy bank and dipped his hand into the water. It was a false impression, but it felt as cold as a mountain stream. Hardly daring to hope, he raised his cupped hand to his lips and after a slight hesitation swallowed deeply.

He said quietly, 'It's pure.'

Bolitho watched the seamen throwing themselves down on their chests and scooping the water over their faces and shoulders, swallowing great gulps of it in their eager excitement.

Stockdale wiped his mouth with satisfaction. 'Good stuff.'

Bolitho smiled. Josh Little would have called it a 'wet.'

'We'll stand easy a while, then signal the ship.'

The seamen drew their cutlasses and drove them into the sand before squatting down against the palms or leaning over the shimmering water as if to make sure it was still there.

Bolitho walked away from them, and as he examined his pistol to ensure that it was free of sand and damp he thought of that moment when she had joined him on *Destiny's* quarterdeck.

It must not end, it could not be allowed to die.

'Something wrong, sir?' Stockdale lumbered up the slope.

Bolitho realized he must have been frowning in concentration. 'Not wrong.'

It was uncanny how Stockdale always seemed to know, to be ready in case he was needed. Yet it was something very real between them. Bolitho found it easy to talk to the big, hoarse prize-fighter, and the reverse was true also, without any hint of subservience or as a means to gain favour.

Bolitho said, 'You go and make the signal.' He watched the pistol half disappear in Stockdale's great fist. 'I need to think about something.'

Stockdale watched him impassively. 'You're young, an' beggin' yer pardon, sir, I think you should *stay* young for as long as you can.'

Bolitho faced him. You never really knew what Stockdale meant with his brief, halting sentences. Had he implied that he should keep away from a woman who was ten years older than he was? Bolitho refused to think about it. Their life was now, when they could find it. They could worry about differences later.

He said, 'Be off with you. I wish it was that simple.'

Stockdale shrugged and strode down the slope towards the beach, his broad shoulders set in such a way that Bolitho knew he was not going to let it rest there.

With a great sigh Bolitho walked back towards the pool to warn his men that Stockdale was about to fire the pistol.

Sailors cooped up in a ship-of-war often became nervous of such things when they were put ashore.

One of the seamen had been lying with his face half under the water, and as Bolitho approached he stood up dripping and grinning with pleasure.

Bolitho said, 'Be ready, men . . .' He broke off as someone gave a piercing scream and the seaman who had been grinning at him pitched forward into the water.

All at once there was frantic pandemonium amounting to panic as the sailors scrabbled in the sand for their weapons and others stared with horror at the drifting corpse, the water reddening around it from a spear thrust between the shoulders.

Bolitho swung round, seeing the sunlight partially broken by running, leaping figures, the glitter of weapons and a terrifying scream of combined voices which made the hair rise on his neck.

'*Stand to!*'

He groped for his hangar and gasped with shock as another seaman rolled down the slope, kicking and spitting blood as he tried to tug a crude shaft from his belly.

'*Oh, God!*' Bolitho shaded his eyes against the bars of sunlight. Their attackers had it behind them and were closing in on the stampeding seamen, that terrible din of screaming voices making it impossible to think or act.

Bolitho realized they were black men, their eyes and mouths wide with triumph as they hacked down another sailor and pounded his face to a bloody pulp with a piece of coral.

Bolitho ran to meet the attack, dimly aware that more figures were rushing past him as if to separate him from his remaining seamen. He heard someone shrieking and pleading, the sickening sound of a skull splintered open like a coconut.

He found he had his back to a tree and was striking out wildly, wasting his strength, leaving himself open for one of those fire-hardened spears.

Bolitho saw three of his men, one of whom had been wounded in the leg, standing together, hemmed in by screaming, slashing figures.

He pushed himself away from the tree, hacked open a black shoulder with his hanger and bounded across the trampled sand to join the embattled seamen.

One cried, ' 'S'no use! Can't 'old th' buggers!'

Bolitho felt the hanger knocked from his hand and realized he had not fastened the lanyard around his wrist.

He searched desperately for another weapon, seeing that his men were breaking and running towards the beach, the injured one hopping only a few paces before he too was cut down.

Bolitho got a terrifying impression of two staring eyes and bared white teeth, and saw the savage charing towards him, scooping up a discarded cutlass as he came.

Bolitho ducked and tried to leap to one side. Then came the impact, too great for pain, too powerful to measure.

He knew he was falling, his forehead on fire, while in another world he could hear his own voice calling out, brittle with agony.

And then, mercifully, there was nothing.

When consciousness finally returned, the agony which accompanied it was almost unendurable.

Bolitho tried to force open his eyes, as if by doing so he could drive away the torment, but it was so great he could feel his whole body contracting to withstand it.

Voices murmured above his head, but through his partially closed eyes he could see very little. A few hazy shapes, the darker shadows of beams directly overhead.

It was as if his head was being crushed slowly and deliberately between two heated irons, torturing his cringing mind with probing pains and brilliant flashes like lightning.

Cool cloths were being dabbed over his face and neck and then across his body. He was naked, not pinioned by force but with hands touching his wrists and ankles in case he struggled.

Another thought made him cry out with terror. He was badly injured elsewhere than in his head and they were getting ready for him. He had seen it done. The knife glittering in the feeble lanterns, the quick cut and turn of the blade, and then the saw.

'*Easy, son.*'

That was Bulkley, and the fact he was here helped to steady him in some way. Bolitho imagined he could smell the surgeon, brandy and tobacco.

He tried to speak but his voice was a hoarse whisper. 'What happened?'

Bulkley peered over his shoulder, his owl-like face with the little spectacles poised in the air like a comic bladder.

'Save your breath. Breathe slowly.' Bulkley nodded. 'That's it.'

Bolitho gritted his teeth as the pain tightened its hold. It was worst above his right eye where there was a bandage. His hair felt tight, matted with blood. Vaguely the picture re-formed, the bulging eyes, the cutlass swinging towards him. Oblivion.

He asked, 'My men, are they safe?'

Bolitho felt a coat sleeve brush against his bare arm and saw Dumaresq looking down at him, his shape made more grotesque by the angle. The eyes were no longer compelling, but grave.

'The boat's crew are safe. Two of your original party reached it in time.'

Bolitho tried to move his head, but someone held it firmly.

'Stockdale? Is he . . . ?'

Dumaresq smiled. 'He carried you to the beach. But for him all of the people would have been lost. I shall tell you later. Now you must endeavour to rest. You have lost a lot of blood.'

Bolitho could feel the darkness closing over him again. He had seen the quick exchange of glances between Dumaresq and the surgeon. It was not over. He might die. The realization was almost too much and he felt the tears smarting in his eyes as he gasped. 'Don't . . . want . . . to . . . leave . . . *Destiny*. Mustn't . . . go . . . like . . . this.'

Dumaresq said, 'You will recover.'

He rested his hand on Bolitho's shoulder so that he could feel the strength of the man, as if he were transferring some of his power into him.

Then he moved away, and Bolitho realized for the first time that he was in the stern cabin and that beyond the tall windows it was pitch-dark.

Bulkley watched him and said, 'You have been unconscious all day, Richard.' He wagged his finger at him. 'You had me somewhat troubled, I can tell you.'

'Then you are not worried for me now?' Again he tried to move, but the hands gripped him firmly like watchful animals.

Bulkley made a few adjustments to the bandages. 'A severe blow to the head with a heavy blade is never a thing to be scoffed at. I have done some work on you, the rest will depend on time and care. It was a close-run fight. But for Stockdale's courage, and his determination to rescue you, you would be dead.' He glanced round as if to ensure that the captain had gone. 'He rallied the remaining seamen when they were about to flee from the beach. He was like a wild bull, yet when he carried you aboard he did it with the gentleness of a woman.' He sighed. 'It must be the costliest cargo of fresh water in naval history!'

Bolitho could feel a new drowsiness closing in to withstand the pounding anguish in his skull. Bulkley had given him something.

He whispered, 'You would tell me if . . .'

Bulkley was wiping his fingers. 'Probably.' He looked up and added, 'You are being well cared for. We are about to weigh anchor, so endeavour to rest yourself.'

Bolitho tried to keep a grip on his senses. About to weigh anchor. Here all day. So the water must have been obtained. Men had died. Many more afterwards, he thought, when Colpoys' marines took their revenge.

He spoke very slowly, knowing his words were getting slurred, but knowing too that he must make himself understood.

'Tell Aur . . ., tell Mrs Egmont that . . .'

Bulkley leaned over him and pulled at his eyelids. 'Tell her yourself. She has been with you since you were brought aboard. I told you. You are well cared for.'

Then Bolitho saw her standing beside him, her black hair hanging down over either shoulder, glossy in the lantern light.

She touched his face, her fingers brushing his lips as she said softly, 'You can sleep now, my lieutenant. I am here.'

Bolitho felt the hands relax their hold from his wrists and ankles, and sensed the surgeon's assistants withdrawing into the shadows.

He murmured faintly, 'I—I did not want you to see me like this, Aurora.'

She smiled, but it made her look incredibly sad.

'You are beautiful,' she said.

Bolitho closed his eyes, the strength gone from him at last.

By the screen door Bulkley turned to look at them. He should be used to pain and the gratitude of recovery, but he was not, and he was moved by what he saw. It was more like a painting from mythology, he thought. The lovely woman weeping by the fallen body of her hero.

He had not lied to Bolitho. It had been very close, and the cutlass had not only made a deep scar above the eye and into the hairline but had scored the bone beneath. Had Bolitho been an older man, or the cutlass expertly used, it would have ended there.

She said, 'He is asleep.' But she was not speaking to Bulkley. She removed her white shawl and very gently spread it across Bolitho's body, as if his nakedness, like her words, was something private.

In *Destiny*'s other, ordered world a voice bellowed, '*Anchor's aweigh*, sir!'

Bulkley put out a hand to steady himself as the deck tilted to the sudden pressure of wind and rudder. He would go to his sick-bay and have several long drinks. He had no wish to see the island as it fell astern in the dusk. It had given them fresh water, but had taken lives in exchange. Bolitho's party at the pool had been massacred but for Stockdale and two others. Colpoys had reported that the savages who had attacked them were once slaves who had possibly escaped when on passage to an island plantation.

Seeing Bolitho and his men approaching, they had doubt-less imagined they were there to hunt them down and award some brutal reprisal. When *Destiny*'s boats, roused by the pistol-shot from the beach and the sudden panic amongst the cutter's crew, had reached the shore, those same slaves had run towards them. Nobody knew if they had realized *Destiny* was not a 'blackbirder' after all and were trying to make recompense. Colpoys had directed the swivel guns and musketoons which were mounted in each boat to rake the beach. When the smoke had drifted away there had been nobody alive to explain.

Bulkley paused at the top of the ladder and heard the clatter of blocks, the pad of bare feet as the seamen hauled at halliards and braces to set their ship on her true course.

To a man-of-war it was only an interlude. Something to be written up in her log. Until the next challenge, the next fight. He glanced aft at the swaying deckhead lantern and the red-coated sentry beneath it.

And yet, he decided, there had been a lot of worthwhile things, too.

12

Secrets

The days which immediately followed Bolitho's return to the living were like parts of a dream. From the age of twelve, since he had first gone to sea as a midshipman, he had been used to the constant demands of a ship. Night or day, at any hour and under all conditions he had been ready to run with the others to whatever duty was ordered, and had been under no illusions as to the consequences if he failed to obey.

But as *Destiny* sailed slowly northwards through the Caribbean he was forced to accept his inactivity, to remain still and listen to the familiar sounds beyond the cabin or above his head.

The dream was made more than bearable by the presence of Aurora. Even the terrible pain which struck suddenly and without mercy she somehow held at bay, just as she saw through his pitiful attempts to hide it from her.

She would hold his hand or wipe his brow with a damp cloth. Sometimes when the agony probed his skull like a branding iron she put her arm beneath his shoulders and pressed her face to his chest, murmuring secret words into his body as if to still the torment.

He watched her whenever she was in a position where he could see her. While his strength held he described the shipboard sounds, the names of the sailors he knew, and how they worked together to make the ship a living thing.

He told her of his home in Falmouth, of his brother and sisters and the long Bolitho ancestry which was part of the sea itself.

She was always careful not to excite him with questions, and allowed him to talk as long as he felt like it. She fed him, but in such a fashion that he did not feel humiliated or like a helpless child.

Only when the matter of shaving arose was she unable to keep a straight face.

'But, dear Richard, you do not seem to *need* a shave!'

Bolitho flushed, knowing it was true, as he usually shaved but once a week.

She said, 'I will do it for you.'

She used the razor with great care, watching each stroke, and occasionally glancing through the stern windows to see if the ship was on even keel.

Bolitho tried to relax, glad that she imagined his tenseness was out of fear of the razor. In fact, he was more than aware of her nearness, the pressure of her breast as she leaned over him, the exciting touch on his face and throat.

'There.' She stood back and studied him approvingly. 'You look very . . .' she hunted through her vocabulary '. . . distinguished.'

Bolitho asked, 'Could I see, please?' He saw the uncertainty. '*Please.*'

She took a mirror from the cabin chest and said, 'You are strong. You will get over it.'

Bolitho stared at the face in the mirror. It was that of a stranger. The surgeon had sheared away his hair from the right temple, and the whole of his forehead from eyebrow to where the hair remained was black and purple with savage bruising. Bulkley had appeared content when he had removed the dressing and bandages, but to Bolitho's eyes the length and depth of the scar, made more horrific by the black criss-cross of the surgeon's stitches, was repellent.

He said quietly, 'It must sicken you.'

She removed the mirror and said, 'I am proud of you. Nothing could spoil you in my heart. I have stayed with you from that first moment when you were carried here. Have watched over you, so that I know your body like my own.' She met his gaze proudly. 'That scar will remain, but it is one of honour, not of shame!'

Later she left his side in answer to a summons from Dumaresq.

The cabin servant, Macmillan, told Bolitho that *Destiny* was due to sight St Christopher's on the following day, so it seemed likely that the captain was about to clarify Egmont's statement and make certain he would stand by it.

The hunt for the missing bullion, or whatever form it had taken since Garrick's seizure of it, seemed of no importance to Bolitho. He had had plenty of time to think about his future as he sweated in pain or had found recovery in her arms. Perhaps too much time.

The idea of her stepping ashore, to rejoin her husband in whatever new enterprise he dictated, and not to see her ever again, was unbearable.

To mark the progress of his recovery he had several visitors. Rhodes, beaming with pleasure to see him again, unabashed as ever as he said, 'Makes you look like a real terror, Richard. That'll get the doxies jumping when we reach port!' He was careful not to mention Aurora.

Palliser came too and made as close as he knew how to an apology.

'If I had sent a marine picket as Colpoys suggested, none of it would have happened.' He shrugged and glanced round the cabin, at the female attire draped near the windows after being washed by the maid. 'But it apparently has its brighter aspects.'

Bulkley and Dumaresq's clerk supervised the first walk away from the cabin. Bolitho felt the ship responding beneath his bare feet, but knew his weakness, the dizziness which never seemed far away, no matter how hard he tried to conceal it.

He cursed Spilláne and his medical knowledge when he said, 'Might be a severe fracture there, sir?'

Bulkley replied gruffly, 'Nonsense. But still, it's early days.'

Bolitho had expected to die, but with recovery apparently within his grasp it seemed unthinkable there was yet another course he might have to take. To be sent home in the next available ship, to be removed from the Navy List and not even retained on half-pay to give some hope of re-employment.

He wished he could have thanked Stockdale, but even his influence had so far failed to get him past the sentry at the door.

All the midshipmen, with the noticeable exception of Cowdroy, had been to visit him, and had stared at his terrible scar with a mixture of awe and commiseration. Jury had been quite unable to hide his admiration and had exclaimed, 'To think that I cried like a baby over my pin-prick!'

It was late evening before she returned to the cabin, and he sensed the change in her, the listless way she arranged his pillow and made certain his water-jug was filled.

She said quietly, 'I shall leave tomorrow, Richard. My husband has signed his name to the documents. It is done. Your captain has sworn that he will leave us to go as we please once he has seen the governor of St Christopher's. After that, I do not know.'

Bolitho gripped her hand and tried not to think of Dumaresq's other promise to the *Heloise*'s master before he had died. Had died from Bolitho's own blade.

He said, 'I may have to leave the ship, too.'

She seemed to forget her own troubles and leaned over him anxiously.

'What is this? Who said you must go?'

He reached up carefully and touched her hair. Like silk. Warm, beautiful silk.

'It doesn't matter now, Aurora.'

She traced a pattern on his shoulder with her finger.

'How can you say that? Of course it *matters*. The sea is your world. You have seen and done much, but all your life still lies before you.'

Bolitho felt her hair touch his skin and shivered.

He said firmly, 'I shall quit the Navy. I have made up my mind.'

'After all you have told me of your family tradition, you would throw it all away?'

'For you, yes, I will.'

She shook her head, the long black hair clinging to him as she protested, 'You must not speak like this!'

'My brother is my father's favourite, and always has been.' It was strange that in moment of crisis he could say it without bitterness or remorse, even knowing it was the truth. 'He can uphold the tradition. It is you I want, you I love.'

He said it so fiercely that she was obviously moved.

Bolitho saw her hand rest on her breast, a pulse beating in her throat which made her outward composure a lie.

'It is madness! I know all about you, but of me you know nothing. What sort of life would you have, watching me grow older while you yearn for the ships, for the chances you threw away?' She placed her hand on his forehead. 'It is like a fever, Richard. Fight it, or it will destroy both of us!'

Bolitho turned his face away, his eyes pricking as he said, 'I could make you happy, Aurora!'

She stroked his arm, soothing his despair. 'I never doubted it. But there is more to life than that, believe me.' She backed away, her body moving in time with the ship's gentle roll. 'I told you earlier. I could love you. For the past days and nights I have watched you, touched you. My thoughts were wicked, my longing greater than I would dare admit.' She shook her head. 'Please, do not look at me like that. Perhaps, after all, the voyage took too long, and tomorrow comes too late. I no longer know anything.'

She turned, her face in shadow as she was framed against the salt-stained windows.

'I shall never forget you, Richard, and I will probably damn myself for turning your offer aside. But I am asking for your help. I cannot do it alone.'

Macmillan brought the evening meal and said, 'Beg pardon, ma'am, but the cap'n an' 'is officers send their respects, an' will you dine with them tonight? It bein' the last time, so to speak.'

Macmillan was really too old for his work, and served his captain in the same fashion as a respected family retainer. He was totally unaware of the tension, the huskiness in her voice as she replied, 'I will be honoured.'

Nor did he see the despair on the lieutenant's face as he watched her walk into the screened-off part of the cabin where her maid spent most of the day.

She paused. 'The lieutenant is stronger now. He will manage.' She turned away, her words muffled. 'On his own.'

With Bulkley's supporting hand at his elbow, Bolitho ventured on to the quarterdeck and looked along the ship's length towards the land.

It was very hot, and the scorching noon sun made him

realize just how weak he still was. Seeing the bare-backed seamen bustling about the upper deck, others straddled along the yards as they shortened sail for the final approach, he felt lost, out of things in a way he had not known before.

Bulkley said, 'I have been to St Christopher's previously.' He pointed towards the nearest headland with its writhing line of white surf. 'Bluff Point. Beyond it lies Basseterre and the main anchorage. There will be King's ships a'plenty, I've no doubt. Some forgotten flag-officer who'll be anxious to tell our captain what to do.'

Some marines marched past, panting loudly in the red coats and heavy equipment.

Bolitho gripped the nettings and watched the land. A small island, but an important link in Britain's chain of command. At another time he would have been excited at a first visit. But now as he stared at the nodding palms, the occasional glimpse of native boats, he could only see what it represented. Here they would part. Whatever his own fate might be, here it was ended between them. He knew from the way Rhodes and the others avoided the subject that they were probably thinking he should be thankful. To have lived through that murderous attack and then be nursed by so beautiful a woman should be enough for any man. But it was not.

Dumaresq came on deck and glanced briefly at the compass and at the set of the sails.

Gulliver touched his hat. 'Nor'-nor'-east, sir. Steady as she goes.'

'Good. Prepare a salute, Mr Palliser. We shall be up to Fort Londonderry within the hour.'

He saw Bolitho and held up his hand. 'Stay if you wish.' He crossed the deck to join him, his glance taking in Bolitho's eyes, dulled by pain, the horrible scar laid bare for all to see. He said, 'You will live. Be thankful.'

He beckoned the midshipman of the watch. 'Get aloft with you, Mr Lovelace, and spy out Fleet Anchorage. Count the ships, and report to me as soon as you are satisfied.' He watched the youth swarm up the ratlines and said, 'Like the rest of our young gentlemen, he has grown up on this voyage.' He glanced at Bolitho. 'That applies more to you than anyone.'

Bolitho said, 'I *feel* a hundred, sir.'

'I expect so.' Dumaresq grinned. 'When you get your own command you will remember the pitfalls, I *hope*, but I doubt if you will pity your young lieutenants any more than I do.'

The captain turned aft, and Bolitho saw his eyes light up with interest. Without looking he knew she had come on deck to see the island. How would she see it? As a temporary refuge or a prison?

Egmont seemed unchanged by his ordeal. He walked to the side and remarked, 'This place has altered little.'

Dumaresq kept his voice matter of fact. 'Garrick will be here, you are certain?'

'As sure as anyone can be.' He saw Bolitho and nodded curtly. 'I see you are recovered, Lieutenant.'

Bolitho forced a smile. 'Thank you, sir, yes. I ache, but I am in one piece.'

She joined her husband and said steadily. 'We both thank you, Lieutenant. You saved our lives. We cannot repay that.'

Dumaresq watched each in turn, like a hunter. 'It is our purpose. But some duties are more rewarding than others.' He turned away. 'To see Garrick taken is all I ask, damn him. Too many have died because of his greed, too many widows are left by his ambitions.'

Palliser cupped his hands. 'Take in the forecourse.'

Dumaresq's calm was slipping as he snapped, 'God damn his eyes, Mr Palliser, what *is* Lovelace doing up there?'

Palliser peered up at the mainmast cross-trees where Midshipman Lovelace sat precariously balanced like a monkey on a stick.

Egmont forgot Bolitho and his wife as he picked upon the captain's changed mood.

'What is worrying you?'

Dumaresq clasped and unclasped his strong fingers across the tails of his coat.

'I am not worried, sir. Merely *interested*.'

Midshipman Lovelace came sliding down a backstay and landed on the deck with a thud. He swallowed hard, visibly shrinking under their combined stares.

Dumaresq asked mildly, 'Must we wait, Mr Lovelace? Or is it something so stupendous you cannot bear to call it from the masthead?'

Lovelace stammered, 'B-but, sir, you told me to c-count

the vessels yonder?' He tried again. 'There is only one man-o'-war, sir, a large frigate.'

Dumaresq took a few paces back and forth to clear his thoughts. 'One, y'say?' He looked at Palliser. 'The squadron must have been called elsewhere. East to Antigua to reinforce the admiral perhaps.'

Palliser said, 'There may be a senior officer here, sir. In the frigate maybe.' He kept his face immobile. Dumaresq would not take kindly to being outranked by another captain.

Bolitho did not care. He moved closer to the quarterdeck rail and saw her put her hand on it.

Dumaresq shouted, 'Where is that damned quill-pusher? Send for Spillane at once!'

To Egmont he said, 'I must discuss a few trivial matters before we anchor. Please come with me.'

Bolitho stood beside her and briefly touched her hand with his. He felt her tense, as if she shared his pain, and said quietly, 'My love. I am in hell.'

She did not turn to look at him but said, 'You promised to help me. *Please*, I will shame us both if you continue.' Then she did look at him, her eyes steady but just too bright as she said, 'It is all wasted if you are to be unhappy and your life spoiled because of something we both value.'

Palliser yelled, 'Mr Vallance! Stand by to fire the salute!'

Men ran to their stations while the ship, indifferent to all of them, continued into the bay.

Bolitho took her arm and guided her to the companionway. 'There will be a lot of smoke and dust directly. You had best go below until we are closer inshore.' How was it possible to speak so calmly on unimportnat matters? He added, 'I must talk with you again.'

But she had already gone down into the shadows.

Bolitho walked forward again and saw Stockdale watching from the starboard gangway. His gun was not required for the salute, but he was showing his usual interest.

Bolitho said, 'It seems I am at a loss when it comes to finding the right words, Stockdale. How can I thank you for what you did? If I offered you reward, I suspect you would be insulted. But words are nothing for what I feel.'

Stockdale smiled. 'You bein' 'ere for us all to see is enough. One day you'll be a captain, sir, an' grateful I'll be.

You'll be needin' a good cox'n then.' He nodded towards Johns, the captain's own coxswain, smart and aloof in his gilt-buttoned jacket and striped trousers. 'Like old Dick yonder. A man o' leisure!' It seemed to amuse him greatly, but the rest of his words were lost in the controlled crash of gun-fire.

Palliser waited for the fort by the anchorage to reply and then said, 'Mr Lovelace was right about the frigate.' He lowered the telescope and glanced grimly at Bolitho. 'But he failed to note that she is wearing Spanish colours. I doubt that the captain will be greatly amused!'

Bulkley said anxiously, 'I think you should rest. You have been on deck for hours. What are you trying to do, kill yourself?'

Bolitho watched the clustered buildings around the anchorage, the two forts, each well placed at either side like squat sentinels.

'I'm sorry. I was thinking only of myself.' He reached up and gingerly touched the scar. Perhaps it would be completely healed, or partially covered by his hair before he saw his mother again. What with her husband returning home with one arm, and now a disfigured son, she would have more than enough to face up to.

He said, 'You did so much for me, too.'

'*Too?*' The surgeon's eyes twinkled behind his glasses. 'I think I understand.'

'Mr Bolitho!' Palliser appeared through the companionway. 'Are you fit enough to go ashore?'

'I must protest!' Bulkley pushed forward. 'He is barely able to stand up!'

Palliser stood facing them, his hands on his hips. Ever since the anchor had been dropped and the boats put down alongside, he had been called from one crisis to another, but mostly down to the great cabin. Dumaresq was extremely angry, if the loudness of his voice was anything to go by, and Palliser was in no mood for argument.

'Let *him* decide, dammit!' He looked at Bolitho. 'I am short-handed, but for some reason the captain requires you to go ashore with him. Remember our first meeting? I need every officer and man *working* in my ship. No matter how you feel, you keep going. Until you drop, or are incapable of movement, you are still one of my lieutenants, is that plain?'

Bolitho nodded, somehow glad of Palliser's temper. 'I'm ready.'

'Good. Then get changed.' As an afterthought he said, 'You may *carry* your hat.'

Bulkley watched him stride away and exploded angrily, 'He is beyond understanding! By God, Richard, if you feel unsteady I will demand that you stay aboard! Young Stephen can take your place.'

Bolitho made to shake his head but winced as the pain stabbed back at him.

'I shall be all right. But thank you.' He walked to the companionway adding, 'I suspect there is some special reason for taking me with him.'

Bulkley nodded. 'You are getting to know our captain very well, Richard. He never acts without a purpose, never offers a guinea which will not profit him two!'

He sighed. 'But the thought of leaving his service is worse than tolerating his insults. Life would seem very dull after Dumaresq's command!'

It was almost evening by the time Dumaresq decided to go ashore. He had sent Colpoys with a letter of introduction to the governor's house, but when the marine returned he had told him that there was only the acting-governor in residence.

Dumaresq had commented sharply, 'Not another Rio, I trust?'

Now, in the captain's gig, with a hint of cooler air to make the journey bearable, Dumaresq sat as before, with both hands gripped around his sword, his eyes fixed on the land.

Bolitho sat beside him, his determination to withstand the pain and the recurring dizziness making him break out in a sweat. He concentrated on the anchored vessels and the comings and goings of *Destiny*'s boats as they ferried the sick and wounded ashore and returned already loaded with stores for the purser.

Dumaresq said suddenly, 'A mite to starboard, Johns.'

The coxswain did not even blink but moved the tiller accordingly. From one corner of his mouth he muttered, 'You'll get a good look at 'er presently, sir.'

Dumaresq nudged Bolitho sharply with an elbow. 'He's a rascal, eh? Knows my mind better than I!'

Bolitho watched the anchored Spaniard as she towered above them. She was more like a cut-down fourth-rate than a frigate, he thought. Old, with elaborately carved and gilded gingerbread around her stern and cabin windows, but well-maintained, with an appearance of efficiency which was rare in a Spanish ship.

Dumaresq was thinking the same and murmured, 'The *San Augustin*. She's no local relic from La Guaira or Porto Bello. Cadiz or Algeciras is my guess.'

'Will that make a difference, sir?'

Dumaresq turned on him angrily, and just as swiftly let his temper subside.

'I am bad company. After what you have suffered under my command, I can spare you civility at least.' He watched the other vessel with professional interest, as Stockdale had studied the other gun crews. 'Forty-four guns at least.' He seemed to recall Bolitho's question. 'It might. Weeks and months ago there was a secret. The Dons suspected there was evidence available as to the *Asturia*'s lost treasure. Now it seems they have more than mere suspicions. *San Augustin* is here to mime *Destiny*'s role and to prevent His Most Catholic Majesty's displeasure if we do not share our confidences.' He gave a grim smile. 'We shall see about that. I have no doubt that a dozen telescopes are watching us, so look no more. Let them worry about us.'

Dumaresq noticed that the landing-place was only fifty yards away and said, 'I brought you with me so that the governor would see your scar. It is better proof than anything else that we are working for our masters in Admiralty. Nobody here need know you gained so distinguished a wound whilst seeking water for our thirsty people!'

A small group was waiting for the boat to maneouvre to the landing-place, some red uniforms amongst them. It was always the same. News from England. Word from the country which had sent them this far, anything which might maintain their precious contact.

Bolitho asked, 'Will the Egmonts be allowed to go, sir?' He lifted his chin, surprised at his own impudence as Dumaresq's gaze fastened on him. 'I should like to know, sir.'

Dumaresq studied him gravely for several seconds. 'It is

important to you, I can see that.' He untangled the sword from between his legs in readiness for climbing ashore. Then he said bluntly, 'She is a very desirable woman, I'll not argue.' He stood up and straightened his hat with elaborate care. 'You need not gape like that. I'm neither completely blind nor insensitive, you know. If I'm anything, it's most likely envious.' He clapped him on the shoulder. 'Now, let's deal with the acting-governor of this seat of empire, Sir Jason Fitzpatrick, and afterwards I may consider *your* problem!'

Grasping his hat in one hand, and supporting his sword in the other, Bolitho followed the captain out of the boat. Dumaresq's casual acceptance of his feelings for another man's wife had completely taken the wind from his sails. No wonder the surgeon could not face the prospect of a quieter and more predictable master.

A youthful captain from the garrison touched his hat and then exclaimed, 'My God, gentlemen, that is a bad wound!'

Dumaresq glanced at Bolitho's discomfort and might even have winked.

'The price of duty.' He gave a solemn sigh. 'It makes itself felt in many ways.'

13

Place of Safety

Sir Jason Fitzpatrick, the acting-governor of St Christopher's, looked like a man who lived life to excess. Aged about forty, he was extremely fat, and his face, which had seemingly defied the sun over the years, was brick-red.

As Bolitho followed Dumaresq across a beautifully tiled entrance hall and into a low-ceilinged room, he saw plenty of evidence of Fitzpatrick's occupation. There were trays of bottles set around, with neat ranks of finely cut glasses close to hand, presumably ready for the acting-governor to slake his thirst with the shortest possible delay.

Fitzpatrick said, 'Be seated, gentlemen. We will taste some of my claret. It should be suitable, although in this damnable climate, who cay say?'

He had a throaty voice, and incredibly small eyes which were almost hidden in the folds of his face.

Bolitho noticed the tiny eyes more than anything. They moved all the time, as if quite independent of the heavy frame which supported them. Dumaresq had told him on the way from the water-front that Fitzpatrick was a rich plantation owner, with other properties on the neighbouring island of Nevis.

'Here, master.'

Bolitho turned and felt his stomach contract. A big Negro in red jacket and loose white trousers was holding a tray towards him. Bolitho did not see the tray or the glasses upon it. In his mind's eye he could picture that other black face, hear the terrible scream of triumph as he had hacked him down with a seaman's cutlass.

He took a glass and nodded his thanks while his breathing returned to normal.

Dumaresq was saying, 'By the authority entrusted in me, I am ordered to complete this investigation without further delay, Sir Jason. I have the written statements required, and would like you to furnish me with Garrick's whereabouts.'

Fitzpatrick played with the stem of his glass, his eyes flitting rapidly round the room.

'Ah, Captain, you are in a great hurry. You see, the governor is absent. He was stricken with fever some months back and returned to England aboard an Indiaman. He may be on his way back by now. Communications are very poor, we are hard put to get our mails on time with all these wretched pirates on the rampage. Honest craft sail in fear of their lives. It is a pity their lordships of Admiralty do not put their minds to *that*.'

Dumaresq was unmoved. 'I had hoped that a flag-officer would be here.'

'As I explained, Captain, the governor is away, other-wise . . .'

'Otherwise there'd be no damned Spaniard anchored here, I'm certain of that!'

Fitzpatrick forced a smile. 'We are not at war with Spain. The *San Augustin* comes in peace. She is commanded by *Capitán de Navio* Don Carlos Quintana. A most senior and personable captain, who is also entrusted with his country's authority.' He leaned back, obviously pleased with his advantage. 'After all, what evidence do you really have? The statement of a man who died before he could be brought to justice, the sworn testimony of a renegade who is so eager to save his own skin he will say anything.'

Dumaresq tried to hide the bitterness as he answered, 'My clerk was carrying further documents of proof when he was murdered in Madeira.'

'Indeed I am genuinely sorry about that, Captain. But to cast a slur against the name of so influential a gentleman as Sir Piers Garrick without evidence would be a criminal act in itself.' He smiled complacently. 'May I suggest we await instructions from London? You may send your despatches on the next home-bound vessel, which will probably be from Barbados. You could anchor there and be ready to act when so instructed. By then, the governor may have returned, and the squadron too, so that you will have senior naval authority to uphold your actions.'

Dumaresq snapped angrily, 'That could take months. By then, the bird will have flown.'

'Forgive my lack of enthusiasm. As I told Don Carlos, it all happened thirty years ago, so why this sudden interest?'

'Garrick was a felon first, a traitor second. You complain about the flocks of pirates who roam the Main and the Caribbean, who sack towns and plunder the ships of rich traders, but do you ever wonder where they find their own vessels? Like the *Heloise*, which was new from a British yard, sent out here with a passage crew, and for what?'

Bolitho listened entranced. He had expected Fitzpatrick to leap to his feet and summon the garrison commander. To plan with Dumaresq how they would seek and detain the elusive Garrick, and *then* wait for further orders.

Fitzpatrick spread his red hands apologetically. 'It is not within my province to take such action, Captain. I am in a temporary capacity, and would receive no thanks for putting a match to the powder-keg. You must of course do as you think fit. You say you had hoped for a flag-officer to be here? No doubt to take the responsibility and decision from *your* shoulders?' When Dumaresq remained silent he continued calmly, 'So do not pour scorn on me for not wishing to act unsupported.'

Bolitho was astounded. The Admiralty in London, some senior officers of the fleet, even the government of King George had been involved in getting the *Destiny* here. Dumaresq had worked without respite from the moment he had been told of his assignment, and must have spent many long hours in the privacy of his cabin pondering on his own interpretation of his scanty collection of clues.

And now, because there was no naval authority to back his most important decision, he would either have to kick his heels and wait for orders to arrive from elsewhere, or take it upon himself. At the age of twenty-eight, Dumaresq *was* the senior naval officer in St Christopher's, and Bolitho found it impossible to see how he could proceed with a course of action which might easily destroy him.

Dumaresq said wearily, 'Tell me what you know of Garrick.'

'Virtually nothing. It is true he has shipping interests, and has taken delivery of several small vessels over the months. He is a very rich man, and I understand he intends to continue trading with the French in Martinique, with a view to extending commerce elsewhere.'

Dumaresq stood up. 'I must return to my ship.' He did not look at Bolitho. 'I would take it kindly if you would accommodate my third lieutenant who has been wounded, and all to no good purpose, it now appears.'

Fitzpatrick lifted his bulk unsteadily. 'I'd be happy to do that.' He tried to hide his relief. Dumaresq was obviously going to take the easier course.

Dumaresq silenced Bolitho's unspoken protest. 'I'll send some *servants* to care for your wants.' He nodded to the acting-governor. 'I shall return when I have spoken with the *San Augustin*'s captain.'

Outside the building, his features hidden in the gloom, Dumaresq gave vent to his true feelings. 'That bloody hound! He's in it up to the neck! Thinks I'll stay anchored and be a good little boy, does he? God damn his poxy face, I'll see him in hell first!'

'*Must* I stay here, sir?'

'For the present. I'll detail some stout hands to join you. I don't trust that Fitzpatrick. He's a local landowner, and probably as thick as thieves with every smuggler and slaver in the Caribbean. Play the innocent with me, would he? By God, I'll wager he knows how many new vessels have fetched up here to await Garrick's orders.'

Bolitho asked, 'Is he still a pirate, sir?'

Dumaresq grinned in the darkness. 'Worse. I believe he is directly involved with supplying arms and well-found vessels for use against us in the north.'

'America, sir?'

'Eventually, and further still if those damned renegades have their way. Do you think the French will rest until they have rekindled the fires? We kicked them out of Canada and their Caribbean possessions. Did you imagine they'd put forgiveness at the top of their list?'

Bolitho had often heard talk of the unrest in the American colony which had followed the Seven Years War. There had been several serious incidents, but the prospect of open rebellion had been regarded by even the most influential newspaper as bluster.

'All these years Garrick has been working and scheming, using his stolen booty to best advantage. He sees himself as a leader if a rebellion comes, and those in power who believe otherwise are deluding themselves. I have had plenty of time to mull over Garrick's affairs, and the cruel unfairness which made him rich and powerful and left my father an impoverished cripple.'

Bolitho watched the gig approaching through the darkness, the oars very white against the water. So Dumaresq had already decided. He should have guessed, after what he had seen and learned of the man.

Dumaresq said suddenly, 'Egmont and his wife will also be landed shortly. They are outwardly under Fitzpatrick's care, but post a guard for your own satisfaction. I want Fitzpatrick to know he is directly implicated should there be any attempt at treachery.'

'You think Egmont is still in danger, sir?'

Dumaresq waved his hand towards the small residency. 'Here is a place of safety. I'll not have Egmont on the run again with some mad scheme of his own. There are too many who might want him dead. After I have dealt with Garrick, he can do as he damn well pleases. The quicker the better.'

'I see, sir.'

Dumaresq signalled to his coxswain and then chuckled. 'I doubt that. But keep your ears open, as I believe things will begin to move very shortly.'

Bolitho watched him climb into the gig and then retraced his steps to the residency.

Did Dumaresq care what happened to Egmont and his wife? Or, like the hunter he was, did he merely see them as bait for his trap?

There were two or three small dwellings set well apart from the residency, and which were normally used for visiting officials or militia officers and their families.

Bolitho assumed that these visitors were rare, and when

they came were prepared to supply their own comforts. The building allotted to him was little more than the size of a room. The frames around the shutters were pitted with holes, made by a tireless army of insects, he thought. Palms tapped against the roof and walls, and he guessed that in any heavy rainstorm the whole place would leak like a sieve.

He sat gingerly on a large, hand-carved bed and trimmed a lantern. More insects buzzed and threw themselves at the hot glass, and he pitied the less fortunate people on the island if the governor himself could be struck down by fever.

Planks creaked outside the loosely fitting door and Stockdale peered in at him. With six other men, he had come ashore, to keep a weather-eye on things, as he put it.

He wheezed, 'All posted, sir. We'll work watch an' watch. Josh Little will take the first one.' He leaned against the door and Bolitho heard it groan in protest. 'I've put two 'ands near the other place. It's quiet enough.'

Bolitho thought of the way she had looked at him as she and her husband had been hurried into the next dwelling by some of the governor's servants. She had appeared worried, distressed by the sudden change of events. Egmont was said to have friends in Basseterre, but instead of being released to go to them, he was still a guest. A prisoner, more likely.

Bolitho said, 'Get some sleep.' He touched the scar and grimaced. 'I feel as if it happened today.'

Stockdale grinned. 'Neat bit o' work, sir. Lucky we've a good sawbones!'

He strolled out of the door, and Bolitho heard him whistling softly as he found his own place to stretch out. Sailors could sleep anywhere.

Bolitho lay back, his hands behind his head, as he stared up at the shadows above the lantern's small glow.

It was all a waste. Garrick had gone from the island, or that was what he had heard. He must be better informed than Dumaresq had believed. He would be laughing now, thinking of the frigate and her unwanted Spanish consort lying baffled at anchor while he . . .

Bolitho sat up with a jerk, reaching out for his pistol, as the planks outside the door squeaked again.

He watched the handle drop, and could feel his heart pounding against his ribs as he measured the distance across the room and wondered if he could get to his feet in time to defend himself.

The door opened a few inches and he saw her small hand around its edge.

He was off the bed in seconds, and as he opened the door he heard her gasp, 'Please! Watch the light!'

For a long, confused moment they clung together, the door tightly shut behind them. There was no sound but their breathing, and Bolitho was almost afraid to speak for fear of smashing this unbelievable dream.

She said quietly, 'I had to come. It was bad enough on the ship. But to know you were in here, while . . .' She looked up at him her eyes shining. 'Do not despise me for my weakness.'

Bolitho held her tightly, feeling her soft body through the long pale gown, knowing they were already lost. If the world fell apart around them, nothing could spoil this moment.

How she had got past his sentries he could not understand, nor did he care. Then he thought of Stockdale. He should have guessed.

His hands were shaking badly as he held her shoulders and kissed her hair, her face and her throat.

She whispered, 'I will help you.' She stood back from him and allowed the gown to fall to the floor. 'Now hold me again.'

In the darkness, somewhere between the two small buildings, Stockdale propped his cutlass against a tree and sat down on the ground. He watched the moonlight as it touched the door he had seen open and close just an hour ago and thought about the two of them together. It was probably the lieutenant's first time, he thought comfortably. He could have no better teacher, that was certain.

Long before dawn the girl named Aurora slipped quietly from the bed and pulled on her gown. For a while more she looked at the pale figure, now sleeping deeply, while she touched her breast as he had done. Then she stooped and kissed him lightly on the mouth. His lips tasted of salt, perhaps from her own tears. Without another glance she left the room and ran past Stockdale, seeing nothing.

*   *   *

Bolitho walked slowly from the doorway and stepped down onto the sun-hardened ground as if he was walking on thin glass. Although he had donned his uniform he still felt naked, could imagine their embrace, the breathtaking demands of their passion which had left him spent.

He stared at the early sunlight, at one of his guards who was watching him curiously as he leaned on a musket.

If only he had been awake when she had left him. Then they would never have parted.

Stockdale strolled to meet him. 'Nothin' to report, sir.'

He eyed Bolitho's uncertainty with quiet satisfaction. The lieutenant was different. Lost, but alive. Confused too, but in time he would feel the strength she had given him.

Bolitho nodded. 'Muster the hands.'

He went to raise his hat to his head and remembered the scar which throbbed and burned at the slightest touch. She had even made him forget about that.

Stockdale stooped down and picked up a small piece of paper which had dropped from inside the hat. He handed it over, his face expressionless.

'Can't read meself, sir.'

Bolitho opened the paper, his eyes misty as he read her few brief words.

Dearest, I could not wait. Think of me sometimes and how it was.

Beneath it she had written, *The place your captain wants is Fougeaux Island.*

She had not signed her name, but he could almost hear her speaking aloud.

'You feelin' weak, sir?'

'No.'

He re-read the small message once again. She must have carried it with her, knowing she was going to give herself to him. Knowing too that it was ending there.

Feet grated on sand and he saw Palliser striding along the path, Midshipman Merrett trotting in his wake and hard put to keep up with the lanky lieutenant.

He saw Bolitho and snapped, 'All done.' He waited, his eyes wary.

Bolitho asked, 'Egmont and his wife, sir. What's happened?'

'Oh, didn't you know? They've just boarded a vessel in the

bay. We sent their luggage across during the night. I'd have thought you would be better informed.'

Bolitho hesitated. Then very carefully he folded the paper and removed the lower half, with the island's name written on it.

Palliser examined it and said, 'It'll be the one.'

He refolded the paper and handed it to Merrett. 'Back to the ship, my lad, and present this with my respects to the captain. Lose it, and I promise you a hideous death!' The youth fled down the path and Palliser said, 'The captain was right after all.' He smiled at Bolitho's grave features. 'Come, I'll walk back with you.'

'You say they've already boarded a vessel, sir?' He could not accept it. 'Where bound?'

'I forget. Is it important?'

Bolitho fell in step beside him. She had provided the information as repayment, perhaps for saving her life, or for sharing his love with her. Dumaresq had used both of them. He felt his face sting with anger. A place of safety, he had called it. More likely one of deceit.

When he reached the ship he found the hands turned-to, the sails loosely brailed and ready to set at short notice.

As instructed, Bolitho presented himself in the cabin where Dumaresq and Gulliver were studying some charts with elaborate care.

Dumaresq told the master to wait outside and then said bluntly, 'In order to avoid my having to punish you for insubordination, let me speak first. Our mission in these waters is an important one for so small a vessel. I have always believed it, and now with that final piece of intelligence I know where Garrick has made his headquarters, his storehouse for arms, unlawful supplies and vessels to disperse them. It *is* important.'

Bolitho met his gaze. 'I *should* have been told, sir.'

'You enjoyed it, did you not?' His voice softened. 'I know what it's like to be in love with a dream, and that is all it could have been. You are a King's officer, and may amount to being a fair one, given time and a bit of common sense.'

Bolitho looked past him towards the windows, at the moored vessels there, and wondered which, if any of them, was Aurora's.

He asked, 'Is that all, sir?'

'Yes. Take charge of your division. I intend to weigh as soon as my quill-pusher has made copies of my despatches for the authorities and for London.' He was lost in his thoughts, the hundred and one things he must do.

Bolitho blundered from the cabin and into the wardroom. It was impossible to picture the cabin as it had been. Her clothes hung neatly to dry, the young maidservant always near in case she was needed. Perhaps Dumaresq's way was the best, but need it be so brutal and without feeling?

Rhodes and Colpoys rose to greet him, and they solemnly shook hands.

Bolitho touched the piece of paper in his pocket and felt stronger. Whatever Dumaresq and the others thought, they could never be certain, or really know how it was.

Bulkley entered the wardroom, saw Bolitho and was about to ask him how his wound was progressing, but Rhodes gave a slight shake of his head and the surgeon called Poad for some coffee instead.

Bolitho would get over it. But it would take time.

'Anchor's aweigh, sir!'

Dumaresq walked to the rail and stared across at the Spaniard, as with her sails booming in a lively breeze *Destiny* tacked round towards the open sea.

He said, 'That will rile the Don. He's half of his people ashore gathering supplies and will not be able to follow us for hours!' He threw back his head and laughed. 'Damn you, Garrick! Make the most of your freedom!'

Bolitho watched his men setting the main-topgallant sail, calling to each other as if they too were infected by Dumaresq's excitement. Death, prize-money, a different landfall, it was all meat to them.

Palliser shouted from the quarterdeck, 'Chase up those hands, Mr Bolitho, they have lead in their limbs today!'

Bolitho turned aft, his mouth framing an angry retort. Then he shrugged. Palliser was trying to help him in the only way he knew.

Skirting treacherous shallows off Bluff Point, *Destiny* spread more sails and headed away towards the west. Later, when Bolitho took over the afternoon-watch, he examined the chart and Gulliver's carefully written calculations.

Fougeaux Island was very small, one of a scattered group some 150 miles west-north-west of St Christopher's. It had been claimed by France, Spain and England in turn, even the Dutch had been interested for a time.

Now it owed allegiance to no country, for to all intents it had no real use. It lacked timber for firewood or repairs, and according to the navigational notes it had less than its share of water. A bare, hostile place with a lagoon shaped like a reaping-hook as its one asset. It could provide shelter from storms, if little else. But as Dumaresq had observed, what else did Garrick require?

Bolitho watched the captain as he prowled restlessly about the deck, as if he could not bear the restraint of his quarters now that his goal was so close. Adverse winds were making progress hard and frustrating, with the ship tacking back and forth for several miles to gain a few cables advance.

But the mention of lost bullion, and the prospect of some share in it, seemed to make up for the back-breaking work of trimming the yards and resetting the sails again and again.

Suppose the island proved to be empty or the wrong one? Bolitho guessed it to be unlikely. Aurora must have known that Garrick's capture was the only way of preventing him from taking his revenge on her husband and herself. Also that Dumaresq had no intention of freeing them without solid information.

The next day found *Destiny* drifting becalmed, her sails hanging flat and devoid of movement.

Far away to starboard was the vague shape of another islet, but otherwise they had the sea to themselves. It was so hot that feet stuck to the deck seams, and the gun barrels felt as if they had been firing in battle.

Gulliver said, 'If we had taken a more northerly passage we'd have been in better luck for a wind, sir.'

'I know that, damn you.' Dumaresq turned on him hotly. 'And risk losing my keel as well, is that what you want? This is a frigate, not some damned fishing boat!'

All that day, and for half of the next, the ship rolled uneasily in the swell. A shark moved cautiously beneath her counter, and several of the hands tried their luck with hooks and lines.

Dumaresq never seemed to leave the deck, and as he passed Bolitho during his watch he saw that his shirt was black with sweat, and there was a livid blister on his forehead which he did not seem to notice.

Halfway through the afternoon-watch the wind felt its way slowly across the glittering water, but with it came a surprise.

'Ship, sir! Fine on the larboard quarter!'

Dumaresq and Palliser watched the tan-coloured pyramid grow above the horizon, the great scarlet cross clearly etched on her forecourse to dispel any doubt.

Palliser exclaimed bitterly, 'The Don, blast his soul!'

Dumaresq lowered the glass, his eyes like stones. 'Fitzpatrick. He must have told them. Now they're hot for blood.' He looked past his officers. 'If Don Carlos Quintana interferes now, it will be his own blood!'

'Man the braces there!'

Destiny shivered and tilted steadily to a freshening breeze, her renewed strength tossing spray up and around her white figurehead.

Dumaresq said, 'Put the people to gun-drill, Mr Palliser.' He stared astern at the other vessel. She already seemed to be drawing much closer.

'And run up the colours, if you please. I'll have no damned Spaniard crossing by bows!'

Rhodes dropped his voice. 'He means it too, Richard. This is his moment. He'd die rather than share it!'

Some of the men near the quarterdeck glanced at each other and murmured apprehensively. Their natural contempt for any navy but their own had been somewhat blunted by the brief stay at Basseterre. The *San Augustin* carried at least forty-four guns against their own twenty-eight.

Dumaresq shouted, 'And get those dolts to work, Mr Palliser! This ship is getting like a sty!'

One of Bolitho's gun-captains muttered, 'I thought we was only after a pirate.'

Stockdale showed his teeth. 'An enemy's an enemy, Tom. When did a flag make any difference?'

Bolitho bit his lip. This was the true responsibility of command at close quarters. If Dumaresq did nothing he could

be court-martialled for incompetence or cowardice. If he
crossed swords with a Spanish ship he might be blamed for
provoking a war.

He said, 'Stand to, lads. Cast off the breechings!'

Maybe Stockdale was right. All you had to worry about
was winning.

The following day the hands were sent to breakfast and
then the decks swabbed down before the sun had crept fully
over the horizon.

The breeze, though light, was steady enough, and had
shifted during the night watches to south-westerly.

Dumaresq was on deck as early as anyone, and Bolitho saw
the impatience in his thick-set figure as he strode about the
deck glancing at the compass or consulting the master's slate
by the wheel. He probably saw none of these things, and
Bolitho could tell from the way that Palliser and Gulliver
gave him a wide berth that they knew the measure of his
moods of old.

With Rhodes, Bolitho watched the boatswain detailing his
working parties as usual. The fact that a larger man-of-war
than their own was trailing astern, and that the little known
Fougeaux Island lay somewhere beyond the lee bow made no
difference to Mr Timbrell's routine.

Palliser's brusque tones made Bolitho start. 'Rig top-chains
before all else, Mr Timbrell.'

Some of the seamen looked up at the yards. Palliser did not
explain further, nor did he need to for the older hands. The
chains would be rigged to sling each yard, as the cordage
which normally held them might be shot away in any sort of
battle. Then the nets would be spread across the upper deck.
The slings and the nets were the only protection to the men
below from falling spars and rigging.

Perhaps it was the same aboard the Spaniard, Bolitho
thought. Although he had seen little evidence so far. In fact,
now that she had caught up, the *San Augustin* seemed content
to follow and watch events.

Rhodes turned abruptly and headed for his own part of the
ship, hissing quickly, 'Lord and master!'

Bolitho swung round and came face to face with the captain.
It was unusual to see him away from the quarterdeck or poop,

and the seamen working around him seemed to press back as if they too were awed by his presence.

Bolitho touched his hat and waited.

Dumaresq's eyes examined his face slowly, without expression.

Then he said, 'Come with me. Bring a glass.' Tossing his hat to his coxswain, he added, 'A climb will clear the head.'

Bolitho stared as Dumaresq began to haul himself out and on to the shrouds, his broad figure hanging awkwardly as he peered up at the spiralling masthead.

Bolitho hated heights. Of all the things which had encouraged him to work for advancement to lieutenant, he thought it was probably that. No longer needed to swarm aloft with the hands, no ice-cold terror as the wind tried to cut away your grip on frozen ratlines, or throw you out and into the sea far below.

Perhaps Dumaresq was goading him, provoking him, if only to relieve his own tension.

'Come along, Mr. Bolitho! You are in stays today!'

Bolitho followed him up the vibrating shrouds, foot by foot, hand over hand. He told himself not to look down, even though he could picture *Destiny*'s pale deck tilting away beneath him as the ship drove her shoulder into a steep roller.

Disdaining the lubber's hole, Dumaresq clawed his way out on the futtock shrouds so that his mis-shapen body was hanging almost parallel to the sea below. Then up past the main-top, ignoring some startled marines who were exercising with a swivel gun, and towards the topgallant yard.

Dumaresq's confidence gave Bolitho the will to climb faster than he could recall. What did Dumaresq know about love, or whether he and Aurora could have overcome all the obstacles together?

He barely noticed the height and was already peering up towards the main-royal yard when Dumaresq paused, one foot dangling in space as he observed, 'You can get the *feel* of her from here.'

Bolitho clung on with both hands and stared up at him, his eyes watering in the fierce sunlight. Dumaresq spoke with such conviction, and yet with a warmth which was almost akin to love itself.

'Feel her?' Dumaresq seized a stay and tugged it with his

fist. 'Taut and firm, equal strain on all parts. As she should be. As any good vessel ought to be, properly cared for!' He looked at Bolitho's upturned face. 'Head all right?'

Bolitho nodded. In his mixture of resentment and anger he had forgotten about his wound.

'Good. Come on then.'

They reached the cross-trees where a lookout slithered down to make room for his betters.

'Ah.' Dumaresq unslung a telescope, and after wiping the lens with his neckcloth trained it across the starboard bow.

Bolitho followed his example, and then felt a touch of ice at his spine, despite the sun and the wind which hissed through the rigging like sand.

It was like nothing he had ever seen. The island seemed to be made entirely of coral or rock, obscenely stripped bare like something which was no longer alive. In the centre was a ridge, rather like a hill with the top sliced off. But misty in distance, it could have been a giant fortress, and the low island there merely to support it.

He tried to compare it with the sparse details on the chart, and guessed from the bearing that the sheltered lagoon was directly beneath the hill.

Dumaresq said hoarsely, 'They're there right enough!'

Bolitho tried again. The place appeared deserted, stamped in time by some terrible natural disaster.

Then he saw something darker than the rest before it was lost in the heat-haze. A mast, or several masts, while the vessels lay hidden by the protective wall of coral.

He looked quickly at Dumaresq and wondered how differently he saw it.

'Little pieces of a puzzle.' Dumaresq did not raise his voice above the murmur of rigging and canvas. 'There are Garrick's ships, his little armada. No line of battle, Mr Bolitho, no flagship with the admiral's proud flag to inspire you, but just as deadly.'

Bolitho took another look through his glass. No wonder Garrick had felt so safe. He had known of their arrival at Rio, and even before that at Madeira. And now Garrick had the upper hand. He could either send his vessels out at night or he could stay put like a hermit-crab in a shell.

Again Dumaresq seemed to be speaking to himself. 'All

the Don cares about is the lost bullion. Garrick can go free as far as he is concerned. Quintana believes that he will excise those carefully selected vessels and what booty remains without firing a shot.'

Bolitho asked, 'Perhaps Garrick knows less than we think, sir, and may try to bluff it out?'

Dumaresq looked at him strangely. 'I am afraid not. No more bluff now. I tried to explain Garrick's mind to the Spaniard at Basseterre. But he would not listen. Garrick helped the French, and in any future war Spain will need an ally like France. Be certain that Don Carlos Quintana is mindful of that, too.'

'Cap'n, sir!' The lookout beneath sounded anxious. 'The Don's makin' more sail!'

Dumaresq said, 'Time to go.' He looked at each mast in turn and then at the deck below.

Bolitho found he could do the same without flinching. The foreshortened blue and white figures of the officers and midshipmen on the quarterdeck, the changing patterns of men as they moved around the double line of black cannon.

For those few moments Bolitho shared an understanding with this devious, determined man. She was his ship, every moving part of her, every timber and inch of cordage.

Then Dumaresq said, 'The Spaniard may attempt to enter the lagoon before me. It is dangerous folly because the entrance is narrow, the channel unknown. Without hope of surprise he will be depending on his peaceful intentions, with a show of force if that fails.'

He climbed with surprising swiftness down to the deck, and when Bolitho reached the quarterdeck Dumaresq was already speaking with Palliser and the master.

Bolitho heard Palliser say, 'The Don is standing inshore, sir.'

Dumaresq was busy with his telescope again. 'Then he stands into danger. Signal him to sheer off.'

Bolitho saw the other faces nearby, ones he had come to know so well. In a few moments it might all be decided, and it was Dumaresq's choice.

Palliser shouted, 'He ignores us, sir!'

'Very well. Beat to quarters and clear for action.' Dumaresq clasped his hands behind him. 'We'll see how he likes *that*.'

Rhodes gripped Bolitho's arm. 'He must be mad. He can't fight Garrick and the Dons.'

The marine drummer boys began their staccato beat, and the moment of doubt was past.

14

Last Chance

'The Don is shortening sail, sir.'

'We shall do likewise.' Dumaresq stood in the centre of the quarterdeck just forward of the mizzen, like a rock. 'Take in the t'gan'sls.'

Bolitho shielded his eyes as he peered up through the tracery of rigging and nets as his own men began to fist and fight the rebellious canvas. In less than an hour the tension had risen like the sun, and now, with *San Augustin* firmly placed on the starboard bow, he could feel it affecting every man who was near him. *Destiny* had the wind-gage, but by overhauling the Spanish captain had placed himself between her and the approaches to the lagoon.

Rhodes strolled aft and joined him between two of the twelve-pounders.

'He's letting the Don get away with it.' He grimaced. 'I must say I approve. I don't fancy a one-sided fight unless the odds are in *my* favour.' He glanced quickly at the quarterdeck and then lowered his voice. 'What do you make of the lord and master *now*?'

Bolitho shrugged. 'I am bounced between contempt and admiration. I despise the way he used me. He must have known Egmont would not betray Garrick's island on his own.'

Rhodes pursed his lips. 'So it *was* his wife.' He hesitated. 'Are you over it, Dick?'

Bolitho looked across at the *San Augustin*, her streaming pennants and the white ensign of Spain.

Rhodes persisted. 'In all this, with the prospect of being blown to gruel because of some stupid event of long ago, you can still fret for the love of a woman?'

Bolitho faced him. 'I'll not get over it. If only you could have seen her . . .'

Rhodes smiled sadly. 'My God, Dick, I'm wasting my time. When we return to England I'll have to see what I can do to roust you out of it.'

They both turned as a shot reverberated across the water. Then there was a splash as the ball threw up a spindly waterspout in direct line with the Spaniard's bowsprit.

Dumaresq snapped, 'God in heaven, the buggers have fired first!'

Several telescopes were trained on the island, but nobody was able to sight the hidden cannon.

Palliser said dourly, 'That was a warning. I hope the Don has the sense to heed it. This calls for stealth and agility, not a head-on charge!'

Dumaresq smiled. 'Does it indeed? You begin to sound like an admiral, Mr Palliser. I shall have to watch myself!'

Bolitho studied the Spanish ship closely. It was as if nothing had happened. She was still steering for the nearest finger of land where the lagoon began.

A few cormorants arose from the sea when the two ships sailed past, like heraldic birds as they circled watchfully overhead, Bolitho thought.

'Deck there! Smoke above th' hill, sir!'

The telescopes trained round like small artillery.

Bolitho heard Clow, one of the gunner's mates, remark, 'That be from a bloody furnace. Them devils is heatin' shot to feed the Dons.'

Bolitho licked his lips. His father had told him often enough about the folly of setting a ship against a sited shore battery. If they used heated shot it would turn any vessel into a pyre unless it was dealt with immediately. Sun-dried timbers, tar, paint and canvas would burn fiercely, while the wind would do the rest.

Something like a sigh transmitted itself along the deck as the *San Augustin*'s ports lifted in unison, and then at the blast of a trumpet she ran out her guns. In the far distance they looked like black teeth along her tumblehome. Black and deadly.

The surgeon joined Bolitho by the twelve-pounders, his spectacles glinting in the sun. Out of deference for the men who might soon need his services, he had refrained from wearing his apron.

'I am as nervous as a cat when this is dragging on.'

Bolitho understood. Down on the orlop deck below the waterline, in a place of spiralling lanterns and entrapped smells, all the sounds were distorted.

He said, 'I think the Spaniard intends to force the entrance.'

As he spoke the other ship reset her topgallants and tacked very slightly to take advantage of the south-westerly wind. How fine her gingerbread looked in the sun's glare, how majestic were the proud pennants and the scarlet crosses on her courses. She was like something from an old engraving, Bolitho thought.

She made the lean and graceful *Destiny* appear spartan by comparison.

Bolitho walked aft until he stood directly below the quarterdeck rail. He heard Dumaresq say, 'Another half-cable, and then we'll see.'

Then Palliser's voice, less certain. 'He might just force the entrance, sir. Once inside he could wear ship and rake the anchored vessels, even use them to protect himself from the shore. Without craft, Garrick is a prisoner.'

Dumaresq considered it. 'That part is true. I have only heard of one man who successfully walked on water, but we need another sort of miracle today.'

Some of the nine-pounder crews nearby rocked back on their knees, grinning and prodding each other over the captain's humour.

Bolitho marvelled that it could be so easy for Dumaresq. He knew exactly what his men needed to keep them alert and keen. And that was what he gave them, neither more nor a fraction less.

Gulliver said to nobody in particular, 'If the Don succeeds, that's a farewell to our prize-money.'

Dumaresq looked at him, his teeth bared in a fierce grin. 'God, you are a miserable fellow, Mr Gulliver. How you can find your way about the ocean under such a weight of despair I cannot fathom!'

Midshipman Henderson called, 'The Spaniard has passed the point, sir!'

Dumaresq grunted. 'You have good eyes.' To Palliser he added, 'He is on a lee shore. It will be now or not at all.'

Bolitho found that he was gripping his hands together so tightly that the pain helped to calm him. He saw the reflected flashes from the *San Augustin*'s hidden gunports, the great gouts of smoke, and then seconds later came the rumbling crash of her broadside.

Puffs of smoke and dust rose like plumes along the hill-side, and several impressive avalanches of rocks tumbled down towards the water.

Palliser said savagely, 'We shall have to come about shortly, sir.'

Bolitho looked up at him. After *Destiny*, Palliser had been hoping for a command. He had made little secret of the fact. But with hundreds of sea officers on the beach and on half-pay, he needed more than an empty commission to carry him through. The *Heloise* could have been a stepping-stone for him. But promotion boards had short memories. *Heloise* lay on the bottom and not in the hands of a prize court.

If Don Carlos Quintana succeeded in vanquishing Garrick's defences, all the glory would go to him. The Admiralty would see too many red faces for Palliser to be remembered as anything but an embarrassment.

There was a solitary bang, and another waterspout shot skywards, well clear of the Spaniard's hull.

Palliser said, 'Garrick's strength was a bluff after all. Damn him, the Dons must be laughing their heads off at us. We found their treasure for them and now we're made to watch them take it!'

Bolitho saw the Spaniard's yards swinging slowly and ponderously, her main-course being brailed up as she edged past another spine of coral. To the anchored vessels in the lagoon she would make a fiercesome spectacle when she presented herself.

He heard someone murmur, 'They'm puttin' down boats.'

Bolitho saw two boats being swayed out from the *San Augustin*'s upper deck and then lowered alongside. It was not

smartly done, and as the men tumbled into them and cast off,
Bolitho guessed that their captain had no intention of heaving
to on a lee shore, with the added threat of a heavy cannon
nearby.

Instead of making for the spur of coral or for the island's
main foreshore, the boats forged ahead of their massive consort and were soon lost from view.

But not from the masthead lookout, who soon reported that
the boats were sounding the channel with lead and line to
protect their ship from running aground.

Bolitho found he could ignore Palliser's bitter outbursts,
just as he could admire the Spaniard's skill and impudence.
Don Carlos had likely fought the British in the past, and this
chance of humiliating them was not to be missed.

But when he glanced aft he saw that Dumaresq appeared
unworried, and was watching the other vessel more as a
disinterested spectator.

He was waiting. The thought struck Bolitho like a fist.
Dumaresq had been pretending all along. Goading the Spaniard
rather than the other way round.

Bulkley saw his expression and said thickly, 'Now I think I
understand.'

The Spaniard fired again to starboard, the smoke gushing
downwind in an unbroken bank. More fragments and dust
spewed away from the fall of shot, but no terrified figures
broke from cover, nor did any gun fire back at the brightly
flagged vessel.

Dumaresq snapped, 'Let her fall off two points to starboard.'
'Man the lee braces!'

The yards squeaked to the weight of men at the braces, and
leaning very slightly *Destiny* pointed her jib-boom towards
the flat-topped hill.

Bolitho waited for his own men to return to their stations.
He must be mistaken after all. Dumaresq was probably changing tack in readiness to come about and make a circular turn
until they were back on their original approach.

At that moment he heard a double explosion, like a rock
smashing through the side of a building. As he ran to the side
and peered across the water he saw something leap in the air
ahead of the Spanish ship and then drop from view just as
quickly.

The masthead yelled, 'One o' th' boats, sir! Shot clean in 'alf!'

Before the men on deck could recover from their surprise the whole hill-top erupted with a line of bright flashes. There must have been seven or eight of them.

Bolitho saw the water leap and boil around the Spaniard's counter and a jagged hole appear in a braced topsail.

Without a telescope it looked dangerous enough, but he heard Palliser shout, 'That sail's smouldering! Heated shot!'

The other balls had fallen on the ship's hidden side, and Bolitho saw the flash of sunlight on a glass as one of her officers ran to peer at the hill-top battery.

Then, as the *San Augustin* fired again, the carefully sited battery replied. Against the Spaniard's heavy broadside, the returned fire was made at will, each shot individually laid and aimed.

Smoke spurted from the ship's upper deck, and Bolitho saw objects being flung outboard and more smoke from her poop as flames took hold.

Dumaresq was saying, 'Waited until she had passed the point of reason, Mr Palliser. Garrick is not such a fool that he wants his channel blocked by a sunken ship!' He thrust out his arm, pointing at the smoke as the vessel's fore-topgallant mast and yard plunged down into the water. 'Look well. That is where *Destiny* would have been if I had yielded to temptation!'

The Spaniard's firing was becoming haphazard and wild, and the shots were smashing harmlessly into solid rock or ricocheting across the water like flying fish.

From *Destiny*'s decks it appeared as if the *San Augustin* was embedded in coral as she drove slowly into the lagoon, the hull trailing smoke, her canvas already pitted with holes.

Palliser said, 'Why doesn't he come about?'

All his anger for the Spaniards had gone. Instead he was barely able to hide his anxiety for the stricken ship. She had looked so proud and majestic. Now, marked down by the relentless bombardment, she was heading into helpless submission.

Bolitho turned as he heard the surgeon murmur, 'A sight I'll not forget. Ever.' He removed his glasses and polished them fiercely. 'Like something I was once made to learn.

        'Far away where sky met sea
        A majestic figure grew
        Pushed along by royal decree
        Her aggressive pennants flew.'

He smiled sadly. 'Now it sounds like an epitaph.'

A rumbling explosion echoed against *Destiny*'s hull, and they saw black smoke drifting above the lagoon and blotting out the anchored vessels completely.

Dumaresq said calmly, 'She'll strike.' He ignored Palliser's protest. 'Her captain has no choice, don't you see that?' He looked along his own ship and saw Bolitho watching him. 'What would you do? Strike your colours or have your people burn?'

Bolitho heard more explosions, either from the battery or from within the Spaniard's hull. Like Bulkley, he found it hard to believe. A great ship, beautiful in her arrogance, and now this. He thought of it happening here, to his own ship and companions. Danger they could face, it was part of their calling. But to be changed in the twinkling of an eye from a disciplined company to a rabble, hemmed in by renegades and pirates who would kill a man for the price of a drink, was a nightmare.

'Stand by to come about, Mr Palliser. We will steer east.'

Palliser said nothing. In his mind's eye he was probably seeing the utter despair aboard the Spanish ship, although with a more experienced understanding than Bolitho's. They would see *Destiny*'s masts turning as she stood away from the shore, and in that they would recognize their own defeat.

Dumaresq added, 'Then I shall explain what I intend.'

Bolitho and Rhodes looked at one another. So it was not over. It had not even begun.

Palliser closed the screen door quickly, as if he expected an enemy to be listening.

'Rounds completed, sir. The ship is completely darkened as ordered.'

Bolitho waited with the other officers and warrant officers in Dumaresq's cabin, feeling their doubts and anxieties, but sharing the chilling excitement nonetheless.

All day, *Destiny* had tacked slowly back and forth in the

blazing sunshine, Fougeaux Island always close abeam, although not near enough to be hit by any battery. For hours they had waited, and some had hoped until the last that the *San Augustin* would emerge again, somehow freeing herself from the lagoon to join them. There had been nothing. More to the point, there had been no terrible explosion and the aftermath of flying wreckage which would have proclaimed the Spaniard's final destruction. Had she blown up, most of the anchored vessels in the lagoon would have perished, too. In some ways the silence had been worse.

Dumaresq looked around their intent faces. It was very hot in the sealed and shuttered cabin, and they were all stripped to their shirts and breeches. They looked more like conspirators than King's officers, Bolitho thought.

Dumaresq said, 'We have waited a whole day, gentlemen. It is what Garrick would have expected. He will have anticipated each move, believe me.'

Midshipman Merrett sniffed and rubbed his nose with his sleeve, but Dumaresq's eyes froze him into stillness.

'Garrick will have made his plans with care. He will know I have sent to Antigua for aid. Whatever chance we had of bottling him in his lair until that support arrived vanished when *San Augustin* made her play.' He leaned on his table, his hands encircling the chart he had laid there. 'Nothing stands between Garrick and his ambitions elsewhere but *this ship*.' He let his words sink in. 'I had few fears on that score, gentlemen. We can tackle Garrick's flotilla when it breaks out, fight them together, or run them down piecemeal. But things have changed. Today's silence has proved that.'

Palliser asked, 'D'you mean he'll use the *San Augustin* against us, sir?'

Dumaresq's eyes flashed with sudden anger at the interruption. Then he said almost mildly, 'Eventually, yes.'

Feet shuffled, and Bolitho heard several voices murmuring with sudden alarm.

Dumaresq said, 'Don Carlos Quintana will have surrendered, although he may have fallen in the first engagement. For his sake, I hope that was so. He will receive little mercy at the hands of those murdering scum. Which is something *you* will bear in mind, do I make myself clear?'

Bolitho found he was clenching and unclenching his hands.

His palms felt clammy, and he knew it was the same sickness of fear which had followed the attack on the island. His wound started to throb as if to remind him, and he had to stare at the deck until his mind cleared again.

Dumaresq said, 'You will recall the first shots at the Spaniard? From a single cannon to the west'rd of the hill. They were deliberately fired badly to encourage the intruder into their trap. Once past the point they used the battery and some heated shot to create panic and final submission. It gives an idea of Garrick's cunning. He was prepared to risk setting her afire rather than allow her amongst his carefully collected flotilla. And Don Carlos might well have persevered against an ordinary bombardment, although I doubt if he would have succeeded.'

Feet moved overhead, and Bolitho imagined the men up there on watch, without their officers, wondering what schemes were being hatched, and who would pay for them with his life.

He could also picture the ship, without lights and carrying little canvas as she ghosted through the darkness.

'Tomorrow Garrick will still be watching us, to see what we intend. We shall continue throughout the day, patrolling, nothing more. It will do two things. Show Garrick that we expect assistance, also that we have no intention of leaving. Garrick will know time is running out and will endeavour to hasten things along.'

Gulliver asked uneasily, 'Won't that be the wrong thing to do, sir? Why not leave him be and wait for the squadron?'

'Because I do not believe the squadron *will* come.' Dumaresq eyed the master's astonishment blandly. 'Fitzpatrick, the acting-governor, may well delay my despatches until he is relieved of his own responsibility. By then it will be too late anyway.' He gave a slow smile. 'It is no use, Mr Gulliver, you must accept your fate, as I do.'

Palliser said, 'Us against a forty-four, sir? I've no doubt Garrick's other craft will be fairly well armed, and may be experienced in this sort of game.'

Dumaresq appeared to grow tired of the discussion. 'To-morrow night, I intend to close the shore and drop four boats. I cannot hope to force the entrance myself, and Garrick will know this. He'll have guns laid on the channel anyway, so I'd still be at a grave disadvantage.'

Bolitho felt his stomach muscles tighten. A boat action. Always chancy, always difficult, even with the most experienced of hands.

Dumaresq continued, 'I will discuss the plans further when we see how the wind supports us. In the meantime, I can tell you this. Mr Palliser will take the cutter and the jolly-boat and land at the sou'-west point of the island. It is the best sheltered part and the least likeliest for an assault. He will be supported by Mr Rhodes, Mr Midshipman Henderson and . . .' his eyes moved deliberately to Slade, '. . . our senior master's mate.'

Bolitho glanced quickly at Rhodes and saw how pale his face seemed. There were tiny beads of sweat on his forehead, too.

The senior midshipman, Henderson, by comparison looked calm and eager. It was his first chance, and like Palliser he would soon be trying his luck for promotion. It would be uppermost on his mind until the actual moment came.

'There will be no moon, and as far as I can discover, the sea will be kind to us.' Dumaresq's stature seemed to grow and expand with his ideas. 'The pinnace will be lowered next, and will make for the reefs to the north-eastern end of the island.'

Bolitho waited, trying not to hold his breath. Knowing what was coming.

It was almost a relief when Dumaresq said, 'Mr Bolitho, you will take charge of the pinnace. You will be supported by Midshipmen Cowdroy and Jury, and an experienced gunner's mate with a complete gun's crew. You will find and seize that solitary cannon below the hill-side, and use it as I direct.' He smiled, but there was no warmth in his eyes. 'Lieutenant Colpoys can select a squad of picked marksmen and take them to cover Mr Bolitho's actions. You will please ensure that your marines discard their uniforms and make do with slop clothing like the seamen.'

Colpoys looked visibly shocked. Not by the prospect of being killed, but at the idea of seeing his marines clad in anything but their red coats.

Dumaresq examined their faces again. Perhaps to see the

relief of the ones who would be staying, the concern of those detailed for his reckless plan of attack.

He said slowly, 'In the meantime, I shall prepare the ship to give battle. For Garrick will come out, gentlemen. He has too much to lose by staying, and as *Destiny* will be his last witness he will be eager to destroy us.'

He had their full attention.

'And that is what he will have to do, before I let him pass!'

Palliser stood up. 'Dismiss.'

They moved to the door, mulling over Dumaresq's words, trying perhaps to see a last glimmer of hope that an open battle might be avoided.

Rhodes said quietly, 'Well, Dick, I think I shall take a large drink before I stand my watch tonight. I do not feel like brooding.'

Bolitho glanced at the midshipmen as they filed past. It must be far worse for them.

He said, 'I have done a cutting-out expedition myself. I expect that you and the first lieutenant will be told to excise one of the anchored vessels.' He shivered in spite of his guard. 'I don't fancy the prospect of taking that cannon from under their noses!'

They looked at each other, and then Rhodes said, 'The first one of us to return buys wine for the wardroom.'

Bolitho did not trust himself to answer but groped his way to the companion-ladder and up to the quarterdeck to resume his watch.

A large shadow sidled from the trunk of the mizzen-mast and Stockdale said in a hoarse whisper, 'Tomorrow night then, sir?' He did not wait for a reply. 'Felt it in me bones.' His palms scraped together in the darkness. 'You'd not be thinkin' of takin' anyone else as a gun-captain?'

His simple confidence helped to disperse Bolitho's anxiety more than he would have thought possible.

'We'll stay together.' He touched his arm impulsively. 'After this, you'll lament the day you ever quit the land!'

Stockdale rumbled a chuckle. 'Never. 'Ere, a man's got room to breathe!'

Yeames, master's mate of the watch, grinned. 'I don't reckon that bloody pirate knows what 'e's in for, sir. Old Stockdale'll trim 'is beard for 'im!'

Bolitho walked to the weather side and began to pace slowly up and down. Where was she now, he wondered? In some ship heading for another land, a life he would never share.

If only she would come to him now, as she had on that other incredible night. She would understand. Would hold him tenderly and drive back the fear which was ripping him apart. And there was another long day to endure before they would begin the next act. He could not possibly survive this time, and he guessed that fate had never intended it otherwise.

Midshipman Jury shaded the compass-light with his hands to examine the swinging card and then looked across at the slowly pacing figure. Just to be like him would be the only reward he could ever want. So steady and confident, and never too impatient or hasty with a quick rebuke like Palliser, or scathing like Slade. Perhaps his father had been a bit like Richard Bolitho at that age, he thought. He hoped so.

Yeames cleared his throat and said, 'Best get ready to pipe the mornin'-watch, sir, though I fear it'll be a long day today.'

Jury hurried away, thinking of what lay ahead, and wondering why he was not apprehensive any more. He was going with the third lieutenant, and to Ian Jury, aged fourteen years, that was reward enough.

Bolitho had known the waiting would be bad, but throughout the day, as *Destiny*'s company laid out the equipment and weapons which would be required for the landing-parties, he felt his nerves stretching to breaking-point. Whenever he looked up from his work, or came on deck from the cool darkness of one of the holds, the bare, hostile island was always there. Although his knowledge and training told him that *Destiny* covered and re-covered her track again and again during the day, it seemed as if they had never moved, that the island, with its fortress-like hill, was waiting, just for him.

Towards dusk, Gulliver laid the ship on a new tack to take her well clear of the island. The masthead lookouts had been unable to sight any sort of activity, so well sheltered was the lagoon, but Dumaresq had no doubts. Garrick would have watched their every move, and the fact *Destiny* had never tacked closer inshore might have helped to shake his confidence, to make him believe that help was already on the way for that solitary frigate.

Eventually, Dumaresq called his officers aft to the cabin. It was much as before, hot and clammy, the air penned in by the shutters so that they were all soon sweating freely.

They had gone over it again and again. Surely nothing on their part could go wrong? Even the wind favoured them. It remained from the south-west, and although slightly fresher than before, gave no hint that it might turn against them.

Dumaresq leaned on his table and said gravely, 'It is time, gentlemen. You will leave here to prepare your boats. All I can do is wish you well. To ask for luck would be an insult to each of you.'

Bolitho tried to relax his body, limb by limb. He could not begin the action like this. Any one fault would break him in pieces, and he knew it.

He plucked the shirt away from his stomach and thought of the time he had purposefully donned a clean one, just to meet her on deck. Perhaps this was the same hopeless gesture. Unlike changing into clean clothing before a battle at sea to avoid infecting a wound, this was something personal. There would be no Bulkleys on that evil island, no one to see the purpose of his reasoning, or to care.

Dumaresq said, 'I intend to lower the cutter and jolly-boat in an hour. We should be in position to drop the launch and pinnace by midnight.' His gaze moved to Bolitho. 'Although it will be a harder pull for your people, your cover will be better.' He checked off the points on his strong fingers. 'Make certain your muskets and pistols remain unloaded until you are sure there will be no accidents. Examine all the gear and tackle you need before you enter the boats. Talk to your people.' He spoke gently, almost caressingly. '*Talk* to them. They are your strength, and will be watching you to see how you measure up.'

Feet padded across the deck above and tackle scraped noisily along the planking. *Destiny* was heaving to.

Dumaresq added, 'Tomorrow is your worst day. You will lie in hiding and do nothing. If an alarm is raised, I cannot save you.'

Midshipman Merrett tapped at the door and then called, 'Mr Yeames' respects, sir, and we are hove to.'

With the cabin pitching unsteadily from side to side, it was rather unnecessary, and Bolitho was amazed to see several of those present grinning and nudging each other.

Even Rhodes, whom he knew to be worried sick about the coming action, was smiling broadly. It was that same madness returning. Perhaps it was better this way.

They moved out of the cabin and were soon swallowed up by their own groups of men.

Mr Timbrell's hoisting-party had already swayed out the jolly-boat, and the cutter followed shortly over the nettings and then into the slapping water alongside. There was suddenly no time for anything. In the enclosing darkness a few hands darted out for brief clasps, voices murmured to friends and companions, a 'good luck', or 'we'll show 'em'. And then it was done, the boats wallowing round in the swell before heading away towards the island.

'Get the ship under way, Mr Gulliver.' Dumaresq turned his back on the sea, as if he had already dismissed Palliser and the two boats.

Bolitho saw Jury talking with young Merrett, and wondered if the latter was glad he was staying aboard. It was incredible to consider how much had happened in so few months since they had all come together as one company.

Dumaresq moved silently to his side. 'More waiting, Mr Bolitho. I wish I could make her fly for you.' He gave a deep chuckle. 'But there never was an easy way.'

Bolitho touched his scar with one finger. Bulkley had removed the stitches, and yet he always expected to feel the same agony, the same sense of despair as when he had been cut down.

Dumaresq said suddenly, 'Mr Palliser and his brave fellows will be well under way by now. But I must not think of them any more. Not as people or friends, until it is over.' He turned away, adding briefly, 'One day you will understand.'

15

A Moment's Courage

Bolitho attempted to rise to his feet, gripping Stockdale's shoulder for support as the *Destiny*'s pinnace lifted and plunged across a succession of violent breakers. In spite of the night air and the spray which continually dashed over the gunwale, Bolitho felt feverishly hot. The closer the boat drew to the hidden island the more dangerous it became. And most of his men had thought the first part had been the worst. Being cast adrift by their parent ship and left to pull with all their might for the shore. Now they knew differently, not least their third lieutenant.

Occasionally, and now more frequently, jagged fangs of rock and coral surged past, the white water foaming amongst them to give the impression they and not the boat were moving.

Gasping and cursing, the oarsmen tried to maintain the stroke, but even that was broken every now and then as one of them had to lever his loom from its rowlock to save the blade from being splintered on a tooth of rock.

The yawing motion made thinking difficult, and Bolitho had to strain his mind to recall Dumaresq's instructions and Gulliver's gloomy predictions about their final approach. No wonder Garrick felt secure. No vessel of any size could work inshore amongst this strewn carpet of broken coral. It was bad enough for the pinnace. Bolitho tried not to think about *Destiny*'s thirty-four-foot launch which was following them somewhere astern. Or he hoped it was. The extra boat was carrying Colpoys and his marksmen, as well as additional charges of gunpowder. What with Palliser's large party which had already been put ashore on the south-west of the island, and Bolitho's own men, Dumaresq was short-handed indeed. If he had to fight, he would also need to run. The idea of Dumaresq fleeing in retreat was so absurd that it helped to sustain Bolitho in some way.

'Watch out, forrard!' That was the boatswain's mate Ellis Pearse up in the bows. A very experienced seaman, he had been sounding with a boat's lead-and-line for part of the way, but was now acting as a lookout as one more rock loomed out of the darkness.

The noise seemed so great that somebody on the shore must hear them. But Bolitho knew enough to understand that the din of the sea and surf would more than drown the clatter of oars, the desperate thrusts with boat-hooks and fists to fight their way past the treacherous rocks. Had there been even a glimmer of moon it might have been different. Strangely enough, a small boat stood out more clearly to a vigilant lookout than a full-rigged ship standing just offshore. As many a Cornish smuggler had found out to his cost.

Pearse called hoarsely, 'Land ahead!'

Bolitho raised one hand to show he had heard and almost tumbled headlong.

It had seemed as if the broken rocks and the mill-race of water amongst them would never end. Then he saw it, a pale suggestion of land rising above the drifting spray. Much larger close to.

He dug his fingers into Stockdale's shoulder. It felt like solid oak beneath his sodden shirt.

'Easy now, Stockdale! A little to starboard, I think!'

Josh Little, gunner's mate, growled, 'Two 'ands! Ready to go!'

Bolitho saw two seamen crouching over the creaming water and hoped he had not misjudged the depth.

Somewhere astern he heard a grating thud, and then some splashing commotion of oars as the launch regained her balance. It had probably grazed the last big rock, Bolitho thought.

Little chuckled. 'I'll bet that rattled the bullocks!' Then he touched the man nearest him. *'Go!'*

The seaman, as naked as the day he was born, dropped

over the side, hung for a few moments kicking and spitting out water, and then gasped, 'Sandy bottom!'

'Easy all!' Stockdale swung the tiller-bar. 'Ready about!'

Eventually, stern on to the beach, the pinnace backed-water, and aided by two men gripping the gunwales surged the last few yards on to firm sand.

With the ease of a man lifting a stick from a pathway, Stockdale unshipped the rudder and hauled it inboard as the pinnace rose once again before riding noisily on to a small beach.

'Clear the boat!'

Bolitho staggered up the beach, feeling the receding surf dragging at his feet and legs. Men stumbled past him, snatching their weapons, while others waded into deeper water to guide the launch on to a safe stretch of sand.

The first seaman who had been detailed to go outboard from the pinnace was struggling to pull on his trousers and shirt, but Little said, 'Later, matey! Just shift yerself up to the top!'

Somebody laughed as the dripping seaman hopped past, and again Bolitho marvelled that they could still find room for humour.

' 'Ere comes the launch!'

Little groaned. 'Hell's teeth! Like a pack o' bloody cler-gymen!' Hoisting his great belly over his belt, he strode down to the surf again, his voice lashing at the confusion of men and oars like a whip.

Midshipman Cowdroy was already clambering up a steep slope to the left of the beach, some men close at his heels. Jury remained by the boat, watching as the last of the weapons, powder and shot and their meagre rations were passed hand to hand to the shelter of the ridge.

Lieutenant Colpoys sloshed through the sand and exclaimed sharply, 'In God's name, Richard, surely there must be a better way of fighting a battle?' He paused to watch his marines as they loped past, their long muskets held high to escape the spray and sand. 'Ten good marksmen,' he re-marked absently. 'Damn well wasted, if you ask me.'

Bolitho peered up at the ridge. It was just possible to see where it made an edge with the sky. They had to get over it and into their hiding-place without delay. And they had about four hours to do it.

'Come on.' He turned and waved to the two boats. 'Shove off. Good luck.'

He deliberately kept his voice low, but nevertheless the men nearest him stopped to watch the boats. Now it would be really clear to all of them. In an hour or two those same boats would be hoisted to the safety of their tier aboard *Destiny* and their crews would be free to rest, to put the tension and danger behind them.

How quickly they seemed to move, Bolitho thought. Without their extra passengers and weapons they were already fading into the shadows, outlined only occasionally by the spray as it broke over their oars.

Colpoys said quietly, 'Gone.' He looked down at his mixed garb of sea officer's shirt and pair of moleskin breeches. 'I'll never live this down.' Then, surprisingly, he grinned. 'But still, it will make the colonel sit up and take notice when I next see him, what?'

Midshipman Cowdroy came slithering back down the slope. 'Shall I send scouts on ahead, sir?'

Colpoys regarded him coldly. 'I shall send two of *my* men.'

He snapped out a curt order and two marines melted into the gloom like ghosts.

Bolitho said, 'This is your kind of work, John.' He wiped his forehead with his shirt-sleeve. 'Tell me if I do anything wrong.'

Colpoys shrugged. 'I'd rather have my job than yours.' He clapped him on the arm. 'But we stand or fall together.' He glared round for his orderly. 'Load my pistols and keep by me, Thomas.'

Bolitho looked for Jury but he was already there.

'Ready?'

Jury nodded firmly. 'Aye, ready, sir.'

Bolitho hesitated and peered down at the small sliver of sand where they had come ashore. The surf was still boiling amongst the reefs, but even the marks of the boats' keels had been washed away. They were quite alone.

It was hard to accept that this was the same small island. Four miles long and less than two miles from north to south.

It felt like another country, somewhere which when daylight came would be seen stretching away to the horizon.

Colpoys knew his trade well. Bulkley had mentioned that the debonair marine had once been attached to a line regiment, and it seemed very likely. He threw out his pickets, sent his best scouts well ahead of the rest and retained the heavier-footed seamen for carrying the food, powder and shot. Thirty men in all, and Palliser had about the same number. Dumaresq would be thankful to get his boat crews back aboard, Bolitho thought.

And yet in spite of all the preparations, the confident manner in which Colpoys arranged the men into manageable files, Bolitho had to face the fact that he was in charge. The men were fanning out on either side of him, stumbling along on the loose stones and sand and content to leave their safety to Colpoys' keen-eyed scouts.

Bolitho controlled the sudden alarm as it coursed through him. It was like being on watch that first time. The ship running through the night with only you who could change things with a word, or a cry for help.

He heard a heavy tread beside him and saw Stockdale striding along, his cutlass across one shoulder.

Without effort Bolitho could picture him carrying his body down to the boat, to rally the remaining seamen and to call for assistance. But for this strange, hoarse-voiced man he would be dead. It was a comfort to have him at his side again.

Colpoys said, 'Not far now.' He spat grit from his teeth. 'If that fool Gulliver is mistaken, I'll split him like a pig!' He laughed lightly. 'But then, if he *is* wrong, I shall be denied that privilege, eh?'

In the darkness a man slipped and fell, dropping his cutlass and a grapnel with a clatter.

For an instant everyone froze, and then a marine called, 'All quiet, sir.'

Bolitho heard a sharp blow and knew that Midshipman Cowdroy had struck the awkward seaman with the flat of his hanger. If Cowdroy turned his back during any fighting, it was unlikely he would ever live to be a lieutenant.

Bolitho sent Jury on ahead, and when he returned breathless and gasping he said, 'We're there, sir.' He waved vaguely towards the ridge. 'I could hear the sea.'

Colpoys sent his orderly to halt the pickets. 'So far so good. We must be in the center of the island. When it's light enough I'll fix our position.'

The seamen and marines, unused to the uneven ground and the hard march from the beach, crowded together beneath an overhanging spur of rock. It was cool and smelled damp, as if there were caves nearby.

In a matter of hours it would be a furnace.

'Post your lookouts. Then we'll issue food and water. It may be a long while before we get another chance.'

Bolitho unclipped his hanger and sat down with his back against the bare rock. He thought of his climb to the main cross-trees with the captain, his first sight of this bleak, menacing island. Now he was here.

Jury stooped over him. 'I'm not sure where to post the lookouts on the lower slope, sir.'

Bolitho pushed the weariness aside and somehow lurched to his feet.

'Come with me, I'll show you. Next time, you'll know.'

Colpoys was holding a flask of warm wine to his lips and paused to watch them vanish into the darkness.

The third lieutenant had come a long, long way since Plymouth, he thought. He might be young, but he acted with the authority of a veteran.

Bolitho wiped the dust from his telescope and tried to wriggle his prone body into a comfortable position. It was early morning, and yet the rock and sand were already hot, and his skin prickled so that he wanted to tear off his shirt and scratch himself all over.

Colpoys slid across the ground and joined him. He held out a fistful of dried grass, almost the only thing which survived here in little rock crannies where the rare rainfalls sustained it.

He said, 'Cover the glass with it. Any reflected light on the lens and the alarm will be raised.'

Bolitho nodded, sparing his voice and breath. Very carefully he levelled the glass and began to move it slowly from side to side. There were several small ridges, like the one

which they were using to conceal themselves from enemy and
sun alike, but all were dwarfed by the flat-topped hill. It shut
off the sea directly ahead of his telescope, but to his right he
could see the end of the lagoon and some six anchored vessels
there. Schooners, as far as he could tell, pinned down by the
glare, and with only one small boat cutting a pattern on the
glittering water. Beyond and around them the curved arm of
rock and coral ran to the left, but the opening and the channel
to the sea were hidden by the hill.

Bolitho moved the glass again and concentrated on the land
at the far end of the lagoon. Nothing moved, and yet somewhere there Palliser and his men were lying in hiding,
marooned, with the sea at their backs. He guessed that the
San Augustin, if she was still afloat, was on the opposite side
of the hill, beneath the hill-top battery which had beaten her
into submission.

Colpoys had his own telescope trained towards the western
end of the island. 'There, Richard. Huts. A whole line of
them.'

Bolitho moved his glass, pausing only to rub the sweat
from his eyes. The huts were small and crude and without any
sort of window. Probably for storing weapons and other
booty, he thought. The glass misted over and then sharpened
again as he saw a tiny figure appear on the top of a low ridge.
A man in a white shirt, spreading his arms wide and probably
yawning. He walked unhurriedly towards the side of the
ridge, and what Bolitho had taken to be a slung musket
proved to be a long telescope. This he opened in the same
unhurried fashion and began to examine the sea, from side to
side and from the shore to the hard blue line of the horizon.
Several times he returned his scrutiny to a point concealed by
the hill, and Bolitho guessed he had sighted Destiny, outwardly cruising on her station as before. The thought brought
a pang to his heart, a mixture of loss and longing.

Colpoys said softly, 'That is where the gun is. Our gun,'
he added meaningly.

Bolitho tried again, the ridges merging and separating in a
growing heat-haze. But the marine was right. Just beyond the
solitary lookout was a canvas hump. It was almost certainly
the solitary gun which had made such a pretence at bad
markmanship to lure the Spaniard past the point.

Colpoys was murmuring, 'Put there to offer covering fire for any anchored prizes, I shouldn't wonder.'

They looked at each other, seeing the sudden importance of their part in the attack. The gun had to be taken if Palliser was to be allowed to move from his hiding-place. Once discovered, he would be pinned down by the carefully sited cannon and then slaughtered at leisure. As if to add weight to the idea, a column of men moved from the hill-side and made for the line of huts.

Colpoys said, 'God, look at 'em. Must be a couple of hundred at least!'

And they were certainly not prisoners. They strolled along in twos and threes, the dust rising from their feet like an army on the march. Some boats appeared in the lagoon and more men could be seen at the water's edge with long spars and coils of rope. It seemed likely they were about to rig sheer-legs in readiness for hauling cargo down to the boats.

Dumaresq had been right. Again. Garrick's men were preparing to leave.

Bolitho looked at Colpoys. 'Suppose we're wrong about the *San Augustin*? Just because we cannot see her doesn't mean she's disabled.'

Colpoys was still looking at the men by the huts. 'I agree. Only one way to find out.' He twisted his head as Jury came breathlessly up the slope. 'Keep down!'

Jury flushed and threw himself beside Bolitho. 'Mr Cowdroy wants to know if he can issue some more water, sir.' His eyes moved past Bolitho to the activity on the beach.

'Not yet. Tell him to keep his people hidden. One sight or sound and we'll be done for.' He nodded towards the lagoon. 'Then come back. Do you feel like a stroll?' He saw the youth's eyes widen and then calm again.

'Yes, sir.'

As Jury dropped out of sight, Colpoys asked, 'Why him? He's just a boy.'

Bolitho levelled his glass once again. 'At first light tomorrow *Destiny* will make a feint attack on the entrance. It will be hazardous enough, but if the *San Augustin*'s artillery is ranged on her as well as the hill-top battery, she could be crippled, even wrecked. So we have to know what we are up against.' He nodded towards the opposite end of the lagoon.

'The first lieutenant has his orders. He will attack the moment the island's defences are distracted by *Destiny*.' He met the marine's troubled gaze, hoping he looked more confident than he felt. 'And we must be ready to support him. But if I had to choose, I would say that yours is the greater value to this escapade. So I shall go myself and take Mr Jury as messenger.' He looked away. 'If I fall today . . .'

Colpoys punched his arm. 'Fall? Then we shall follow so swiftly, Saint Peter will need to muster all hands!'

Together they measured the distance to the other low ridge. Someone had rolled up part of the canvas and one wheel of a military cannon was clearly visible.

Colpoys said bitterly, 'French, I'll lay any odds on it!'

Jury returned and waited for Bolitho to speak. Bolitho unbuckled his belt and handed it to the marine.

To Jury he said, 'Leave everything but your dirk.' He tried to smile. 'We're travelling like gentlemen of the road today!'

Colpoys shook his head. 'You'll stand out like milestones!' He removed his flask and held it out the them. 'Douse yourselves and then roll in the dust. It will help, but not much.'

Eventually, dirty and crumpled, they were ready to go.

Colpoys said, 'Don't forget. No quarter. It's better to die than to be taken by those savages.'

Down a steep slope and then into a narrow gully. Bolitho imagined that every fall of loose stones sounded like a landslide. And yet, out of sight from the lagoon and the ridge where he had left Colpoys with his misgivings, it seemed strangely peaceful. As Colpoys had remarked earlier, there were no bird droppings, which implied that few birds came to this desolate place. There was nothing more likely to reveal their stealthy approach than some squawking alarm from a dozen different nests.

The sun rose higher, and the rocks glowed with heat which enfolded their bodies like a kiln. They stripped off their shirts and tied them around their heads like turbans, and each gripping his bared blade, ready for instant use, they looked as much like pirates as the men they were hunting.

Jury's hand gripped his arm. ''There! Up there! A sentry!''

Bolitho pulled Jury down beside him, feeling the midshipman's tension giving way to sick horror. The 'sentry' had been one of Don Carlos' officers. His body was nailed to a post facing the sun, and his once-proud uniform was covered in dried blood.

Jury said in a husky whisper, 'His eyes! They put out his eyes!'

Bolitho swallowed hard. 'Come on. We've a way to go yet.'

They finally reached a pile of fallen boulders, some of which were scarred and blackened, and Bolitho guessed they had been hurled down by *San Augustin*'s opening broadside.

He eased his body between two of the boulders, feeling their heat on his skin, the painful throbbing of the scar above his eye as he pushed and dragged himself into a cleft where he would not be seen. He felt Jury pressing behind him, his sweat mingling with his own as he slowly lifted his head and stared at the lagoon.

He had been expecting to see the captured Spaniard aground, or being sacked and looted by the victorious pirates. But there was discipline here, a purpose of movement which made him realize what he was watching. The *San Augustin* was at anchor, and her upper deck and rigging were alive with men. Splicing, hammering, sawing and hoisting fresh cordage up to the yards. She could have been any man-of-war anywhere.

Her fore-topgallant mast, which had been shot away in the short battle, was already being replaced by a professional-looking jury-rig, and from the way the men were working, Bolitho knew they must be some of her original company. Here and there about the ship's deck stood figures who did not take part in the frantic activity. They stood by swivel-guns or with muskets at the ready. Bolitho thought of the tortured, eyeless thing on the hill-side and tasted the bile in this throat. No wonder the Spaniards worked for their captors. They had been given an horrific lesson, and doubtless others besides, to break any resistance before it began.

Boats glided alongside the anchored ship, and tackles were lowered immediately, with big nets to hoist cases and great chests over her bulwarks.

One boat, separate from all the rest, was being pulled slowly around the *San Augustin*'s stern. A small, stiff-backed man with a neatly clipped beard was standing in the sternsheets, pointing with a black stick, jabbing at the air to emphasize a point for the benefit of his companions.

Even in distance there was something autocratic and arrogant about the man. Someone who had gained power and respect from treachery and murder. It had to be Sir Piers Garrick.

Now he was leaning on the boat's gunwale, pointing with his stick again, and Bolitho saw that the *San Augustin*'s bilge was showing slightly, and Garrick was probably ordering a change of trim, some cargo or shot to be shifted to give his new prize the best sailing quality he could manage.

Jury whispered, 'What are they doing, sir?'

'The *San Augustin* is preparing to leave.' He rolled on his back, oblivious to the jagged stones as he tried to think clearly. '*Destiny* cannot fight them all. We must act now.'

He saw the frown on Jury's face. He had never thought otherwise. *Was I like him once? So trusting that I believed we can never be beaten?*

He said, 'See? More boats are coming down to her. Garrick's treasure. It has all been for this. His own flotilla, and now a forty-four-gun ship to do with as he will. Captain Dumaresq was right. There is nothing to stop him.' He smiled gravely. 'But *Destiny*.'

Bolitho could see it as if it had already happened. *Destiny* standing close inshore to provide a diversion for Palliser, while all the time the captured *San Augustin* lay here, like a tiger ready to pounce. In confined waters, *Destiny* would stand no chance at all.

'We must get back.'

Bolitho lowered himself through the boulders, his mind still refusing to accept what had to be done.

Colpoys could barely hide his relief as they scrambled up to join him on the ridge.

He said, 'They've been working all the time. Clearing those huts. They've slaves with them too, poor devils. I saw more than one laid flat by a piece of chain.'

Colpoys fell silent until Bolitho had finished describing what he had seen.

Then he said, 'Look here. I know what you're thinking. Because this is a damnable, rotten useless island which nobody cares about and precious few have even heard of, you feel cheated. Unwilling to risk lives, your own included. But it's like that. Big battles and waving flags are rare. This will be described as a skirmish, an "incident", if you must know. But it *matters* if we think it does.' He lay back and studied Bolitho calmly. 'I say to hell with caution. We'll go for that cannon without waiting for the dawn tomorrow. They've nothing else which will bear on the lagoon. All the other guns are dug-in on the hill-top. It will take hours to shift 'em.' He grinned. 'A whole battle can be won or lost in that time!'

Bolitho took the telescope again, his hands shaking as he trained it on the ridge and the partly covered cannon. It was even the same lookout as before.

Jury said huskily, 'They've stopped work.'

'No wonder.' Colpoys shaded his eyes. 'See yonder, young fellow. Isn't that a cause enough for dying?'

Destiny moved slowly into view, her topsails and topgallants very pale against the hard blue sky.

Bolitho stared at her, imagining her sounds now lost in distance, her smells, her familiarity.

He felt like a man dying of thirst as he sees a wine jar in a desert's image. Or someone on his way to the gallows who pauses to listen to an early sparrow. Each knows that tomorrow there will be no wine, and no birds will sing.

He said flatly, 'Let's be about it then. I'll tell the others. If only there was some way of informing Mr Palliser.'

Colpoys backed down the slope. Then he looked at Bolitho, his eyes yellow in the sunlight.

'He'll know, Richard. The whole damned island will!'

Colpoys wiped his face and neck with his handkerchief. It was afternoon, and the blazing heat thrown back at them from the rocks was sheer torment.

But waiting had paid off. Most of the activity around the huts had ceased, and smoke from several fires drifted towards the hidden seamen and marines, bringing smells of roasting meat as an additional torture.

Colpoys said, 'They'll rest after they've eaten.' He glanced at his corporal. 'Issue the rations and water, Dyer.' To Bolitho he added quietly, 'I estimate that gun to be a cable's distance from us.' He squinted his eyes as he examined the slope and the steep climb to the other ridge. 'If we start, there'll be no stopping. I think there are several men with the cannon. Probably in some sort of magazine underground.' He took a cup of water from his orderly and sipped it slowly. 'Well?'

Bolitho lowered the telescope and rested his forehead on his arm. 'We'll risk it.'

He tried not to measure it in his mind. Two hundred yards across open ground, and then what?

He said tightly, 'Little and his crew can take care of the gun. We'll attack the ridge from both sides at once. Mr Cowdroy can take charge of the second party.' He saw Colpoys grimace and added, 'He's the senior one of the pair, and he's experienced.'

Colpoys nodded. 'I'll place my marksmen where they'll do the most good. Once you've taken the ridge, I'll support you.' He held out his hand. 'If you fail, I'll lead the shortest bayonet-charge in the Corps' history!'

And then, all of a sudden they were ready. The earlier uncertainty and tension was gone, wiped away, and the men gathered in their tight little groups with grim but determined faces. Josh Little with his gun-crew, festooned with the tools of their trade, and extra charges of powder and some shot.

Midshipman Cowdroy, his petulant face set in a scowl, had already drawn his hanger and was checking his pistol. Ellis Pearse, boatswain's mate, carried his own weapon, a fearsome, double-edged boarding-cutlass which had been made specially for him by a blacksmith. The marines had dispersed amongst the rocks, their long muskets probing the open ground and further towards the flat-topped hill-side.

Bolitho stood up and looked at his own men. Dutchy Vorbink, Olsson, the mad Swede, Bill Bunce, an ex-poacher, Kennedy, a man who had escaped jail by volunteering for the Navy, and many others he had come to know so well.

Stockdale wheezed, 'I'll be with you, sir.'

Their eyes met.

'Not this time. You stay with Little. That gun has got to be taken, Stockdale. Without it we might as well die here and now.' He touched his thick arm. 'Believe me. We are all depending on you today.'

He turned away, unable to watch the big man's pain.

To Jury he said, 'You can keep with Lieutenant Colpoys.'

'Is that an order, sir?'

Bolitho saw the boy's chin lift stubbornly. What were they trying to do to him?

He replied, 'No.'

A man whispered, 'The sentry's climbed down out of sight!'

Little chuckled. 'Gone for a wet.'

Bolitho found that his feet were already over the edge and his hanger glinting in the sunlight as he pointed towards the opposite ridge.

'Come on then! *At 'em, lads!*'

Heedless now of noise and deception, they charged down the slope, their feet kicking up dust and stones, their breath rasping fiercely, as they kept their eyes fixed on the ridge. They reached the bottom of the slope and pounded across open ground, oblivious to everything but the hidden gun.

Somewhere, a million miles away, someone yelled, and a shot whined across the hill-side. More voices swelled and faded as the men by the lagoon stampeded for their weapons, probably imagining that they were under attack from the sea.

Three heads suddenly appeared on the top of the ridge even as the first of Bolitho's men reached the foot. Colpoys' muskets banged seemingly ineffectually and from far away, but two of the heads vanished, and the third man bounded in the air before rolling down the slope amongst the British sailors.

'Come on!' Bolitho waved his hanger. '*Faster!*'

From one side a musket fired past him, and a seaman fell clutching his thigh, and then sprawled sobbing as his companions charged on towards the top.

Bolitho's breath felt like hot sand in his lungs as he leapt over a crude parapet of stones. More shots hammered past him, and he knew some of his men had fallen.

He saw the glint of metal, a wheel of the cannon beneath its canvas cover, and yelled, 'Watch out!'

But from beneath the canvas one of the hidden men fired a fully charged musketoon into the advancing seamen. One was hurled on his back, his face and most of his skull blasted away, and three others fell kicking in their own blood.

With a roar like an enraged beast, Pearse threw himself from the opposite of the gun-pit and slashed the canvas apart with his double-edged blade.

A figure ran from the pit, covering his head with his hands and screaming, 'Quarter! Quarter!'

Pearse threw back his arm and yelled, 'Quarter, you bugger! Take that!' The great blade hit the man across the nape of the neck, so that his head dropped forward on to his chest.

Midshipman Cowdroy's party swarmed over the other side of the ridge, and as Pearse led his men into the pit to complete his gory victory, Little and Stockdale were already down with the cannon, while their crew ran to discover if there was any life in the nearby furnace.

The seamen were like mad things. Yelling and cheering, pausing only to haul their wounded companions to safety, they roared all the louder as Pearse emerged from the pit with a great jar of wine.

Bolitho shouted, 'Take up your muskets! Here come the marines!'

Once again the seamen threw themselves down and aimed their weapons towards the lagoon. Colpoys and his ten marksmen, trotting smartly in spite of their borrowed and ill-matched clothing, hurried up to the ridge, but it seemed as if the attack had been so swift and savage that the whole island was held in a kind of daze.

Colpoys arrived at the top and waited for his men to take cover. Then he said, 'We seem to have lost five men. Very satisfactory.' He frowned disdainfully as some bloodied corpses were passed up from the gun-pit and pitched down the slope. 'Animals.'

Little climbed from the pit, wiping his hands on his belly. 'Plenty o' shot, sir. Not much powder though. Lucky we brought our own.'

Bolitho shared their madness but knew he must keep his grip. At any moment a real attack might come at them. But they had done well. Better than they should have been asked to do.

He said, 'Issue some wine, Little.'

Colpoys added sharply, 'But keep a clear eye and a good head. Your gun will be in action soon.' He glanced at Bolitho. 'Am I right?'

Bolitho twitched his nostrils and knew his men had the furnace primed-up again.

It was a moment's courage, a few minutes of reckless

wildness. He took a mug of red wine from Jury and held it to his lips. It was also a moment he would remember until he died.

Even the wine, dusty and warm though it was, tasted like claret.

' 'Ere they come, sir! 'Ere come th' buggers!'

Bolitho tossed the mug aside and picked up his hanger from the ground.

'Stand to!'

He turned briefly to see how Little and his crew were managing. The cannon had not moved, and to create panic it had to be firing very soon.

He heard a chorus of yells, and when he walked to the crude parapet he saw a mass of running figures converging on the ridge, the sun playing on swords and cutlasses, the air broken by the stabbing crack of muskets and pistols.

Bolitho looked at Colpoys. 'Ready, marines?'

'*Fire!*'

16

Only a Dream

'Cease firing!'

Bolitho handed his pistol to a wounded seaman to reload. He felt as if every fibre in his body was shaking uncontrollably, and he could scarcely believe that the first attack had been repelled. Some of those who had nearly reached the top of the ridge were lying sprawled where they had dropped, others were still dragging themselves painfully towards safety below.

Colpoys joined him, his shirt clinging to his body like a wet skin. 'God!' He blinked the sweat from his eyes. 'Too close for comfort.'

Three more seamen had fallen, but were still alive. Pearse was already supplying each of them with spare muskets and powder-horns so that they could keep up a rapid fire for another attack. After that . . . ? Bolitho glanced at his gasping, cowering sailors. The air was acrid with powdersmoke and the sweet smell of blood.

Little bawled, ' 'Nother few minutes, sir!'

So fierce had been the attack that Bolitho had been forced to take men from the gun-crew to help repel the charging, yelling figures. Now, Little and Stockdale, with a few more picked hands, were throwing their weight on wooden staves and handspikes to work the cannon round towards the head of the anchorage.

Bolitho picked up the telescope and levelled it on the six motionless vessels. One, a topsail schooner, looked very like the craft which had put paid to the *Heloise*. None showed any sign of weighing, and he guessed that their masters were expecting the hill-top guns to smash this impudent invasion before more harm could be done.

He took a mug of wine from Pearse without seeing what he was doing. Where the hell was Palliser? Surely he must have realized what they were attempting? Bolitho felt a stab of despair. Suppose the first lieutenant believed the gunfire and pandemonium implied that Bolitho's party had been discovered and was being systematically wiped out. He recalled Dumaresq's own words before they had left the ship. *I cannot save you*. It was likely Palliser would take the same view.

Bolitho swung around, trying to hide his sudden desperation as he called, 'How much *longer*, Little?' He realized that the gunner's mate had only just told him, just as he knew that Colpoys and Cowdroy were watching him worriedly.

Little straightened his back and nodded. 'Ready.' He stooped down again, his eye squinting along the gun's black barrel. 'Load with powder, lads! Ram the charge 'ome.' He was moving round the breech like a great spider, all arms and legs. 'This 'as got to be done nice an' tidy like.'

Bolitho licked his lips. He saw two seamen taking a shot-carrier towards the small furnace, where another man waited with a ladle in his fists, ready to spoon the heated ball into the carrier. Then it was always a matter of luck and timing. The ball had to be tipped into the muzzle and tamped down on to a double-thick wad. If the gun exploded before the rammer could leap clear he would be blown apart by the ball. Equally, it might split the barrel wide open. No wonder captains were terrified of using heated shot aboard ship.

Little said, 'I'll lay for the middle vessel, sir. A mite either way an' we might 'it one or t'other.'

Stockdale nodded in agreement.

Colpoys said abruptly, 'I can see some men on the hill-top. My guess is they'll be raking *us* presently.'

A man shouted, 'They're musterin' for another attack!'

Bolitho ran to the parapet and dropped on one knee. He could see the small figures darting amongst the rocks and others taking up positions on the hill-side. This was no rabble. Garrick had his people trained like a private army.

'*Stand to!*'

The muskets rose and wavered in the glare, each man seeking out a target amongst the fallen rocks.

A fusilade of shots ripped over the parapet, and Bolitho knew that more attackers were taking advantage of covering fire to work around the other end of the ridge.

He darted a quick glance at Little. He was holding out his hands like a man at prayer.

'Now! *Load!*'

Bolitho tore his eyes away and fired his pistol into a group of three men who were almost at the top of the ridge. Others were fanning out and making difficult targets, and the air was filled with the unnerving din of yells and curses, many in their own language.

Two figures bounded over the rocks and threw themselves on a seaman who was frantically trying to reload a musket. Bolitho saw his mouth open in a silent scream as one attacker pinioned him with his cutlass and his companion silenced him forever with a terrible slash.

Bolitho lunged forward, striking a blade aside and hacking down the man's sword-arm before he could recover. He felt the shock jar up his wrist as the hanger cut through bone and muscle, but forgot the screaming man as he went for his companion with a ferocity he had never known before.

Their blades clashed together, but Bolitho was standing amongst loose stones and could barely keep his balance.

The deafening roar of Little's cannon made the other man falter, his eyes suddenly terrified as he realized what he had done.

Bolitho lunged and jumped back behind the parapet even before his adversary's corpse hit the ground.

Little was yelling, 'Look at that 'un!'

Bolitho saw a falling column of water mingled with steam where the ball had slammed down between two of the vessels. A miss maybe, but the effect would rouse panic quickly enough.

'Sponge out, lads!' Little capered on the edge of his pit while the men with the cradle dashed back towards the furnace for another ball. 'More powder!'

Colpoys crossed the blood-spattered rock and said, 'We've lost three more. One of my fellows is down, too.' He wiped his forehead with his arm, his gold-hilted sabre hanging from his wrist.

Bolitho saw that the curved blade was almost black with dried blood. They could not withstand another attack like the last. Although corpses dotted the slope and along the broken rim of the parapet, Bolitho knew there were many more men already grouping below. They would be far more fearful of Garrick than a ragged handful of seamen.

'*Now!*' Little plunged his slow-match down and the gun recoiled again with a savage explosion.

Bolitho caught a brief blur of the ball as it lifted and then curved down towards the unmoving vessles. He saw a puff of smoke, and something solid detach itself from the nearest schooner and fly into the air before splashing in the water alongside.

'*A hit! A hit!*' The gun-crew, black-faced and running with sweat, capered around the gun like madmen.

Stockdale was already using his strength on a handspike to edge the muzzle round just that small piece more.

'She's afire!' Pearse had his hands above his eyes. 'God damn 'em, they're tryin' to douse it!'

But Bolitho was watching the schooner at the far end of the lagoon. She of all the vessels was in the safest anchorage, and yet even as he watched he saw her jib flapping free and men running forward to sever the cable.

He reached out, not daring to take his eyes from the schooner. '*Glass! Quickly!*'

Jury hurried to him and put the telescope in his fingers. Then he stood back, his eyes on Bolitho's face as if to discover what was about to happen.

Bolitho felt a musket-ball fan past his head but did not flinch. He must not lose that small, precious picture, even though he was in danger of being shot down while he watched.

Almost lost in distance, and yet so clear because he knew them. Palliser's tall frame, sword in hand. Slade and some seamen by the tiller, and Rhodes urging others to the halliards and braces as the schooner broke free and fell awkwardly downwind. There were splashes alongside, and for a moment Bolitho thought she was under fire. Then he realized that Palliser's boarders were flinging the vessel's crew overboard, rather than lose vital time putting them under guard.

Colpoys shouted excitedly, 'They must have swum out to the vessel! He's a cunning one is Palliser! Used our attack as the perfect decoy!'

Bolitho nodded, his ears ringing with the crack of musket-fire, the occasional bang of a swivel. Instead of steering for the centre of the lagoon, Palliser was heading directly for the schooner which had been hit by Little's heated shot.

As they tore down on her, Bolitho saw a ripple of flashes and knew that Palliser was raking the men on her deck, smashing any hope they might have had of controlling the flames. Smoke was rising rapidly from her hatch and drifting down towards the beach and its deserted huts.

Bolitho called, 'Little! Shift the target to the next one!'

Minutes later the heated ball smashed through a schooner's frail hull and caused several internal explosions which brought down a mast and set most of the standing rigging ablaze.

With two vessels burning fiercely in their midst, the remainder needed no urging to cut their cables and try to escape the drifting fireships. The last schooner, the one seized by Palliser's boarding party, was now under command, her big sails filling and rising above the smoke like avenging wings.

Bolitho said suddenly, 'Time to go.' He did not know why he knew. He just did.

Colpoys waved his sabre. 'Take up the wounded! Corporal, put a fuse to the magazine!'

Little's slow-match plunged down again, and another heated ball ripped across the water and hit the vessel already ablaze. Men were leaping overboard, floundering like dying fish as the great pall of smoke crept out to hide them from view.

Pearse lifted a wounded marine across his shoulder, but held his boarding-cutlass in his other hand.

He said, 'Wind's steady, sir. That smoke will blind the bloody battery!'

Panting like wild animals, the seamen and marines scrambled down the slope, keeping the ridge between them and the hill-top battery.

Colpoys pointed to the water. 'That'll be the closest point!' He fell on his knees, his hands to his chest. 'Oh God, they've done for me!'

Bolitho called two marines to carry him between them, his

mind cringing to the din of musket-fire, the sound of flames devouring a vessel beyond the dense smoke.

There was shouting, too, and he knew that many of the schooner's people had been ashore when the attack had begun and were now running towards the hill-side in the hope of reaching the protection of the battery.

Bolitho came to a halt, his feet almost in the water. He could barely suck breath and his eyes streamed so badly he could see little beyond the beach.

They had done the impossible, and while Palliser and his men took advantage of their work, they were now able to go no further.

He knelt down to reload his pistol, his fingers shaking as he cocked it for one last shot.

Jury was with him, and Stockdale, too. But there seemed less than half of the party which had so courageously stormed the ridge and taken the cannon.

Bolitho saw Stockdale's eyes light up as the magazine exploded and hurled the gun bodily down the slope amidst a landslide of corpses and broken rocks.

Midshipman Cowdroy stabbed at the smoke with his hanger. '*Boat!* Look, there!'

Pearse lowered the marine to the ground and waded into the water, his terrible cutlass held above his head.

'We'll take it off 'em, lads!'

Bolitho could feel their desperation like a living force. Sailors were all the same in one thing. Get them a boat, no matter how small, and they felt they could manage.

Little dragged out his cutlass and bared his teeth. 'Cut 'em down afore they slips us!'

Jury fell against Bolitho, and for an instant he thought he had been taken by a musket-ball. But he was pointing incredulously at the smoke and the shadowy boat which was poking through it.

Bolitho nodded, his heart too full to understand.

It was Rhodes standing in the bows of the long-boat, and he saw the checkered shirts of *Destiny*'s seamen at the oars behind him.

'*Lively there!*' Rhodes reached down and seized Bolitho's wrist. 'All in one piece?' He saw Colpoys and shouted, 'Lend a hand there!'

The boat was so full of men, some of them wounded, that there was barely five inches of freeboard, as like a drunken sea-creature it backed-water and headed once more into the smoke.

Between coughs and curses Rhodes explained, 'Knew you'd try to reach us. Only chance. My God, you raised a riot back there, you rascal!'

A burning schooner drifted abeam, and Bolitho could feel the heat on his face like an inferno. Explosions rolled through the smoke, and he guessed it was either another magazine or the hill-top battery shooting blindly across the lagoon.

'What now?'

Rhodes stood up and gestured wildly to the coxswain. 'Hard a-starboard!'

Bolitho saw the twin masts of a schooner right above him, and with his men reached out to catch the heaving-lines which came through the smoke like serpents.

Groaning and crying out in pain, the wounded were pushed and hauled up the vessel's side, and even as the long-boat was cast adrift with a man who had died in sight of safety as her only passenger, Bolitho heard Palliser shouting orders.

Bolitho felt his way through the smoke and met Palliser and Slade by the tiller.

Palliser exclaimed, 'You look like an escaped convict, man!' He gave a brief smile, but Bolitho saw only the strain and the relief.

Rhodes was kneeling beside the marine lieutenant. 'He'll live if we can get him to old Bulkley.'

Palliser raised one hand and the helm went over very slightly. Another schooner was just abeam, her sails drawing well as she stood away from the blazing hulks and headed for the entrance.

Then he said, 'By the time they've discovered we've taken one of their own, we'll be clear.'

He turned sharply as the *San Augustin*'s towering masts broke above the smoke. She was still at anchor, and probably had every able man from the island on board waiting to fend off the drifting fire-ships and douse the results of any contact with them.

Palliser added, 'After that, it will be someone else's problem, thank God!'

A ball splashed down near the larboard bow, and Bolitho guessed that Garrick's gunners had at last realized what was happening.

As the smoke thinned, and parts of the island merged clean and pale in the sunlight, Bolitho saw they were already past the point.

He heard Pearse whisper, 'Look, Bob, there she be!' He lifted the head of a wounded seaman so that he could see *Destiny*'s braced topsails as Dumaresq drove her as close as he dared to the reefs.

Pearse, a boatswain's mate who had fought like a devil, who by command of his captain had laid raw the back of many a defaulter with his cat-o'-nine-tails, said very quietly, 'Poor Bob's dead, sir.' He closed the young seaman's eyes with his tarry fingers, adding, ' 'Nother minute and 'e'd 'ave bin fine.'

Bolitho watched the frigate shortening sail, the rush of men along her gangway as the two vessles tacked closer together. *Destiny*'s figurehead was as before, pure and pale, her victor's laurels held up as if in defiance to the smoke-shrouded island.

And all Bolitho could think of was the dead seaman named Bob, of a solitary corpse left drifting in the long-boat, of Stockdale's anxiety at being ordered away from his side when he was needed. Of Colpoys, and the corporal nicknamed Dipper, Jury and Cowdroy, and others who had been left behind.

'Take in the fores'l!' Palliser watched the *Destiny*'s wary approach with grim satisfaction. 'There were times when I never thought to see *that* lady again.'

Josh Little crossed to Pearse's side and said roughly, 'We'll 'ave a wet when we gets aboard, eh?'

Pearse was still looking at the dead seaman. 'Aye, Josh. An' one for 'im, too.'

Rhodes said, 'The lord and master will have his way now. A fight to the finish.' He ducked as a heaving-line soared aboard. 'But for myself, I wish the odds were fairer.' He looked across at the great pall of smoke which surrounded the flat-topped hill as if to carry it away. 'You're a marvel, Dick. You really are.'

They examined each other like strangers. Then Bolitho

said, 'I was afraid you'd hold back. That you'd think we were all taken.'

Rhodes waved his arm to some of the seamen along *Destiny*'s gangway. 'Oh, didn't I tell you? We knew what you were doing, where you were, everything.'

Bolitho stared at him in disbelief. 'How?'

'Remember that main-topman of yours, Murray? He was their sentry. Saw you and young Jury as you left cover.' He gripped his friend's arm. 'It's true! He's below now with a splinter in his leg. Had quite a story to tell. Lucky for you and young Jury, eh?'

Bolitho shook his head and leaned against the schooner's bulwark to watch the two hulls come together in the swell.

Death had been that close, and he had known nothing about it. Murray must have taken the first available vessel out of Rio and had ended up with Garrick's pirates. He could have raised the alarm, or could have shot them both down and become a hero. Instead, something which they had once shared, another precious moment, had held them together.

Dumaresq's voice boomed through a speaking-trumpet. 'Roundly there! I shall be aground if you cannot shift yourselves!'

Rhodes grinned. *'Home.'*

Captain Dumaresq stood by the stern windows of his cabin, his hands behind him, as he listened to Palliser's account of the pitched-battle and their escape from the lagoon.

As he signalled for Macmillan to pass round more wine to his stained and weary officers, he said gravely, 'I put a landing-party ashore to prick Garrick's balloon. I did not expect you to make an invasion all on your own!' Then he smiled broadly, and it made him look sad and suddenly tired. 'I shall think of you and your lads at dawn tomorrow. But for you, *Destiny* would have been met with such a resistance that I doubt I could have worked her clear. Things are still bad, gentlemen, but at least we *know*.'

Palliser asked, 'Do you still intend to despatch the schooner to Antigua, sir?'

Dumaresq regarded him thoughtfully. *'Your* schooner, you mean?' He moved to the windows and stared at the dying sun reflected from the water. Like red gold. 'Yes, I am afraid it is another prize I must take from you.'

Bolitho watched, his mind strangely alert in spite of the strain, the bitter memories of the day. He recognized the bond between captain and first lieutenant as if it were something solid and visible.

Dumaresq added, 'If *San Augustin* is little damaged we must fight her as soon as we can. When Garrick's lookouts see the schooner standing away he will know that time is running out, that I have sent for aid.' He nodded grimly. 'He will come out tomorrow. That is my belief.'

Palliser persisted, 'He will be supported by the other schooners, maybe two survived the fires.'

'I know. Better that than wait for Garrick to sail against us with a completely overhauled ship. I'd ask for better terms, but few captains get the chance to choose.'

Bolitho thought of the men who had been sent over to the schooner. All but a few were wounded, and yet there had been something defiant about them, something which had raised a cheer from *Destiny*'s gangways and rigging.

For reasons of his own, Dumaresq had sent Yeames, master's mate, in command of the prize. It must have been a hard blow for Slade.

Bolitho had been moved when Yeames had approached him before the last boatload had been ferried across. He had always liked the master's mate, but had thought little beyond that.

Yeames had held out his hand. 'You'll win tomorrow, sir, I've no doubt o' that. But mebbee we'll not meet again. In case we do, I'll want you to remember me, as I'd be proud to serve you when you gets your command.'

He had gone away, leaving Bolitho confused and proud.

Dumaresq's resonant voice broke through his thoughts. 'We shall clear for action at dawn tomorrow. I shall speak with the people before we close the enemy, but to you especially I give my thanks.'

Macmillan hovered by the screen door until he caught the captain's eye.

'Mr Timbrell's respects, sir, an' will you want to darken ship?'

Dumaresq shook his big head slowly. 'Not this time. I

want Garrick to see us. To *know* we are here. His one
weakness, apart from greed, is anger. I intend that he shall
grow angrier before morning!'

Macmillan opened the door, and gratefully the lieutenants
and midshipmen made to withdraw.

Only Palliser remained, and Bolitho guessed he would
share the more technical details with the captain without their
interruption.

With the door shut once more, Dumaresq turned to his first
lieutenant and gestured to a chair.

'There's something else, isn't there?'

Palliser sat and thrust out his long legs. For a moment more
he kneaded his eyes with his knuckles and then said, 'You
were right about Egmont, sir. Even after you put him aboard
a vessel outward-bound from Basseterre he tried to warn
Garrick, or to reason with him. We'll probably never know.
He obviously transferred to a smaller, faster vessel and took
the northerly route through the islands to reach here before
us. Whatever happened, his words were lost on Garrick.'

He delved into his pocket and withdrew the gold necklace
with its double-headed bird and gleaming ruby tails.

'Garrick had them butchered. I took this from one of our
prisoners. The seamen I told you about explained the rest to
me.'

Dumaresq picked up the heavy necklace and examined it
sadly.

'Murray, he saw it?'

Palliser nodded. 'He was wounded. I sent him in the
schooner before he could speak with Mr Bolitho.'

Dumaresq walked to the windows again and watched the
little schooner turning stern on, her sails as gold as the
necklace in his hand.

'That was thoughtful. For what he has said and done,
Murray will be discharged when he reaches England. I doubt
if his path will ever cross with Mr Bolitho's again.' He
shrugged. 'If it does, the pain will be easier to bear by then.'

'You'll not tell him, sir? Not let him know that she is
dead?'

Dumaresq watched the shadows reaching across the heaving water to cover the schooner's hull.

'He'll not hear it from me. Tomorrow we must fight, and I

need every officer and man to give all he has. Richard Bolitho has proved himself to be a good lieutenant. If he survives tomorrow, he'll be an even better one.' Dumaresq raised one of the windows and without further hesitation tossed the necklace into *Destiny*'s wake. 'I'll leave him with his dream. It's the very least I can do for him.'

In the wardroom Bolitho sat in a chair, his arms hanging at his sides as the resistance ran out of him like fine sand from a glass. Rhodes sat opposite him, staring at an empty goblet without recognition.

There was still tomorrow. Like the horizon, they never reached it.

Bulkley entered and sat down heavily between them. 'I have just been dealing with our stubborn marine.'

Bolitho nodded dully. Colpoys had insisted on staying aboard with his men. Bandaged and strapped up so that he could use only one arm, he had barely the strength to stay on his feet.

Palliser came through the door and tossed his hat on to a gun. For a moment he looked at it, probably seeing it tomorrow with this place stripped bare, the screens gone, the little personal touches shut away from the smoke and fire of battle.

Then he said crisply, 'Your watch, I believe, Mr Rhodes? The master cannot be expected to do everything, you know!'

Rhodes lurched to his feet and grinned. 'Aye, aye, sir.' Like a man walking in his sleep he left the wardroom.

Bolitho barely heard them. He was thinking of her, using her memory to shield his mind from the sights and deeds of that day.

Then he stood up abruptly and excused himself from the others as he went to the privacy of his cabin. He did not want them to see his dismay. When he had tried to see her face there had been only a blurred image, nothing more.

Bulkley pushed a bottle across the table. 'Was it bad?'

Palliser considered it. 'It'll be worse yet.' But he was thinking of the jewelled necklace. On the sea-bed astern now. A private burial.

The surgeon added, 'I'm glad about Murray. It's a small thing in all this misery, but it's good to know he's clear of blame.'

Palliser looked away. 'I'm going to do my rounds and turn in for a few hours.'

Bulkley sighed. 'Likewise. I'd better request to borrow Spillane from clerk's duties. I shall be short-handed, too.'

Palliser paused in the doorway and regarded him emptily. 'You'd best hurry then. He'll maybe hang tomorrow. Just to stroke Garrick's anger further. He was his spy. Murray saw him searching old Lockyer's body at Funchal when it was brought aboard.' Weariness was slurring Palliser's words. 'Spillane guessed, and tried to incriminate him over Jury's watch. To drive a wedge between fo'c'sle and quarterdeck. It's been done before.' With sudden bitterness he added, 'He's as much a murderer as Garrick.'

He strode from the wardroom without another word, and when Bulkley turned his head he saw the first lieutenant's hat was still lying on the gun.

Whatever happened tomorrow, nothing would ever be the same again, he thought, and the realization saddened him greatly.

When darkness finally shut out the horizon and the flattened hill above Fougeaux Island had disappeared, *Destiny*'s lights still shone on the water like watchful eyes.

17

Into Battle

Overnight Fougeaux Island seemed to have shrunk in size, so that when the first faint light filtered down from the horizon it looked little more than a sand-bar across *Destiny*'s starboard bow.

Bolitho lowered his telescope and allowed the island to fall back into the shadows. Within an hour it would be bright sunlight. He turned his back and paced slowly up and down the quarterdeck. The business of preparing the ship for battle had been unreal, an almost leisurely affair carried out watch by watch during the night.

The seamen knew their way around the masts and hull so well that they had little left to do which required daylight. Dumaresq had thought that out with the same meticulous care he planned everything he did. He wanted his men to accept the inevitability of a fight, the fact that some if not all of them would never make another voyage in *Destiny*. There was only one alternative passage, and it was marked on the master's chart. Two thousand fathoms, straight down.

Also, Dumaresq intended his people to be as rested as possible, without the usual nerve-wrenching stampede of clearing for action when an enemy showed himself.

Palliser appeared on the quarterdeck, and after a cursory glance at the compass and each sail in turn he said, 'I trust the watch below is completing breakfast?'

Bolitho replied, 'Aye, sir. I have ordered the cooks to douse the galley fire as soon as they are done.'

Palliser took a glass from Midshipman Henderson, who had been assisting with the morning-watch.

Midshipman Cowdroy had been similarly employed during the night. As next in line for promotion, they might find themselves as acting-lieutenants before *Destiny*'s cooks relit their fires.

Palliser scrutinized the island carefully. 'Terrible place.' He returned the glass to Henderson and said, 'Aloft with you. I want to be told the moment Garrick tries to leave the lagoon.'

Bolitho watched the midshipman swarming up the ratlines. It was getting lighter rapidly. He could even see the boatswain's top-chains which he had slung on each yard, the additional tackles and lines hauled up to the fighting-tops for urgent repairs when needed.

He asked, 'You believe it is today, sir?'

Palliser smiled grimly. 'The captain is certain. That's enough for me. And Garrick will know it is his only chance. To fight and win, to get away before the squadron sends support.'

Vague figures moved about the upper deck and between the guns. Those black muzzles, now damp with spray and night mist, would soon be too hot to touch.

Petty officers were already discussing last-moment changes to crews, to replace those who had died or were on their way to safety aboard the captured schooner.

Lieutenant Colpoys was right aft by the taffrail with his sergeant as seamen trooped along the gangways to pack the hammocks tightly in the nettings as protection for those who shared the quarterdeck in times like these. An exposed, dangerous place, vital to any ship, an aiming-point for marksmen and the deadly swivel-guns.

Midshipman Jury took a message at the quarterdeck ladder and reported, 'Galley fires doused, sir.'

He looked very young and clean, Bolitho thought, as if he had taken great care over his dress and bearing.

He smiled. 'A fine day for it.'

Jury looked up at the masthead, searching for Henderson. 'We have the agility if nothing else, sir.'

Bolitho glanced at him, but saw himself just a year or so back. 'That's very true.' It was pointless to add that the wind was only a breeze. To tack and wear with speed you required the sails drawing well. Wind and canvas were the stuff of a frigate.

Rhodes climbed up to the quarterdeck and glanced curiously at the smudge of land beyond the bowsprit. He was wearing his best sword, one which had belonged to his father. Bolitho thought of the old sword which his father wore. It appeared in most of the portraits of the Bolitho family at Falmouth. It was destined to be Hugh's one day, very soon now if his father was coming home for good. He turned away from Jury and Rhodes. Somehow, he did not have the feeling he would live to see it again. He was alarmed to discover he could accept it.

Palliser came back and said sharply, 'Tell Mr Timbrell to rig a halter from the main-yard, Mr Bolitho.' He met their combined stares. 'Well?'

Rhodes shrugged awkwardly. 'Sorry, sir. I just thought that at a time like this. . . .'

Palliser snapped, 'At a time like this, as you put it, one more corpse will hardly make much difference!'

Bolitho sent Jury for the boatswain and thought about Spillane and what he had done. He had had plenty of opportunity to steal information and pass it ashore in Rio or Basseterre. Like the captain's coxswain, the clerk was more free than most to move as he pleased.

Garrick must have had agents and spies everywhere, maybe even at the Admiralty where one of them had followed every move towards putting *Destiny* to sea. When the ship had made ready to sail from Plymouth, Spillane had been there. It would have been easy for him to discover the whereabouts of Dumaresq's recruiting parties. He had only to read the posters.

Now, like lines on a chart, they had all been drawn here to this place. A cross on Gulliver's calculations and bearings. Something destined rather than planned.

Most of the men on deck looked up as the boatswain's party lowered a hangman's noose from the main-yard to the gangway. Like Rhodes, they would have little stomach for a summary execution. It was outside their code of battle, their understanding of justice.

Bolitho heard one of the helmsmen mutter, 'Cap'n's comin' up, sir.'

Bolitho turned to face the companionway as Dumaresq,

wearing a freshly laundered shirt, with his gold-laced hat set firmly on his head, strode on to the quarterdeck.

He nodded to each of his officers and the men on watch, while to Colpoys, who was attempting to draw himself to attention, he said curtly, 'Save your strength, you obstinate redcoat!'

Gulliver touched his hat. 'Nor' by east, sir. Wind's still light though.'

Dumaresq eyed him impassively. 'I can see that.'

He turned to Bolitho. 'Have the hands lay aft at six bells to witness punishment. Inform the master-at-arms and the surgeon, if you please.' He waited, watching Bolitho's emotions and his efforts to conceal them. 'You've still not learned deceit, it seems?' One of his feet tapped on the deck. 'What is it, the execution?'

'Yes, sir. It's like an omen. A superstition. I—I'm not sure what I mean.'

'Evidently.' Dumaresq walked to the rail and looked along the upper deck. 'That man tried to betray us, just as he attempted to destroy Murray and all he believed in. Murray was a good man, whereas—' He broke off to watch some marines beginning a slow climb to the fore and main-tops.

'I'd like to have seen Murray before he left, sir.'

Dumaresq asked sharply, 'Why?'

Bolitho was surprised at Dumaresq's reaction. 'I wanted to thank him.'

'Oh. That.'

Midshipman Henderson made all of them look up. 'Deck there! Ship standing out from the island, sir!'

Dumaresq dug his chin into his neckcloth. 'At last.'

He saw Midshipman Merrett by the mizzen. 'Go fetch the Articles of War from my servant. We'll get this matter over with and then clear for action.'

He patted his scarlet waistcoat and gave a soft belch. 'That was a nice piece of pork. And the wine will help to start the day.' He saw Bolitho's uncertainty. 'Bring up the prisoner. I'd like him to see his master's ship before he swings, God rot him!'

Sergeant Barmouth placed a line of marines across the poop, and as the pipe for all hands to lay aft and witness punishment echoed between decks, Spillane, escorted by the master-at-arms and Corporal Dyer, appeared from the forecastle.

The seamen, already stripped to their trousers and ready for the drums to beat to quarters, parted to allow the little group through.

Beneath the quarterdeck rail they halted, and Poynter reported harshly, 'The prisoner, sir!'

Bolitho made himself look at Spillane's upturned face. If anything, it was completely empty, as if the neat and usually composed man was unable to accept what had happened.

Bolitho recalled how Spillane had come to his cabin with the message from *Aurora*, and wondered how much he had passed on to Garrick.

Dumaresq waited for his officers to remove their hats and then said in his resonant voice, 'You know why you are here, Spillane. Had you been a pressed man, or one forced into the King's service against your will it might have been different. You, however, volunteered, knowing you were intending to betray your oath and where possible bring disaster to your ship and your companions. Yours was a conspiracy to commit murder on a grand scale. Look yonder, man.'

When Spillane remained stricken and staring at him, Dumaresq snapped, 'Master-at-arms!'

Poynter gripped the prisoner's chin and swung him round towards the bows.

'That ship is commanded by your master, Piers Garrick. Take a long look, and ask yourself now if the price of treachery was worthwhile!'

But Spillane's eyes were fixed on the swaying halter. It was doubtful if he saw anything else.

'Deck there!' Henderson's normally powerful voice sounded unsteady, as if he was afraid of breaking into the drama below him.

Dumaresq glared up at him. 'Speak, man!'

'The *San Augustin* has corpses hanging from her yards, sir!'

Dumaresq swarmed into the shrouds, snatching a telescope from Jury as he passed.

Then he climbed down to the deck very slowly and said, 'They are the ship's Spanish officers.' He darted a quick glance at Bolitho. 'Hung there as a warning, no doubt.'

But Bolitho had seen something else in Dumaresq's eyes. Just briefly, it had been relief, but why? What had he expected to see?

Dumaresq returned to the quarterdeck rail and replaced his hat. Then he said, 'Remove that halter from the main-yard, Mr Timbrell. Master-at-arms, put the prisoner down. He will await judgement with the others.'

Spillane's legs seemed to collapse under him. He clasped his hands together and said brokenly, 'Thank you, sir! The Lord bless you for your kindness!'

'Stand up, you bloody hound!' Dumaresq looked at him with disgust. 'To think that men like Garrick can corrupt others so easily. By hanging you, I would have been no better than he. But hear me. You will be able to listen to our progress today, and I suspect that will be an even greater punishment!'

As Spillane was hustled away, Palliser said bitterly, 'If we sink, that bugger will reach the bottom first!'

Dumaresq clapped him on the shoulder. 'Very true! Now, beat to quarters, if you will, and try to knock two minutes off your time!'

'Ship cleared for action, sir!' Palliser touched his hat, his eyes gleaming. 'Eight minutes exactly.'

Dumaresq lowered his telescope and glanced at him. 'Short-handed we may be, but each man-jack is working the harder for it.'

Bolitho stood below the quarterdeck watching his guncrews by their tackles, seemingly relaxed, although the waiting was far from over.

The distant ship had spread more sail to stand well clear of the island, but as *Destiny* lifted and fell gently in the swell, the *San Augustin* appeared to be motionless. Would she turn and run for it? There was always a chance her stern-chasers might cripple the pursuing frigate with a lucky shot.

Midshipman Henderson, isolated from the preparations far below his perch, had reported that two other sail had cleared the lagoon. One was the topsail schooner, and Bolitho wondered how Dumaresq could be so sure Garrick was in the big man-of-war and not in the schooner. Perhaps he and Dumaresq were too much alike after all. Neither wishing to be a spectator, each eager to inflict a quick and undeniable victory.

Little walked slowly behind the starboard battery of twelve-pounders, stooping occasionally to check a tackle or to ensure that the ship's boys had sanded the decks sufficiently to prevent the crews from slipping when the pace grew warm.

Stockdale was at his own gun, his men dwarfed by his great bulk as he cradled a twelve-pound ball in his hands before replacing it in the shot-garland and selecting another. In a manner born, Bolitho thought. He had often seen old gun-captains do it. To make certain the first shots would be perfect. After the opening broadsides it was usually each crew to itself and devil take the hindmost.

He heard Gulliver say, 'We have the wind-gage, sir. We can always shorten sail if the enemy comes about.'

He was probably speaking merely to release his own anxieties or to await a suggestion from the captain. But Dumaresq remained silent, watching his adversary, glancing occasionally at the masthead pendant or the sluggish wave curling back from *Destiny*'s bows.

Bolitho looked forward and saw Rhodes speaking with Cowdroy and some of his gun-captains. The waiting was endless. It was what he expected, but he never grew used to it.

'The schooners have luffed, sir!'

Dumaresq grunted. 'Hanging back like jackals.'

Bolitho climbed up to peer over the gangway which ran above the starboard battery to link quarterdeck to forecastle. Even with the packed hammock nettings and the nets spread above the deck there was little enough protection for the seamen, he thought.

Almost the worst part was the empty boat-tier. Apart from the gig and the quarter-boat towing astern, the rest had been left drifting in an untidy line. In action, flying splinters were one of the greatest hazards, and the boats made a tempting target. But to see them cast adrift put the seal on what they had to face.

Henderson called, 'The corpses have been cut down, sir!' He sounded hoarse from strain.

Dumaresq said to Palliser, 'Like so much meat. God damn his eyes!'

Palliser answered evenly, 'Maybe he wishes to see *you* angry, sir?'

'Provoke me?' Dumaresq's anger faded before it could spread. 'You could be right. Hell's teeth, Mr Palliser, it should be Parliament for you, not the Navy!'

Midshipman Jury stood with his hands behind his back watching the far-off ship, his hat tilted over his eyes as he had seen Bolitho do.

He said suddenly, 'Will they try to close with us, sir?'

'Probably. They have the numbers. From what we saw on the island, I would guess they outmatch us by ten to one.' He saw the dismay on Jury's face and added lightly, 'The captain will hold them off. Hit and run. Wear them down.'

He glanced up at Dumaresq by the rail and wondered. No emotion, and yet he must be scheming and planning for every possible set-back. Even his voice was as usual.

Jury said, 'The other two craft could be dangerous.'

'The topsail schooner maybe. The other one is too light to risk a close encounter.'

He thought of what would have happened but for their desperate action on the island. Was it only yesterday? There would have been six schooners instead of two, and the forty-four-gun *San Augustin* might have had time to mount more guns, maybe those from the hill-top battery. Now, whatever the outcome, their captured schooner would carry Dumaresq's despatches to the admiral at Antigua. Too late for them perhaps, but they would ensure that Garrick remained a hunted man for the rest of his life.

How clear the sky looked. Not yet too hot to be oppressive. The sea too was creamy and inviting. He tried not to think of that other time, when he had pictured himself running and swimming with her, finding happiness together, making it last.

Dumaresq said loudly, 'They will attempt to dismast us and lay us open to boarding. It is likely that the larger of the schooners has been armed with some heavier pieces. So make each shot tell. Remember that many of their guncrews and seamen are Spaniards. Terrified of Garrick they may be, but they'll not wish to be pounded to gruel by you!'

His words brought a murmur of approval from the bare-backed gun-crews.

There was a ragged crash of cannon-fire, and Bolitho turned to see the *San Augustin*'s starboard guns shoot out long orange tongues, while the smoke rolled over the ship and partially hid the island beyond.

The sea foamed and shot skywards, as if the power was coming from beneath the surface instead of from the proud ship with the scarlet crosses on her courses.

Stockdale said, 'Rough.'

Several of the seamen around him shook their fists towards the enemy, although at three miles range it was unlikely anyone would see them.

Rhodes strolled aft, his beautiful sword at odds with his faded sea-going coat.

He said, 'Just to keep them busy, eh, Dick?'

Bolitho nodded. Rhodes was probably right, but there was something very menacing about the Spanish vessel for all that. Perhaps because of her extravagant beauty, the richness of her gilded carvings which even distance could not conceal.

He said, 'If only the wind would come.'

Rhodes shrugged. 'If only we were in Plymouth.'

Another broadside spouted from the Spaniard's hull, and some balls ricocheted across the sea's face and seemed to go on forever.

There was an even louder shout of derision, but Bolitho saw some of the senior gun-captains looking worried. The enemy's iron was dropping short and was not that well directed, but as both vessels were moving so slowly on what would likely remain a converging tack, it made each barrage more dangerous.

He pictured Bulkley and his loblolly boys on the shadowy orlop deck, the glittering instruments, the brandy to take away the agony, the leather strap to prevent a man biting through his tongue as the surgeon's saw did its work.

And Spillane, in irons below the waterline, what was he thinking as the thunder rolled against the timbers around him?

'Stand by on deck!' Palliser was staring down at the double line of guns. 'Run in and load!'

This was the moment. With fixed concentration each gun-captain watched as his men put their weight on the tackles and hauled them away from the sides.

Bulky cartridges were passed rapidly to each muzzle and rammed home by the loader.

Bolitho watched the one nearest to him as he gave the cartridge in his gun two extra sharp taps to bed it in. His face was so set, so absorbed, that it was as if he was about to take on an enemy single-handed. Then the wad, followed by a gleaming black ball for each gun. One more wad rammed down, just in case the ship should give an unexpected roll and tip the ball harmlessly into the sea, and they were done.

When Bolitho looked up again, the other ship seemed to have drawn much closer.

'Ready on deck!'

Each gun-captain held up his hand.

Palliser shouted, 'Open the ports!' He waited, counting seconds, as the port-lids rose along either side like reawakened eyes. *'Run out!'*

The *San Augustin* fired again, but her master had let her fall off to the wind and the whole broadside fell a good half mile from *Destiny*'s larboard bow.

Rhodes was striding behind his guns, giving instructions or merely joking with his men, Bolitho could not tell.

With *San Augustin* now lying off their larboard bow on an invisible arrowhead, it was hard to keep his crews busy and prevent them from standing to look to the opposite side to see what was happening.

Palliser called, 'Mr Bolitho! Be ready to send some of your hands across to assist. Two broadsides and we will alter course to larboard and allow your guns a similar chance.'

Bolitho waved his hands. 'Aye, sir!'

Dumaresq said, 'Alter course three points to starboard.'

'Man the braces there! Helm a-weather!'

With her canvas flapping and cracking, *Destiny* responded, the *San Augustin* seeming to go astern as she showed herself to the crouching gun-captains.

'Full elevation! *Fire!*'

The twelve-pounders hurled themselves inboard on their tackles, the smoke rolling downwind towards the enemy in a frothing screen.

'Stop your vents!' Rhodes was striding more quickly now. 'Sponge out and load!'

The gun-captains had to work doubly hard, using a fist or

two if necessary to contain their men's excitement. To put a charge into an unsponged barrel where some smouldering remains from the first shot were still inside was inviting sudden and horrible death.

Stockdale pounded the breeching-ring of his gun. 'Come on, boys! *Come on!*'

'Run out!' Palliser was resting his telescope on the hammock nettings to study the other ship. 'As you bear! *Fire!*'

This time broadside was uneven, with each captain taking his time, choosing his own moment. But before they could watch the fall of shot men were already dashing to braces and halliards, while aft Gulliver urged his helmsmen to greater efforts as *Destiny* changed tack, standing as close to the wind as possible without losing her maneouvrability.

Bolitho's mouth had gone dry. Without noticing he had drawn his hanger and was holding it to his hip as the deck tilted, and then slowly but steadily his gun-captains saw *San Augustin*'s gilded beak-head edge across their open ports.

'On the uproll!'

San Augustin's side erupted in darting tongues, and Bolitho heard the wild shriek of langridge or chain-shot passing high overhead. He found time to pity Midshipman Henderson clinging to the cross-trees with his telescope trained on the enemy while the murderous tangle of chain and iron bars swept past him.

'*Fire!*'

Bolitho saw the sea bursting with spray around the other ship, and thought he saw her main-course quiver as at least one ball ploughed through it.

As his men threw themselves on handspikes and rammers, yelling for powder and shot, oblivious to everything but the hungry muzzles and Palliser's voice from the quarterdeck, Bolitho glanced at the captain.

He was with Gulliver and Slade beside the compass, pointing at the enemy, the sails, at the drifting smoke, as if he held every act and each consequence in his palm.

'*Fire!*'

Down *Destiny*'s starboard side, gun by gun, the twelve-pounders crashed inboard, their trucks squealing like enraged hogs.

'Stand by to alter course! Be ready, Mr Rhodes! Larboard battery load with double-shot!'

Bolitho ducked away from running seamen and bellowing petty officers. Their constant, aching drills on the long passage from Plymouth had taught them well. No matter what the guns were doing, the ship had to be worked and kept afloat.

Once again the guns roared out their challenge, a different sound this time, jarring and painful, as the double-shotted barrels responded to their charges.

Bolitho wiped his face with his wrist. He felt as if he had been in the sun for hours. In fact, it was barely eight bells. One hour since Spillane had been sent below.

Dumaresq was taking a risk to double-shot his guns. But Bolitho had seen the two schooners working their way to windward, as if to close with *Destiny* from astern. They had to hit *San Augustin,* and hit her hard, if only to slow her down.

Dumaresq shouted, 'Fetch the gunner! Lively there!'

Bolitho winced as water cascaded over the opposite gangway, and he felt the hull jump to a massive pounding. Two hits at least, perhaps on the waterline.

But the boatswain was already yelling orders, and his men were running past the marine sentries who guarded each hatchway, to examine the hull and to shore up any damage.

He saw the gunner, blinking like an owl in the sunlight, his face creased with anger at being called from his magazine and powder rooms even by the captain.

'Mr Vallance!' Dumaresq's face was split in a fierce grin. 'You were once the best gun-captain in the Channel Fleet, is that not so?'

Vallance shuffled his felt slippers, very necessary footwear to avoid kicking up sparks in so lethal a place as the magazine.

'That be true, sir. No doubt on it.' Despite the noise, he was obviously pleased to be so remembered.

'Well, I want you to personally take charge of the bow-chasers and put paid to that topsail schooner. I'll bring the ship about.' He kept his voice level. 'You'll have to look alive.'

Vallance shuffled away, jerking his thumb to beckon two of the gun-captains from Bolitho's battery without even asking permission. Vallance was the best of his kind, even if he was usually a taciturn man. He did not need Dumaresq to elaborate. For when *Destiny* tacked round to engage the schooners she would present her full length to the enemy's broadside.

Destiny's bow-chasers were nine-pounders. Although not as powerful as several other naval guns, the nine-pounder was always considered to be the most accurate.

'Fire!'

Rhodes' crews were sponging out again, and the seamen shone with sweat which cut runnels through the powder-dirt on their bodies like marks of a lash.

The range was less than two miles, and when Bolitho looked up he saw several holes in the main-topsail and few seamen working to replace some broken rigging while the battle raged across the narrowing strip of water.

Vallance was up in the bows now, and Bolitho could picture his grizzled head bobbing over the larboard nine-pounder, remembering perhaps when he had been a gun-captain himself.

Dumaresq's voice cut through a brief lull in the firing. 'When you are ready, Mr Palliser. It will mean five points to larboard.' He pounded his fists together. 'If only the wind would come!' He thrust his hands behind him again as if to control their agitation. 'Loose the t'gan'sls!'

Moments later, answering as best she could to the flapping canvas, *Destiny* tacked round to larboard, and in seconds, or so it seemed, the schooners lay across her bows.

Bolitho heard the crash of a nine-pounder, and then the other on the opposite bow as Vallance fired.

The topsail schooner seemed to stagger, as if she had run headlong on to a reef. Foremast, sails and yard all crumpled together to swamp her forecastle and slew her round out of command.

Dumaresq yelled, 'Break off the action! Bring her about, Mr Palliser!'

Bolitho knew that the second schooner was hardly likely to risk sharing her consort's fate. It was a masterful piece of gunlaying. He saw his men sliding down the stays to the deck after setting the extra sails, and wondered how *Destiny* would appear to the enemy's gun-crews as they peered through the smoke and saw one of their number crippled so easily.

It would hardly affect the difference of armament between the two ships, but it would put heart into the British seamen when they most needed it.

'Steady as she goes! Nor' by east, sir!'

Bolitho shouted, 'It'll be our turn next!' He saw several of the seamen turn to grin at him, their faces like masks, their eyes glazed by the constant crash of gunfire.

The deck seemed to leap beneath Bolitho's feet, and with astonishment he saw a twelve-pounder from the opposite battery toppled on to its side, two men crushed and screaming under it, while others ducked or fell sprawling to flying splinters.

He heard Rhodes yelling to restore order and the responding bang of several guns, but the damage had been bad, and as Timbrell's men ran to haul away the broken timber and upended gun, the enemy fired again.

Bolitho had no way of knowing how many of *San Augustin*'s shots found their mark, but the deck shook so violently he knew it was a massive weight of iron. Woodwork and pieces of broken metal clattered around him, and he covered his face with his arms as a great shadow swooped over the deck.

Stockdale pulled him down and croaked, 'Mizzen! They've shot it away!'

Then came the thundering crash as the complete mizzen-mast and spars scythed across the quarterdeck and down over the starboard gangway, snapping rigging and entangling men as it went.

Bolitho staggered to his feet and looked for the enemy. But she seemed to have changed position, her upper yards misting over as she continued to shoot. *Destiny* was listing, the mizzen dragging her round as men ran and stumbled amongst the tangled rigging, their ears too deafened by the noise to react to their orders.

Dumaresq came to the quarterdeck rail and retrieved his hat from his coxswain. He glanced quickly around the upper deck and then said, 'More hands aft! Cut that wreckage clear!'

Palliser seemed to rise out of the chaos like a spectre. He was gripping his arm which appeared to be broken, and he looked as if he might collapse.

Dumaresq roared, '*Move yourselves!* And another ensign to the mainmast, Mr Lovelace!'

But it was a boatswain's mate who swarmed up the shrouds through the smoke to replace the ensign which had been shot down with the mizzen. Midshipman Lovelace, who would have been fourteen years old in two weeks' time, lay by the nettings, torn almost in half by a trailing backstay.

Bolitho realized that he had been standing quite motionless while the ship swayed and shuddered about him to the jar of gun-fire.

He grasped Jury's shoulder and said, 'Take ten men and assist the boatswain!' He shook him gently. 'All right?'

Jury smiled. 'Yes, sir.' He ran off into the smoke, calling names as he went.

Stockdale muttered, 'We've less than six guns which'll bear on this side!''

Bolitho knew that *Destiny* would be out of control until the mizzen was hacked free. Over the side he could see a marine still clinging to the mizzen-top, another drowning as he watched, dragged under by the great web of rigging. He turned and looked at Dumaresq as he stood like a rock, directing the helmsmen, watching his enemy and making sure his own company could see him there.

Bolitho tore his eyes away. He felt shocked and guilty, as if he had accidentally stolen Dumaresq's secret.

So that was why he wore a scarlet waistcoat. So that none of his men should see.

But Bolitho had seen the fresh, wet stains on it which had run down on to his strong hands as his coxswain, Johns, supported him by the rail.

Midshipman Cowdroy clambered over the debris and yelled, 'I need more help forrard, sir!' He looked near to panic.

Bolitho said, 'Deal with it!' What Dumaresq had said to him about the stolen watch. *Deal with it.*

Axes rang through the smoke, and he felt the deck lurch upright as the broken mast and attendant rigging drifted clear of the side.

How bare it seemed without it and its spread of canvas.

With a start he realized that *San Augustin* lay directly across the bows. She was still firing, but *Destiny*'s change of direction which had been caused by the mizzen dragging her

round, made her a difficult target. Balls slammed down close
to the side or splashed in the sea on either beam. *Destiny's*
guns were also blind, except for the bow-chasers, and Bolitho
heard their sharper explosions as they reopened fire in deadly
earnest.

But another heavy ball smashed under the larboard gangway, toppling two guns and painting the decks red as it cut
down a group of men already wounded.

Bolitho saw Rhodes fall, try to recover his stand by the
guns and then drop on his side.

He ran to help him, shielding him from the billowing
gun-smoke as the world went mad around them.

Rhodes looked directly at him, his eyes free of pain, as he
whispered, 'The lord and master had his way, you see,
Dick?' He looked up at the sky beyond the rigging. 'The
wind. Here at last but too late.' He reached up to touch
Bolitho's shoulder. 'Take care. I always knew. . . .' His
eyes became fixed and without understanding.

Blindly Bolitho stood up and stared around at the destruction and the pain. Stephen Rhodes was dead. The one who
had first made him feel welcome, who had taken life at face
value, day at a time.

Then, beyond the broken nettings and punctured hammocks
he saw the sea. The sluggish swell was gone. He peered up at
the sails. Holed they might be, but they were thrusting out
like breast-plates as they pushed the frigate forward into the
fight. They had not been beaten. Rhodes had seen it, *the
wind,* he had said. The last thing he had understood on this
earth.

He ran to the side and saw *San Augustin* startlingly close,
right there on the starboard bow. Men were shooting at him,
there was smoke and noise all around, but he felt nothing.
Close to, the enemy ship was no longer so proud and invul-
nerable, and he could see where *Destiny's* claws had left their
mark.

He heard Dumaresq's voice following him along the deck,
commanding, all powerful even in its pain. *'Ready to starboard, Mr Bolitho!'*

Bolitho snatched up Rhodes' beautiful sword and waved it
wildly.

'Stand to! Double-shotted, lads!'

Musket-balls hammered across the decks like pebbles, and here and there a man fell. But the rest, dragging themselves from the wreckage and leaving Rhodes' guns on the larboard side, shambled to obey. To load the remaining twelve-pounders, to crouch like dazed animals as foot by foot the *San Augustin*'s towering stern loomed over them like a gilded cliff.

'*As you bear!*'

Who was shouting the orders? Dumaresq, Palliser, or was he himself so stunned by the ferocity of the battle that he had called them himself?

'*Fire!*'

He saw the guns sliding inboard, the way their crews just stood and watched the destruction as every murderous ball ploughed through the Spanish man-of-war from stern to bow.

None of the gun-captains, not even Stockdale, made any attempt to reload. It was as if each man knew.

The *San Augustin* was drifting downwind, perhaps her steering shot away, or her officers killed by the last deadly embrace.

Bolitho walked slowly aft and on to the quarterdeck. Wood splinters were everywhere, and there were few men left at the six-pounders to cheer as some of the enemy's rigging collapsed in a welter of sparks and smoke.

Dumaresq turned stiffly and looked at him. 'I think she's afire.'

Bolitho saw Gulliver, dead by his helmsmen, and Slade in his place, as if he had been meant for master from the beginning. Colpoys, his red coat over his bandaged wounds like a cape, watching his men standing back from their weapons. Palliser, sitting on a cask, while one of Bulkley's men examined his arm.

He heard himself say, 'We'll lose the treasure, sir.'

An explosion shook the stricken *San Augustin,* and figures could be seen jumping over the side and trampling down anyone who tried to stop them.

Dumaresq looked down at his red waistcoat. 'So will they.'

Bolitho watched the other ship and saw the smoke thickening, the first glint of fire beneath her mainmast. If Garrick was still alive, he would not get far now.

Bulkley arrived on the quarterdeck and said, 'You must come below, Captain. I have to examine you.'

'*Must!*' Dumaresq gave his fierce grin. 'It is not a word I choose——' Then he fainted in his coxswain's arms.

After all that had happened it seemed unbearable. Bolitho watched as Dumaresq's body was picked up and carried carefully to the companionway.

Palliser joined him by the quarterdeck rail. He looked ashen but said, 'We'll stand off until that ship either sinks or blows up.'

'What shall I do, sir?' It was Midshipman Henderson, who had somehow survived the whole battle at the masthead.

Palliser looked at him. 'You will assume Mr Bolitho's duties.' He hesitated, his eyes on Rhodes' body by the fore-mast. 'Mr Bolitho will be second lieutenant.'

A greater explosion than all the previous ones shook *San Augustin* so violently that her fore and main-topmasts toppled into the smoke and the hull itself began to turn turtle.

Jury climbed up and joined Bolitho to watch the last moments of the ornate ship.

'Was it worth it, sir?'

Bolitho looked at him and at the ship around them. Already there were men working to put the damage to rights, to make the ship live again. There were a thousand things to do, wounded to care for, the remaining schooner chased and caught, prisoners to be rescued and separated from the Spanish sailors. A great deal of work for one small ship and her company, he thought.

He considered Jury's question, what it had all cost, and what they had discovered in each other. He thought too of what Dumaresq would have to say when he returned to duty. That was a strange thing about Dumaresq. Dying was like defeat, you could never associate it with him.

Bolitho said quietly, 'You must never ask that. I've learned, and I'm still learning. The ship comes first. Now, let's be about it, otherwise the lord and master will have harsh words for all of us.'

Startled, he looked at the sword he still grasped in his hand.

Perhaps Rhodes had answered Jury's question for him?

Epilogue

Bolitho tugged his hat down over his eyes and looked up at the great grey house. There was a squall blowing up the Channel, and the rain which stung his cheeks felt like ice. All the months, all the waiting, and now he was home again. It had been a long, hard journey from Plymouth after *Destiny* had dropped anchor. The roads were deeply rutted, and there had been so much mud thrown up on the coach windows Bolitho had found it difficult to recognize places which he had known since boyhood.

And now that he was back again he felt a sense of unreality, and, for some reason he could not determine, one of loss.

The house was unchanged, just as it had looked when he had last seen it, almost a year ago.

Stockdale, who had driven with him from Plymouth, shifted his feet uncertainly.

'Are you sure it's all right fer me to be 'ere, sir?'

Bolitho looked at him. It had been Dumaresq's last gesture before he had left the ship, before *Destiny* had been put into the hands of the dockyard for repair and a well-deserved overhaul.

'Take Stockdale. You'll be getting another ship soon. Keep him with you. A useful fellow.'

Bolitho said quietly, 'You're welcome here. You'll see.'

He climbed up the worn stone steps and saw the double-doors swing inwards to greet him. Bolitho was not surprised, he had felt in the last few moments that the whole house had been silently watching him.

But it was not old Mrs Tremayne the housekeeper but a young maidservant he did not recognize.

She curtsied and blushed. 'Welcome, zur.' Almost in the same breath she added, 'Cap'n James is waitin' for you, zur.'

Bolitho stamped the mud from his shoes and gave the girl his hat and boat-cloak.

He strode through the panelled hall and stepped into the big room he knew so well. There was the fire, blazing brightly as if to hold the winter at bay, gleaming pewter, the filtered smells from the kitchen, security.

Captain James Bolitho moved from the fire and put his hand on his son's shoulder.

'My God, Richard, I saw you last as a scrawny midshipman. You've come home a man!'

Bolitho was shocked by his father's appearance. He had steeled himself against the loss of an arm, but his father had changed beyond belief. His hair was grey and his eyes were sunken. Because of his sewn-up sleeve he was holding himself awkwardly, something Bolitho had seen other crippled sailors do, fearful of having someone brush against the place where a limb had been.

'Sit down, my boy.' He watched Bolitho fixedly, as if afraid of missing something. 'That's a terrible scar you have there. I must hear all about it.' But there was no enthusiasm in his voice. 'Who was that giant I saw you arrive with?'

Bolitho gripped the arms of his chair. 'A man called Stockdale.'

He was suddenly aware of the quiet, the deadly, clinging silence.

He asked, 'Tell me, Father. Is something wrong?'

His father walked to a window and stared unseeingly through the sleet-washed glass.

'There have been letters, of course. They'll catch up with you one day.' He turned heavily. 'Your mother died a month ago, Richard.'

Bolitho stared at him, unable to move, unwilling to accept it.

'Died?'

'She had a short illness. A fever of sorts. We did all we could.'

Bolitho said quietly, 'I think I knew. Just now. Outside the house. She always gave the place light.'

Dead. He had been planning what he was going to tell her, how he would have quietened her concern over his scar.

His father said distantly, 'Your ship was reported some days back.'

'Yes. Then fog came down. We had to anchor.'

He thought suddenly of the faces he had left, how much he needed them at this moment. Dumaresq, who had gone to the Admiralty to explain the loss of the treasure, or to be congratulated for depriving a potential enemy of it. Palliser, who had got his command of a brig at Spithead. Young Jury, with a break in his voice when they had shaken hands for the last time.

'I heard of some of your exploits. It sounds as if Dumaresq made quite a name for himself. I hope the Admiralty see it that way. Your brother is away with the fleet.'

Bolitho tried to contain his emotion. Words, just words. He had known his father would be like this. Pride. It was always a question of pride with him, first and foremost.

'Is Nancy at home?'

His father looked at him distantly. 'You won't know that either. Your sister married the squire's son, young Lewis Roxby. Your mother said it was on the rebound after that other wretched business.' He sighed. 'So there it is.'

Bolitho leaned back against the chair, pressing his shoulders against the carved oak to control his sorrow.

His father had lost the sea. Now he was alone, too. This great house which looked across the slopes of Pendennis Castle or out across the busy comings and goings of Carrick Roads. Each a constant reminder of what he had lost, of what had been taken from him.

He said gently, '*Destiny* has paid off, Father. I can stay.'

It was as if he had shouted some terrible oath. Captain James strode from the window and stood looking down at him.

'I never want to hear that! You are *my* son and a King's officer. For generations we've left this house, and some have never come back. There's war in the air, and we'll need all our sons.' He paused and added softly, 'A messenger came here just two days back. An appointment already.'

Bolitho stood up and moved about the room, touching
familiar things without feeling them.

His father added, 'She's the *Trojan*, eighty guns. There's
going to be a war right enough if they're recommissioning
her.'

'I see.'

Not a lithe frigate, but another great ship of the line. A new
world to explore and master. Perhaps it was just as well.
Something to fill his mind, to keep him busy until he could
accept all which had happened.

'Now I think we should take a glass together, Richard.
Ring for the girl. You must tell me all about it. The ship, her
people, everything. Leave nothing out. It's all I have now.
Memories.'

Bolitho said, 'Well, Father, it was a year ago when I joined
Destiny at Plymouth under Captain Dumaresq. . . .'

When the young maidservant entered with the glasses and
wine from the cellar, she saw the grey-headed Captain James
sitting opposite his youngest son. They were talking about
ships and foreign parts. There was no sign of grief or despair
in their reunion.

But she did not understand. It was all a question of pride.